I hesitated, u...
flar...

For a moment, I was p... ...e
sudden promise of thi... ...w
of night. It left me raw and aching; my hips trembled with
the urge to submit to him. I blinked, and realized he had
moved closer.

Crap.

I stood my ground. Maybe if I didn't move, he'd back
down and I'd pass whatever preternatural bullshit test he
was running.

Or maybe I was in big trouble.

His cheeks curved up in amusement as he reached out
to run a lightly callused thumb over my lower lip. "Pretty
Dreamer," he crooned, leaning close so that his exquisite
pout lay within inches of my lips.

Yup. Big trouble.

I swallowed hard. My brain worked overtime to come up
with something . . . *anything* . . . to say, but all I could manage was a strangled groan, helpless against the rolling wave
of pleasure that pulsed low in my belly.

The room began to spin, and I staggered backwards. My
foot slipped on a loose pile of paper, my hands gripping the
edge of the counter to keep from falling. The dark stranger
captured my wrist, fingers digging hard enough to make the
bones ache, trying to steady me, his face ashen.

"Hold on, Abby."

I had only a moment to wonder how he knew my name
before my vision faded into blackness. . . .

A Brush of Darkness is also available as an eBook

A BRUSH OF
DARKNESS

ALLISON PANG

POCKET BOOKS
New York   London   Toronto   Sydney

Pocket Books
A Division of Simon & Schuster, Inc.
1230 Avenue of the Americas
New York, NY 10020

First Pocket Books paperback edition February 2011

POCKET and colophon are registered trademarks of Simon & Schuster, Inc.

For information about special discounts for bulk purchases, please contact Simon & Schuster Special Sales at 1-866-506-1949 or business@simonandschuster.com.

The Simon & Schuster Speakers Bureau can bring authors to your live event. For more information or to book an event contact the Simon & Schuster Speakers Bureau at 1-866-248-3049 or visit our website at www.simonspeakers.com.

Designed by Esther Paradelo
Cover illustration by Nathalia Suellen. Design by Lisa Litwack.

Manufactured in the United States of America

10 9 8 7 6 5 4 3 2 1

ISBN 978-1-4391-9832-2
ISBN 978-1-4391-9841-4 (ebook)

To Dan, Connor, and Lucy—you are my Heart.
And to my mother, whatever CrossRoads she may wander.

Acknowledgments

For all that writing is a seeming solitary occupation, the act of getting a book published is a team effort, and to that effect I've got quite a few people to thank. It's almost a given that I'm going to forget someone, but I shall do my best.

To my editor, Danielle Poiesz, for taking something good and insisting I make it great, and for having the confidence in me to do it right. And for the chocolate, the power of which can never really be underestimated.

To my agent, Colleen Lindsay, for making me remove all the bacon. Well, some of the bacon, anyway, since the power of bacon can't really be underestimated, either.

To Jeffe Kennedy, for being my midnight sounding board, supreme idea-bouncer, and all-around Good Person.

To Liz Pelletier, for being my drive-by girl, my pitch queen, and also for making sure I didn't expose myself to comma shame.

To Staci Myers, for talking me down off the cliff more times than I care to count, and above all, for believing in me.

To my beta readers—Dawn McClure, Kirsten Higman, and Jane Houle—your honest feedback was beyond invaluable and much appreciated, and your continuing support and good wishes mean so very much to me.

To Darchala Chaoswind, for making such pretty pictures.

And to K. A. Krantz, Danica Avet, La-Tessa Montgomery, and Simon Larters—for making me laugh and reminding me of what the important things are.

Between twilight and dawn
B'twixt heaven and hell
Travel the CrossRoads
Whence the OtherFolk dwell . . .

One

Cat piss and cabbages.

It was the only way to describe it, really. Even on a good day, the bookstore smelled like a mix of dust and dirty feet. The AC had coughed its last an hour ago, leaving me the proud employee of an ad hoc sauna. A drip above the lintel had forced me to keep the door closed to avoid a miniature lake from forming on the warping hardwood floor. The remainder of the morning was doomed to be a soggy, stinky mess.

The weathered sign hanging from the shutter outside read PROSPECTUS INTELLIGENTSIA TABERNUS. I called it the Pit for short. Probably unkind, but God knows the place reeked like one this morning. Still, the stale odor didn't seem to stop my steady stream of customers from leaving wet trails and dripping umbrellas in their wakes, though I suspected their visits were more of an effort to get out of the rain than driven by any great desire to find a coverless copy of a Dean Koontz novel.

The rain let up just before lunch and with it went the last of my customers, an old man waddling into the wet with a paper sack full of ancient sailing books.

Bliss.

Time for some retro Tom Jones. I loaded up my latest playlist on the silver iPod mounted on the counter and wriggled my way to the front window, tinny speakers blaring. Flipping over the CLOSED FOR LUNCH sign, I mock strutted my way to the minifridge in the storage room for a couple of Cokes and a sandwich, my hips swaying counterpoint. I was half a can and three verses into "She's a Lady" before the main door creaked open again.

The bells chimed in their plaintive way, somehow cutting through the rumbling growl of the music. A man drifted across the threshold. The grace of his movements caused the hair on the back of my neck to rise. He seemed a shadow, sucking up all the light from the room. The exquisite darkness of his ebony eyes swept over me, primitive and uncompromising. And overdone as all hell. Still. The silken fall of his hair just brushed the top of his shoulders and I've always been a sucker for good grooming and potential wangst.

What the hell. I'd bite.

"What's new, pussycat?" I purred.

"I need to talk to Moira." The timbre of his words pushed past me, heated and hollow.

"I'm afraid Moira isn't here."

His eyes narrowed, the line of his jaw shifting almost imperceptibly. The alarms in the back of my head suddenly went off. I'm not shy, but the thrum of desire that started beating through my veins as he approached the counter wasn't normal or natural. If this guy was human I'd swear off bacon for a month.

I turned down the music in a futile attempt to distract myself from the elegant curve of his cheekbones and the smooth paleness of his skin. He glided toward me, each rolling step filled with a lazy arrogance. A faint shimmer of silver dusted his hair, fading in the damp light that trickled through the front bay window. I blinked.

He'd been traveling the CrossRoads. I'd never been there myself, but the silver snowflakes were a dead giveaway he'd been moving between worlds.

My smile was polite, but I couldn't quite keep the stiffness from my voice. "If you'd like, I can take your information and I'll let her know you stopped by." I tapped my pencil on the notebook in front of me. He'd asked for Moira by name, not her official title of Protectorate. I was under no obligation to answer his questions, and as far as I was concerned, the less involved I got in the offshoots of Faery politics, the better.

Truthfully, some of the OtherFolk freaked me the hell out, especially when they insisted on walking around in broad daylight like this. For that matter, I didn't even know *what* he was. Looks aside, he couldn't have been a vampire. Even vampires with TouchStones didn't go walking around at noon. Not like that, anyway. Fae, maybe? Lycanthrope? Oh, what difference did it make? Usually the best policy was to just be polite and wait for them to go away.

That being said, I really hated it when they started trying to magic me up. It's rude and nothing pissed me off faster than when one of them tried to get in my face about it. I knew they couldn't always help it, but this guy wasn't even attempting to tamp it down. Glamour oozed out of him, the magic rolling over me in soft waves of lust. Kinda pleasant in its own way, but distracting as all get out. My mouth tightened; I was suddenly very impatient.

A frown marred his handsome features, and he looked down as though seeing me for the first time. "When will she be back?"

"She's *not* here," I repeated, a hint of annoyance creeping into my tone. I'm not exactly the most outspoken person in the world, but store clerk or not—human or not—I wasn't some invisible piece of dog shit on the bottom of his shoe either.

"I don't know when she'll be back," I added. The truth of it galled me because I really didn't. The Faery woman had left nearly four months ago and, except for that last note taped on her office door, I hadn't heard from her at all. But this guy didn't need to know that. Hell, none of them needed to know that. I could barely get the OtherFolk to give me the time of day as it was. God only knew what they'd do if they realized Moira wasn't here to hold them in line. "If you'd like to sample some of her . . . other wares, I'll be reopening the shop around back from midnight to one A.M."

"Will you, now?" He stepped closer and I shivered, the quiet power coiling behind the words dancing over my skin.

Sweat beaded on my forehead, cool and clammy. "They don't call it the Midnight Marketplace for nothing." I thrust out my chin in subtle challenge, ignoring the rising panic that fluttered at the base of my throat. Piss him off, Abby. That will be brilliant.

His face was quiet and brimming with secrets like a Cheshire cat's. "You're her TouchStone, aren't you?"

"Of course I am," I agreed pleasantly. "And now that we've established the obvious, let's get back to business. Who are you?"

"Tsk." He waggled a finger at me, and I rolled my eyes. Something about the gesture was very familiar, but if I'd met him before I couldn't recall. Then again, I'd only been Moira's TouchStone for six months and I'd seen an awful lot, much of which had become a muddled mess of fancy sparkles and obscenely beautiful people. Anchoring an OtherFolk to the mortal realm wasn't an easy—or straight-forward—task.

"Fine, I get it. Names have power and all that, but it makes it a bit hard to leave a message, don't you think?" I pointed out.

A flicker of a smile showed on that perfect mouth as his gaze roamed about the bookstore. The store itself was fairly plain, but it had high arches, a giant stone fireplace with overstuffed cushions on the floor, and thick crown molding around the top where the paint was peeling off. I had told Moira the whole thing needed remodeling, or at least some fresh paint, but she insisted the place had "character." Shabby chic, maybe. Sounded like laziness to me, but whatever. It wasn't my store. I just worked there.

The man wandered through the stacks for a moment. I seized the opportunity to take his measure, or at least attempt to stare at his ass, which was currently encased in delectable black leather pants. Or I assumed it was, based on what I could see below the fall of his duster. Had it been anyone else wearing it, I would have said they were trying way too hard, but he was working it pretty well so I gave him a pass.

The duster hung open, inviting an easy view of his chest, a white T-shirt sticking to the muscled ridges of his abdomen. *Definitely* my type. His dark eyes flicked sideways at me, the edges crinkling in silent laughter, and I shrugged, not bothering to hide the fact that I'd been checking him out. Hell, he'd probably been expecting it.

He lingered over a coverless paperback about a French vampire. It was one of those overblown stories that had been really popular about ten years ago, complete with ruffling white shirts, long dark ringlets, and outrageous accents. Even a duster or two, actually. I'd thought it marvelous and horribly sexy when I'd read it, my sixteen-year-old heart near fit to bursting at the idea of some dashing angel of the night feeding from my inner thigh.

The reality had been a whole lot messier. It didn't involve my inner thigh either.

He blew the dust off the pages, snorting softly when he read the title. I'd always thought Moira had an absolutely craptacular taste in books. From the looks of it, he agreed. My opinion of him rose a notch.

"It has a happy ending, you know," I said.

His brow furrowed, lips pursed at me, before his attention flicked back to the book. "Does it?"

"All the good romances do."

"There are no happy endings. And vampires are over-rated, bloodsucking tools."

"Can't argue with that." I laughed. "But the vamp in this one runs off with an emotionally constipated angel, so I suppose it all works out in the end. If you don't like that sort of thing, maybe I can interest you in one of these great 'how-to-massage' books from the seventies. It has pictures, if that makes it easier for you to understand."

He ignored me, his expression cryptic. "Very clever of her." He tapped the book with his fingers.

"Clever of who?"

"Moira. Hiding in plain sight like this." His hand made an eloquent gesture as if to encompass the room. "And all thanks to her little mortal TouchStone, so willing to throw herself away—and for what?" He pointed at me. "Rumors of a magic iPod and seven years of agelessness?"

I bristled. "*Enchanted* iPod, thank you very much. And what I'm willing to throw myself away for is absolutely no concern of yours." The barb had taken, however, and I looked down at the counter before that little sliver of regret could show itself.

He chuckled softly. "Not as good as you had hoped, is it?"

"Neither is your outfit. Did you learn to dress that way

in Leather for Bad Boys one-oh-one?" My upper lip curled in derision, suddenly bold in knowing my place. "Sounds to me like someone doesn't have a TouchStone of his own." I noted the time with a little sound of pity. 11:57 A.M. "How are those CrossRoads treating you?" I asked. At this time of day, any other folk traveling the CrossRoads sans Touch-Stone would have a helluva time.

"Not nearly well enough, apparently." His gaze met mine. "Shall I show you?"

I hesitated, watching those dark eyes flare gold with power. For a moment, I was pinned beneath them, drowning in the sudden promise of things best left to the protective shadow of night. It left me raw and aching; my hips trembled with the urge to submit to him. I blinked and realized he had moved closer.

Crap.

I stood my ground. Maybe if I didn't move, he'd back down and I'd pass whatever preternatural bullshit test he was running.

Or maybe I was in big trouble.

His cheeks curved up in amusement as he reached out to run a lightly callused thumb over my lower lip. "Pretty Dreamer," he crooned. He leaned close to my face so that his exquisite pout lay within inches of my lips. An electric jolt shot from my breasts to my groin, sliding over my flesh with wicked intent.

Yup. Big trouble.

I swallowed hard, my eyes closing of their own volition. Inside, my brain was working overtime to come up with something—*anything*—to say, but all I could manage was a strangled groan. I was helpless against the rolling wave of pleasure pulsing low in my belly.

The room began to spin, and I staggered backward. My foot slipped on a loose pile of paper, and I grabbed the edge of the counter. The world tilted with a familiar lurch, and my jaw clamped down against the vertigo.

He captured my wrist, fingers digging hard enough to make the bones ache. Fire lanced all the way to my elbow as my eyes snapped open with a cry. The arrogant stranger lunged over the counter to steady me, his face ashen. Whatever he'd intended, this wasn't it. The thought was somewhat comforting.

"Hold on, Abby," he whispered.

I had only a moment to wonder how he knew my name before my vision faded into blackness.

. . . *his fingers were sliding down my thigh, his voice husky with whispered promises as his tongue slipped into my mouth. I spread myself beneath him in wanton desperation, filled with the ache of well-used flesh. He moved over me, inside me, through me. I was losing myself in the golden thrum of his eyes as he thrust into me. Somewhere in the distance was the chiming of bells, and my bones vibrated with the implication. I fell away, wrapped in his scent and the dim edge of twilight as something snapped into place . . .*

"Enough." His voice reverberated like a thunderclap, abruptly breaking the . . . trance? Dream?

"And here I pegged you as the shy, unassuming type." I pulled back from him as the darkness receded, gagging at another wave of dizziness. Admittedly, I hadn't taken my seizure meds that morning, but whether the reaction was caused by my condition or his influence didn't matter. It hadn't felt like a seizure anyway. Balance slowly regained, I glanced up at him, and slid my hands into my pockets to hide my trembling fingers. "What the hell was that?"

Surprise flickered across his face, quickly replaced by

something a bit more appraising. "I don't know," he said finally. "It wasn't supposed to happen."

His gaze lingered on me, somehow managing to be impudent and measured at the same time, but the overconfident cockiness was gone.

"Wow. I find myself strangely not reassured by that." I crossed my arms, hunching my back protectively. I was Moira's TouchStone, by God, marked by a sacred OtherFolk bond that should be beyond contestation and this asshat had just violated every precept that I was aware of.

I was outraged.

was livid, even.

I was hopelessly out of my league.

The golden edges of his eyes faded away. "Are you all right?"

The sudden change in his demeanor left me suspicious. "Right as rain. Why the . . . you know?" I tapped my head and tried not to blush.

"Side effect. I'm afraid I got a little carried away." He eyed me cautiously, all peaches-and-cream polite. "For what it's worth, I'm sorry."

"Understatement of the week." I reached out, clinging to the edges of the counter like a barnacle at high tide. "And how the hell did you know who I was?"

His mouth twitched. "Name tag."

Idiot.

I shut my eyes, cheeks burning. "Where's a nice bottomless pit when you need one?"

A sharp rap sounded from outside and I started. The figure at the door was young and female and far too perky for a rainy day.

"Shoo," I hissed at the stranger, uncertain of how much attention he would attract. "Shouldn't you be moving along now? The CrossRoads will be closing any minute."

He shrugged and leaned against the wall, a wolfish grin on his face. He raised a finger to his lips as he motioned toward the door.

I rolled my eyes. Leave it to me to attract the tall, dark, and obnoxious ones. I pointed at the sign in the window, hoping whoever it was would cut me some slack and come back after my uninvited guest had left. No such luck.

"Wow." A head poked through the doorway. "It totally stinks in here. You should open the door or something." Blond, top-heavy, and rather leggy on the whole, she looked like she'd wandered off the set of a *Girls Gone Wild* audition, wrapped up in denim cutoffs and Skechers. Her eyes were wide and imploring, the color of warm hazelnuts. Innocent.

"Ah, yes," I said, ignoring the soft snort coming from the corner. "You know, we're kind of closed right now."

"Yeah, well, I need some information. Do you have any books on Celtic myths?" She breezed her way in and trotted up to the counter with the self-serving air of the young and stupid.

I chewed on the question, a low throb at the base of my skull signaling an oncoming headache. Or a seizure. Crapshoot as to which one was going to come first. I wasn't going to get rid of the headache, but I could eliminate the pain in the ass standing in front of me. "There should be a copy of Lady Gregory's *Gods and Fighting Men* back behind the mirror. It would be a good place to start. Unless you're looking for something specific?"

"Well . . . uh. Actually, I was kinda hoping you might have something a little more . . . *real*?"

I raised a brow at this. Truth be told, I did; I had books that would damn near bite your nose off if you put them too close to your face. But those were locked away in the back, not for public consumption. Moira had drilled that into my head often enough, but I would have figured it out on my own. I'm lazy, but I'm not a moron.

"Real?" I mimicked.

"Yeah." She leaned in so I could see the roots of her hair. Her voice dropped to a conspiring whisper. "You know . . . *OtherFolk*?" She turned her head to take in the quantity of shelves. "You have a lot of books here." Her gaze became slightly unfocused as it slid past the corner, and I realized my visitor must be hiding behind a Glamour.

"I'm not quite sure what you mean," I said, deciding to play dumb.

"Oh, I get it." She winked at me. "It's okay. Brandon sent me. Said you would set me straight. Something about TouchStones?"

"Brandon," I repeated, my voice careful and quiet. I would have to have a little chat with that sometimes furry bartender. I don't mind helping out, but I didn't have time for another one of his strays. "And just how did you run into him?"

"I tried to get into the Hallows last night." She flushed beneath my stare. "Everyone knows this town is full of weird shit. Why shouldn't I be a part of it?"

"Did you find your way there by yourself?" I phrased it casually, but my estimation of her slowly began to rise when she nodded. There was a pretty heavy Glamour on the OtherFolk nightclub, geared toward warning away an ignorant mortal public. If she'd had the determination to push her way through it . . .

Still. Even if she was right about people being aware, I wasn't going to go shouting it from the rooftops. The OtherFolk guard their secrets well. Spilling them was a really awesome way to end up on someone's private shitlist. And that didn't even include the one currently laughing his ass off in the corner.

"Listen, you don't want to get involved with them. Trust me. It messes with your head and the only thing you'll have when you're done is a big pile of regret." I held up my hand to forestall what would surely be a whining protest. "However, seeing as Brandon sent you my way, I'll throw you a bone." I resisted the impulse to giggle at my own pun, though something told me the werewolf wouldn't have approved. "What did you say your name was?"

"Katy." One perfectly waxed brow arched, daring me to make an issue of it. It would have been more impressive if the expression on her face wasn't flitting between hope and suspicion.

"How old are you, Katy?"

"Seventeen." I glanced over at the mirror in the corner, as though to argue with my reflection. Seventeen. Jesus. Had I ever been that eager to throw myself off the cliff? I let my gaze go slightly fuzzy, the blue of my eyes fading into the glass of the mirror, the pale, freckled face curving away into some far-off piece of my past.

Yes.

My reflection stared back without blinking. The mirror itself had always given me the creeps. It was carved of black wood with silver gilt edges, on a curved stand with a wide base. There was nothing particularly ominous about it at the moment, just my face peering from its cold depths, familiar and smooth. I shook my head and turned back to the girl.

Girl, hell. I wasn't all that much older than she was, but her innocence nearly overwhelmed me. I was jaded and weary standing next to her like that. Funny what a difference a few seconds can make on your outlook. One moment you're cruising along enjoying the sweet carelessness of youth, and the next you've got a gimpy leg and a metal plate in your head, and everything you've ever known is in shambles. Life can be a real bitch, I guess.

"All right. Come with me."

She let out a muffled squeal and followed me behind the mirror. "Are there any here now? You know. Watching us?"

My hand hesitated inches away from the book I wanted. The stranger's merriment wrapped around me like a ribbon, and I bit down hard on the inside of my cheek. "Oh, no. I don't think so. It's nearly noon, after all. They don't like being caught out in the daylight hours." I glanced behind me, avoiding the corner by the door. Her mouth twisted into a scowl of disappointment, and I gave her a wry shrug as I pulled out a volume of poetry. "Believe it or not, in a lot of ways they're just like us. It's not like they're hiding in your closet or under your bed." I paused. "Or at least, not most of them."

Her upper lip curled as she looked at the book. "What's this?"

"A book. And you're going to read it." I flipped through several pages, marking them with a couple of spare Post-its from my pocket before handing it to her.

She stared at me and then glanced at the first marked page. After a moment of silence she began to read aloud:

O see ye not yon narrow road,
So thick beset wi' thorns and briers?
That is the Path of Righteousness,
Though after it but few inquires.

And see ye not yon braid, braid road,
That leis across the lily leven?
That is the Path of Wickedness,
Though some call it the Road to Heaven.

And see ye not yon bonny road
That winds about the fernie brae?

That is the Road to fair Elfand,
Where thou and I this night maun gae.

But, Thomas, ye shall haud your tongue
Whatever ye may hear or see;
For speak ye word in Elfyn-land,
Ye'll ne'er win back to your ain countrie.

Her brow furrowed impatiently. "Yes, yes, I know this part. I've read this before, you know."

"Then you should have some of the answers you're looking for." She looked at me quizzically. I sighed and went on. "How many paths are there?"

"Three. Duh."

I closed my eyes. "Yes. What are they?"

"Faeryland, Heaven, Hell. Yeah, I get it. Light Path, Dark Path, and Middle Earth or whatever. What does it have to do with the CrossRoads?"

"Everything," I said quietly. "Thomas stood at the CrossRoads with the Faery Queen and he chose her. Not the angels. Not the daemons. The Fae."

"And that means?"

"The Fae are in control. Or at least they have the most influence, the most to gain from TouchStones. They are the Keepers of the CrossRoads, the liaisons between the Other-Folk and us."

Thomas the Rhymer had been the first mortal Touch-Stone to record a Contract with the OtherFolk. And he had fulfilled that contract—for a full seven years—gaining the gift of Prophecy as a result. The irony of the situation wasn't lost on me. From his perspective, the Fae were probably the most amusing of the bunch. Heaven knew just about every angel I'd ever met damn near had a stick up his ass. And really? However pretty the daemon girls are, it's almost always a guarantee they're going to come back and eat your soul one dark night, and who wants to deal with that?

"You can Contract with whoever you wish, of course, but the Fae watch over it all. Depending on who and what you choose, though, there may be political ramifications." My mouth thinned. "And if it goes badly, then the Faery Protectorate has to get involved."

She chewed on her lip thoughtfully. "And what would my Contract with Brandon be?"

I shrugged. I had no idea what sorts of things a werewolf might require of his TouchStone, though I could think of a few responsibilities she probably wouldn't want to take on. "Regardless of the specifics of each individual Contract, the mere fact that the two of you are TouchStoned will allow him to move between our world and the CrossRoads without waiting for the Hours. Aside from that, I can't say. Each Contract is individualized."

Katy's eyes darted toward the door. "So *that's* what he meant. If he has a TouchStone, he doesn't have to worry about being weaker in the daytime?"

"That's one part of it," I agreed. "Each Path has their own Hour, where traveling is easiest. TouchStones ease that transition. Something about having a soul, I suppose. The angels prefer Dawn. The daemons, Midnight."

"And the Fae like Twilight, I suppose. What about noon? How does that fit in?"

"There's a fourth Path," I said, watching her try to work it out. "Can you tell me what it is?"

"Um, no?" She scowled. "It doesn't say anything about a fourth Path."

"Yes it does," I said. "Come back and tell me when you figure it out. It's all in there, I promise."

Katy gave me a dubious look and clutched the book tightly. "How much is it?"

"On the house," I said, waving her off.

"And if I do this, you'll take me to the CrossRoads?"

"I can't do that. Most of the Doors are hidden, so that's something you'll have to figure out on your own." *That, and the fact you've never been there,* my inner voice said snidely. The Doors to the CrossRoads themselves were fluid enough—transitory gateways that opened and shut at the Hours—but finding them was another matter altogether. "Truthfully, it's probably best if you TouchStone to Brandon first. And take it from me—read the Contract and understand just what you're getting into. Being a TouchStone isn't for the faint of heart."

A fierce smile spread across her face. "I'll be back soon." She squinted as she peered at my shirt. "Abby?"

"That's me," I said dryly, pulling at my name tag. The eavesdropping man candy pointed at me and then tapped his head. I suppressed a sneer.

"Thank you so much, Abby. You won't be disappointed, I promise." Katy beamed at me and I couldn't help but feel like the wolf in Red Riding Hood's story. *The better to eat you with, my dear?* But no, that wasn't right, either. I recognized that determined look in her eye, and even though I was fairly new to the whole OtherFolk scene, there was a part of me that would have loved to have had help instead of stumbling through it like I was.

And fucking it up royally, even.

"Will you be around tonight? You know, in case I figure it out?"

I snorted. There's enthusiasm for you. "Not really. I'm going to an art gallery showing at the Waterfront. And I need to go get shoes for it first." Small talk was not my forte, but I seemed to have momentarily adopted a friend.

"Oh," she said. "Well, you should check out that new place on the corner of Canon and King. They've got some really nice stuff. And turn on the fan or something—it's gross in here."

"I'll do that," I said with a wan smile. She thanked me again and left, the door clinking shut behind her. I took a deep breath. It *was* entirely too damn hot in here. Of course, the main reason for that was still in the corner. Watching me.

I was going to have to remedy that *soon*.

"Well, this has been fun, but technically I'm working, so unless you're going to buy something, you need to leave. Since you couldn't be bothered to give me your name, I'll just tell Moira that an extra from the porno version of *Something Wicked This Way Comes* was looking for her."

"Extra? Hell," he muttered. "I'd be the star."

I coughed. "Emphasis on the word 'comes,' of course."

The amusement rippled from him, rich and dark, but there wasn't anything menacing about it now. "I suppose I deserve that. Did you want that name?"

"Color me excited," I retorted. "Seems only fair, though. Generally I prefer a handshake and a hello *before* I hop into metaphysical bed with someone."

"I don't." He shrugged and held out his hand. "Brystion." He trilled the *r* sound, giving it an exotic rumble. *Brrrist-e-on.*

"Just Brystion?" I let my hand slip into his, holding my breath as I waited for the mind roll to happen again. When it didn't, I relaxed. His skin was warm to the touch, but somehow not unpleasant even with the heat of the day.

"For now. And don't worry about telling Moira, Abby."

"Why?" My pulse jumped at the delicious way my name rolled off his tongue.

He smiled. "Because she already knows, now," he said gently, shaking his head at my ignorance.

Before I could ask him what he meant, he was gone. I craned my neck toward the window, catching a glimpse of his dark form striding down the street, heedless of the on-coming drizzle—or the dull thudding of my heart.

Two

The woman in the painting was soft and pale and naked. There was a proud thrust to her jaw as she stared down at me, her dark eyes half-lidded and smoky with kohl. I would have had to slaughter a horde of Avon ladies in ritual sacrifice to have skin that luminous and milky white.

She was a flawless collection of curves, her nipples hard and rosy, one hand reaching up to run perfect fingers through a cascade of midnight hair. Delicate wings arched from her back. The feathers were stained a brilliant crimson and spread in guarded invitation. She was chained, bound to the bed she knelt on, the crisp edges of the sheets in violent relief against the darkness in the corners of the room. The iron did not seem to faze her, but I shivered beneath the challenge in her shadowed eyes: *I will give you what you want if you give me what I need . . .*

I swallowed and read the title placard, strangely grateful that I was the only one standing here at the moment. It seemed more respectful that way, a private sort of voyeurism.

Debt Paid in Full.

"No, thanks." My eyes lingered on the graceful flare of

her hip before edging over to the iron shackles at her wrists. I like my kink straightforward, but I've never been one for mind games. Whoever she was, the scarlet woman was formidable and wrapped in a raw sexuality I would never possess.

Still, my feet were frozen in place, her ebony gaze holding me there until it felt like *I* was the one in chains. I doubted she'd ever been mortal. I certainly didn't recognize her. Not that that meant much in itself—it's hard to pin names on people who could change shape or Glamour themselves into something else. Or refuse to give names at all. I snorted softly, my heart pattering, as Brystion materialized in my mind. I still had no idea what he'd been talking about, but then, I suppose that was nothing new. Moira's recent absence had left me hanging in the knowledge department, proper protocol notwithstanding.

Legends and myths, half-truths and lies. All of it swirled into an obnoxious mishmash of information. Most of the OtherFolk liked it that way; it kept them mysterious and hard to pin down.

It also made them damn hard to contact, especially when I needed to call in the debts for the Marketplace. That was something Moira usually took care of, but I'd noticed that since the Protectorate had been gone, there had been a spike in items purchased on credit. I was beginning to think some of our customers were trying to take advantage of the situation.

Luckily, the highly polished marble floors of the Portsmyth Waterfront Fine Arts Gallery appeared to be free of any OtherFolk influence at the moment, and that was peachy keen with me. My attention remained locked on the winged beauty, something inside me shattering with pity.

Topher was three times a fool for trying to capture her on anything as mundane as mere canvas. In the Faery world, you never got something for nothing. If the talent burned bright enough, an OtherFolk muse might be tempted to leave behind a bit of their immortal essence, but at what cost?

A chill skittered its way down my spine, breaking me from my stupor. I welcomed the distraction, uprooting myself to move on to the next painting—*Melusine Bathes.*

Redheaded and petite, the subject was lounging in a massive hot tub of green and gold marble. Her torso was that of a human woman, her hips curving into the body of a silver snake. A leather corset hugged her waist, tight and glossy black, the shadows offset by a rainbow headscarf and violet teashade glasses. The snake-woman held an elegant violin to her cheek, a golden key poking from between succulent lips.

"It's truly dreadful, isn't it?"

I tweaked the curly red locks of the woman who suddenly brushed up against me. "I think he captured you rather well, Mel. The violin is a nice touch."

Melanie St. James, mortal fiddler for a number of local bands—OtherFolk and otherwise—lightly punched my shoulder. "But a snake? Why a snake? I told Topher I wanted to be painted as a Faery."

"Technically, I think Melusine *was* a Faery, and a rather famous one at that. She just happened to become scaly in the bathtub." My mouth twitched. "According to Wikipedia, anyway."

"You *would* know that." Mel pushed her violet glasses farther up the bridge of her nose. "You're late, you know. I've been here for over an hour." She peered dubiously into her wine glass, swirling it with a practiced flourish. "And this stuff tastes like the bastard love child of grapes and rubbing alcohol."

"Your first mistake was choosing wine over champagne."

I snagged a flute of the bubbly from a passing server. "And I fell asleep." I stifled a yawn, the bubbles dancing on my tongue as I took a modest sip. I'd had every intention of catching a shower and then shoe shopping, but somehow all I'd managed was to stagger up to my apartment after work and pass out on the bed. By the time I woke up, I barely had enough time to toss on some fresh clothes and hoof it to the gallery. I wiggled my recently manicured toes in my sandals as if to prove the point.

"*That* is kind of weird." I motioned at the key between her painted lips. The letters G-A-G were lightly etched on each burnished prong. "Maybe he's trying to tell you something?"

She rolled the stem of her wine glass between her fingers, brows drawn. "Who the hell knows? I offered to set up in the corner and add a little ambiance to the place tonight, but he turned me down."

"Not everyone can appreciate the subtle tones of *Apocalyptica*, I guess." I eyed the violin case on her back with a twinge of envy. The instrument never looked like much, battered as it was, but there was always a sly gleam along the woodwork whenever the light touched it. Rumor had it Melanie had pulled a Charlie Daniels to get it, but I'd never had the courage to ask her. Some things are just private, and probing as to whether your friend really *had* outplayed the Devil seemed a bit rude.

"*Apocalyptica* uses cellos," she corrected primly with an aggrieved sniff.

I shrugged and gestured toward the painting of the woman with the red wings. "Any idea who that is?"

"She's hot, but no." Melanie's gaze lit up with mischief. "Seen yours yet?"

"Uh . . . no?"

She erupted into a fit of tipsy giggles and looped her arm

through mine, steering me away like a rudderless boat. We stumbled through the roving jungle of viewers and velvet ropes. My drink nearly spilled at least half a dozen times.

"Here we are." She tilted her head at the canvas, hazel eyes whirling in expectation.

If my goal had been to capture flies, I would have succeeded marvelously. As it was, I could only blink dumbly as my jaw slacked and the blood rushed to my face. "Ah. He seems to have made me naked." A naked mermaid, in fact. The scales of my tail were like spun glass, luminous and shining. Dark green strands of seaweed were entwined in my auburn hair, sweeping over my shoulders and around the sculpted edges of my hips. And yes. There was my chest in all its diminutive glory.

"Christ. The least he could have done was cover them up with seashells or something," I complained.

"I think they're kind of cute." Mel winked at me. "Like little teacups." I glared at her and she laughed again. "Oh, come on. It's not like it really matters. I doubt anyone but us would know it was you."

I pointed to the pink and blue streaks decorating the mermaid's tresses. "Of course not."

"Ah, well . . . I suppose there is that." She tapped the pencils jutting out from the bun I'd hastily twisted together as I'd run out the door. "That's, uh, a new look for you, isn't it? And you're going to have to dye your bangs again." She flicked the pencils. "The color is fading."

"Maybe. I was actually thinking of letting them grow out." My gaze drifted back toward the painting, myriad tiny details popping out at me, easily missed on first glance. Many of the brushstrokes were shadowy, particularly the edges around my mermaid self; it was as though I were captured in a delicate blue bubble of light, the depths fading away into inky blackness. Silhouettes of darker things lurked there as well. I wet my lips. If I peered closer, would I see them? The dark fins and gleaming teeth, the rolling dead eyes?

Trust Topher to paint the source of my nightmares.

I sipped at my champagne numbly, trying to focus on something else.

Up, Abby. Look up. A massive galleon sailed on the waves far above my piscine semblance. There was a dark figure standing at the prow, hands extended in heartsick longing toward the crashing whitecaps.

The title was *Waiting for Ships*. Damned if I knew what that meant, but something about the whole image had my fingers itching to touch the hidden spot above my left ear. The hair didn't grow over it quite right anymore, but the scar tissue was slowly fading and I'd learned to hide it pretty well. Then again, I'd learned to hide a lot of things pretty well. Topher had been kind enough not to paint it, but if I squinted I could almost see it anyway.

"He really didn't do you justice," a dark voice drawled behind us, breaking me out of what was well on its way to becoming a rather large wallow in self-pity.

"Back for more, I see," I said, not bothering to turn around. I could recognize that voice anywhere. "And whatever do you mean?"

"I think you know," Bryston murmured. His soft chuckle rippled around us as he slid next to me. Our shoulders were near enough to touch, but just hovering outside the boundary of propriety. The duster was gone and the heat from his arm brushed against my skin. I heard Mel breathe in sharply when she saw him, but I didn't look at her. I didn't look at him either, draining the rest of my glass in a single swallow.

The three of us stood there, not moving, staring at my naked boobs for at least another five minutes.

"Well. Did you get enough of a look, or did you need to do that mind-touching thing again?" I asked bluntly.

"I told you that was an accident." He paused, eyes lighting up with a salacious gleam. "Did you want me to?"

"Not unless you're serving bacon for breakfast."

He frowned, and his attention moved past me as he tilted his head toward Melanie. "Are we still on for tomorrow night?"

I did a double take as a flare of jealousy sparked through my veins.

She grinned at him, deliberately ignoring the hairy eyeball I threw at her. "Of course. You'll be doing the second set, if that's all right with you."

"It'll do." His mouth curved up in a sly smile. "I'm going to go look around. Catch you later, Abby."

"I'll bet you will." I studied my feet as he sauntered away, darting a last look at his retreating backside.

"I didn't know you knew him." Melanie's eyes followed him too, glowing with blatant admiration.

"I don't actually know who he is." I exchanged my empty champagne glass for a full one. "He came into the Pit today. Seems a right arrogant shit, if you ask me." My lips pursed, unwilling to reveal just *how* arrogant. "Although he's certainly in the right place. Stick a ribbon on that ass and you could mount it on the wall. It's damn near a work of art by itself."

We ogled said body part with a companionable sigh. We weren't the only ones. Small pockets of silence fell around the gallery as the crowd parted for him. He ignored the hungry glances and smug murmurs, taking a few unhurried moments at each painting before gliding away.

"Cheeky bugger." I purposefully turned my back on him. "Whoever he is."

Melanie chuckled. "Brystion is eye candy of the highest caliber, my dear, not just some OtherFolk man whore."

"If you say so. I say if it walks like a duck—"

"You *have* to have heard of him," she said incredulously. "He's only the hottest piece of ass this side of the Cross-Roads." She watched him slip into the crowd and then sighed. "That's a new look for him though. Normally he's blond."

I made a noncommittal sound. "That's what he looked like earlier today. You said blond?" Something niggled at the back of my mind as I tried to picture him with blond hair. I couldn't really say that I liked the effect, and yet there was something so familiar . . .

"Ah, that's right." I snapped my fingers. "He was the lead singer for that Dark Path band. What was it? Lolly-Folly or something?"

"Ion's Folly," Mel snorted. "You know, short for Brys*tion*?"

"Maybe I should drop by the Hallows more often," I smirked.

"Yeah, well, don't get your hopes up. They broke up a few months ago. But you probably would have known who he was if you hadn't been so busy trying to be Buffy the Vampire Layer the last time you were there."

I winced. "Cute. Cut the crap, Mel. What am I dealing with?"

She took another sip of wine. "He's an incubus, Abby."

A ripple of unease fluttered in my belly as certain things fell into place. "Seriously? Like sits on your chest and sucks out your soul and all that?"

"I don't know. I've never slept with him." Her fingers reached up to twirl her hair, wrapping one fat curl around her thumb. "There are rumors, but from what I understand he's pretty choosy." She glanced over her shoulder and frowned, her tongue running over the edge of her teeth. "Strange to see him here though. He almost never hangs out on this side of the CrossRoads without a TouchStone."

"He didn't seem to have one earlier today." I slid my hand over my lips with a little twitch.

"Yeah," she agreed. "I don't think he's had one since the band broke up."

"Well, maybe he just wanted to rub elbows with *you*."

"I rub elbows with him nearly every night he's at the Hallows. Believe me, I'm over it." Her face became sly. "Why so interested? Hoping to do a little wall mounting of your own?"

"I'm not. Not really," I amended. "He was looking for Moira earlier. I was just curious where I could find him if I needed to." My voice was as nonchalant as a cat licking cream from its whiskers and probably about as convincing.

"I'll bet," she said dryly. "He's playing a set with us tomorrow night. You should come."

"It's not really my scene, you know. Not since Jett's Contract." A shudder ran through me at the memory of the vampire's feral grin.

"I know," she interjected, a touch of sympathy tingeing her words. "And the bloodsucker still hangs around there, but honestly, Abby, he can't hurt you if you don't let him."

"I'll think about it." My mind dangled a little worm of remembrance across my consciousness. "Ah, crap, I may need to stop by anyway. Brandon sent me another one."

"Still looking for a TouchStone, eh?"

"Yeah. Not sure why he thinks I'd be such a good judge of them. This is the fourth one this month."

"Well, maybe you need to have less stringent tests?"

"Tests? Hell, I give them a copy of True Thomas's stuff and see if they come back. None of them have. But this one might be different." I snagged yet another glass of champagne off a waiter's tray. "She actually managed to make her way to the Hallows on her own."

"Promising. What's her name?"

"Katy. Perky and blond. Just the way he likes them."

"Typical," she grunted. "But whatever floats his boat, I guess. You should bring her by tomorrow."

"Oh, no." I shook my head. "I'm no babysitter. If Brandon wants her so badly he can damn well invite her himself."

"All right." She squeezed my shoulder. "I need to go, actually. I've got a Contract to meet in about twenty minutes. Duty calls and all that."

Aside from her singular playing talent, Melanie also had the ability to open Doors to the CrossRoads with her music, regardless of the time of day or location, though she'd never really explained the exact mechanics of it to me. She was in nearly constant demand as a result, but she tried to balance it with short-term Contracts.

"Anyone I know?"

She shrugged. "Doubtful. I hardly know who they are half the time. They pay the fee, we Contract, and then they tell me where they want to go. And that's that." Her stance twisted abruptly, the way it always did when we got to a subject she didn't really want to talk about. "You gonna be okay here?"

"I always am."

She shifted the violin on her back with a shrug. "Sure you are. You're a TouchStone. You practically fart moonbeams and piss rainbows. But seriously, take a night off from playing World of Warcraft and come dancing or something." Her face sobered for a moment as she turned to go. "I think it would be a very good thing if you were seen there, even if it's just once a week. Let people know you exist?"

"My dancing days are over, Mel," I said, watching my best friend strut through the crowd. For a moment, I wanted to call her back, to spill the beans about everything—my inability to figure out what I was doing, that odd little note tacked on Moira's office door . . .

Be back soon, Abby. Hold back the fort.

It hadn't made any sense to me four months ago and it still didn't. I also had no idea what her idea of "soon" was. The mostly immortal tended to overlook the little things— like the concept of time—I'd noticed.

In the end, I let Melanie walk away. She didn't understand; none of my friends really did. I was the Protectorate's golden child, wasn't I? How pathetic would it be to admit I was failing at this too? But then, it wasn't like I had much choice in the matter anymore. I had no one to blame but myself.

I sighed and looked at my watch. Still a little while to go before I had to go back to open the Marketplace. I craned my head above the rest of the crowd but there was no sign of Bryston—or Topher for that matter—so I wandered about the rest of the gallery, aimlessly sipping champagne.

I drifted past paintings of other friends, swept away in a haze of feathers and scales, horns and hooves. The irony of portraying humans as the very beings that surrounded them struck me as amusing. A slightly drunken giggle escaped me, attracting the attention of a sharp-nosed eggplant of a woman at the front of the gallery. Stifling another laugh, I bit down on my lip and focused on a small kiosk with a map of Portsmyth etched in sepia tones. I covered my mouth with my hand, quelling my sudden burst of strange humor. "Too much alcohol," I murmured to myself. *Too little sleep*, the voice in my head retorted dryly.

You Are Here.

I looked at the red star and snorted. I certainly was. I ran my finger over the star, absently taking in the circular shape of the town, its narrow streets a remnant of an older time, with cobblestones and horse-drawn carriages, candled lanterns and muddy gutters. On impulse, I traced a path from the gallery to the Pit, pausing over the OtherFolk landmarks that I knew. They weren't on the map, of course, but I'd found the hidden alley that led to the Hallows, the sunken garden of the Judgment Hall, and the Door at the base of the church that stood on its little hill. I'd never been through it, but I knew Moira had used it regularly. I turned away abruptly, heading back to the main exhibit, humor gone in a wave of impotent despair. Had she used it when she left this last time?

I found myself drawn to the scarlet woman again. I stood there for a long while, trying to guess what she had been thinking when it was painted. Her face was a grim reminder that I was just as bound to this place as she appeared to be, even if my chains weren't as solid.

"I knew she was kinky, but I never thought she'd willingly submit to chains," Bryston muttered behind me. I hadn't heard him arrive, but the smooth timbre of his voice was more than enough to give him away.

Another flare of jealousy stung me as I looked at the woman's pale curves. "Ex-girlfriend?" I guessed, the words clipped and taut.

He let out a deep chuff. "I'm not quite that kinky either." He paused. "She's my sister."

Three

I looked at Brystion and then back at the painting, the unease growing in my belly. "Your sister? Would that make her a succubus?"

"Of course." His lip curled in derision. "Figured that out all by yourself, did you?"

I shrugged. "Not really. Melanie told me what you were—the rest was my own clever deduction. That's what friendly people do, by the way— tell each other things. You know, as opposed to leering around dark corners all mysterious."

"Your first mistake was assuming I was friendly," he growled, pushing the dark fall of his hair from his forehead with a sharp tug.

I snorted, the alcohol making me careless. "If invading my mind and trying to fuck me senseless isn't friendly, I'd hate to see what happens when you actually *like* someone."

The light in his eyes emptied, leaving them dark and lifeless. I suddenly wished that I'd kept my mouth shut. The earlier masque of flirtation and faux self-deprecation melted away, leaving him cold. Untouchable. Other . . .

I shook myself. No matter how damned beautiful he

was, I had to remember that what I was dealing with was *not* human.

There was a hint of his sister about him, a pride I hadn't seen before. His jaw tensed under my scrutiny. I reached out to touch his arm and then thought better of it. Which is really just a nice way of saying I wimped out, but there it is. "What is it?"

His mouth flattened, snaking into a tight line. "You. You're so damned ignorant."

I blinked. "Maybe so, but at least I'm not an arrogant prick. Or maybe I'm not quite as stupid as you think. Either way, you have a nice evening now."

He caught my wrist as I turned to go and I took a swig of my champagne. He stroked the silver bracelet overhanging my palm. "And just what do you mean by that?" His face was as expressionless as the backside of a boulder.

I stepped back, rubbing my wrist against my skirt where his fingers had left a hot tingle.

He glared down at me, but I refused to look away, ignoring the sudden tremble in my knees. "Why, for the love of all that is holy, would Moira choose *you* as her representative here?"

"You'd have to ask her," I said, the sting of shame burning my cheeks. "After all, I'm just a mere mortal."

His nostrils flared. "I'm through playing games, Abby. Where is she?"

"You tell me. According to you I shouldn't worry about it because 'she already knows.' Unless," I said, slowly trying to piece it together, "she really *doesn't*. Your funky little magic seduction thing didn't work, did it?"

"Oh, it worked," he muttered. "Maybe a little too well."

I pushed a loose strand of hair behind my ear. "Well, I'm not sure what you mean. I'm certainly not on my knees if that's what you wanted. Or is that what's got your panties all in a bunch? Your mojo," I said, fluttering my fingers at him, "didn't work and now you're all atwitter?"

He snatched my free hand with the uncompromising snap of a hawk's talons. "Your stupidity is breathtaking. I'm surprised you've even managed to live this long."

"Moot point, given that I'm rather ageless at the moment, so a howdy-do and fuck you too," I drawled sweetly. A security guard eyed us from the front door but I waved him off, plastering a smile on my face. Getting arrested for a peace violation wasn't going to win me any favors with Moira. Protocol of secrecy and all that. "Let. Go. Of. Me."

Bryston's eyes flashed gold but he did as I said. I grabbed his arm and shuffled him to a curtained alcove. There were a number of them scattered about the art gallery—comfortable little nooks of gleaming wood and bland silk, undoubtedly used to make artistic conversation over a cup of mocha pretentiousness. My gaze flicked toward him, something inside me aching as I studied his face. Whatever his issues were, they didn't have as much to do with me as he was letting on.

Nearby, there was a bench and a little table with a pot of red dahlias on it. I set my drink on the table and wiped my damp fingers on my blouse. "No offense, but you're pretty stupid yourself. You get caught manhandling the Touch-Stone of the Protectorate in a public place like this and someone is going to kick your ass."

"You're bluffing."

"Try me." I sat down, watching him take a glass of his own from a tuxedo-clad waiter. "I don't make the rules, Bryston, but I do know that there are certain . . . protections that she has in place. She can't afford to look weak, even if she's not here. An attack on me is an attack on her. I may seem stupid to you, but even I know that much." I took a dainty sip of my drink.

"And your point is?"

"I'm all you've got, at the moment. So be a big boy and try using your words this time."

He tossed back the champagne like water, sliding down to sit beside me. I couldn't help but watch the way his mouth lingered on the rim of the glass, condensation glinting down the stem. "You're a fool."

"You're making this so hard for me. Do I sit here and bask in the glory of your ego or do I get up and walk out the door?" I drummed my fingers softly on the table. "Let me think."

"You're nowhere near as safe as you think you are." He jabbed a finger at me. "Whatever 'protection' you think you've been afforded, don't rely on it unless *you* have a way to back it up."

"Duly noted." I took another sip of champagne, letting it swirl around my mouth. "That's pretty bold talk from someone who damn near assaulted me this afternoon. If you're so concerned about my well-being there are better ways of showing it."

He leaned forward so his face hovered within inches of mine. "And you're pretty bold for someone who's lying through her teeth."

I froze. Shit. Did he know? I set the glass down carefully, smoothing out my skirt until I managed to compose my expression. "Perhaps you should tell me what the hell you're really talking about."

"My sister is missing."

I exhaled slowly, my eyes darting toward the painting. "All right. That's a good start. How does that concern me?"

"It doesn't," he snapped, drawing himself upright. "It *should* concern Moira, but as you said, she's not here. So I'm stuck with you."

"Listen, I'm sure your sister is a lovely . . . succubus, but I fail to see why Moira needs to be involved with—"

"Don't patronize me, little TouchStone," he said coldly. "You set this meeting up; I expect some answers."

"I never set anything up. Certainly not knowingly, anyway." I bit down on my thumb, chewing the nail. Clearly I had overstepped some OtherFolk protocol of which I was currently ignorant. Again.

"You made it fairly obvious this afternoon." He eased back against the bench. "Why else would you have made sure I knew where you would be tonight? It's open and public, and certainly busy enough," he pointed out. "It makes sense."

"I'm sorry." I hissed between my teeth. "I had no such manipulations in mind. This is just something I was supposed to go to. I mean, I also said I needed to buy shoes—how did you manage to interpret that bit of information covertly? Plan on being my shadow over at Fashion Footwear?"

"If I'd needed to. But then . . ." His gaze dropped pointedly down to my feet. "You didn't go."

"You've been following me?"

"Of course." He stroked the rim of his glass suggestively. "You're hiding something."

"Everyone's hiding something." I stood up abruptly and set my drink on the table, apprehension lancing down my spine. "You know what? I'm done trying to figure out what you're talking about . . . *Brystion*. If that even is your real name. If you need help, ask for it. If you want to keep being all tragic and broody and mysterious, than save it until Moira comes back, because I sure as hell don't have the patience to deal with it now." I hesitated, hating to admit my weakness. "And you're right. I don't know what I'm doing, but I'm trying the best I can. I don't know what you want, but whatever it is, you must be pretty desperate."

He uncoiled from the chair, eyes narrowed. "Explain yourself."

"What's to explain?" I snorted. "You braved the Cross-Roads at noon—without a TouchStone. That smacks of desperation to me. Even on top of that, you could have formally requested the Protectorate's help and I'd be honor-bound to help you. But you haven't, have you?" His face became stony and I knew I'd hit a nerve. "You didn't want anyone to know what you were doing," I continued, my heart skating along the edges of my own special brand of recklessness. "Not many OtherFolk around at noon to see you dropping by . . ."

"I'll give you that much, perhaps." He carelessly pushed his hair away from his face.

"And you appear to have snagged a TouchStone simply to what? Stalk me? What kind of a Contract could you have made in such a short time?"

"None of your business."

"Fair enough." I took a final sip of my champagne. I would have to ask Charlie what was involved in an incubus Contract; visions of something deliciously dark and sordid pressed the edges of my mind. Not that it mattered anyway. Multiple Contracts were frowned upon, but hey, a girl can dream, right? Too bad the personality didn't seem to match the package.

He said nothing for a moment and then his hand lightly tripped up my back as he pressed hard against me. His eyes bored into mine, capturing me with the heat of a thousand suns. "You're a Dreamer, Abby. I could drink your dreams like milk." He inhaled as though taking in my scent. "I could make you hotter than you've ever been. Make you boneless and wet and utterly sated, so that every breath you take is pleasure."

"Haven't we done this before?" I swallowed weakly. "What do you want from me?"

His nose nuzzled my cheek, lips brushing over my ear.

"Tell me what I need to know, and I'll make it happen. Every night, for the rest of your life."

"At which point you kill me. No, thanks." I pressed my hands against his chest. "I don't bargain with OtherFolk, Bryston. Not without a Contract. We pathetic mortals almost always get the shaft with your magic crap. Besides," I noted dryly, "your TouchStone will get jealous."

He slumped back into his seat. "Somehow I think she won't mind," he sighed. I almost felt sorry for him. *Almost.* It didn't change the fact that I couldn't help him if he didn't tell me what was going on. It also didn't change that he'd just tried to mojo his way past my defenses for the second time that day. I should have been utterly furious, but I wasn't. Just weary.

"When was the last time Moira held Court?"

"Ah . . . a while ago," I said, not wanting to admit just how long it had been. Four or five months at least, but she'd had one informal Hearing right before she left. "She's been rather busy lately and I don't think—"

He captured my hand, holding my wrist gently. "Don't lie. I'll kill you if you lie to me."

I opened my mouth, words of denial fading away beneath the gunmetal hardness in the words. He meant it.

"All right," I said hoarsely. I stood there, perched between fight or flight as every pallid heartbeat rushed through my ears. His nostrils flared. Perhaps he sensed my weakness. Tell me. Trust me. He stroked his thumb downward, the tremble of his flesh on mine filling me with the tumultuous urge to spill all that I held sacred. Moira's disappearance, my inability to sleep, the rotting edge of jaded appreciation that I seemed to trip over in my everyday life, the fact that I was completely and utterly in over my head . . .

"Who are you?" I wondered aloud.

He flinched. "No one," he said, his gaze drawn to the other end of the gallery with a resigned sort of anger.

"Ah, there you are, Abby!" Blinking stupidly, I glanced up to see a beaming Topher sliding through the crowd. Although he was impeccably dressed, even the slickness of an Armani suit couldn't hide the gauntness of his face or the shine of his balding pate. Dark circles ringed his eyes, and his cheekbones were hollow and hungry.

"It's Himself, then, is it?" I quipped in an Irish brogue that would have killed a leprechaun. I rose up on tiptoe to greet him with a kiss on the cheek. Very chichi.

"Abby, so glad you could make it." His eyes lingered on Brystion, and then he winked at me. "Nice to see you brought a friend."

"Strictly business." I corrected him without looking at the incubus. "How are you feeling these days?"

"Ah, well, you know how it is." He shrugged. "Some weeks are better than others, but each day is a gift, I always say."

"Yes." My mind strayed to a not-so-distant, giftless day of my own. "It is."

"So, who is your gorgeous, 'strictly business' friend?" I could almost see Topher trying to sketch the perfect lines of the man beside me, but something told me Brystion wasn't one to allow himself to be captured so easily.

"How horribly rude of me." For a moment I was tempted to just leave it at that, but I turned toward the incubus, manners and protocol butting heads with a rush of indignation and fear. "Brystion, this is Topher Fitzroy, the resident artistic genius responsible for this exhibit. Topher, this is Brystion . . ." My voice trailed away awkwardly. "Just Brystion, I guess?"

"First-name basis only, my dear, is a fine thing." The artist grinned. His smile faded when he looked at Brystion. "Is something the matter?"

I glanced over in surprise. A dark shadow had crossed over the incubus's face. "You say you're responsible for that?" His hand gestured toward the painting of his sister.

"Of course," Topher said, his expression suggesting the question wasn't even worthy of being asked. "It was a special commission and well worth every penny, if I do say so myself." He gazed at the painting fondly, but there was a tightness about his eyes where his smile never quite reached.

Brystion drew a ragged breath. "She would *never* have sat for you. You don't have the soul for it." He loomed over the artist, the edges of his skin blurring away for a moment. I blinked. He was about to drop his Glamour.

Shit. Not that I knew just what an incubus actually looked like, but judging by the darkness that was sliding up the back of his neck, it wasn't overly human. Hysterical visions of people running for the exits pursued by a massive cock and balls filled my mind, and I let out a gasp of laughter despite myself.

"That's enough." I let my voice drop into something soothing and quiet, the way Moira did when she was trying to stave off an argument between Paths. I inserted myself between the two men, stroking the crest of Brystion's wrist with a careful thumb.

The daemonic races in particular respond to physical stimulation, even if it be a simple stroke of the hand. A tiny distraction may be the difference between life and death. Moira's lilting voice echoed through my mind, even as I remembered the elegant scrawl of her notes on the tattered book she'd given me to study.

The incubus started beneath my touch, but his attention remained fixed on Topher. "Your Dreams are empty, mortal," he rumbled, eyeing the other man like he'd found the remains of something dead and furry beneath his foot.

With a shake, he pulled away from me, his eyes growing
dark once more as the lines around his body shifted back
into his Glamour.

"I beg your pardon?" Topher's lips paled beneath the
soft light of the gallery. For a moment, his face came alive
with that old spark, and I marveled to see it. A flush of
anger colored his cheeks and chased away the pall of death
that had surrounded him for months. He was brilliant for
a span of seconds and then it faded, leaving him wan and
drained. He raised his head proudly. "I assure you, I can
and *did* paint her, just as was requested. Succubus or not,
she sat for me by choice."

"I doubt that. Where is she?"

Topher's face became impassive. "Short of this picture, I
have not seen her since the night she posed for me."

Bryston snorted. "You did a shit job on Abby's as well.
Whatever talent you once had is gone. Have some dignity
and get on with your life."

The artist's mouth flattened into a sour line. "My dear,"
he said, waving over the security guard. "I'm going to have
to ask your friend to leave. He's causing a scene, and I'm
afraid my nerves can't take it. Would you mind escorting
him out?"

I shrugged helplessly at him, my cheeks burning beneath
the onslaught of stares from the other patrons. I tugged at
Bryston's shirt, my face stony. "Come on, then. Let's go."

He was silent as I led him outside, but the anger that
radiated from him made me want to retreat to my bedroom
and hide beneath the blankets. It didn't stop me from opening my mouth again though.

"Hey, awesome job at embarrassing the living shit out of
me in front of my friend."

"There is no way Sonja would have gotten near him, let
alone sat willingly in chains. In *chains*, Abby!"

"Okay, but that doesn't give you the right to be a dick. You said she was missing. Did it ever occur to you to be nice to someone who might have seen her recently?" He made a sound halfway between a sigh and a growl, keeping pace with me as I headed back to the Pit. Not quite an acknowledgment of guilt, but not admitting anything either. Typical male.

We walked in silence for several blocks, my feet knowing the way back without my having to think about it. Past the pawnshop and the Bagel Café, Fiddler's Green Fine Irish Gifts and the Opera Alley where the buskers performed. A glass player sat there tonight, perched behind a table full of elegant crystal, his fingers nimbly plying his trade. It was late enough that most of the shops were closed, but we moved through the waning crowds without issue, the vibrato of the glass music echoing eerily between the buildings as we walked.

"And I happen to *like* mermaids, you know," I said finally, unable to stand the quiet. I didn't know what else to talk about but the paintings.

"He made your tits too small," he grunted as we turned the corner, ignoring my muffled snort of mock outrage. "That and the expression on your face . . ." He paused, studying me from beneath his sweep of dark lashes. "You seemed . . . sad."

My shoulders tightened beneath the added scrutiny. "Yes, I suppose I was." The sign hanging from the shutter of the Pit creaked lightly in the breeze, the faded paint gleaming under the dim streetlight. "You almost lost it in there, didn't you?"

"You're changing the subject." He shoved his hands into his pockets and shifted away from me.

"Yes. Is that a common thing for incubi? I've never seen that happen before."

He exhaled sharply and then sighed, leaning up against the glass window of the storefront. "No. It shouldn't have happened. I suppose I owe you for stopping it." His head tipped backward, his eyes shutting. One eye cracked back open at me, a soft halo of gold flaring from beneath the lid. "So do you normally dance at work?"

"Now who's changing the subject?" I folded my arms over my chest in the universal gesture of *I'm horrified. Please fuck off.* "And I hardly think waggling my hips up the aisle counts as much of a show." My face blazed hot in the darkness. "How much did you see?"

"Enough." He chuckled bemusedly. "Why Tom Jones?"

I blinked. "Why . . . what?"

"Tom Jones. You were listening to him when I came into the store." His eyes lit up with amusement and I bristled.

"Yeah, I was. What's your point? It's a free country."

"Word on the street is that your little enchanted iPod there can play just about every song in existence. Why in the hell would you choose to listen to Tom Jones?"

"It reminds me of my mother," I said softly. "He was her favorite. She . . . died . . . rather recently."

"I'm sorry. I didn't mean to pry." His voice gentled. For a moment, I hated him for it. Hated the way that awful aching guilt pushed its way to the forefront, hated the way it echoed in the familiar words of pity, the murmurs of condolences, the sound of screeching metal and slurred, drunken apologies.

Helpless, I let the memory wash over me, a bittersweet wave tinged by the copper taste of blood and the blinding gleam of headlights. It was wrapped in the perfect stillness of the asphalt and pine trees through the cracked windshield, overcome by the repetitious seat-belt chime and the cloying scent of fluid leaking from the engine and the remainder of my mother's brainpan in my lap.

"I don't want your sympathy, Brystion." I backed away from him, my eyes beginning to burn. I blinked rapidly against the threatening tears. "I don't want anything from you at all."

He opened his mouth as if to say something, but I fumbled at the lock, turned the key, and didn't look back as I stepped inside and slammed the door behind me.

Four

Damn the incubus, anyway.

I was in a foul mood. The evening had been about as successful as diving into an empty swimming pool. Based on
the wretched slide of emotions tearing at my heart, I think I
would have chosen the pool.

I pushed the thoughts away and turned my attention to
the controlled chaos of the Midnight Marketplace. I had
enough trouble as it was without putting my mother's death
under the Freudian microscope.

"Chaos" may actually be too kind a word. If the bookstore was shabby and used, the Marketplace was anything
but. Glittering and warm, it had an aura of homeness that
shone about the place. Rich woods, soft carpets, and magnificent tapestries—all of it lush and comfortably mystical.
Small balls of witchlight floated up by the ceiling, adding a
sparkling glow to everything the pastel hues touched.

OtherFolk could visit the Marketplace at will, beyond the limits of the CrossRoads and without the use of
TouchStones. I wasn't entirely sure how it worked, only
that the store resided in its own little dimension. It was
separate from our world, but anchored here by me. Or more

realistically, by Moira, using me as her TouchStone. The Doorway itself was really the key to the whole thing. By whatever magics Moira employed, the Door only appeared at midnight in the courtyard behind the bookstore, the frame gleaming silvery blue against the back wall. The irony of it all was that only a mortal could open it. Yay, me.

The Marketplace was in full swing this evening. I usually enjoyed the hustle and bustle of the crowd, the strangeness of the pointed ears and feathered wings, goat hooves and lion's tails. But tonight I couldn't help but wonder at Bryston's words, not liking the uncomfortable tingle that tightened around my chest.

Was it really true? Did they all think I was some kind of idiot? A front for a Protectorate who no longer wished to protect?

My hands twitched on the counter and I took a deep breath. For all I knew the incubus was a lying piece of shit who was only trying to manipulate me for his own ends.

And doing a damn good job of it, apparently.

I eyed the ancient oak door speculatively, wondering if he would show up here as well. Some perverse part of me hoped he would.

The door chimes rang out and I glanced up, hiding a mild twinge of disappointment when it wasn't Bryston. Only for a moment though, and then I gave the Gypsy a genuine smile as he sauntered through the doorway. He was one of my regulars. He rarely spoke, leaving anything that needed to be said to the fiery gleam in the almond depths of his eyes.

He muttered a question in that liquid voice of his, and I shrugged. "It hasn't come yet, but we'll be getting a delivery tonight. Might be in there."

A wan smile spread across his face as he bowed and made his way to his usual corner in the back of the store. A few moments later an elegant strain of a mystical Romany czardas wove its way through the room. There was a pause and a near audible sigh from the other patrons as the haunting notes rang out with a distant, secret sorrow. He came here on most delivery nights, searching for an answer that I had no way of giving him.

I bit my lip and tried to lose myself in the roll of the music, the last of my anger at Brystion sluicing away and leaving me with a hollow ache in my chest. All I could feel was the pain of the recent past. How long had it been since the accident? Eight months? A year?

Being ageless had a peculiar effect on mortals. The days seemed to slide by, blurring one into the next. I'd lost track of time and it was very disconcerting. It was easy to see why OtherFolk were often so jaded, but that really wasn't an excuse. Maybe Brystion had been right. If I couldn't manage to keep myself together for six months, how was I ever going to last seven years?

The specifics of my Contract were rather clear on that account though. I served Moira in whatever capacity she dictated. In return, I no longer aged. Not quite the same as being immortal, but I'd taken the offer without too much thought.

There was always a price though. A price I'd have to learn to deal with.

"How much is this?" A gnarled hand thrust what looked like a pile of loose seaweed in my face. Her knuckles were large, wrinkled tree knobs, but her manicure blazed in a perfect shade of emerald green. The hag's piggish eyes gleamed at me from beneath a greasy fall of salt-and-pepper hair. She shifted her substantial weight, grunting impatiently.

"One moment." I flipped over the lavender tag hanging from the center of the pile. **D7**. I searched through my spreadsheet until I found the matching value. "That's Mermaid's Tangle. Two coppers a strand." I did a quick figure in my head as I counted up the strands. "This will be about one gold piece if you buy the whole hank."

"Outrageous," the hag snapped. "What is Moira thinking with these kinds of prices?"

"I'm sure I don't know, ma'am," I said, keeping my voice bland. I was in no rush to piss anyone else off this evening, and I could already tell where this was going. "I'll be happy to take down your opinions and pass them along."

"Excuse me, miss?"

I glanced over at the courier elf standing beside the counter. He wasn't our usual delivery guy, and I didn't recognize him. Tall, with auburn hair and green eyes. Bored, disdainful eyes. There was some kind of animal carrier thing sitting on the counter in front of him.

"Uh, yes?"

His name tag read "Hi, my name is Glorfindel. Ask me about our specials at the Gap of Rohan."

My lips pursed. "That's not really your name, is it? I mean, I know Tolkien is sort of the godfather of elves, but isn't that a little over the top?"

He flushed, his hand jerking over the badge protectively. "Management makes us wear them. My real name is Alisair. You can call me Al."

I grunted, understanding that particular predicament a little too well. "What is that?" I pointed a skeptical finger at the carrier, hearing a soft bleat come from inside.

"Sign here, please." The elf ignored my question and handed me a parchment form.

"Oh, no," I said firmly. "We don't take livestock. It's against store policy." And mine. The last thing I needed was to be stuck taking care of vegetable lambs or barnacle geese or some other such nonsense. I damn near killed everything

I touched, anyway. The sad little garden out back was proof enough.

"Let me check the order." He frowned, flipping through the stack of documents in his arms. I felt a momentary twinge of glee. For all that most OtherFolk look down on technology, I couldn't help but feel superior for a moment. Give me an Excel spreadsheet any day of the week.

Ignoring the hag as she tapped her foot, I bent over to take a careful look inside the carrier.

"Is that what I think it is?"

He snorted. "I wouldn't wager on anything that you might be thinking, but yes, that's a miniature unicorn. Rather expensive species to be shipped and a very ornery fellow at that."

I peered closer, meeting the tiny beast's silvery blue eyes, losing myself in the delicate hooves and seashell horn, spiraled and sharp. Its face was a strange mix of goat and deer and something else, its tufted tail flicking like an irritated tiger's against the side of the carrier. It wore a jeweled silver collar and what looked like a blue topaz shining from its throat. "It's lovely," I murmured, myriad little-girl dreams filling my voice with longing.

The hag curled her upper lip. "Unless you're a virgin, girly, don't get your hopes up." The brownie in line behind her covered his mouth with a dark-skinned hand, and I rolled my eyes.

"I'll keep that mind," I retorted dryly.

"Indeed," the courier agreed. "And 'it' is actually a 'he,' according to the invoice."

I snapped my attention back to the pointy-eared prig. "That's all well and good . . . Al . . . but we didn't order him, so you'll have to take him back."

"I'll have to check with my manager." He pushed his hair back to tap the Bluetooth headset curled over his right ear. "Let me get the rest of the deliveries and you can sign off on that part."

"Okay." I moved the carrier away from the counter's edge. "I'll be waiting." He disappeared into the crowd and back out the door. I eyed his headset bemusedly. Maybe I'd been wrong about the technology thing.

The hag cackled at me as I rang her up. With a last chuckle, she hunched away, clutching her purchase to her breast. The rest of the line moved briskly after that, as I marked down the purchases of the brownie and a scaled dragon man, two pale angels and something I could only recognize as a shambling mass of flesh. It smelled like a mix of a freshly made zombie and dried pig feces. My dinner roiled in protest as the scent slammed into my face. I swallowed hard to keep from gagging. The blob burbled at me, a stray tentacle dragging something slimy up to the register. I couldn't even tell what it was in the mucusy mess trailing behind.

"On the house." I forced a smile. That gray slug track it left behind was going to be a bitch to clean up.

A shadowy figure stepped up to the counter next, hands empty. Inwardly I cringed. The Marketplace was supposed to be a place where the OtherFolk could be themselves, such as they were. Glamours weren't allowed, or at least not major ones. It gave everyone equal footing, or so Moira's theory went. It was never a good sign when they tried to hide themselves. Well, unless it was a medusa or something. I'd deal with a cloaked face over being turned to stone any day.

The figure paced about, paying careful attention to the carrier. "How much for the unicorn?"

"It's not for sale, I'm afraid. There was a mistake at the—" The what? Manufacturer's? Mystical Petting Zoo? "Shipping company," I finished up lamely. "He's going back in a few minutes. I'm sorry. I don't know where you can get one, but maybe Al can help you."

"I'll pay you double what he's worth," the figure said. "Even triple."

My eyes narrowed. What was it with dark and mysterious men that just couldn't seem to listen today?

"The answer is no," I snapped.

"You don't understand. I *need* that animal." The guttural voice became desperate and wheedling. I wavered, pity warring with bitchiness. What would Moira do? My gaze roamed around the store, and I realized it had grown quiet. They were all watching to see what I would do. I exhaled softly. Any action by me would be seen as an action by Moira. Another bleat emerged from the box, and I shook myself.

"Listen, I don't care if you're Voldemort under that thing. We don't sell livestock. Period."

The snigger that erupted from the back of the store abruptly cut off as Alisair reappeared, frowning. "You were right, there's no record of this animal being requested or purchased by the Marketplace. Strange. Ah, well." He shrugged. "Wires get crossed all the time. I'll just take him back and we'll sort it out." I couldn't quite help feeling a pang of regret. After all, it's not every day a girl gets to see a childhood fantasy brought to life. I opened my mouth to speak when the hooded figure lurched for the carrier. Its gloved hands curled around the handle. "I'm sorry, but I *must* have it."

"Back off, there, sticky fingers." The elf bristled, snatching the carrier back. They struggled for a moment, the unicorn making a panicked cry as he slid helplessly back and forth. My eyes darted between them.

"That's enough, both of you." I pointed at the door. "Take it outside before one of you breaks something."

There was a snap and a crack as the figure heaved backward. The plastic carrier split open, spilling out one very disgruntled unicorn. He twisted in midair like a cat and landed on all four hooves.

"Now you've done it." Alisair glowered at the figure as the unicorn sidled toward the door. "Do you have any idea how hard it is to capture one of those?"

"Nobody move!" The music cut off with a discordant flourish and I winced at the arched brow of the Gypsy. "Sorry." I raised my voice, craning my head over the shelves, trying to remember whatever bits of unicorn lore I knew. "Is anyone here a virgin?"

Silence.

Of course not.

"You're no help." I knelt on the floor, my left knee grinding in protest. "No one make any sudden moves." All I needed was for this thing to take off through the store and gore someone. Although, really, how bad could it be? He was only fifteen inches tall.

"Shhhhh." I slowly held out one hand to the little beast. I wasn't a virgin by any means, but I was the only mortal female in the store, so that was going to have to do.

His tail lashed from side to side, his nostrils flaring. "I don't blame you," I said, pretty sure I wouldn't enjoy being dumped on the floor either. He sniffed my hand, his breath tickling the back of my knuckles. We hovered there for a moment, and then he turned away with a snort.

The elf tittered. "Told you."

"Beggars can't be choosers. Besides, I never said I was a virgin." I looked up at the cloaked figure from the corner of my eye, my face flaming. "And don't think *you'll* be getting him, even if you help." It stared at me impassively, and then pulled back the hood of the cloak to reveal azure scaled skin and cat-slit eyes.

An old-world daemon. Great.

"We'll see." It smiled, revealing a frightfully large number of teeth. "If we have no maidens here, you'll need a golden bridle. Or a jeweled snare," it added helpfully.

"What you need is to let that poor creature go." A blond fae pushed her way to the front of the store. Her diaphanous wings quivered in indignation. She wore combat boots and a T-shirt proclaiming *Pave the Rainforest*.

"Who are you?" I asked.

"I'm Didi. Second in command of Pixies for PETA. And he's *not* livestock. He's a living, breathing being, deserving of your respect and compassion." She crossed her arms. "I demand that you free him from his bonds of captivity."

"Right." The urge to run screaming from the room bubbled up in my chest, tightly wrapped in a slight wave of hysteria. My eyes flicked toward the daemon. His grin became broader.

"And what do *you* want him for?" I forced myself to meet the daemon's eyes.

His smile never wavered. "Bachelor party."

"I don't even want to know." I held up my hand before he could say anything else, my stomach churning at the thought. The pixie stomped her foot but I waved her off. "Enough. Let's just catch him first."

"I refuse to be party to this . . ." She flounced away toward the back of the store in a swirl of pink glitter, followed by what appeared to be a cluster of chipmunks, jeweled beetles, and one very confused baby seal.

"All right, come on then." I scrambled forward. "Oh, no you don't." The unicorn edged away, his tiny hooves scraping over the floor. My hands slid over fur as soft as dandelion fluff, his silken muscles bunching madly as he squirmed. "Gotcha!"

A low ringing echoed through my ears, strangely sub-dued, my limbs vibrating as though something snapped into place. Immediately the unicorn stopped moving and became heavy in my arms. He shifted and blinked blearily at me; he was as stunned as I.

"Wha . . . what is that?" I was lost in the sapphire brilliance of his eyes, my head suddenly dizzy. I slumped on the floor, overtaken by the scent . . .

. . . the scent of a hidden forest glade, dew-tipped violets over my tongue, and the creeping shadow of delicate ferns shading us from the harsh light of the golden afternoon . . .

"Touching. Sign here, please."

"What are you talking about? I caught . . . him." I gazed back down at the unicorn, the angst and heat of the moment rolling out of me in a wave of giddiness.

"You caught him, all right." Alisair flicked the rim of his baseball cap, which declared him a Cincinnati Bengals fan. "You just became his TouchStone. That makes him nonreturnable. So if you don't mind, I'd really like to be going now."

"I don't understand." I shuffled to my feet, cradling the unicorn in the crook of my arm. I stroked his head, my fingers scratching at the base of his ears. He began to . . . purr? Hum? "How can I become his TouchStone without a Contract? Besides, I'm already Contracted to Moira."

"Good question." The elf shoved a pen in my face, his voice a study in complete indifference. "Wish I could stay to chat, but I've got more deliveries to make. Truly, you're fascinating for a mortal."

"You don't have to be rude." I took the pen and signed my name next to Moira's seal on the parchment. He rolled up the scroll and left, muttering something under his breath. The daemon stared at me hard enough to burn holes through my skin.

"Well," I said, unable to completely keep the smugness from my voice, "I guess you're going to have to leave empty-handed."

He let out a humorless laugh. There was a hint of brimstone about it, like it contained the promise of damnation wrapped in silk. "Don't be too sure of that," he said, his eyes resting on me for a moment. He sniffed the air, a forked tongue flicking out toward the unicorn, scenting him.

I shifted the unicorn in my arms, turning him away from the daemon. "That's enough," I said. "Buy something or leave."

He straightened up as Didi fluttered by, scaled face brightening. "Ah, well, perhaps I've found something just as good, eh?" With a chuckle that would have turned milk sour, the daemon licked his lips and followed the pixie out the door.

I shuddered, knowing it wasn't right, but also knowing there was very little I could do about it. Whatever pathetic amount of authority I had ended as soon as they crossed the threshold. But I had bigger things to worry about. A murmur of voices rippled in my ear, a cacophony of elbows and polite coughs and "highly unusual," and "I wonder what Moira will make of this," and "it's not right . . . it's just not right."

I was suddenly eager to be done with this day. It was nearly 1:00 A.M. Close enough. "We're closing," I announced loudly. "Make your purchases and we'll see you soon."

There were a few grumbles, but most of the patrons filed out sharply enough. An unassuming fellow wearing spectacles and a scarf brought up the rear. A tiny pair of horns burst from his brow, nearly covered by the soft chestnut waves of his hair. He bought tea and a tin of biscuits before disappearing into the night, a winged cat at his heels.

Apparently some daemons really liked their chai.

The Gypsy was the last to leave, pausing at the counter to tip his violin at me. His gaze held a gleam of amusement when it fell upon the unicorn. He eyed me suggestively and then laughed softly.

"Yeah, yeah," I muttered. "Everyone's a critic."

He chuckled again, teeth flashing. I gestured at the boxes that Al had left beside the counter. "Looks like your special order didn't come in again. Maybe next time?"

He nodded and bowed before gathering up his violin and slipping out the door. I breathed a sigh of relief at the sudden silence.

"Finally."

My heart pattered with another little thrill as I remembered the unicorn in my arms. He curled his upper lip and bleated plaintively.

"Are you hungry?" I suddenly realized I had no idea what to feed him, let alone any concept of taking care of his basic needs. It's not like I could run to PetSmart for unicorn treats.

I set him down for a moment, my fingers lingering in the cirrus fluff of his mane. I had a few more minutes and then I'd have to leave too, or I'd be stuck in the store until it reopened. I'd already done that once, and I wasn't eager to repeat the experience, even if I did manage to enchant my iPod as a result.

Whatever Brystion and the rest of them thought, the iPod hadn't been part of the bargain between me and Moira. The concept had amused her enough that she'd let me keep the damn thing despite the fact that I'd nearly wrecked the store trying to get out.

I looked over at the pile of deliveries. I slit open the top box with a knife and ran a quick eye over the basic merchandise. Nothing that couldn't wait. Yawning, I rubbed my eyes. "Time for bed." A feather-light touch brushed my shin and I gazed down absently, then looked away and shuddered.

"Forgive me if I'm wrong," I said, my voice strangled. "I mean, I know I'm an idiot and all, but I'm pretty sure unicorns aren't supposed to hump people's ankles."

The unicorn made a shrugging motion as if to say, *What can you do?*

"I'll show *you* what I can do, you little shit." I stepped away, shoving at him with my foot. "Get off me." Unperturbed, he shook himself like a dog and trotted over to the door. He pawed at it with a dainty cloven hoof. If he hadn't just been taking some rather extreme liberties with my person, I would have thought it horribly cute.

I held the door open and gestured politely. "After you, I'm sure." No way was I was going to let him walk behind me. Chest pushed out, he paraded into the courtyard, his silver horn glinting in the moonlight. I shut the door behind us, pausing for a moment until the edges began to glitter with the telltale sign of a Doorway. It melted away in a slurry of sparkles and fading witchlight. A few seconds later there was nothing left but bare stone and brick.

A prickle crept over the back of my neck and I turned to look behind me. The courtyard was empty, but I couldn't quite help remembering the way that daemon had looked at me like I should have been something he found at a steakhouse. I hoped the pixie had gotten away.

The unicorn brayed at me and snorted. "Yeah, yeah," I muttered, chalking up my uneasy feeling to nerves and exhaustion. Scooping up the unicorn, I mounted the stairs to the apartment. It had been a hell of day.

Based on the way my head began throbbing, the night wasn't going to be much better.

Five

His skin was silver, dappled in moonlight and shadows, a mastery of long lines and pale musculature rising and falling with each hurried breath. There was a rhythm to it, like the crash of the sea upon a hidden shore; it gave him away, belied the calmness of his elegant cheekbones, the arrogant arch of his mouth. The pulse at his neck flashed once, twice. I ached to run my lips over it, to taste that soft sheen of sweat at the hollow of his collarbone.

I took one step closer and then another, reached out to thread my fingers through his silken hair. It glittered beneath the light, twining over his broad shoulders to trail around my wrist like the ebony jesses of some exotic bird of prey. His hand slid over mine, capturing my palm to press it over his chest.

"Look at me," he demanded, tipping my chin upward. I arched a brow at his tone of voice, but I didn't pull away. I didn't look at him either, not directly, and I could feel him tense in anticipation. My lips curved into a savage smile, and I wondered if my little act of rebellion would finally unleash what I knew was hovering beneath the surface. My gaze drifted to the standing mirror, slowly rising up the reflected length of his body; I lingered over the tempting curve of his ass, his taut *muscles coiled and trembling. His grasp tightened around my wrist, and I chuckled, daring him to make the next move.*

"Checkmate," I murmured, as his breath came hard and ragged. He snarled softly, lips brushing over my forehead. His hand slid down the small of my back to press me up against his growing erection, pushed tight in the confines of his leather pants. I let my hand stroke boldly downward, my fingers aching to set him free, to grasp his turgid magnificence.

I rocked my hips into his groin as my gaze drifted up to feast on his sensual mouth before settling on his eyes, dark and golden.

Those . . . eyes . . .

I gasped in recognition, pulling away, falling as my name dropped from his lips in a seductive, knowing tone.

"Abby . . ."

I bolted upright, sheets tumbling to my quaking thighs, skating the edge of that last wave of pleasure. I knew all it would take was a slight movement and I would be tumbling into the realm of orgasm. My hips twitched violently, pushing upward, straining toward the hand that was already creeping down the flat of my belly.

"No," I told myself firmly.

No.

I was *not* going to lie here and masturbate to the Prince of Broody Darkness. The *horribly* sexy Prince of Broody Darkness.

Even I have to draw the line somewhere. And getting off in my sleep to mysterious OtherFolk was where I drew it—especially with ones that insisted on being total asshats the night before. Besides, who the hell ever used the phrase "turgid magnificence" in the real world?

I cracked an eye at the clock and groaned. 8:00 A.M. Still too early for a mere mortal to be awake and far too late to go back to sleep. I flopped onto my belly. Eventually the hot and bothered part of my brain ran off to dip its head in an ice bucket and I was able to think. My body appeared to be much more unforgiving and continued to thrum in dismay. I tried to ignore the way my hips ached to grind into the mattress. My lips pursed as a thought struck me. What if that *hadn't* been a dream? What if Bryston had actually . . . been here?

"Go away," I said, rolling my eyes at my own idiocy. "If you're there, I don't want any."

The silence mocked me. *Liar* . . .

And yet, I couldn't quite shake the idea that it had been more than just a dream. After all, he *was* an incubus. The thought that he might actually have taken his stalking into the realm of my dreams was disconcerting enough to have me roll out of bed pretty quickly. I shambled into the bathroom and gazed blearily into the mirror. Was he in there? No flash of gold seared me from my reflection.

I peered closer. Was there a hint of something reflected in my face? Frustration? Amusement? No, I decided. Except for the dark circles beneath my eyes, there wasn't anything different about me at all. I shrugged and tottered toward the shower. The water turned on with a hiss and bang of creaky pipes.

As I stood there, I shut my eyes and let the water sluice over me, the tiny bathroom filling with steam. Suddenly I realized I hadn't had any nightmares for the first time since the death of my mother. I reached up, touching my forehead, the ghost of a tingle brushing over the skin where he'd kissed me.

It would almost be worth it. I sighed as I lathered my hair into a soapy sculpture. The concept of having a singularly quiet night was beyond tempting, and if I added a few orgasms into the mix, why then, so much the better. But I had a feeling it could never be that simple. Everything came with a price.

Everything.

I shut the water off with a jerk, squeezing my hair viciously. I snatched a towel from the rack and rubbed it over my skin until I was dry. Stalking back into the bedroom, I tossed on a clean pair of jeans and a Hello Kitty ninja T-shirt.

A soft bleat caught my attention and I looked down to see the unicorn nested deep in my lower dresser drawer.

"Er," I muttered stupidly at him as he wallowed in a pair of lacy briefs. "That's quite enough of that . . . you." He rolled his upper lip at me in disdain. Whatever. Another chunk of my childhood dreams had just run down the reality drain in the form of a horny unicorn, no less. Just my luck.

I padded lightly on the hardwood floor as I made my way into the kitchen, my stomach rumbling. I deftly ignored the large manila envelope sitting on the round table, the same way I'd ignored it every morning for the last two weeks. I'd turned it over so I didn't have to read it, but I knew what it meant with its crisp, neat writing on the front and the attorney-at-law label at the top left. Undoubtedly there was something in there that I had to sign or process, but that would mean admitting certain things.

Like the fact that my mother wasn't ever coming back.

If I ignored it long enough, one of these mornings it would just be gone. So far this theory was failing miserably, but I had plenty of time to wait. I wasn't going anywhere, was I?

Mysterious envelope or no, breakfast was in order. I threw the kettle on for some tea and rummaged around the fridge. It was small as far as appliances went, but it never actually ran out of food. It didn't have anything too exotic, but the staples were always in there and always fresh. Another perk from Moira. My TouchStone duties seemed to burn a lot of calories. Something about the way the Contract worked, I guess, although whether it was the magic of the bond or just the fact that I rarely got a moment to myself, I didn't know. A never-empty icebox set that off nicely, but I'd still lost a few pounds over the last couple of months.

One heated frying pan later and I was well on my way to cooking a heaping pile of bacon and cheesy scrambled eggs. I'd tried for an omelet, but as usual I'd ended up with nothing more than a runny mess. One of these days I'd just admit that I couldn't cook, but until then I was going to keep trying. I piled some toast together with jam and topped off the whole thing with a mug of steaming English Breakfast.

Something sharp pricked my ankle, and I jumped. "Oh, it's you," I muttered as the unicorn snorted up at me. "You want some?"

He made a little movement that looked like a nod and trotted off toward the table, leaping onto one of the chairs. I hesitated. "What the hell." I skimmed a few strips of bacon onto an extra plate. There was a part of me that felt a little uncomfortable with feeding what was surely an herbivore nothing more than the remnants of a cloven-hoofed cousin, but based on the way the little beast licked the grease off the plate I didn't have much to worry about.

We sat at the table together, the unicorn and I, chewing in silence as I mulled over the details of yesterday. "I think I'm screwed," I told him ruefully, sliding back into my chair to sip my tea. "Totally and utterly screwed. And I think I need to give you a name."

Tapping his horn on his plate, he made a little grunt that sounded an awful lot like "more." I tossed him a spoonful of eggs, sucking on my lower lip as he buried his face in the cheese. Between the underwear, the leg humping, and the single-minded eating, it was almost like living with a tiny, preternatural fratboy. All I needed was to trip over some empty cans of Natty Light.

Today was my late day, but my stomach churned with restlessness. Charlie would be working the early shift at the bookstore this morning, and she was always good for a chat. I slipped on my Crocs and refilled my mug after dumping the dishes into the sink.

"You're staying here," I told the unicorn. "Last thing I need is for you to start showing . . . your affections . . . to the general public." He rolled his eyes, but ambled off the chair and back into the bedroom, hooves tapping like little hammers.

I clutched the mug to my chest as I left the apartment, creaking down the outer steps. I'd broken several coffee cups since I'd moved in, mostly due to carelessness. Well, that and the occasional seizure. I rolled my head on my shoulders, stifling the urge to run my fingers over the scar. My mother used to joke about me spinning until my brains fell out when I was a kid, but I supposed a metal plate would be just fine for stopping that sort of thing.

The morning was brilliant, everything still damp and dewy from yesterday's rain. It was going to be humid later, but there was a crispness to the air that spoke of cooler times approaching. I breathed it in, enjoying a few moments of quiet, but there was an edge to it. The calm before the storm, maybe.

There was no mark upon the back wall to indicate the silver Doorway to the Marketplace had ever been there, but I could almost see it gleaming on the brickwork in an ivy-twined lattice of magic. The remainder of the courtyard was small and square and utterly boring. Moira liked to think of it as quaint. I called it "Abby can't garden for shit." The few flowers left after the scorching July heat were wilted but defiant. If I had any brains at all I'd look at getting a few gnomes in to do some pruning.

The Pit had a back-door opening beneath the stair,

leading into the storeroom and the makeshift closet that doubled as Moira's office. I unlocked it with a jingle of keys, giving the morning sunshine one last regretful look. There were days when living above the bookstore was an advantage, but for some reason I couldn't think of one right now.

There were no customers this early in the morning, but Charlie was humming away, busy with a more mundane set of inventory boxes. UPS had come early. Charlie's short, chestnut hair was cut into a pixie bob I'd never be able to pull off. It was cute and perky and perfectly framed her heart-shaped face. Her complexion was what they call "sun-kissed," but not in the freckled mess I always seemed to get. Hers was just a gorgeous nut-brown smoothness. I cleared my throat to let her know I was there. She startled and then smiled broadly.

"You're up early, Abby. I didn't expect to see you for at least a few more hours."

"I know." I set my mug down on an empty shelf as I knelt beside her. "I couldn't go back to sleep, so I thought I might come down and help you out with this. Should have done it yesterday, anyway."

"More nightmares?"

"Not quite. Not unless you call being pawed by an incubus a bad thing."

"Ah, yes." She wiped her dusty hands on her jeans, her mouth a little O of distaste. "Melanie mentioned that you'd had a bit of a run-in with Brystion last night."

"Does *everyone* know who this guy is except me?" I rolled my eyes at her. "The way he played hard to get, you'd think it was supposed to be some big secret."

"Maybe he was just dicking with you. He's been known to be a real prick sometimes, although since his last Touch-Stone left him it's just gotten worse."

"She left him?"

"That's the rumor, anyway. She ran off with the drummer of Ion's Folly, the way I heard it."

"Ah." I nodded wisely. "I guess that explains why they broke up."

"Could be," she drawled, pulling out a stack of books. "Wow. Who the hell chooses this crap? You or Moira?"

"That's all Moira, I'm afraid. The most she lets me do is narrow down the genre choice. This month it was alien romance or western history."

"God." She held out a book as though it might shit on her. "*His Tentacled Love*? Are you kidding me?"

"Apparently not. How about *The Spawning*?" I waggled my fingers at her. "Like hentai for grown-ups."

"Speaking of spawning, how'd it go with Brystion?"

"How did what go? He's an ass."

"But he showed up in your dreams last night?"

"Don't be a perv. It was just a dream. At least, I hope it was. I don't know. I get the feeling he's kind of stalking me." I dug out another stack of books, not really reading the titles. "I mean, I suppose he's got good reason. His sister is missing, and he wants the Protectorate's help to find her."

"Well, surely Moira wouldn't turn him down. What did she say?"

"She . . . uh . . . doesn't know."

Charlie's eyes narrowed. "What do you mean she doesn't know? You didn't tell her?"

"She's been a little hard to get a hold of." I studied the ceiling for a moment. By the tone of my friend's voice, it was almost as if I'd been caught with my hand in the cookie jar. But in my case, the Oreos were likely to grow teeth and gnaw my fingers off. "Like not at all. I don't know where she is."

The confession rushed out of me with a whoosh. Instead of feeling relieved, though, the weight of the last few months pressed down on me even more. My throat clenched like a fist had been shoved down my gullet and my head started its telltale throb.

"Abby?" Charlie's voice warbled at me from a distance, rushing down the dark corridor of my consciousness. I couldn't move, but I could sense her by my side, grasping my shoulders.

Only a little one . . .

Seconds, minutes, hours. I never really could tell how long I stayed out during an episode, but suddenly my eyes were open, exhaustion hitting me full in the face. Charlie had laid me out on the floor, my limbs heavy and dull.

"Hey, you okay?" Charlie's face came into focus, her dark chocolate eyes wide.

"Yeah. Just . . . tired. Want to sleep." My eyelids sank for a moment. "Seizures always make me drowsy," I mumbled. "Least I didn't piss myself this time. How long was I out for?"

"A few minutes. Jesus, Abby, I thought you were getting better."

"Happens. I'm tired. Or maybe drained is a better way of describing it. But I get them more when I'm tired." *And when you take your meds haphazardly,* a snide voice reminded me. "I just need to get more sleep."

"That could be," she agreed, "but being a TouchStone expends energy. And you're not just a normal TouchStone, Abby—you're the TouchStone of the Protectorate, which is a lot more intense. Most mortals can only handle short-term Contracts, and certainly not more than one."

"If you say so." I rubbed at my head, ignoring her eye roll.

"Ever wonder why so many brilliant musicians and artists seem to die at such a young age?"

I blinked stupidly at her, my muddled thoughts tripping over themselves. "Too many Contracts?"

"Absolutely. OtherFolk are drawn to anyone with major talent, particularly the Fae. Sometimes they're not overly careful about how much energy they take."

Bryston's words echoed in my mind for a moment, something suddenly becoming uncomfortably clear.

You're a Dreamer, Abby. I could drink your dreams like milk.

"Yeah, yeah, I get it. The whole rainbow connection thing—the poets, the dreamers, and me. Moot point since I'm not any of those things. Not anymore. And I'm certainly not interesting enough for anyone else to want to Contract with me. Except Fuckfang." I struggled to sit, letting Charlie pull me upright. The world tilted sideways for a moment and then straightened as I leaned against one of the stacks. I tipped my head back. "And he only thought . . . well, never mind what he thought." I frowned. "Doesn't matter anyway."

I met her liquid eyes with a sour smile. "So where does this leave me? Moira's missing. A succubus has disappeared and her horny incubus brother seems bent on trying to invade my mind." *And a unicorn is upstairs getting busy in my underwear drawer,* I added silently, wondering if I should tell her I'd TouchStoned to him. I glanced at her worried face. I'd shelve it for now.

"You're going to have to talk to Robert about this," Charlie pointed out.

My heart tripped over itself trying to launch its way out of my throat. Robert was Moira's personal bodyguard and her first lieutenant. Charlie was his TouchStone, but how they had come to that particular Contract I didn't know. What I *did* know was that Robert swore like a sailor, drank like a fish, and still dropped his *r*s with a good dose of

Boston pride. He had a wicked temper and guarded Moira's interests like a hawk. For being the living embodiment of such a bundle of clichés, he also seemed to intensely dislike me, though damned if I'd ever figured out why.

"Are you sure? I didn't think it was worth getting him involved."

"Are you kidding me?" Her eyes grew wild for a moment. "Robert's been in a foul mood lately, and I didn't know why. I mean, I knew he was worried when she didn't answer his calls, but he didn't want to make a fuss because . . . well . . . she's Fae, and they're just weird. Besides, you've been sitting here acting as though everything was fine. He thought you'd let him know if there was something wrong." She turned toward me, shaking her head. "Abby, why didn't you come to us?"

I gave the other woman a helpless shrug. "She left a note. I mean, she said she'd be back. How was I supposed to know? Christ, for all the contact Robert's had with me, they could have both taken off and I wouldn't have known."

"I've forgotten how new you are to all this," she said. "All kidding aside, you're in a bad position, Abby. What do you think the rest of the OtherFolk are going to do when they realize Moira isn't here?"

"Nothing good, I'm guessing," I said grimly.

She patted my hand thoughtfully. "I think you should take the rest of the day off. Go on upstairs and rest, but come to the Hallows tonight. I'll make sure Robert's there, and you two can try to figure out what the best course of action is. It wouldn't hurt for you to be seen either. After all, if there's something untoward going on, showing them that you're not rattled by it couldn't hurt."

"Unless I get killed for it." My lips curved into a self-mocking smile. "But I'll be there."

Six

Hot stuff, Abby." The bartender grinned broadly at me, his teeth gleaming in the amber light of the nightclub. This would have been slightly more reassuring if it weren't for the distinctly wolfish snout pressing out from his face. His tongue lolled between sharp canines as he laughed at my expression, one hairy paw taking the ten-dollar bill I handed him. "You look damn good enough to eat, darlin'. All you need is a little red hood."

"Not that hot, Brandon." I stifled a groan at his words. My fingers curled around the Mudslide he pushed across the bar, smearing the condensation on the frosted mug. I let my lips drift over the straw, the heady sweetness of chocolate and Bailey's flooding my mouth. My gaze flicked to the mirror behind the counter. No harm in checking myself out, right?

I was as dressed up as I get, in wedge-heeled, sling-back sandals and denim capris. My shirt was a cut-off, leaving my belly slightly exposed. I hadn't worked out in ages, but years of *pliés* and *pas de chat* had left my abs with more than a hint of tautness. Maybe not as muscular as before, but I didn't mind.

I'd pulled my hair into something more stylishly tousled, and I even brushed on a little eye shadow. Not too much though. Funny how tossing a little glitter on your eyelids suddenly looks garish when you're standing next to a gorgeous fox-woman or an ethereal nixie. Of course, there were some real ugly creatures that hung around this place too. Not that it really mattered. Glamour or not, beautiful or hideous, the OtherFolk all had an aura of otherworldliness that the rest of us couldn't touch.

The woman at the other end of the bar was certainly doing her damnedest though. She had hair the color of ripe chestnuts and golden skin, her dark-smudged eyes and green velvet dress giving her a sort of absinthe-Faery-meets-streetwalker vibe. She was holding court among a gaggle of vampires. They were drooling all over her, but I couldn't tell if that was because she was an artist of some sort, or just because of the 38DD implants bolted to her chest. I shuddered.

I turned back to the werewolf and snorted. "She seems like your type, Brandon. How come you're not trying to talk her into being your TouchStone?"

"She's just a groupie," he declared, licking his chops. "She'd be lovely for a few nights, I'm sure, but I'm looking for something a bit more permanent."

"And you thought an underage girl would be the best choice?"

He winced, and his wolf ears flattened sheepishly. "I know, I know," he sighed. "But Katy seems so . . . *right*. And she found this place on her own. That has to count for something, doesn't it? Besides, she's awfully sweet. I miss that sometimes."

I nodded and let my gaze travel to the door. The Glamour draped like a veil at the entrance of the alley leading to the Hallows reminded me of swimming through spiderwebs of boredom and ennui. Mortals that weren't TouchStones—or who hadn't had their eyes opened to the OtherWorld—tended to walk on by, glances sliding away as if it didn't exist. Inside, it was like any other bar. Smoky. Hazy. Hot and sweaty with dancers and drinkers, wingmen and fat chicks. Normal. Well, except for the pointed ears and fanged smiles, that is.

Up on the stage Melanie played "Last of the Wilds" by Nightwish, her hand rocking over the strings of her violin, its wood a burnished silver color beneath the lights. She twirled about like a gothic pixie, all black corset and Doc Martens.

Elves crowded the stage, whirling in a flurry of impossible colors, cheering her on with hungry eyes. For all that the OtherFolk acted so high-and-mighty around us, they certainly lapped it up when one of us shone.

Melanie was one of the brightest.

A sudden handwave caught my attention as Charlie gestured me over to her table. I held up my drink in assent and grabbed my purse. "I'll see you around, Brandon." His ears flicked toward me curiously as he wiped off the glass-topped bar.

"You'll help me out then?"

"It's the fourth one this month, dude. Maybe you should try something different."

"Just this last time, I promise." He blinked winsomely at me. "I really think she's the one."

I laughed despite myself. "Spare me the puppy-dog eyes, wolf-boy. I'll see what I can do."

"It's nice to see you here again, Abby," he said, his grin playful now. "You should stop by more often."

"Probably." I rewarded him with a genuine smile. Brandon was a nice sort. A little hairy for my taste, but given some of the OtherFolk quirks I'd seen, I probably could have lived with it.

I slipped through the swarm of dancers, narrowly avoiding an elbow to the jaw from a satyr dancing a rather obscene version of the Electric Slide. "Watch it," I shouted above the hum of the music, but he simply gave me a once-over and turned away. Ouch. Rejected by a smelly goat-man. Somehow I thought I'd live, though an inopportune glance at his groin told me *someone* had certainly been eating his Wheaties.

"Hey there, Sparky." Robert's voice drawled out the *r*s, so it came across as "Spahhky." I liked the way it sounded, despite the usual hostility that lingered beneath. There was a dangerous lilt to it tonight, and I struggled not to wipe my suddenly damp hands on my pants.

"Robert." I smiled, taking another sip of my drink to mask my apprehension. As far as angels go, I suppose he was fairly typical—blond, blue eyed, broad shouldered, and well muscled. He tended to dress casually, and tonight was no exception. He cut a nice figure in his button-flys and Sean John shirt. And wings. Huge-ass, glossy white wings that stretched nearly all the way to the ground. At the moment they were neatly arched and partially folded. If they were mine I would have been worried someone might step on them, but Robert gave off an aura of "don't touch" that apparently translated between realms. Of course, the fact that he had full authority from Moira to smite anything he damn well pleased probably had a lot to do with it.

"Charlie tells me there's an . . ." He paused, the words crisp and specific. "An issue."

I swallowed another mouthful of Mudslide, squirming beneath the sharpness of his gaze. "I don't know if it's really an *issue*. Moira just didn't tell me when she was coming back." I struggled to keep my smile. "Honestly, I just thought it was something she did."

"Ah well, sure. And she does disappear from time to

time, usually to take care of things in Faery, but she's always been good about letting me know beforehand. This is worrisome." He chugged his beer and fixed his jewel-bright eyes on me again. "You say you haven't heard from her at all?"

I pulled the piece of parchment from my purse and slid it over to him. "Just this note. But she didn't mention anything about telling you or if she was in trouble. I'm sorry. I thought you knew."

"Hold *back* the fort?" He snorted. "The Fae never get anything right." His sizable bulk pressed across the table and his voice dropped low. "I don't like it. This whole thing just stinks, especially given what happened with her last TouchStone."

Charlie nudged him with her elbow. "Bobby," she hissed. "You don't need to get into that."

A cold shiver ran down my spine at her words. I wasn't completely ignorant of the situation, but I'd never gotten a straight answer from anyone on it. "Get into what? What happened with her last TouchStone?"

Charlie raked a steely gaze over the angel, and he had the good sense to hastily resume nursing his beer. I swallowed a laugh. That had been a "no nookie tonight" look if I'd ever seen one. She sipped her Cosmopolitan before glancing over at me. A typical stalling tactic and we both knew it. "We don't know, actually. He'd been with Moira for years. They were really close." Her eyes darted toward the angel. "Like us."

Lovers.

"A permanent Contract?" I raised my brows. "I didn't think Moira was the type. Besides, she damn near bit my head off when she found out about my little . . . indiscretion with Jett. Why would she get involved with her Touch-Stone?"

The angel snorted, sliding his empty bottle toward the

center of the table. "Hypocrites, the lot of them. There's not a damn Faery in the world that doesn't talk sideways out of their mouth; Moira is no exception. Don't get me wrong"—he held up a hand as I started to bristle—"she's been a great Protectorate, but she's as flighty as the rest of them. As far as what happened to Maurice . . ." He shrugged. "Nobody knows. One day they were as thick as thieves and the next . . . gone."

"We always figured it was some sort of lovers' quarrel, but we never dreamed she'd break the Contract." Charlie bit her lip. "It was the eight-hundred-pound gorilla in the room, Abby. He'd been with her for *years*. And the next thing we knew, you showed up and . . . well, you didn't really seem to know anything at all. We didn't know what to think."

I focused on the MudSlide resting between my knees; Bryston's words to me about my ignorance the night before were suddenly becoming clear. "And I'm just a straw horse, is that it? A shadow replacement for the status quo?" The words rang hollow in my mouth, the bitter truth leaving an aftertaste of shame and bile.

"That's not it, Abby, but even you have to admit things don't add up. Why would she replace such a loyal companion with . . . well, you? You're perfectly lovely, but if she was going to be gone for such an extended period, she probably should have had a TouchStone with more experience."

"I didn't ask for this," I reminded them, ignoring the dagger slice of betrayal that lanced through my gut. "I didn't know what I was getting into when I signed the Contract. I didn't even know what a TouchStone *was*, let alone what the duty entailed. And I sure as fuck didn't think I'd be stuck doing it all alone."

"I know." Charlie reached out to squeeze my arm. "Unfortunately, declaring ignorance isn't going to help right now. We didn't realize she had left you without any resources."

Robert's head snapped toward me. "You've been running the Marketplace by yourself all this time?"

"Well, it's not like there's anyone else lining up for the job, now is there?" I retorted.

"You should have come to us. To *me*." His hand slammed on the table, the empty bottle tipping on its side. "That's what I'm here for."

I bared my teeth at him and then bit down hard on the straw. "Really? Because somehow I don't see you stooping to scrub the hoof prints off the hardwood floor of the Marketplace."

He shot me a piercing look, ignoring my last comment. "I'm going to have to insist that you curb your activities for a while until we can see about getting you some kind of bodyguard."

"What if I don't want to?" I frowned at him. "I'm not some kind of child; this is my life too, you know."

"You're our last link to Moira," he said. "I don't know what happens if something happens to you."

Charlie reached out and gently stroked his arm. "We'll figure it out. You know we will." Her eyes were full of sympathy and pride, gentle with sorrow.

I could only nod, turning away as my senses reeled with this latest impact. Apparently I was responsible not only for the existence of my TouchStone mistress, but for that of everyone else attached to her. "What do you know about unicorns?" I asked randomly.

"Unicorns are from the Light Path. They can't be corrupted." The angel shifted, leaning across the table, as I struggled not to let out a bark of laughter.

"Oh the humanity," I muttered. "Listen, I really think we should take—" My words were cut off, drowned by the strum of an electric guitar wailing over the speakers. All attention snapped toward the stage, suddenly gone dark as the houselights dimmed. A spotlight pointed at the center, its silver light pooling over the scuffed dance floor, shining off the condensation on my glass.

Melanie appeared, pushing back a few damp strands of hair from her forehead. She smiled, her teeth glinting, as she stared out into the crowd. I felt a twinge of homesickness, watching her. My heart ached, remembering how it felt to be the core interest of a venue, the way the lights partially blinded you, but you didn't care because you knew you were the reason they were there.

She curtsied at the wave of catcalls and cleared her throat, tapping the microphone with her violin bow. "Ladies and gents, mortal and Other, I have the distinct pleasure of introducing an old favorite, in his first performance since Ion's Folly disbanded." There was a murmur of excitement at this, a rumbling wave of anticipation.

Robert snorted next to me. "Tool."

"Hush," Charlie hissed, elbowing him in the shoulder. The angel's face hardened, and he crossed his arms. I missed whatever else Melanie said in the little exchange, but it didn't really matter because in the next instant the lights flooded the stage as Bryston appeared to a screaming wave of applause.

The incubus basked in it, a sly smile on his face. He clearly nodded to a few patrons, resulting in definite female voices squealing out his name. "What's the big deal?" I shouted to Charlie over the din.

She shook her head and pulled at her ears. "Wait," she mouthed, pointing back at the stage. I looked back at Robert, but the angel had gone sulky, his brows furrowed.

And then the music started and I held my breath for a moment as the incubus took the microphone. The rest of the band was reduced to nothing more than silhouetted shadows behind him. I'm not sure what I was expecting, but the voice that poured out of him wasn't it. The low, seductive sweep of notes pressed its way through the Hallows, echoed in the pulsing rhythm of my heart. My stomach was full of butterflies, hot and nervous, and I leaned forward despite myself. Around me, the subtle pull grew stronger. A quick glance showed the effect wasn't solely on me. Even Charlie looked vaguely uncomfortable, shifting in her seat to recross her legs.

Bryston smirked as his gaze swept over the crowd, his fingers drifting over the mic.

"This bed is on fire with passionate love . . ."

I snorted. Leave it to an incubus to sing "Laid." I blinked as our eyes met, watched the flare of gold ring around his pupils. The sounds dropped away and for a moment it was just the two of us in the dark. My arms wrapped around my shoulders instinctively, as if he could see my nakedness, wondering if the same longing was written on my face. My vision went smoky, hazy, blurring in the sudden rush of bodies as they swayed around me.

Blinking rapidly, I shook my head, wrenching my attention back to Charlie and Robert. "Is it even worth trying to discuss any more of this?" I leaned toward her, my words nearly lost in the din. My chair rocked and I ducked as a . . . Viking? No, a Valkyrie pranced by, her muscular frame shoveling me out of the way in her hurry to get to the dance floor.

"I'm not sure there's much else to talk about." Robert snapped out a wing, startling an elven waitress into nearly spilling her drink. "I'll put out some feelers and see if Moira's gone back to Faery. It could be as simple as Court politics."

"Maybe."

His eyes gleamed unpleasantly, and I knew we both suspected it wouldn't be that easy. "In the meantime, I'd like you to report anything else untoward. I'm counting on you for this, Abby."

Charlie coughed low in her throat, her gaze dipping toward the incubus onstage for a moment. "Yeah," I muttered. I knew I could be dense, but Charlie was about as subtle as a brick through a window sometimes.

The tempo of the music had changed and I glanced behind me, watching as Brystion gyrated onstage to Led Zeppelin's "The Lemon Song," his hand cupping the microphone suggestively. I didn't know why I didn't want to talk to Robert about the incubus—it was stupid not to. And yet my mouth wouldn't open. "I think I'm gonna go," I said finally, ignoring Charlie's stare.

My eyes met Brystion's again, and I couldn't help giving him a little nod. One dark brow rose in return, and the music changed again. It became darker, slower. The song beat at my brain, but not in words I could recognize.

I stood up, every heartbeat urging me to step toward him, make my way to the dance floor and submit to his will, to drown in the ocean of flesh writhing beneath his mien. I took a step and felt a cool grasp on my wrist. I looked down, trying to shake it off. It was Robert. He said something that sounded like my name, but it didn't matter. All I wanted was . . . there. On the stage, all graceful limbs and muscled torso, gyrating to the beat of the drums. My hips swung wide in answer.

Yes . . .

"No," I whispered, and moved toward the dance floor. I brushed by the other dancers, limbs moving in a remembered grace. If the crowd parted before me, I didn't question it, no more than I questioned the way the incubus seemed to uncoil off the stage, oozing down the steps.

Melanie's mouth quirked at me and then she shrugged, her head inclining toward the guitarist who immediately began an extended solo.

My hand drifted forward, an explosion of heat rocketing up my arm when Brystion captured it. And then I was spinning as he turned me out and drew me back, his golden eyes blazing. I pulled away, uncertain. Something didn't seem quite right, but I wasn't sure I wanted to stop. "What are you doing?" I murmured.

"Dancing." Amusement flickered across his face as he pressed his hips tightly against mine.

"Well, yes, I can see that. But why?"

"Why not?" When I only stared at him, he shook his head and lowered his mouth to my ear. "Because you looked like you wanted to."

Before I could answer this, glass shattered as a bottle slammed on top of the bar. I blinked, realized we were standing alone in the center of the dance floor, with the music gone and Brystion's arm paused mid-twirl.

What the hell? I glanced at him and then toward the bar, startled to see a snarling Brandon emerge toward us, his hackles raised.

"I'll fucking kill him." Robert's voice came as though from a distance, muffled and heated. I inhaled slowly, risking a quick glance behind me. The angel pushed through the crowd, his wings outspread, even as Brystion slowly moved in front of me.

"Not in here," the werewolf rumbled. "You know the rules. No fighting in my bar." His canines gleamed in the reflection of the bottle in his hand. "The only one who gets to break heads around here is me."

The angel and the incubus ignored him, circling slowly in a systematic sizing up. It was like watching dogs made of dynamite sniff each other's backsides, and I could only wonder who was holding the match. Bryston's eyes had gone dark again, his pose suddenly relaxed as though he knew something. Judging by Robert's posture, the angel knew it too, the stiffness in his shoulders broadcasting his displeasure.

Brandon turned toward me, the unwritten message plain. His bar, yes, but this was Moira's bodyguard and her domain. This needed to stop, and now. And apparently I had to do it. I tugged on the angel's shirt. "Robert. It's all right."

"No, Abby," he snarled back. "It's really not. And this little shit knows it."

Brystion snorted. "I've done nothing that isn't within my rights. Run along now, angel, and see if you can't find the head of a pin to dance on. I hear the jury is still out on just how many of you can do the Electric Slide without falling off."

I choked back a laugh despite myself. Somehow I didn't think Thomas Aquinas had meant his philosophical wonderings to be used as an ethnic slur, but there it was.

Robert slipped around the incubus as though searching for a weakness, but whatever it was, I couldn't see it. Brystion leaned in and whispered something, his face mocking.

Robert stiffened, one hand drifting down to the longsword at his hip. His fingers caressed the hilt in warning. "As Moira's TouchStone, this is your call, Abby." His tone clearly told me what he thought I should do, overriding the statement.

I was half inclined to agree with him. The only problem was that I had no clue what either of them was talking about. Clearly there was a larger game going on here and I didn't know who all the players were. I sent a questioning glance toward Charlie. She gave a nearly imperceptible shake of her head. This one was on me.

Great. I stifled the urge to cover my face with my hands. I exhaled slowly. "I think you should let Bryston get back to his set and the rest of these fine people to their chosen entertainments." I raised a brow at the two of them, praying that they'd both take the hint. "The incubus and I will discuss things afterward."

Relief flashed in Bryston's eyes, but it was gone nearly before I saw it. Robert's jaw tightened, his teeth grinding together. "So be it." He leaned forward to snarl something at the incubus. Bryston nodded shortly, his gaze flicking back toward me for a moment, but I couldn't hear what they were saying. Robert's thumb jabbed in my direction and his voice suddenly grew loud. ". . . and if you don't, I'll fucking kill you, you understand?" Bryston covered his mouth, stifling a yawn.

"This cloak-and-dagger bullshit is really starting to wear thin, Charlie." I turned away from the two men with a weary sigh, making my way back to our table.

"I didn't know this was going to happen," she retorted tightly, tracking Robert as he returned to his seat, his wings snapping shut.

"What was *that* all about?" I rested my head on my arms, ignoring the rush of eyes on my back. My skin crawled beneath those hidden judgments, but I shook it off. "So much for not attracting attention to the situation."

He ignored the jab, staring at his fingers as though imagining them wrapped around a certain daemon's throat. Finally he looked up at me, blue eyes fiery. "Just remember that I was against this. When Moira comes back, we're going to hash this out, you and I."

"What are you talking about?"

The angel pointed toward the stage where Bryston and the band were tweaking the instruments to start back up again. "You chose *him*. Ask *him* what I'm talking about."

His upper lip curled into a sneer. "Good luck getting any
answers from a freaking Dreameater."

I chose him? I glanced out of the corner of my eye, confused. I hadn't chosen anyone. All I wanted was to stop the
bullshit, not get into a preternatural cockfight. "Fine," I
muttered. "Fuck you too." I stood, draining what was left of
my drink, my head spinning slightly.

"Abby . . ." Charlie reached out for me, but I shook my
arm away.

"Don't." She looked as though she might cry. "Don't,"
I repeated softly. "This isn't your choice to make." I set my
mug on the table and headed for the door, pushing past a
gaggle of nymphs. They had fins and scales, so I guessed
that made them undines. "Excuse me," I said politely,
working my way around them.

"Bitch."

I rolled my eyes. "Yes, yes, of course I am. Thanks for
pointing that out. Now if you wouldn't mind, I've got some
forks to stab into my skull."

"He'll use you like a dirty tissue," one of them sniffed.
"All you're worth anyway."

"I weep for it." I elbowed past them. I'd nearly passed
the bar when Bryston's voice boomed through the speakers
again, rich and dark, as he asked for silence.

"I'm sorry for my . . . indiscretion," he said, his fingers
stroking the mic stand curiously, his face a strange mix of
seduction and amusement. "It was not my intent to start
any trouble. As some of you know, I've been away for a bit
and not entirely myself, but that's all changed now."

His eyes flared gold and went half-lidded, his words a
lazy drawl. "I owe someone a very sincere apology. I'm not
very good with that sort of thing, so I'm going to do it with
a song."

He leaned over and said something to Melanie. A

bemused expression crossed her features. I couldn't hear her, but it looked like her mouth moved to say "Are you sure?" At his nod, she shrugged and raised the violin to her chin, bow poised as she waited for his signal. I rolled my eyes and turned toward the door. I'd had enough of cryptic words, unspoken threats, and hidden magics. I was going *home*, goddammit, and crashing for a few hours if it killed me.

My fingers brushed the knob and then I stopped. Turned. The music had started, its familiar beat causing my hands to tremble as I raised them to my lips. Brystion grinned as the chords swelled, finger pointed at me.

A giggle escaped me, and then another, and then great gasps of hysterical laughter erupted as I stumbled back to the bar. Tom Jones. The dickhead was playing Tom frigging Jones. For *me*.

I half sat on a stool, my knees shaky, as I watched the dance floor fill back up. Up on stage, Brystion tipped his head toward me, his mouth curved in hidden promise, hips gyrating in a blatant one.

"Sex bomb, sex bomb. . ."

His hand motioned me forward, pulling me toward him again, but I only shook my head. There didn't seem to be anything other than simple music this time, but I'd had my share of fun for one night.

One dark brow rose when I didn't move, and I gave him an apologetic shrug. The song wrapped up with a flourish and the stage went dark, the bar filled with shouts and whistles.

I slipped Brandon another ten-spot in thanks and adjusted my shirt, slipping out the door without looking back.

Seven

The streetlights flickered dimly in the overhanging fog, the waterfront lost in a comfortable shadow. It was dark and intimate and *solitary* and that suited me just fine. I'd had my fill of sweaty bodies and alcohol-stained breath for one evening. I'd had my fill of drama too.

I leaned over the edge of the dock to listen to the slap of the tide. The way the water gently lapped at the boats always soothed me, the taut hitch of the ropes rising and falling with each small swell. A light breeze tinged with the scent of brine and tar blew gently off the water; it laughed its way through the tangle of my hair, lifting it off my forehead in blessed relief.

Brystion emerged from the darkness to loom against the railing beside me. We didn't touch. I found a strange contentment in sharing the night sea with him, although he had his back to the bay. After a while he looked down, his arms crossed. "What are you thinking about?"

I stared at the distant lights far across the bay and shrugged. "Have you ever seen a mermaid?"

He made a bemused sound. "No," he admitted after a moment. "But they exist . . . probably not as you imagine though." His boots scuffed across the wooden boards, and he rested his arms on the edge of the pier. His duster made a ruffling flap in the wind as I watched his profile gleam beneath the watery street lamps. He was so damn beautiful it made my chest hurt to look at him.

"Nothing is ever how I imagined it would be." A wry smile tugged at my lips. "Did you want to talk about what just happened in there?"

The incubus paused, and I knew immediately that it had been the wrong thing to say. His face shuttered, those dangerous eyes becoming blank and careful. "No."

"What's the matter? Afraid to admit you might actually be attracted to me?"

"Purely business," he said shortly.

"Ah, and what a wondrous job you're doing of that," I said. "My dreams haven't been this full of overblown flesh and angst since I was a teenager." I tapped my fingers on my forehead. "It's been like a brothel of the damned in there, but without the payoff. Or is that the general idea? Get me all hot and bothered and then just walk away? Hope I'll beg you for a magical orgasm in return for some information?"

He sneered, but I still caught the flicker of chagrin that chased its way across his face. I chuckled softly when he stiffened. "You don't have to do that, you know." I rubbed my hands up and down my elbows to ward off the chill tingling its way across my skin.

"Do what? Ask you for help?" He snorted, but there was a hint of despair in it. "That's a laugh, isn't it? You can barely help yourself. How the hell do you think you'd be able to help me do *anything*?"

"Well, for starters, if you actually considered just treating me like a person, I tend to respond to that pretty well." I hunched my shoulders as the breeze picked up. "You can even drop the walking sex-god act. You don't need to impress me. And to be honest, it's getting rather irritating."

"It's not an act." He turned away for a moment and then abruptly took off his coat. "Here." He thrust it at me.

"What?"

"You're cold," he growled.

"Good observation skills too, I see."

"Just. Take. The. Fucking. Thing." Bryston fixed his eyes on me, the pupils flaring gold, staring me down until I finally conceded. I draped it around my shoulders. It was heavy and warm and smelled of old leather and something else. Like cinnamon and honey, but darker. More primitive.

"Thank you," I murmured, nestling into it. The tension drained away from his shoulders. "So are you planning on telling me what this is really all about? I mean, I'd hate to think I just stood up to Robert for nothing."

"Why?"

"Why what? Seems pretty straightforward to me. I don't know about you, but I don't particularly care for having my ass beat down."

"Not you." His hand waved dismissively at me. "I meant why did you stand up to him for me?"

It was a good question. I didn't know. I said as much, shrugging beneath the leather.

He closed his eyes. "You're a liar, just like me. Just like the rest of them."

I stared at him. Whatever this was, it was about more than just me. It had to be. Charlie's words came back to me. ". . . *ran off with the drummer* . . ." Someone had hurt him, badly. I reached out and gripped his wrist. His skin was warm, almost burning, but I didn't know if that was an incubus trait or just because my hands were cold.

"Sometimes," I agreed. "But usually only to myself."

His eyes snapped open. "Why?"

I retreated, wrapping the coat around me a little tighter. The irony of that little move struck me as funny, but I couldn't laugh. Instead, I started to walk, indicating he should follow me with a tilt of my head. The story never got any easier to tell, but I found it somewhat bearable if I was pacing. "I used to be a dancer." I started slowly, my feet marching in time to my words. I focused on the cadence, my voice mechanical. "I danced all through elementary school, high school. I did plays, musicals, fine art workshops, you name it. I was good. Damn good," I amended. "I won scholarships, awards, whatever. I even made it to Juilliard for a few semesters." My stride quickened. "I actually met Melanie there, but she didn't stay long. It wasn't really her style."

"No," he agreed. "She plays the Wild Magic. There's no way to trap that within walls, let alone capture it within the regulations of a classroom."

I gazed at him in surprise. "Wild Magic?"

"It's part of what allows her to open Doors. But you're changing the subject."

"Right. Anyway, I went to Juilliard for a while before becoming a principal for the American Ballet Theatre."

"And then?" The words were soft and dark, gently prodding. I took a shuddering breath.

"And then. And then my mother came to pick me up one evening for dinner. It was lovely, she was lovely, the evening was all perfectly lovely." My voice dropped to a hoarse whisper. "The drunk asshole who plowed his truck into my mother's Ford Focus? Not so fucking lovely." I stopped walking, stopped talking, and for a moment all I could see was the blurring streak of headlights against the windshield and the squalling wrench as the side of the car was pushed forward, punching through the passenger side door, metal and bone ravaged beyond repair, beyond help, beyond the tremulous sighs of my breath in my ears.

I wiped madly at my eyes. I'd reached the end of the pier, and I turned on my heel to head back the way I'd come. "I woke up in the hospital two weeks later with a knee that bends a little farther than it should and a metal plate in my head." I tapped the side above my left ear with a humorless grin. "And of course, my mother died, so I suppose I should mention that too."

If he heard the sarcasm in my words, he gave no sign of it. "And the man who hit you?"

"In prison. There's going to be another hearing, I think, but that's got nothing to do with me. Fucker already had two prior convictions." Rage rippled through my chest, spreading over limbs until my hands shook. "The dance company didn't want me back. I tried, but the leg just wouldn't hold me well enough. And the damage to my head . . . they don't know how bad it is, but I have seizures sometimes, or horrible vertigo. It's unpredictable."

We reached the end of the dock where we'd started and I sighed, slipping out of his coat. "So, yes, I lie to myself. All the time, really, but I'll be honest with you, I'm pretty shitty at it." I blinked back another rush of tears, giving him a wan smile as I pushed the coat back at him.

He frowned at me. "Keep it," he said. "I don't really need it anyway."

I shrugged, but didn't put it back on; I folded it over my arms. My watch beeped in warning. "I should probably get back to the store and get ready to open up the Marketplace."

"You really don't have a choice, do you?"

"Nope. The Contract stipulates what I have to do, so I do it. On the other hand, the Marketplace isn't open every night, so it's not quite as bad as it seems." A slight blush slid over my cheeks. "Will you . . . uh . . . be stopping by later tonight? Assuming that actually *was* you and not just a dream."

Silent laughter rippled around me. "Did you want me to?"

"I don't know. Just what was it you were trying to accomplish?"

"Loaded question." He turned toward the water, his gaze growing distant. "To get your attention, I guess." He eyed me sideways. "Did it work?"

"A little." My lips pursed. "A bit odd waking up to find myself on the brink of getting off, but I suppose as wake-up calls go, it's a pretty nice one."

"Not enough to drive you over the edge," he noted slyly.

"No. I don't like unknowns. At the time, I didn't know what your motivation was. For that matter, I still don't."

"It's becoming rather complicated, actually." He exhaled sharply. "But the overall is still the same. My sister is missing. She was looking for the others."

"Others?"

He nodded, kicking away a loose stone. "More succubi have gone missing. Or showing up dead is more like it. It just took us a little while to figure out the timeline. Sonja was on the trail of someone when she disappeared. If the pattern holds true, I don't think I have much time. A week, maybe less."

"And you just thought to come to Moira now? Why all the secrecy?"

His lips twisted wryly. "Come now, Ms. TouchStone of the Protectorate. Surely you're aware of the bad blood between the Paths."

I was. Of course I was. One only had to see the antagonism between the incubus and the angel earlier to understand it. Three Paths, indeed . . . and, yet, even that trichotomy seemed far too simple to truly explain it. *Angels, Daemons, and the Fae to balance the scales.* "You don't trust Moira?"

"She has a pindancer as her First. Would you, if the

positions were reversed? For all we knew, she sanctioned the kidnappings."

"You can't really believe that."

"I don't know what to believe. I came here to see if Moira would mete out justice, and she's not here." He swiveled back to face me, a terrible longing etched in the golden flare of his eyes. "But you are. Will you help me?"

"And here I thought you didn't think I could help anyone," I retorted dryly.

"Touché," he said. "Though you did manage to push an archangel around quite nicely. Might be hope for you yet."

I paused, the moments measured by the tick of several heartbeats. Could I afford it? Did it matter? As far as I knew, I still had no actual obligation to do anything, but somehow I couldn't imagine Moira just sitting back and letting something like this happen without at least investigating. Finally, I nodded, not quite trusting my voice. He let out a sigh of relief, a gentle smile turning up the corner of his mouth.

"Thank you," he murmured, reaching out to stroke my cheek.

"You don't have to do that, you know." I pulled my head away. "If I do this, I'll do it on my own, not because of any weird sexual thing you're doing. I'm not fond of pity fucks, metaphysical or otherwise."

"I wasn't trying to seduce you. The offer was genuine." He pushed his hand through his hair. "It's a little disconcerting to be turned down by a mere mortal."

"Just a mortal," I snorted. "Real nice. I'll see what I can do about soothing your ego, O gracious and tactful one." I chewed on my lower lip thoughtfully and gave him a sly smile. "Of course, you probably shouldn't feel too bad. After all, I *am* wearing a magical amulet now."

His mouth pursed. "You are?"

"Sure. It's made of silver and moonbeams and blessed by

a flatulent dwarf," I intoned gravely. "It's a guaranteed 'plus four' against Incubus Seduction."

"You're an ass."

"Kiss, kiss, darling." I fluttered my eyelashes, puckering my lips in mock affection.

His hand snarled into my hair, fingers twined tightly at the base of my head. "This is a complication I don't want, Abby." He growled the words, but there was no mistaking the desire that smoldered behind his now glowing eyes.

"The bulge in your pants says otherwise," I retorted, perversely nudging my hips against him. A little voice in the back of my mind was going into apoplectic fits at my boldness. As far as I was concerned, the incubus had been acting like some sort of preternatural cocktease since we'd met and I'd had enough.

He let out a stifled groan, his other hand snaking down to grip my ass. "You'll regret it," he breathed, releasing his hold on my hair to trace a curious thumb over my jaw. His face drifted closer until his mouth brushed mine. I shuddered at the delicate intrusion. His fingers slid up to the small of my back.

"Probably." I sighed, my mind happily unable to focus on anything but the way he was nipping at my lower lip. "I regret a lot of things."

The incubus stared at me, an unnamed emotion flickering across his face, and then his lips were on mine, fierce and possessive.

He devoured me utterly. There was only the sweetness of his tongue, probing hot and wet into the velvet contours of my mouth. It swept shallow, lingering to taste the soft edges, and then moved deeper, pulsing and rhythmic to match the rapid beating of my heart. I jerked forward to bury my hands in his hair, my ragged breathing giving way to a low cry of longing.

"How's that ego?" he purred.

"Rock hard from the feel of it," I gasped. "Just the way I like it."

A low chuckle was his only response, his hand sliding back to my ass. I groaned when he pushed me against the edge of the pier. He lifted me up, grinding his erection into my groin, teasing me with everything it promised. My legs circled his hips.

"Brystion . . ." His name disappeared into the night, captured in the breeze even as he bent his head to sweep his lips down my neck, and he reached up beneath my shirt to press a hardened nipple.

My back arched instinctively. Whatever his attitude, the incubus certainly knew his business, and the heat that burned at my core wanted it. Badly. And yet . . . I was on a dark pier, dry-humping a guy I barely knew, in return for what? Helping him find his missing sister?

My ardor cooled and I put my hands on his face. "Stop." I shivered. "This isn't right. Not for me. Not yet."

"I wasn't going to just take you on the ground like a common street whore," he grumbled, releasing me reluctantly. "Give me *some* credit." His whole body trembled beneath my fingers, vibrating with desire mixed with tightly wound control. "You taste . . . delicious."

"I what?"

He looked at me somewhat sheepishly. "I told you before, Abby. You're a Dreamer. It's a gift, of sorts." His voice softened. "Like being a musician or a dancer, but it's something you're born with."

Robert's words suddenly came back to me. "And you're a Dreameater?"

"That's one word for it," the incubus snapped. "But I'd prefer you not use it around me."

"Fine." I picked up his coat from the ground and

wrapped it around me again. "But you really ought to have more patience with me. I'm new at this sort of thing." I shook my head. "You know what? Forget it. This sex thing just complicates everything and I just . . . I just can't deal with one more level of complexity. If you're really feeling that chivalrous, isn't there anything else you can trade me?"

"I can heal your dreams, if you want. Or show you how to channel them." He closed his eyes for a moment and breathed in deeply. "There's a distinct shadow to you, Abby. You have nightmares, don't you?"

I swallowed. "Yes. Every night since I came out of the coma."

His eyes narrowed. "Did you have one last night?"

"Actually . . . no. Was that your doing?"

"It didn't take much. It was like being at a buffet," he purred. "With every little bit of you just ripe and waiting for me. Not that I sampled anything," he added hastily. "Or not much, at least."

I rubbed my neck, the pulse of my heartbeat slamming against my fingertips. "Never mind that. What would you say to drawing up a Contract? My help in return for some dream ass-kicking?" I shivered at my own boldness. Robert would be shitting cats if he knew I was considering Contracting to someone other than Moira. Impossible or not, it had already happened once with the unicorn, so what would it matter?

My words were not lost on the incubus and he looked at me shrewdly. "You would do that?"

"For a good night's sleep, I would do just about anything." I cringed at the hollow desperation of my voice. "But no funny stuff, okay? Just . . . whatever you can do to help would be fine."

"Trial run tonight, perhaps? I'll behave." He raised his

hand to his heart. "Scout's honor. If it works out, I can stop by tomorrow with the paperwork."

"Somehow I doubt you were ever a Boy Scout, but okay. If you're sure your current TouchStone won't mind, that is. I don't want to . . . get between you two."

"It won't bother her a bit. I promise." His finger traced over my cheek as he melted away into the darkness. "Until tonight."

Eight

Water lapped at my hips, fresh and blue and brilliant. The sand slid through my toes, the song of some ancient wisdom caught up in the grinding of seashells beneath my heels. One step and then another and then I was floating, the waves cresting against my skin, salt water dripping from my hair. Warm and aching beneath the sun, I swam, dimly aware of the coastal shelf falling away beneath me.

It was always the same. No matter how I raged at myself to stop it, to stay on the shore, I inevitably ended up in the ocean, lazy and careless. I opened my eyes and my mouth clamped down on the scream threatening to claw its way from my throat. Black now, the watery depths became nothing more than a pool of ink from which no light glittered. In the distance, the shore teased me with its safety, a golden patch on the horizon. I hovered over the abyss, my limbs like cement, my heart slamming against my ribs.

Would they be able to hear it? The syncopation of my organs pulsed the blood through my veins like the distressed flutter of a fish as it struggled against the current. I eyed the island, knowing I would never make it. I knew I would try anyway, knew I would fail. The current stopped, leaving me in a pool of silence, the water still and even. I held my breath, the barest movement threatening to broadcast my presence in the telltale ripples that would surely mean my doom.

Something brushed past my feet, and I bit my lip at its sandpaper sharpness. Like teeth for skin, biting and hooking into my flesh. I fought the urge to yank my foot away and closed my eyes.

Make it stop. Make it stop. Make it stop.

My mouth formed the words in an empty prayer. There was another sharp tickle—a tug—jolting me from my ankle to my thigh. I looked down, already knowing what I would see, the scream forming on my lips. Blood poured from my midsection, my legs gone, cut out from under me.

When the fin broke the watery surface, my mind blanked, my arms flailing uselessly. I struggled toward that golden shore, the current suddenly picking up again. Sometimes I almost made it.

Not tonight.

The shark snapped at me, pain replacing fear, and all around me was the taste of blood and salt and death, my wailing voice ebbing into a haunted gurgle as it finally pulled me under the darkness . . .

I shrieked, the sound carried away by the howling wind. I stood alone—the ocean gone, the shark gone—perched on the edge of a rocky cliff. There was nothing around me but a void. Voiceless, I tried to move, but my legs were rooted to the ground. Paralyzed, I waited.

She always came now, looming out of the shadows. The warped edges of her face were shattered and bloody and broken.

Mother . . .

She reached out, her corpse-chilled fingers like crumbling bone against my cheek. I started shaking, my legs jerking underneath me as she moved closer. The tattered edges of her hair flicked across my nose, my lips, choking me.

"Why?" she cried.

"I don't know." I stepped off the cliff and hurtled into the unknown . . .

Warm arms captured me from behind.

"Bryston," I sobbed, shudders racking my limbs as he turned me around. I scrabbled for purchase around the solidity of his body, clinging to him as though I could slip out of my skin and seek shelter in his.

"I've got you," he murmured in my ear, the cold darkness spinning away with a flare of shimmering ripples.

"The CrossRoads?" I'd never found my way to the silver-gilt roads that ran between the worlds, but I'd heard enough about what they looked like to at least venture a guess.

He nodded, his brow furrowed. "Of course. The Dreaming is merely another way to get there, but not one that mortals can normally take." He carried me, his legs pacing with rhythmic certainty. The silver-dappled road stretched without end, a spider's web of ley lines curling into the distance, but all around us were shadows. "Are you all right?"

"I guess. I usually wake up by now." I shivered, instinctively wrapping my arms around his neck. He chuckled. His gaze flicked back to the road and I wondered what he was looking for.

"You weren't kidding about the nightmares," he muttered. "That's about one of the worst manifestations I've seen in a long time. Your mother?"

I nodded. "Yeah. I don't know if it's real or if it's just me. I hate it. I'm sure it's my subconscious trying to tell me something."

"It could be, or it could be something more." He stopped and cocked his head as though he was listening for something. "Ah," he sighed. "There it is."

"Where are we going?"

"Your Heart. This isn't the way I would normally go. Skirting the edges of the CrossRoads with your Shadow Self is dangerous enough, but whatever is causing your nightmares *really* doesn't want to let you go."

"My Shadow Self?"

"You're still asleep," he pointed out, tapping me gently on the arm. "This is merely a projection of you from your dreams. Coming here is a short-term escape, but not one you should repeat. Stay long enough and your real body will die."

A cold shiver ran through me at his words. "I never saw the funeral," I said softly. "Never got to say good-bye, really. I couldn't even bring myself to look at the gravesite." I bit my lip and tasted blood. I'd sat in the damn car for hours after I'd been released from the hospital, just parked in the cemetery, but no matter how hard I tried I couldn't get out of the car. Finally, I'd driven away, never looking back. "I'm a coward, I guess."

"No. You simply don't want to admit defeat." He shifted me in his arms. "Do you want to walk?"

"Getting heavy, am I?" My tone was self-mocking, but I nodded anyway.

He gracefully set me on my feet. "No, the roads are getting muddied somewhat. It will just be easier if you're touching them."

I was barefoot, and the silver cobblestones were warm and tingly, like sea foam upon an ocean of darkness. The trails glittered and shifted in the distance as though they might drift away. I wiggled my toes, stirring up a pile of silver dust. "Is it always like this?" I asked.

"Parts of it." The incubus stared off into shadows but didn't release my hand. "This way. We need to move." He pulled me along, my feet making no sound against the road.

"What happens if it catches us?" My eyes darted from

side to side, searching for any sign of the wretchedness we'd left behind.

"It won't, but we need to go. The longer we linger here, the more likely we'll be snared by something else." He didn't elaborate on what that something else was, and I didn't press the issue. He could damn well tell me later, when we were safe. Or at least awake. "It's this way. Hold on tight." His hand gripped mine harder, our fingers entwined as we plunged into the darkness, away from the road.

I struggled to speak, but we were back in the void and I had no voice. He must have sensed my panic because he squeezed my hand lightly. I could barely see the edges of his face, just the dim outline of the glowing whites of his eyes. I focused on them until my own eyes dried out and I was forced to blink.

We stopped in front of a house. Or rather, we stopped in front of a large Victorian guarded by a massive iron gate.

I stared at the porch, my hands lightly gripping the bars, my mind struggling to reconcile its familiarity, with its chipped yellow paint and battered edges, its swinging chair, the broken light fixture twinkling in welcome.

I jumped when Brystion materialized beside me. "Do you have to keep doing that? You know, that whole creature of the night thing?"

He shrugged, inclining his head toward the house. "Old memories?"

"Yes." I tapped my fingers on the gate again, swallowing the lump in my throat. "It's the house I grew up in. What is this place?" I looked around, but there was only my house sitting there in the darkness, surrounded by an open patch of yard and then clusters of thick trees that stretched out farther than I could measure. It smelled like pine and old cedar and the faintest whiff of my grandmother's roses.

"The Dreaming, of course." He arched a brow at me, amused. "Where else would we be?" There was something amorphous about him now, as though he merely took a human shape for my benefit.

"I don't know. I just thought it would be different—clouds or mist or something." His mouth twitched, and I flushed. "Well, how the hell should I know? It's not like I've ever been here."

"Actually, you have. Every mortal comes here when they sleep—they just don't remember it. It's subconscious. This"—he gestured toward the house—"is the Heart of your Dreaming. A home base of sorts."

I nodded slowly, peering out into the darkness hovering beyond a little rocky path that twisted down a sloping hill. "And the rest of it?"

"That's up to you. These are *your* dreams, after all. They are what you make of them."

I shivered when the tang of the sea hit my nose, and I gestured at the path. "The nightmares are that way." Somehow I knew it to be true; if I were to follow it, I'd come to a rocky cliff, golden dunes, and a swirling sea of darkness. And the sharks.

I tugged on the chain around the gate after deciding I didn't really want to pursue that particular line of thought. "Why is this locked?"

"Seems you don't trust me enough to let me in." He frowned, as though he were admitting something he'd rather not. "Your subconscious is wiser than you know."

"Like vampires and thresholds, I guess. Convenient." My eyes narrowed, watching him. Maybe a little *too* convenient. "And yet, you were able to pop into my dreams last night pretty easily." And fill them with a scene even the cheesiest romance novels would have been ashamed of.

"You weren't actually in your Heart then." His head

tilted toward the rocky path. "You were headed that way. Fair game, as far as Dreameaters go," he added dryly.

My skin shivered at the thought. Had I been aware of him? "How is coming here going to help me with my nightmares? Assuming I actually make it inside at some point."

The incubus sighed. "I can teach you how to come here when you sleep, so that your dreaming will be clear. It won't solve the issue of what is causing your nightmares, but you will have a safe place to retreat."

I shifted uneasily. It sounded good, but the idea of giving a daemon free rein in my mental wonderland caused an uneasy roil in my gut. Yet, what choice did I really have? I'd given him my word.

An uncomfortable silence ticked by as I stared back at the house, wondering just what he wasn't telling me. My gaze flicked back toward him. " 'Safe' is a relative term."

"Ah, well, you're in my domain now, Abby." The incubus leaned up against the railing, something in his mien suddenly smug. "That means I have the control here."

I arched a brow at him. "Even in my Heart?"

His lips drifted into a gentle smile. "That is up to you, I suppose. I know what I would prefer."

"I'll bet you do," I muttered. "We're going to have to work on that shyness problem of yours, incubus. I'm getting tired of hanging out with such a wallflower."

"Indeed." He leered. "Want to help me out with that?"

I shoved him lightly. "Not tonight. I should probably get back. After all, we've got a succubus to rescue, don't we?"

The amusement drained from his face and for a moment I was sorry I'd killed the vibe. On the other hand, business was business. He'd come through enough for me to see what he was offering. The chance to offset my nightmares was a heady offer by itself. Sex, or the promise thereof, wasn't going to be part of the equation. *At all.*

"We should probably head back to the art gallery in the morning. Maybe I can convince Topher to give us a little more info on Sonja's whereabouts. I'm sure once he understands the situation, he'll be more forthcoming," I suggested.

"Maybe," Bryston said flatly.

"You never know." I shrugged. "I can meet you when it opens, if you want. Technically, I'm supposed to open the Pit tomorrow, but somehow I'm thinking this is a bit more important. Speaking of which." I tugged on his shirt to get his attention. "How do I get back? And will I come here every time I fall asleep?"

"Time passes differently here, sometimes. As to whether you come back here . . ." He watched me for a long moment.

I started to fidget and clamped down harder around the bars. "What?"

"Nothing," he said finally. "The Heart of your Dreaming is part of you, so you have nothing to fear from it, but if you should find yourself back at the CrossRoads, call for me." Gold flecked the outer edges of his eyes, and his voice became husky. "I will find you, always."

I shivered beneath that dark gaze. "That's the sort of promise you can only make to a TouchStone."

"Yes."

I blinked. A TouchStone?

His fingers traced my shoulder, trailing up my neck to my lips, cutting off anything else I might have said. "Wake up," he whispered.

I sat up with a jerk, startling the unicorn from where he'd curled up against my side. "Crap!"

Nothing but silence met my shout. Well, actually the unicorn made a little *meh* sound at me and rolled over, but that didn't count.

I flopped onto my back with a whoosh, arms curling back beneath my head. Not a bloody chance in hell of falling back asleep. The first rosy rays of dawn were already creeping underneath the blinds. Besides, if I fell back asleep, would I end up there? With *him*? And would that be such a bad thing?

Damn it all.

Assuming I believed the incubus, I'd somehow become his TouchStone. Then it hit me. Yesterday morning in the Pit, that little mind-roll with the . . . well, the naked stuff. Or at least the vision, the snapping sound. It was the only possible explanation.

My own stupid luck. And my own stupid fault for not having realized it earlier. But then, it wasn't like that'd ever happened before.

I eyed the unicorn wryly. Okay, well, it would seem I'd done it twice—by touch. Not Contract. That wasn't normal, was it? I'd certainly never heard Melanie talk about it before. Or anyone else, for that matter. And, of course, the only other option was currently sprawled behind my knees and snoring like a chain saw. Not like *he* was going to sit up and converse over a pot of English Breakfast.

On the other hand, hadn't I suggested a possible Touch-Stone Contract between me and the incubus? So why the fuss now that it had already happened?

Because he's holding the cards, my inner voice piped up. It was a fair cop, but that didn't mean I had to like it. At least with a Contract I knew what to expect. This was like free-falling without a parachute.

I wondered how long it would be before Robert figured it out—if he hadn't already. I had a sinking feeling the angel knew more than he'd let on. As far as I was concerned, *both* men lost points for that one. How hard would it have been to explain what was going on?

How hard would it have been to ask? my internal voice prodded snidely.

"I'm an idiot," I told the unicorn. He cracked an eye at me and snorted. "Well, you don't have to agree with me." He turned away with a self-aggrandizing sigh and I shook my head. "No help at all."

I slid out of bed and headed to the bathroom. First thing I wanted was a hot shower, and then maybe something to eat. After that . . . well, I supposed I'd just have to see.

Nine

The sunlight gleamed on the burnished copper sign of the Portsmyth Waterfront Fine Arts Gallery as I waited outside on the steps. The brine of the bay rolled over the cobblestone streets in a thick fog that spoke of potential rain later. My sandaled heel tapped fast on the polished marble. "Stop that," I muttered to it, willing it to still. A subdued breakfast hadn't done anything to calm my nerves and I still wasn't sure what I was going to say.

The lack of a formal Contract left the door open to a whole series of unknowns. For some reason the one with the unicorn hadn't bothered me nearly as much. But then again, all he did was eat and laze about. The incubus, on the other hand . . .

Even if I asked him, how could I trust his word? Brystion had obviously known for at least a day or so—and he'd waited until I was *asleep* to tell me.

"Not good," I sighed, sipping the last bit of my Dark Cherry Mocha. Thank the gods for Starbucks, anyway.

"What's not good?" Brystion perched beside me like the shadow of a crow, his movements quiet.

"Your hair," I muttered, concentrating on the steaming cup.

He let out a bemused snort. "And here I thought you liked dark and mysterious."

"Says you."

"Dreams don't lie, Abby."

"Yeah? Well, apparently you do." I gulped down the last of the coffee in two quick swigs. "And it sucks."

"You never asked," he said defensively. "And you were rather instrumental in the act. For all I know, you orchestrated it."

"Back to this, I see. One moment you're accusing me of having a brick for a brain and the next you assume I somehow made myself your TouchStone through a mistaken brush of your hand?" My empty cup spun between my fingers as I debated the wisdom of chucking it at him. "And for what? Certainly not the pleasure of your company."

He exhaled softly, leaning back to rest on his elbows so that he was draped over the steps. "I don't know."

"Well, that's a start, anyway. See, here's the thing. I get that you all need to have your secrets . . ." I flicked the cup at him, unsurprised when he batted it away with a careless hand. "But I'm not sure how you think keeping me in the dark about something as important as this is going to help anyone." He glanced over at me, and I stared back, refusing to look away.

"It's a defense mechanism," he finally murmured, tracing a circle on his knee. "In truth, the concept makes me a trifle uneasy, though I suspect you've gotten the worst side of that particular bargain."

"Yeah. You might say that." I hesitated. "And . . . um . . . since we're both airing out the dirty laundry, there's another problem."

"Do tell," he drawled, resignation flicking across his face.

I sucked in a ragged breath. "The truth of the matter is that Moira is missing too. So if this doesn't work, I'm not sure how much help I'm going to be."

"I know."

I blinked. "You know?"

He turned sideways, stretching out so that his feet crossed at the ankles with the length of his calf pressed against my knee. "From the moment we touched in the bookstore."

"Touched, eh? I thought you said that was just a side effect."

He shrugged. "Moira has shields around you. I was poking them with the metaphysical equivalent of a big stick. If she had been anywhere within 'hearing' distance, she would have squashed me like a bug." His mouth twisted wryly as he rested his head on his arms. "Which means she either doesn't know or doesn't care. Or is in a position where she can't act."

"Did you know that it would happen like that?"

He slumped. "No. I knew you'd bonded to me the moment we touched in the store the other day, but I didn't know how to deal with it. I've been waiting for the hammer to drop for days now. How long has Moira been gone?"

"Four months," I said softly, wincing beneath his stare, waiting for the outburst of anger that never came.

"I wondered." He hesitated and then slowly sat up. "I don't think Robert knows about us—the TouchStone thing."

"Then what was that freakout at the Hallows all about last night? Somehow I doubt it was to protect my maidenly honor."

"Not yours," he agreed. "Moira's. In case you hadn't

noticed, I was a tad . . . forward. It probably looked pretty bad to have the Protectorate's TouchStone seduced in front of everyone like that."

"I'd hardly count a few moments of dancing as seduction."

"Clearly I didn't do it long enough," he murmured, his gaze slowly raking over my body as he pulled me to my feet. He gestured toward the glass doors of the gallery. "Shall we?"

"Just one question." I headed up the last of the steps with a yawn, ignoring the prickle of heat taking root in my belly.

"All right."

"If you masturbate, would that make you an incubator?" I eyed him sideways, struggling not to laugh at his nonplussed expression or the sharp bark of mock outrage that followed.

His mouth curved suddenly, his eyes growing golden and lazy. "Guess you'll just have to find out."

Only a few other patrons circled the gallery that morning. No champagne or chocolate strawberries—just us and the paintings. I skirted past two heavyset men carefully taking a covered painting through the main foyer. I turned and slid against the wall. Several other canvases were wrapped in sheets, leaning against the kiosk haphazardly. Clearly we were arriving during a change of display, although I'd always been under the impression that sort of thing was done after hours.

Bryston stood behind me, his presence raw and heated. It felt sexual, protective, almost suffocating in its power.

"Christ, dude. Turn it down already," I muttered to him. "Or just piss on me and mark your territory and get it over with."

"I have a tendency to get carried away," he said sheepishly. Instantly I felt the hunger withdraw and I sighed. I could breathe again.

"So I've noticed." I waved him off before he could say anything else and headed toward the wing with the TouchStone paintings. The succubus portrait had curtains drawn before it, but the others remained lit. "Hmm . . ." I frowned, pulling up the edge of the cloth.

"Excuse me! Excuse me, please. You need to step away from the painting."

"Whoa." I dropped the curtain, stepping back as the small, stout woman from the other night elbowed her way past. She still looked like an eggplant in her dark purple suit and sensible shoes. "I'm sorry." I put on my best ignorant tourist face. "I just wanted to see the picture. It was on view the other night."

"Yes, well, it's been sold and the buyer no longer wants it on display," she sniffed. "Now please, you're going to need to leave."

"I don't think so," Brystion said quietly, his gaze flicking down to her name tag. "We need to see that painting."

"I'm going to call security if the two of you don't get out here," she warned, her face puffing up.

Brystion's lips pursed, his voice suddenly husky. "Come on," he murmured, "what's the harm in letting me take a look? Surely you trust me, right?" He stepped toward her, and although I couldn't see his face, I sure as hell could see hers. She paled beneath the onslaught of that commanding seduction, her expression suddenly going slack.

"What are you doing?" I hissed, but he slid away from me, bearing down on the woman in a nimbus of sexual energy.

"Michelle," he crooned, and I shivered at the raw lust that rippled from him.

"Yes," she whispered. Her breathing became rapid, and her glasses slid haphazardly off the bridge of her nose as she tipped her face up to him. She was a good few inches taller than me but still shorter than him. He reached out to stroke the side of her face, his fingers lingering in her mousy brown hair.

Jealousy flared through me like a burning brand, followed by a slick chaser of anger. If he knew of my reaction he gave no sign.

"Shhhhh," he breathed, his lips hovering mere inches from hers. I bit down hard on my cheek, the copper-edged blood filling my mouth. "Can I look at the picture, Michelle?"

"Ah, of course," she sighed, her eyes never leaving his face. "Anything you want, Mister . . . Mister?"

"Ion." He smiled at her. "You may call me Ion, if you wish."

"Ion," she chirped happily, tugging at the rope pull that controlled the curtain. "It really is a most wonderful painting, Mr. Ion. The details are exquisite, and oh, those feathers! Why, they look like you could just reach out and blow them away."

"Son of a bitch." I heard a soft gasp and turned swiftly. The eggplant was gaping like a fish, blinking as though she'd been doused with a bucket of cold water. The crackling heat of a moment before was gone, shut off like a faucet. Icy fingers gripped my gut as I approached the painting.

"Brystion?" I extended my hand to his shoulder. He trembled beneath my touch, his eyes cold and flat and empty. I swallowed hard, heard it echoed in the soft exhalation of the woman beside me.

"Look," he said tightly, his voice cracking with anger. "Look at that and tell me that bullshit artist doesn't have something to do with Sonja's disappearance."

Puzzled, I glanced up. "What the hell?" The girl in the painting was the same as before—proud and naked—but damn if those eyes didn't have some dark shadows under them this time. The wings were still there—extended and bloodred—but now there was something clustered on the bed beside her. I peered at it, my eyes adjusting to what was surely an improbability. Feathers. A scattering of feathers rested on the white coverlet. "Those weren't there before, were they?"

His shoulder tightened beneath my fingers. "No. Look closer at her wings," he snarled. "She's dying."

"Are you sure?"

"I know what death looks like, Abby, and I sure as hell don't need you to patronize me about it." He gestured at the painting. "She's losing her feathers. That means she's running out of energy." He bared his teeth at me. "They're starving her."

His upper lip curled harshly as he turned to Michelle. "I want you to get that two-bit hack of an artist out here. *Now.*" His words snapped like the crack of bones beneath a boot heel.

Michelle started, her face flushing. "I'm sorry . . . Mister . . . Ion, but that's not possible right now. I'm afraid he's out for the day."

"Ah." I stepped smoothly between them, my hand tightening on his arm in warning. "Do you think maybe you could tell us who commissioned this fabulous painting?"

Her face shuttered. "That's private. The buyer wishes to remain anonymous. It is not our policy to give out that sort of information."

"Well, it's just that I was thinking I might like to buy it instead. I sat for Topher myself, you know." I pointed to the mermaid painting, dazzling her with my most charming smile. Admittedly, I'm not that charming, but I figured I'd give it a shot.

Michelle gave me a withering look, the dazed light in her eyes fading away as she focused on me. "How nice for you," she muttered, her gaze flicking to the mermaid and then back at me. "We don't give that information out," she repeated, the words mechanical, rote. "I will tell Mr. Fitzroy that you stopped by."

Bryston gave me a sideways look. "This sounds familiar."

"Yeah, well, just look at how well it's turned out for you," I retorted as he turned toward the other paintings. He didn't acknowledge my words and that pissed me off even more. Michelle made another little sniff. "What?" I snapped, tapping my watch. "By my reckoning you're open and it's a free country, so don't get your panties all in a bunch."

"You're horribly rude," she said primly. "I shall be sure to inform Mr. Fitzroy that he has absolutely dreadful taste in models."

"You do that." I rolled my eyes at her. "Thanks for your help. *Not*," I whispered beneath my breath as she swished away. Bryston was staring at my painting, shoulders rigid. "You gonna be okay?" I slid behind him.

He shook his head. "It's something to do with these paintings," he muttered. "I can feel it. It's all wrong." He turned to me abruptly. "When did you say you sat for him?"

"I didn't, but it was a few months ago." I frowned, taking a closer look at my picture. There didn't seem to be anything particularly different in it. I was still there, complete with fish tail, complete with ship. Complete with deadly promises.

"What is it?"

"There." I shuddered, my fingers trembling as I pointed at the darkest corner of the painting. "Do you see that?"

"It's a shark." He reached out to trace the edges of the shadowy figure. I couldn't tear my eyes away from the perfect triangle of the dorsal, bitterly edged like a knife. I sucked in a deep breath, my wrist to my lips as I turned away. He looked at me sharply. "Like your nightmares?"

My arms wrapped about my shoulders as I pushed the rising panic away. "Hell, you were there last night."

"You're suppressing something," he said. "And it's manifesting in the form of a shark."

"You a doctor now?" The scowl crept over my face before I could stop it. "I don't care what the fuck it is, Brystion, I just want it to stop."

He swore softly. "What about the other ones?"

I pushed past the incubus, and bit my lip. "Melanie's looks about the same. I don't really see anything different about it." I glanced over at the other one. "The Angel's Charlie," I snorted. Charlie was still there, seated in a feather-strewn bedroom, her eyes dark and sad. An open window looked out on a moonlit sea, a ship silhouetted against the starry sky. The curtains lifted as though the wind was blowing. "Not very original, is it?"

"I could have told you that," Brystion said. "But I agree. I don't think this one looks any different from the other night." His lips pressed together grimly. "But yours . . ." Our gazes met and a pinch of fear lined his eyes. "Why did you sit for him?"

"I already told you. Topher wanted to do a TouchStone series. It was his way of coming back to the business, I guess."

"Coming back? What the fuck would he be coming back from?"

I shrugged. "From what I understand, he got really sick. I've heard rumors of everything from hep C to AIDS, but who knows? He'd come into the bookstore every once in a while and chat up Moira. Maybe buy an old art book or two. He seemed harmless, but there was an air about him, like he just expected to die, you know?"

My mind wandered for a moment, thinking of how the artist had always had a smile when he came to see us. His face may have been gaunt, but his eyes were large and bright. Sometimes he would tease Moira with little sketches, capturing her face in enigmatic expression, poignant and beautiful. "And then one day he dropped by, maybe two months after I got to Portsmyth, and it was like a cloud had been lifted," I continued. "I couldn't have told you what it was, but he seemed lighter, more relaxed. Almost younger, even. He asked if I would mind sitting for him. He said he wanted to capture the inner light of what made a TouchStone."

Brystion's head snapped down at me. "He wanted to what?"

"Capture our inner light," I said, feeling foolish. "Whatever the hell that's supposed to mean. I figured it was just some sort of artistic jargon."

"I'm surprised Moira would allow it, if he phrased it like that."

"Ah, well." I looked away. "Moira was gone by then, Brystion. This was just something the three of us decided to do on our own."

"How long ago was that again?"

"Just under four months, I guess." I added the weeks on my fingers. "Yeah, that sounds about right. Why?"

He turned back to the curtained painting of his sister. "Because that's when the first succubus disappeared," he snarled. He turned abruptly, tapping his fingers together.

"How many of them were there?" I asked.

"Three that I know of, but like I said, it took us a while to figure out the pattern."

"Where did you find the . . . bodies?" Indelicate, maybe, but I didn't think he was going to volunteer the information directly.

"The Dreaming," he said shortly. "We are born from it and that's where we go when we die." The incubus paused, his face troubled. "They were . . . husks. As though they'd been sucked dry. And they disintegrated at our touch."

"So there wouldn't have been any direct evidence that you could have taken to Moira as proof," I mused.

He shook his head grimly. "None other than our word."

"Shit." The lines were adding up here, and I didn't like it one bit. "So now what?" I glanced back at the eggplant. She tapped at her watch and then pointed to the door. Clearly, we'd worn out our welcome. "We have to go."

"I hope you have a pleasant day." The eggplant's lips twisted sourly.

"Oh, no doubt," I rumbled back at her. Polite obviously wasn't working. "Listen, if Topher gets in later today, could you please tell him to give Abby Sinclair a call? I really need to talk with him."

"I'll see what I can do." She crossed her arms, and I knew she wouldn't do anything of the sort. Brystion's eyes lit up and he took a step toward her.

"Knock that shit off," I snapped. "We'll find another way."

Without waiting for a reply, I pushed past him. My arm swung wide behind me, my watch snagging the cloth of one of the nearby paintings leaning against the wall. Shaking my hand, I hissed in irritation as the sheet pulled away. "I'm sorry. Let me just put this back." I stooped to retrieve it and I froze, the cloth falling from my fingers.

Moira's elven face stared back at me, her crystalline eyes piercing. I had only a moment before the eggplant shoved me out of the way, quickly covering the open corner. "Get out now," she snapped. "Before you cause real damage to something." Gesturing at one of the beefcakes who'd just emerged from the back, she pointed at the painting. "Please get this on the truck with the others."

Where the hell had that painting come from? Surely it hadn't been part of the original display? I glanced up at Bryston. He'd seen it too, or at least seen my reaction. I shook my head at him as his gaze slid thoughtfully toward Michelle again.

"Let's go." This time I made it through the rolling glass doors and into the waiting sunlight, the incubus at my heels.

He jogged into my shoulder. "What the hell was that all about? It worked the first time, didn't it? I could have had that woman eating out of my hand."

"Is that how it works, then? You just seduce people to your will? Is that how it's going to be between us?"

"That's disgusting," he snorted, his face ripe with offense. "You're my TouchStone. That would break the Contract."

"Oh, yes. It's *all* about that Contract, isn't it? Which we don't actually have," I pointed out. "How convenient for you." I pushed the hair from my forehead, trying to figure out how to get this conversation back on track. "Look, I know I have no claim on you. But doing that—" I gestured back at the gallery. "I don't know. It just seems wrong."

His eyes blazed for a moment, his lips pulled back in a feral, mocking semblance of a smile. "Don't you tell me what's wrong, Abby. I will do what I have to do to save my sister. If Glamouring a few old biddies into thinking I'll have sex with them is what does it, you'd damn well better believe I will. I am what I am." His hand ran down his chest, pressing lightly against the cotton shirt. "And I will not pretend to be otherwise simply to sooth your morals or your mind. I do what I have to in order to survive—no more, no less."

I stared at him, taken aback by the impassioned onslaught. "All right," I said slowly, suddenly feeling like the Pensivies in front of Aslan's tent. "Not a tame lion. I get it. Let's just get back to figuring out what's going on, shall we?" Inside, my mind was gibbering on and on about the unholy mess I was making of things, but I pushed the noise away. "I don't suppose you happened to see that painting of Moira on the floor there."

He exhaled, his shoulders dropping. "I saw. What do you make of it?"

"I don't know. I certainly didn't see it there last night." I chewed on my lower lip as I tried to remember the tiny bit of detail that I'd seen. The flowered light switch on the wall . . . I snapped my fingers. "Her office. It looked like she was sitting in her office. Back at the Pit," I explained. "She has one there for some of the more domestic type stuff."

I'd never gone in there without Moira, and certainly not since she'd left. There hadn't been a reason to. "Did you hear what I said?" Bryston was staring back at the gallery, distant.

"Yes," he said absently. "Let's go take a look at that truck out back. Maybe we can figure out where it's going."

"Or hitch a ride in the back?" I said it lightly, but my stomach churned at the notion. Part of my Contract with Moira stipulated that I couldn't leave the borders of the city. The results of disobeying were bound to be unpleasant. "Why don't you just Glamour yourself like you did the other day in the bookstore? You could find out that way."

His face shuttered. "Not possible right now. They've already seen me. It will be too hard to confuse their minds directly in the daylight like this. Come on. We're going to have to do this the old-fashioned way." He slipped his arm through mine, strolling us casually down the steps and around the block. I risked a glance back at the glass doors, but there was no sign of the eggplant.

I sighed heavily as we rounded the corner, just in time to see the back of a moving van pull away from the loading dock. MIGHTY MOVERS was painted on the side in faded red letters. "Well, crap."

"That's about right," he muttered, his eyes boring into the metallic plating of the back as though he might burn a hole in it.

I squinted at the license plate. "It's a local truck. We might be able to call around and see if we can find out where they rented it from. In the meantime, we can check Moira's office for any information that would indicate where she is. Assuming there's any sort of connection."

"There is. I'd stake my life on it."

"Well, let's just hope it doesn't come to that." I started back down the alley. "Truthfully, it's not you I'm so much worried about as your ass. It's like the Eighth Wonder of the World or something. Be a shame to deprive future generations of Dreamers, don't you think?" My stomach rumbled. "Come on, I'm starving."

A snort escaped him. "Nice to know you care."

I patted my belly and shrugged. "Yeah, well. A girl's gotta have priorities."

Ten

"About time you showed up." Katy scowled at me from the stoop of the Pit. "You're late." She was draped over the steps of the stoop with the boneless grace of a teenager, all petulant angst and impatience.

"It's not exactly like I've got a line around the block to buy a pallet of Time-Life books, now is it?" I retorted, digging into my pockets for the keys to unlock the front door, juggling the remainder of my sandwich in my hands. "I had things I needed to do this morning. It happens."

"But I have questions and I—" Her voice dropped when she saw Brystion, her eyes widening. "Oh, I'm sorry. I didn't realize you had a guest."

I rolled my eyes as the incubus turned a full-wattage smile on her, stunning her into a dreamy sort of silence. For some reason this didn't irritate me nearly as much as I would have thought.

The door opened with a grunt, the lower corner swollen from the humidity. I propped it open with a stack of ancient hardcovers and sighed when the breeze fluttered through to blow away the dusty smell. "That ought to do it." I headed behind the counter, starting to organize the few things Charlie had left from the day before.

Katy's giggles rippled from the front and I peered over the stacks to see her perched on one of the reading chairs, hanging on to whatever story Brystion was telling. I cleared my throat, gesturing to the back of the store when I caught his gaze.

"Guess that's your cue," he said, winking at her.

"Don't hurt yourself," I muttered.

Katy sauntered up to the counter, the book of poetry resting in the crook of her arm. She had a strut that would make men weep, all hips and ass and long legs and short shorts. She made it seem effortless. A mild twinge of envy swept over me and I frowned. What the hell was wrong with me today?

"Did you like the book?"

She shook her head, setting it gently on the counter. "I didn't get it at all. There's nothing in here about a fourth Path." Her eyes narrowed indignantly. "I think you just gave me this book to get rid of me."

"Never," I murmured, somehow managing to keep a straight face. "Honestly, the information on how to get to the CrossRoads really is in there . . . you just need to figure it out."

"You're lying."

"No, actually she's not." Brystion's dark voice glided up behind us in a silken wave of desire. My legs trembled in response and I was very glad I'd worn a longer skirt today. Katy jumped, her jaw dropping as she turned to stare at him, clearly as affected by the rush of power as I was.

"He's . . . you . . . you're OtherFolk," she finally gasped.

"Ding, ding! We have a winnah!" He tapped the counter in emphasis.

"But . . . I thought . . . I thought you only could appear at the four Hours."

"You thought wrong, then." He glanced over at me in amusement. "Where'd you find this one, Abby? She's even more ignorant than you are."

"You say the most romantic things," I said, a flush crossing my cheeks. "And you're being an ass. Go wait in the storage area. I'll be back in a minute."

His eyes lit up with a wicked twinkle as he sauntered past us, one hand drifting behind him to trail lazily over my hip. I snorted in bemusement as he disappeared into the storeroom.

Katy uncrossed her arms. "He's a real jerk, you know that? You can do better."

"So I've been told." I glanced at her thoughtfully. "You know how to make change?"

She blinked, puzzled. "Sure. Why?"

I tossed her my name tag. "You're me for the next few hours. Think you can handle it? We only take cash, so it should be pretty easy."

"What, run the store so you can go off and get busy with the walking orgasm?"

"I heard that," a dark voice echoed sourly from the back. There was a heartbeat of silence and then a sigh. "Even if it is true."

"I think you're getting the better end of the bargain," I muttered. "But I've got some things I have to do, and this way we both win."

She crossed her arms. "And what do I get out of it?"

"What you wanted. Watch the store for me now and I'll take you to the Hallows tonight."

"Seriously?"

"Scout's honor," I promised, trying not to look back over my shoulder. "Brandon's been asking about you, actually."

Her cheeks pinked prettily. "Well, in that case . . ." She fastened the name tag to her shirt and smiled. "Hi, my name is Abby. How can I help you today?"

"Perfect. Here." I dug my iPod out of my purse and hooked it up to the speakers. "It's . . . um . . . enchanted. Just tell it what you want to listen to and it will play for you."

"Whoa." A grin split her face. "Now we're talking."

I headed back to where Brystion had disappeared as BuckCherry's "Crazy Bitch" suddenly crackled through the sound system. Maybe not the best choice for enticing customers, but I wasn't going to argue. "Just call for me if you need anything; otherwise, prices are noted on the books."

She waved me off, hips swaying as she started grooving behind the counter. Good enough.

Brystion was slouched against the door frame as I shuffled through the storage area. "Having fun holding up that wall?" I breezed past him, averting my eyes from his at the last moment.

"It's a living," he said mildly. "Where's this office?"

"Through here." I led him down the faded hallway, past a small bathroom, to Moira's office. I hesitated in front of the door, as though I could still see the parchment taped to the frosted glass.

"Sorry," I muttered at Brystion. "I don't usually come in here." I glanced at him, surprised to see something sympathetic in his eyes. Shaking my head at my foolishness, I hip-checked the door so it clicked open.

Moira's office was just how I remembered it. Parchment scrolls were stacked neatly on the desk, framed by feathered quills and bottles of ink. A crystal oil burner was pushed off to one side. "She's pretty old school," I said, hitting the switch just inside the door. "And not particularly fond of technology."

"So it would appear." Brystion started nosing around the bookshelves, blowing away the light covering of dust on the bindings. "Nothing that interesting here." He frowned. "You really think this is where the painting was set?"

"I can't say for sure, but I know I saw this switch on the wall in it. And who knows when the thing was painted? There wasn't a date on the corner I saw." I shrugged. "For all I know it was painted after I got here or ten years ago."

He grunted and moved to the other side of the room to inspect some of the Celtic tapestries hanging there. I carefully began to flip through the loose papers on Moira's desk, setting aside the random inventory statements and property assessments. Something sharp pricked my finger. "Ouch," I hissed, sucking the tip in reflex.

"You okay?"

"Yeah, just cut myself on something. It's not deep." I pulled out a loose sheaf of parchment, watching as a pile of glass spilled out from beneath it. The remainder of a picture frame followed suit.

"What's that?" Brystion gingerly picked around the glass, removing the tattered black-and-white photo from the shattered frame. We peered at it, our foreheads nearly touching.

"It's Moira," I said. It was obviously from many years ago. She was dressed in traditional Victorian bustle and leg-of-mutton sleeves. Her sharp eyes and pointed ears stared coolly back at us from beneath a fashionable hat. "From the late 1800s, I'd guess. But who's that?"

Beside her stood a handsome man, dapper in his livery and top hat. One gloved hand was linked through hers possessively.

Brystion flipped the photo over. *Maurice and Moira at the pier. March, 1896.* It was written in Moira's delicate script.

"Hmmm. Looks like it's actually a variation of the boardwalk behind the art gallery," he said.

"Could be. She's been here a while. Looks like Maurice was too, whatever happened to him."

Brystion shot me a look. "What do you mean?"

"According to Charlie and Robert, he disappeared not too long before I arrived in Portsmyth. They suspect he and Moira had a falling-out."

"That's a lot of disappearances in a very short time," the incubus pointed out. "Anyone try to find him?"

"I don't know. I didn't even know anything about him really. Just his name." I glanced back at the picture. "Moira didn't ever talk about him."

He sighed heavily. "As much as I hate to say it, I think we're going to need to get Robert involved. Things are starting to unravel rather quickly. If we're going to put all the pieces back together, we should probably let him in on it."

I nodded, yawning. "Let's see if we can find any details about that van first. Then we'll have something solid to present. And maybe a nap," I added. "I don't know about you, but I'm friggin' tired."

"Understandable. Being a long-term TouchStone is hard work." His face became pensive. "It takes a lot out of mortals—more so for you, though, I think."

"Yeah, I'm hungry a lot."

He looked at me dubiously. "You're rather thin, if you ask me."

"Way to make a girl feel good, dude. I've always been thin. Dancer, remember? But I eat like a pig these days. Hell," I snorted, "I *eat* a lot of pig these days." My stomach rumbled at the thought. "It doesn't seem to matter much, though; I just can't seem to keep any weight on."

He gave me a troubled smile, tight and hard around

the edges. "It's the danger of being a TouchStone," he said abruptly. "It's in your nature to give until there is nothing left." He stared at me, eyes unblinking, gold shimmer about their edges.

I felt my cheeks burn. "Ah, can you just wait here a moment? I'm going to go upstairs and get my laptop and then we can try to track down Mighty Movers." I dashed past him and down the hallway toward the back door without waiting for an answer.

The unicorn was in my underwear drawer again.

"Who invited you, anyway?" I picked him up, rescuing him from the pair of hot-pink panties wrapped over his face. "Pervert," I muttered, ignoring his rather baleful expression when I set him back on the floor. "Go on." I nudged him away, shutting the drawer with an audible click. As many times as I'd found him in there over the last two days, you'd think I'd have gotten smart and put a lock on it. I'd even moved the underwear to the top drawer, but the damn thing managed to get up there as well.

He waggled his beard at me and trotted off, before disappearing under the bed. Strange beast, really, but who was I to question? As long as he stayed out of my way, we could manage as roommates for a while. Hell, for all I knew there was a mountain of tiny unicorn poop piled up beneath my box spring, but as long as it didn't smell I wasn't going to look too closely.

"That's a little forward, don't you think?"

I jumped, turning around swiftly to see Brystion leaning against the door frame. He eyed the panties with a sly smile, reaching out to stroke the latch of the door with a suggestive swirl. "I thought I was up here for business purposes. But I suppose there's business and then there's *business*."

Stifling the urge to throw the offending garment at him,

I tossed it in the corner for the laundry. Too much magical beastie hair. Again. "I told you to wait downstairs." I gestured back through the doorway, trying for nonchalance. Judging by the expression on his face, I failed completely.

He shrugged. "Maybe I wanted to see your bedroom."

"Well, you've seen it now, Hello Kitty underwear and all, so get out."

"Tut-tut." He waggled a finger at me. "Is that any way to talk to your dream lover?"

"Would-be dream lover," I reminded him, grabbing my laptop off the dresser. "You're going to have to do better than that if you want to get into my metaphysical pants."

"Don't you mean 'try harder?'" The smile became a leer and I rolled my eyes. Just my luck to get stuck trying to work with someone who *knew* he was a walking wet dream. The incubus smirked, but retreated to the kitchen, drifting like a shadow. I pretended not to watch him go and he pretended not to notice my not watching. It wasn't much of an arrangement, really, but it would have to do for now.

I set the laptop up at the kitchen table. Not much point in hauling it back downstairs if we were already here. I turned it on and then headed for the fridge as he took a seat. "Want something to drink?"

He rubbed his hands over his face. "Yeah. What do you have?"

"Hard to say—I never really know what's going to be inside. One of the perks of being TouchStone to the Protectorate, I suppose."

He stared at me dubiously. "I'm surprised you would risk it. There are a lot of stories about eating enchanted Faery food, you know."

I rolled my eyes. "Please. It never goes empty, but that's as far as it goes. If Moira was trying to enchant me with some kind of food Glamour, don't you think she could do a hell of a lot better than Oscar Mayer for the presentation?"

A hint of laughter touched the edges of his mouth. "There is that."

I snagged him a Coke from the door, popped it open and set it on the table. The happy Windows music jingled at me and I went over and logged in.

"This might take a few minutes," I said, pulling up Google to start my search for Mighty Movers. Bryston slid his chair closer to me to peer over my shoulder. "Hmmm. We could have a problem here. Says this moving company has been out of business for at least six months."

"Any contact info?" he asked.

"If I pull up a cached page, yeah. There's a phone number here. Assuming it's still connected, maybe they can tell us who they sold the trucks to."

"Long shot, but I guess it's worth trying."

I pulled my cell phone out of my purse. I sneaked a glance at him while I waited for the phone to finish dialing. He stared at the laptop with an air of despondency. After a few seconds I got a disconnected message and I sighed. "No go."

He grunted. "That's that. Suppose we better get a hold of Robert and see if he's got any leads on his end."

"Yeah." We sat in silence for the next few minutes, lost in our respective thoughts. I assumed he would have gotten up at that point, but instead he merely sat there, sipping his soda. Suddenly agitated at the quiet, I got up and filled the kettle with water for tea.

"Such strange things," he murmured finally, running his fingers along the edge of the laptop screen.

"What, you don't have computers in the Pornographic Land of Nod?"

He gave me a withering stare. "I meant technology in

general, actually. It's kind of taken the fun out of the job, you might say."

"Um . . . Dream sex isn't fun?" I frowned. "Then what's the point?"

"In the old days it was different. People used their imaginations—books, poetry, art—every night was something new. But now . . ." The corner of his mouth curled into a self-deprecating smirk. "I mean, how many times can you become Captain Jack Sparrow without feeling at least a little jaded?"

"Come again?"

"That would be the point," he agreed. "Ah, yes, I'd forgotten we haven't gotten that far in our little bedroom games." I bristled, but the look in his eyes said that he hadn't forgotten a damn thing.

Tracing a circle on the table, he sighed. "As a race, incubi's primary job is to drink energy from mortals. Such energy can be used for sustenance or even the creation of another incubus, if there's enough there. In return, we provide sexual satisfaction through fantasy. With the advent of technology, the fantasy takes a dip. There's no originality in dreams anymore. It is . . . unfulfilling."

"So you change your appearance to become the fantasy, then?"

"Of course." His eyes turned black and he shuddered, skin rippling beneath his clothes. I blinked. Captain Jack Sparrow was sitting in my kitchen. Fucking Jack Sparrow!

"Holy crap!" I was starting to like this fantasy thing a whole lot more.

His face became resigned and I almost felt sorry for him. He gave another twitch, and the pirate's features melted away, becoming Bryston's again. "It's harder to do that in the real world," he admitted, "but if you're good enough at it . . ."

"You're that good, then?"

"Obviously."

"So what does this have to do with me?"

"Those images are without substance. They take no effort for Dreamers to come up with, therefore there is no sustenance behind them. Such a feeding is empty . . . hollow." He reached out to take my hand as I turned to get the kettle. "It's been a long time since I've met such a vivid Dreamer, Abby." His thumb rolled over my palm, making me shiver. "And I'm so very, very hungry." There was something feral in his eyes as he spoke, and it sparked an answering hunger deep in my belly.

His nostrils flared, like he'd caught the scent of prey.

Me.

I pulled away, trying not to let my agitation show. He let me go, but his eyes followed me as I moved through the kitchen, steeping my tea, getting out the sugar. "Anyone ever tell you it's hard to concentrate when you're doing that?"

"It's what I am. Why should I change simply because it makes you uncomfortable?"

I had no answer for that. After all, wasn't I the advocate for being true to one's self? I tried changing the subject. "So, if you can change your appearance based on a fantasy, is that what you really look like?"

He stiffened. "No. I don't think you'd particularly like my true form, Abby. At the very least I doubt you would be so comfortable as to have me in your kitchen."

I nearly laughed. Clearly he had no idea just how formidable that face of his was. Or maybe he did. "So is that just a Glamour or whatever? You know, an illusion?"

"No. The change is complete—as complete as I can make it, anyway."

"I didn't know. I can't say I've seen many incubi in the Marketplace."

"We have no real reason to go there. Like the rest of the OtherFolk, we cannot exist here long without a Touch-Stone. Only mortals can give us what we need." His voice became soft.

"What happened to your last one?" I asked abruptly. To hell with not probing. "Melanie said she ran off with the drummer of your band. Is that true?"

His eyes hardened. "Yes. But I suspect she had a reason."

"That makes no sense," I mused. "I thought mortals couldn't break the Contract."

"It depends on how it's written. And besides, I'm the one who broke it."

I did a double take. "You did? But why?"

He was quiet for a long moment and then scowled at me. "I cheated on her," he said finally. "But not in the way you're thinking."

"Like you'd know that." My heart sank at his words, but I wasn't sure why. It wasn't like I could possibly have expected anything better from a daemon.

"I might," he retorted softly. "Walking the Heart of a Dreamer tends to show me a number of things, even when the Dreamer might just as readily forget them."

My hackles rose at his assumption. "Bullshit."

He blinked. "What?"

"I said bullshit. You don't get to just waltz in here act-ing like you know me, simply because you spent . . . what? A few hours in my dreams? You know *nothing* about me, incubus." I closed the laptop and slid it away. "You drop all this information about me, that you get to see my Heart, my dreams, my nightmares. Hell," I snorted, "you've prac-tically seen me naked, and you've been pawing at me like I'm your own private call girl. What gives you the right?" I glared at him, strangely indignant for the unknown woman. "Why did you cheat on her?"

"I had to." He lurched to his feet, pacing around the kitchen like a caged lion. "I loved her, in my own way."

"Loved?"

"Is that so hard to imagine?" His voice grew husky for a moment, but his eyes were obsidian when he glanced over at me. Grief, betrayal, confusion—all of it was written there. I dropped my gaze.

"I never thought about it. You're . . . daemonic." A flash of guilt tightened my throat as he flinched beneath my words.

"Does that make me any less alive? Any less feeling? A denizen of the Dark Path is not always evil, just like one of the Light may not always be good. Your own race is certainly proof enough of that." His dark hair had fallen over his face, hiding him in shadow. I ached to push it back. "I cannot change what I am, Abby, no more than you can change what you are. No more than Elizabeth could change what she was." He sighed, slumping down in the seat beside me. "Or what she wasn't."

Realization snapped like a rubber band to my face. "She wasn't a Dreamer, was she?"

"No. I was starving. And she . . . she tried so hard, but it just wasn't enough."

My mouth twitched despite myself. "High-maintenance incubus, eh? Figures. So then what? You just flounced around looking for other Dreamers?"

"Of course not. I was very discreet."

"Not discreet enough, apparently," I pointed out.

"Yes. And when it became apparent that it wasn't going to work out, I let her go." There was no doubt in my mind that there was a hell of a lot more to this story than he was letting on, but maybe I'd pressed him hard enough. Then again . . .

"So, uh, do you usually Contract your feedings through your TouchStones?"

A wry sort of amusement crossed his face. "Yes. Interested in the job?"

"No. Just curious." A flush prickled over my cheeks as he raised a brow. "What's involved?"

"Trade secret." He winked. "I could tell you, but then I'd have to kill you."

"Pity."

"Yeah," he muttered. "It would be. I bet you'd be good at it, though." He'd moved closer, his leg brushing mine. "Want to find out?" One hand slid over my wrist, thumb stroking the trembling pulse that hammered through my veins.

I stared at him, frozen. Was he serious? Bluffing? Did it matter? I searched his face, but if I expected a direct answer it wasn't forthcoming.

The question hovered between us, crushed into the minute space of our breathing. "Oh, what the hell." And I kissed him.

Eleven

Desire filled my belly, electric and alive. Warm . . . so warm, so goddamned hot. Whatever I thought I'd be doing flew out the window the moment his tongue darted into my mouth. No sex? What the fuck had I been thinking? I moaned softly, low in my throat, as his hand came up, stroked my face, gripped my chin. "So . . . different," I gasped, felt his mouth smile against mine.

"Yes," he growled, nipping at my lower lip before pulling back. His eyes were ringed with gold now, thrumming with desire. His mouth brushed over my cheek, his hand sliding to the back of my head. "Because *you* have chosen this . . . chosen me. I cannot help but respond." He suckled on my ear.

"Christ," I muttered hoarsely. "That sounds like a line from a two-bit porn movie. No wonder you were so cocky before."

"It's a gift." He grinned, lifting me onto the table. My teacup shattered with a crash, but I barely heard it. My skirt was sliding up my legs as his hands cupped my ass. "I will bring you absolute pleasure in return for what you give me."

"Do tell." I shuddered, my hips rising to meet him, a flood of heat pulsing between my thighs. "Is this your doing?" My lower half squirmed beneath him. Somewhere in the back of my mind, a warning bell went off. This was too much, too fast, but oh, it felt so good . . .

"Some of it," Brystion admitted, grinding into me. His mouth covered mine again, and for a moment I didn't care about anything but the delicious thing he was doing with his fingers as they grazed the inner length of my thigh.

"I thought this sort of thing was only supposed to happen while I was sleeping."

"Usually. I can wait," he said softly, pulling back to look at me, the gold light of his eyes dimming. "If you'd prefer that."

"It's just a little fast. Not that I'm not horribly turned on," I added hastily. "But my last . . . relationship with an Otherfolk guy really didn't go so well." *If you could even call it that,* I added silently. *More like being a living blood buffet.* "It wasn't much of a Contract either. But this . . . this . . . God, Ion, I've never felt anything like this."

He nodded, his mouth twisting wryly. "A bit of wooing, perhaps?"

"At least a bit." I nodded, nipping at his chin. "I don't mind a one-night stand or two, but if this is even remotely permanent . . ."

He sighed, his eyes fading to black. "I understand, but I can't wait much longer. We don't have to have sex, but I *am* going to need to feed. Here or in the Dreaming, it doesn't matter to me. But if not you, then someone else."

"Tonight," I promised, sneaking a glance at my watch. It was nearly 1:00 P.M. "Give me until tonight. I just need to wrap my head around it, that's all."

"Doesn't look like it's your head that needs wrapping, Sparky." Robert's voice drawled coolly from the doorway.

The angel leaned against the doorjamb, his upper lip curled in thinly veiled disgust.

I jerked my skirt down as Brysion pulled away, ignoring the flush of fire in my cheeks. "Anyone ever tell you it's polite to knock?"

"Anyone ever tell you you shouldn't leave the door unlocked?" Robert's shoulders thrust back with single-minded purpose. He was here on business, and the sharpness of his gaze smacked of an owl discovering his mouse.

The angel was wingless, wearing ordinary street clothes. A hint of feathers crept over the edges of his coat like a crest of silver hummingbirds, and the sword at his side hummed with sheathed menace.

My jaw dropped beneath the heat of his words, hearing the worst of my fears suddenly thrown at me. "And you're the fucking Queen of England, are you? What gives you the right to just barge in here?" I spared a glance at the incubus, who remained stoically quiet. "I am allowed to have a private life, you know."

"Well, I had news for you. About Moira, actually. And I thought you might want to know that while you've been up here spreading your legs, someone's ransacked the Pit."

"What?" My gut went cold.

"Yeah. The front door was wide open and the back door looks like it was kicked in. It's a damned mess down there. But clearly you were in the middle of something important, so I'll just let you get back to it, shall I?"

"Is Katy all right?" I barked.

The angel frowned. "Who's Katy? The place was empty. I figured it was just—"

Whatever he'd been about to say faded from my hearing as I jumped to my feet and dashed out the door, Brystion at my heels. The door to the storage room hung loosely on its hinges. It creaked ominously as I thundered past it, scattering loose papers and packing peanuts everywhere. One of the inventory boxes appeared to have imploded down the hallway, leaving a distinct trail of pulp and pages scattered in front of Moira's office. The scent of sulfur hung like a miasma of stale eggs and did nothing to improve the already rank odor of mildew and dust.

"Katy? Katy!" There was no answer, and no sign of the girl anywhere except a lock of her blond hair, as though someone had pulled it out during a struggle. I ducked behind the counter. My iPod lay on the floor, still valiantly chugging along even though the speakers had been ripped out of the wall.

My legs suddenly swayed out beneath me. "She's gone," I said, somehow tottering to one of the overstuffed chairs before collapsing, my head spinning with shock.

Bryston poked his head out the front door to look down the street, catching a curious glance from a passerby. "Maybe she got away."

"Maybe you were supposed to be a decoy to Moira's TouchStone so your infernal kin could wreck the place." Robert blew out of his mouth, shaking his head as if to clear it. "That's brimstone. That means daemons." He glared at Bryston. "A lot of them."

"That's bullshit," I retorted.

"Is it? Who's to say he hasn't been planning this all along?" Robert's eyes glittered angrily. "I seem to recall a certain Dreameater promising to leave you alone and get out of town."

"Can't imagine where you would have heard that," Bryston interjected smoothly. "I did no such thing. You told me what you wanted, but I never said what I would do." He took the seat next to mine, lounging with an indolent smirk. "Not my fault if you misinterpreted."

I glared at them both. "Could we please cut the crap and

concentrate on the matter at hand? You guys can go beat the shit out of each other later." I ignored the sour looks they shot me. "I don't have time to stroke your egos right now. We need to find Katy and make sure she's all right."

"I still say she escaped," Brystion mused. "Why would they come after her anyway?"

I shook my head. "I don't know. It doesn't make any sense. They didn't take anything that I can see." I got to my feet and paced in front of the door as the two men continued to trade barbs. A quick check with Robert confirmed that he hadn't seen anything coming through the Door from the CrossRoads, but there were hidden ways and Glamours over half the city, so that didn't mean anything. I kicked a shredded paperback from my path, frowning as something sharp spun away. I stooped for a closer look, my blood running cold as I picked up my name tag.

Wordlessly, I held it out to Robert. He peered at it. "What is this?"

"They weren't after Katy," I said, my voice thick. "They were after me. She was wearing my name tag."

Brystion stared at me. "You gave her your name tag? Brilliant."

"How the hell was I supposed to know? Do you see a damn sign out there inviting daemons to fucking kidnap the help? Dammit. We should have been down here!" I paced over to the front of the store, angry at him, angry at myself. And scared shitless.

"It's not your fault," the incubus said softly.

"No, it's not," I snarled. "You were the one that had to try to get all up my lady softness,"

."Didn't see you fighting it." His eyes flared for a moment and then he looked away.

I slammed the front door, locked it, and turned over the CLOSED sign. Slumping against the wall, I took stock of the room. One sitting chair had been shredded, the upholstery vomiting stuffing all over the carpet. Jesus, what was I going to tell Brandon?

"Why would they be after me?" I wondered aloud.

Robert's upper lip curled, and he moved with inhuman grace toward Brystion. "Damned good question. Let's see if the Dreameater knows. Better yet, I think I'll take him with me to the Judgment Hall."

"What are the charges?" the incubus snapped.

"Conspiring to kidnap the Protectorate, of course," Robert said with a withering smile. "You clearly violated Moira's TouchStone in an effort to seduce her to your cause."

"Bullshit." I shoved the angel away. Or tried to. It was like trying to use a plastic shovel to chisel a brick wall, and about as effective. "This isn't solving anything. I thought we were supposed to be trying to figure out where Moira was. And Sonja," I amended, sparing a quick glance at her brother.

And now Katy, my inner voice nudged. I winced. "And Katy," I said softly. "I fail to see how arresting anyone is going to help us out here. Besides, we've found out some information about the missing succubi . . . and possibly Moira."

"Have you?" Robert frowned at me as I explained about Moira's painting in the gallery and the way Sonja's painting appeared to be changing. "And you think Topher has something to do with this?"

"I don't know. I haven't seen him since the other night and he's not answering his phone. But something isn't right with those paintings. I don't suppose Charlie had anything to say about it when hers was done?"

"Not that I remember." He shook his head, his fingers trailing back down the hilt of his sword thoughtfully. "You may be right about the connection, though I certainly don't know how." He straightened, grim lines etched into his forehead. "I made a few discreet inquiries along the CrossRoads. Moira is not in Faery, as best we can tell. Or anywhere else, for that matter."

"And you don't think she might have just left? Gone on vacation?" Brystion drawled from the storage room doorway. "The gods know if I had to look at your ugly mug every day, I'd probably leave too."

"No, she wouldn't have left," the angel snapped. "Not without telling me."

"But Robert . . . she did," I pointed out. "She tacked a note on the door and she left." I glanced over at Brystion, rolling my eyes at him. Nothing like waving a red flag in front of a bull. Or in Robert's case, a bull with horns that flipped up to shoot 50-caliber bullets. And had flame-throwers in his hooves.

Robert's nostrils flared out like said bull and for a moment I wondered if he might not just charge past me. He sucked in a deep breath. "There's a formal inquiry in the works. We're to meet with the Faery liaison tomorrow to discuss the issue," he said finally. "It's an official Hearing, so I'll need you to present whatever information you have then. Maybe a better pattern will unfold when we've got something to look at. In the meantime, I'll be taking your friend here into custody."

"You and what army, pindancer?" Brystion's jaw hardened.

"That one." Robert gestured toward the storage room where another Celestial suddenly materialized. The beefy angel loomed there, blocking any way of escape. "It will go easier on you if you just turn yourself in, you know." Robert's voice was smug, daring Brystion to try something.

"Too convenient." The incubus bared his teeth at the

newcomer, the angel returning in kind as he captured Brystion's arms behind him. Bryston wasn't exactly fighting him, but I could see the redness in his face, and the sharp movement of his wrists as they were bound behind his back. His lips pursed in self-mocking amusement, but there was nothing funny about that shadowed gaze or the way it swept past me in helpless rage.

"But that makes no sense! He's been *helping* me." I slammed my hand down on one of the stacks, wincing when the bottom shelf collapsed beneath the blow.

"He knows too much, first of all. I can't have him running his mouth and letting it slip that Moira is gone."

"You do it all to save your own skin." An involuntary hiss pressed through Bryston's teeth when the other angel yanked down hard on the rope.

Things were spinning out of control faster than I liked. How far would it go? I sucked in a deep breath. "You can't," I blurted. "I'm his TouchStone."

The room froze, all three men staring at me like I'd grown another head. Bryston closed his eyes as though I'd doomed him.

"What did you just say?" Robert's voice was ice. His gaze nailed me to the floor.

I thrust my chin at him. In for a penny, in for a pound and all that. "I'm his TouchStone."

"Prove it. Show me the Contract, and I'll let him go."

I stared at him helplessly. "I don't have one. We . . . uh . . . did it by accident. When we . . . touched."

"No doubt," the angel smirked. "I think you're full of shit. No Contract, no deal. But you can explain it to the liaison tomorrow, though I doubt she'll be glad to hear it."

"What time is the Hearing?" My heart dropped. I had no way to prepare for this, no way of knowing what Moira would want. I certainly had no authority over the

Judgment Hall, let alone any real influence with the Faery Court. I was fucked. "What about Katy? While you guys have been having your little pissing contest, she could have been dragged halfway across hell knows where." Guilt lanced through my chest. Brandon wasn't going to be very happy with me.

"I'll send out a contingent immediately," Robert agreed. "That many daemons should leave an easy enough trail."

"Yeah, you guys are brilliant trackers," Bryston said. "You obviously keep tabs on people really well around here."

The angel shot him a look of death.

"I want to go with them," I said, interrupting what was surely going to be another example of verbal masturbation. "I can't just sit here. I need to do *something*."

"You're not going anywhere." Robert crossed his arms. "I'll be sending someone to stand guard here tonight and to fix some of the damage, but you're not to leave your apartment, understood? Not even for the Marketplace. There are too many unknowns; I want you where we can keep an eye on you."

"I actually agree with him," the incubus muttered. "Hell hath finally frozen over."

"Enough out of you." Robert snapped his fingers. Bryston snarled as the other Celestial's hand gripped his shoulder, pulling him back into the courtyard. I followed, escaping Robert's sudden snatch at my wrist. Helpless, I watched as the two of them slipped through the garden gate, a sudden shimmer making my eyes water as a shower of silver frost sprinkled over the grass.

Figures they would take the Door, I thought sourly. The CrossRoads was the one place where I couldn't follow. I whirled on Robert, heedless of his sword or his size. "You don't understand, you stupid prick. He needs my help. There's something else going on—"

The angel's mouth compressed into a tight line as he carefully looped his arm through mine, gripping like a vise. "You're right. There is. And until we get this straightened out, Sparky, this is just the way it's going to be. I don't know what kind of little deal you've worked out with him, but I can assure you the Court will not be amused."

"You could have just asked," I said. "I've done nothing wrong, and you've got no right to treat me like this."

The back of my head slammed into the brick wall with an unexpected ferocity, and I cried out despite myself. Robert leaned in close, his nose brushing my cheek. It was a lover's gesture, but there was nothing romantic about the way his fingers bit into my arm. "Listen, little girl," he breathed, his teeth clipping the words. "I'm going to figure out what game you're playing and when I do . . ." He pulled back, pinning me beneath a wave of blue fury. "If I find that you've betrayed the Protectorate, I'm going to paint the walls of the Hallows with your blood."

I shifted, even debated kicking him the balls, but he must have seen something in my expression because he slipped just out of reach. "Try it." He grinned, his hands trembling eagerly. A heartbeat passed and then a second and then I dropped my gaze. Fucked, yes. Stupid, no.

"Thought not." He paused. "I'm going to insist you stay upstairs for the rest of the day. For your own safety, of course."

"Of course," I snarled back. "What about Brystion?"

"The incubus is no longer your concern. Better for you both if he'd just done as I'd asked." Robert watched me impassively, mockingly waving one hand in a warped form of misplaced gallantry as we mounted the stairs to my apartment. "Go on now. I'll send Charlie to get you in the morning and take you over to the Judgment Hall. Maybe if you talk to the elvish liaison beforehand you can avoid any additional . . . unpleasantness."

"I'm not a prisoner, Robert," I said acidly.

"Not yet," he agreed. "But I think that's going to change." He shoved me lightly inside, the door slamming behind me with the finality of a jail cell.

Twelve

And then the fucker locked me in here." I stomped through the kitchen for the millionth time, torn by anger, frustration, and guilt. All of it was wrapped up into the aching edge of the evening, since I knew that tomorrow would be here all too soon. "What the hell am I supposed to do now?"

There was a pause on the other end of the line. "Shit," Melanie's husky voice thrummed through the receiver. "That's pretty heavy, Abby. Did you try calling Charlie?"

"No," I sighed. "We kind of had a little fight the other night, and well, you know . . ." My voice trailed off awkwardly. "What with the whole Robert thing and all."

"Yeah, I hear that. You want me to check it out? I have to tell you, though, I think you're getting in way over your head here. You're sure you don't know where Moira is?"

"Twenty-five-thousand-dollar question. AWOL, I guess."

"All right, hang tight. I'm going to call some people. I'll get back to you as soon as I can." We said good-bye and the line went dead in my hand. I hung up with a frustrated groan, slouching at the kitchen table.

The conversation with Brandon earlier had not gone well. Oh, he'd put on a brave enough tone of voice over the phone, but I could nearly taste his disappointment on my tongue. Disappointment at what had happened, disappointment in me.

I'd rattled off the information for the Hearing, but I couldn't tell if he was really listening to my words. He'd earned the right to be there even if he didn't show.

The shame of my failure burned my heart.

I strayed over to the front window, glancing down at the shadows. The curved silhouette of a woman hovered just outside the streetlight, the ambiance brushing over her skin in sickly yellow hues. I detected the faint glitter of scales on her cheekbones as she tipped her face toward me, acknowledging my silent question with the smallest of motions.

Well, that took care of that. She didn't look like anything particularly magical, but with my luck she was some kind of shapeshifting dragon. My upper lip curled. Robert didn't fuck around. It was a pretty good bet that there was someone out back too.

A soft bleat from the floor caught my attention, and I glanced down to see the unicorn pawing at me with a tiny hoof, his nose twitching. I ground my teeth as I fought the urge to kick him across the room. One more goddamned magical thing.

"And what the hell do you want?" His ears flattened and I realized I'd probably offended the hell out of him, but at the moment I didn't give a shit. "I suppose you're hungry?"

He sighed and gave a rather good imitation of a shrug and wandered over to the fridge. "Fine," I muttered, whipping out a bowl and some Corn Pops from the pantry. "Sorry." I set the bowl down. "I don't feel much like cooking." He sniffed the golden cereal with disdain but proceeded to nibble on it anyway. "Such a trouper."

The phone rang and I snagged it, the unicorn forgotten. "Talk to me, Mel."

"We have what you want." The muffled words choked out of the receiver.

"Who is this?" The anger from before rushed out of me, even as my knees went weak. "Where's Katy?" Long shot that they'd answer, assuming she was what they meant.

"The CrossRoads. Two hours. Anyone else shows up and she's dead." The phone clicked off, leaving me with nothing more than a dial tone. I stared at it.

"But I can't . . ." Assuming I even used the Door in the garden to get to the CrossRoads, I had no idea how to navigate them, no way of getting back. No way of fighting daemons. Not to mention that I was pretty sure the Cross-Roads counted as beyond the borders of Portsmyth.

The phone trilled again. "Abby, it's me." Melanie's voice sounded dark. Worried. Afraid.

"What is it? What did you find out?" I tried to keep my own voice calm, but there was a slight hysterical edge to it that I couldn't control. Should I tell her about the call? Would it inadvertently lead to Katy's death if I stumbled my way through another fuckup? I bit my tongue and waited to hear Melanie's news.

"It's Moira. Robert did some more investigating after he met up with . . . you." I snorted loudly, but she ignored it. "No one knows where she is, Abby. The Fae all thought she was here, and when they found out she wasn't . . . well, let's just say the metaphysical shit has hit the fan."

"Crap. But I don't get it. I know she's the Protectorate and all, but why is that such a big deal to them? Can't they just send another one?" And get me out of this forsaken Contract?

Melanie made a sound of frustration. "Jesus, Abby, don't you know who her mother is?"

"Um, no. She never told me."

"The Queen of Elfland. Moira's a motherfucking Faery princess. And she's missing. And you're the last person who probably saw her. Make sense to you *now*?"

I exchanged a glance with the unicorn. "Oh, shit."

"Damn right, oh, shit."

An icy ribbon ran down my back. Robert's actions suddenly made a horrible sort of sense. As Moira's First, he was sure to be blamed if anything befell the Protectorate.

"And Bryston?" I blurted the words without thinking.

She paused, the silence stretching out for a few awkward moments. "Are you really his TouchStone?" The words were quiet and without judgment, and my inner heart thanked her.

"Yeah, I am." I didn't offer up more of an explanation and she didn't ask. The question was there, hovering over the wire between us. When I said nothing else, she sighed.

"Well, just be careful, I guess. They're going to be looking for answers tomorrow, and I don't think they'll care how they get them."

"That's ridiculous. I know what I'm doing . . ." My voice trailed away as I remembered the way Bryston had seduced the eggplant woman. Remembered the first meeting with the incubus. The night at the Hallows. Was I really sure? Or was it possible that he'd been playing me from the start with the power of his seduction? And yet . . .

The sheer desperation at the loss of his sister. The way he carried me through the CrossRoads. The protective streak that seemed to be cropping up in the form of angel-bashing and coats. Was he just after a free meal? Or a hostile takeover?

I wiped at my forehead, thoughts whirling. The truth of it was that I really had no idea who he was or what he wanted. I glanced over at the unicorn; he was still crunching cheerfully away on the Corn Pops.

"Only one way to find out," I murmured.

I wandered into the bedroom. Perhaps if things were different or less intense or less . . . needful, it wouldn't be such a big deal. But I hated to be forced into things, and I was currently being tossed headfirst into the tiger room. With A.1. sauce for shampoo.

"You still there, Abby?" Melanie's tone was thick with worry. "You want me to come over?"

I shook my head and then snorted at my own idiocy. Duh. "No, I think I've got it covered. Are you going to be at the Hearing tomorrow?"

"I can be. Assuming they let me in, but I'm usually pretty good about getting strings pulled."

"I could definitely use the support." I forced a smile to myself. "Never know, I might need a quick exit. I also might have a lead on Katy, but I need to work out the details." I hesitated and then told her the rest of it, promising to call her back when I knew what I was going to do.

I hung up the phone, suddenly desiring quiet. Too many goddamned questions and not an answer in sight. My head spun with the implications. Moira. Sonja. Katy. What was the link?

Clearly, I owed it to Katy to try to set her free, but without a way to get there . . .

I sighed, staring at my phone. I would have to call Melanie back. Call Robert. Call someone else. Anyone else. Failure, indeed.

And yet, hadn't I managed to get to the CrossRoads through my dreams last night? Admittedly, it had been Bryston's doing, but that meant it was possible. If I could calm down enough to fall asleep, I might be able to do it.

But weren't you warned not to do it? I shushed my inner voice. It was the only way.

My heart started tripping like a hamster on crack at the thought. Time for more desperate measures. I eyed the phone again. What were the chances I'd need backup?

Pretty damn good. But who? And what was I supposed to tell them? *Meet me at the CrossRoads in two hours . . . but I don't know exactly where, and I don't know what I'll be doing. And, oh yeah. There's gonna be daemons and if you show up too soon they're going to kill my friend.*

My upper lip curled as I flipped the phone up and started texting Melanie.

CALL ROBERT. 2 HRS. GOING 2 FIND KATY ON XROADS. ION WILL KNOW HOW 2 FIND ME. FML.

"Time to put your money where your mouth is, incubus," I muttered, shutting off the phone. I didn't want any interruptions.

I padded into the bathroom and flipped open the medicine cabinet. I'd had a lot of trouble sleeping after my accident, nightmares notwithstanding. Pain had become a rather intimate friend. I didn't particularly like taking drugs, but I just couldn't see any other way. My fingers expertly flipped over the little orange vials as I mouthed the names. *Percocet. Vicodin. Oxycontin. Valium. Alavert. Flexeril. Neurontin.*

I hadn't taken any of the painkillers in quite a while, and I avoided the Alavert on pure stubbornness, but maybe the Valium would do. I rolled the vial between my fingers for a moment and debated how many to take. I didn't want to put myself completely under. Too far and I had the feeling I'd be so out of it I wouldn't reach the Dreaming at all. Maybe just half a pill.

A warning bleat sounded softly by the foot of the door.

"And what do you want?" The unicorn's vivid blue eyes sparkled as he imperceptibly shook his head. "What? I can't take something to help me sleep?" He tapped his horn against the doorjamb. "You have a better idea?" This time he made a little whinny that sounded surprisingly like *Come on, stupid.*

I set the drugs back on the counter. "This had better work, whatever it is." He tossed his head, the silvery-white mane rippling down his neck. His hooves clipped the floor as he trotted over to the bed. With a leap that belied his tiny size, the unicorn landed gracefully on the mattress. Turning toward me, he pawed at the blankets, his horn pointing toward the pillow. I raised a brow. "If you're bent on seducing me, there are probably better ways of going about it."

He shot me a withering look, the bleat becoming more insistent. "Fine, but if I wake up to you humping my hip, you and I are going to have words, understand?" He exhaled in exasperation as I crawled into bed and propped my chin on my arm. "Okay, now what? I have to tell you, I'm really not feeling much like sleep."

He paid no mind to my words but proceeded to turn about in a little circle, making a nest in the sheets beside me. The unicorn had a woodsy smell, like young pine and cedar, and fresh dew on newly blooming violets. On instinct my hands reached forward to stroke his back. He stiffened, but then sighed, muscles going limp as he relaxed against me. A delicate rumble emanated from his chest and I blinked.

"Unicorns don't purr, you know." Of course, my knowledge of unicorns seemed to be a bit off these days. I was pretty sure they weren't supposed to frolic in lingerie either, but shows how much I know. The purring grew louder, filling my ears like thunder, but it was oddly soothing.

"So soft," I murmured, my breathing matching the rhythmic sound. "So . . . soft . . ."

* * *

My blood slid sluggish and shadowed, a feathered semblance of itself tickling my veins. My fingers tingled and my toes ached, and all around me the air was thick and misted, coating my lungs like black brandy. I was falling, floating away in an empty sea of darkness.

The Dreaming.

Were those shadows around me? Finned and fierce with dead doll eyes and razor-wire teeth?

I was surrounded by corpse-white bellies and dead flesh hanging from gobbling mouths. My nightmares, given shape once again. Even the unicorn couldn't surpass them, it would seem; however, he had managed my slumber.

No island this time, no undersea shelf to hide behind. The predators loomed from the void. Where was my Heart? Confusion reigned over the terror that tightened my throat. Something brushed by my head, almost like a caress. Biting down a strangled scream, I wriggled away, limbs struggling like a tadpole in amber. No direction now but down . . .

A glimmer caught my eye, a river of light flowing long and narrow far below me. I thrust toward it, breaking through a scattering of gossamer webs clinging to my hair like tiny fingers. My nightmares receded, the stream swiftly grew larger, as I descended. I wasn't quite falling and wasn't quite floating—more like a gentle drift. Going down the rabbit hole. Alice would have nothing on this. It was a road, I realized a few moments later, set with silver and granite paving stones.

My naked feet landed carefully on the path, and a surge of warmth shot up into my legs, stirring up dust motes of silver sparkle.

"Well, hell," I breathed, looking up at the heedless dark of the sky.

I'd done it.

Thirteen

The strange euphoria quickly began to wear off as I peered into the blackness around me. Nothing. It was anticlimactic, at best.

"Bryston?" His name trembled off my lips, shivering away as though it didn't want to break the silence. It was stupid, I know, since if things went the way they were supposed to, he wouldn't be here at all.

With a sigh, I stumbled forward, ignoring a tiny wave of vertigo. I didn't know how to get to my Heart, but one thing was certain—I wasn't going to get anywhere if I just stood like a lump. On the other hand, I was probably walking into a trap, so either way I was screwed. For a moment I regretted not bringing a weapon, but somehow I doubted I would have been able to.

Something I'd have to ask Bryston later.

The road curved a bit, but there was no landscaping that I could see. Only the fog of shadows, oppressive and disconcerting.

Keep calm, Abby . . . and don't leave the road.

"Fat chance," I said aloud. The road twisted again and

then it seemed to split, but as I got closer I realized it was a four-way intersection. An actual *crossroads*.

"Damn." I cursed myself for keeping my eyes shut last time I was here. Not that it would have helped much. For all I knew there were crossroads like this all over the place.

I stared out into the darkness, wondering how I was going to find Katy's captors. Maybe they would just find me.

I passed through two more intersections, each time letting the feeling of the road beneath my feet choose my path. The cobbles were getting warmer now and, strangely enough, I saw signs of life. Small tufts of silver grass lined the road, and in the distance I saw the creeping edges of vines and thorn bushes, hedgerows and thickets. A green snail with a burnished shell oozed its way over a damp pile of leaves. I squatted over it for a closer look, jumping back when it looked up, eye stalks wavering furiously. "Bluebells forever," it muttered.

"Curiouser and curiouser," I retorted, curling my upper lip at it. "All I need now is a damn Cheshire cat." The snail ignored me and I continued on my way.

It was growing lighter, but it wasn't quite sunlight and it wasn't really moonlight either. Twilight?

I looked down. Dirt. "What the hell?" I turned around, but the road stopped abruptly, leaving me standing on warm earth, the silver grass tickling the bottoms of my feet. Now what? Brystion had said not to leave the CrossRoads, but he didn't say anything about what you were supposed to do if they just ended.

I peered into the woods, but there was nothing to indicate which way to go. Soft sighs rippled from the underbrush, echoed by crackling leaves. Moist things grew beneath the hedgerows, their scents damp and earthy.

Should I try to go back? Would I end up in "fair elfland"

if I pressed forward? Or Heaven? Or someplace much, much worse?

"Fuck it." No one ever got anywhere by going backward. And even if I did go back, I had no idea how to return to the mortal world. I glanced at my watch, not surprised to see it had stopped. No way of knowing how long I'd been wandering around, then. No way of knowing when my backup was going to be here. An uneasy tingle in my arms made me rub my elbows.

"Not one of your brighter ideas," I finally admitted to myself.

I left the road, following the pressed trails of what looked like deer tracks, switchbacking around the gentle slope of the hillside. There were actual trees now—slender birch, the white bark gleaming in the silver light, and delicate ash saplings. At least the scenery had changed.

There was another copse of trees up ahead, a quiet ring of plant life and tiny silver mushrooms. "Hello?" I said it louder this time.

"You have such delicious dreams," a husky voice whispered in my ear. My eyes snapped open, and I whirled around. Or I tried to. My heart slammed against my rib cage. Not Bryston. So totally *not* Bryston.

"You!" I instantly recognized the unicorn-obsessed daemon from the Marketplace.

"Oh, yes." His smile became broader, pointy teeth gleaming. "Now who's disappointed?" He drew me in tighter to him. "So tasty," he crooned. "And so *alone*. I'm going to devour you into little pieces, but your soul, I think, I will save. Would you like that? I'll wear it like a skin upon my back."

"Let her go, Hzule." Another voice rumbled out of the darkness. The trees parted to reveal three more daemons, all scales and horns and Versace.

And teeth. A shitload of teeth. A small figure was clutched between them, her blond hair hanging over her face.

"Let. Go." I croaked the words and tried to move, but my feet were wedged in molasses.

"Which one?" Hzule snorted, flicking his hands out so I stumbled to my knees. I scrambled away from him.

"What have you done to her?" I got to my feet as Katy raised a tear-streaked face to me. Terrified, but at least not injured that I could see. "Let her go," I said, my confidence growing.

The one who had spoken before curled his lip at me as he puffed on a swiftly burning cigarette. "A trade. You for her."

I had suspected as much, but that didn't stop my stomach from clenching at the thought. "Why?"

He shrugged. "So we can get paid. It's nothing personal."

Hzule grunted something under his breath and I shot him a nasty look. "For most of you, maybe." I approached the daemons who held Katy, a purple welt blooming over her cheek. I bit my lip. "How awesome of you to beat a child."

"She put up a fight," Cigarette said, flicking his ash at me. "I assume we can expect better from you?"

My eyes narrowed. I needed to stall for time. Pissing them off might work splendidly. "Guess that all depends on your definition of 'better.' I'm curious though. Why did you take her?" I jabbed a thumb at Hzule. "After all, he already knew what I looked like."

"I was the lookout," Hzule said, shooting daggers at Cigarette. "Though if I'd been allowed to run point, we wouldn't be having this conversation."

Cigarette turned a darker shade of viridian. "She had on the name tag, asshole. He told us she wore a name tag."

I cocked my head to the side, my interest piqued.

Hzule snorted before I could say anything. "And I told you she had pink hair, dumbass."

"I'm color-blind."

I sidled closer to the solo daemon that was now holding Katy. He rolled his eyes at me. Clearly this wasn't an unusual occurrence, then. I filed away that information for later. "So, if I come with you, what happens to her?"

"We'll let her go. We'll have to rip out her tongue, of course, so she can't spill the beans, but the rest of her will be unharmed. Or at least no more than she already is."

Katy tilted her head up to look at him and started to struggle, her mouth working frantically at her gag. He clamped down hard on her shoulders.

"That's enough," I snapped, pushing him away. "Let her go."

Surprisingly, he did. I caught Katy before she fell, the two of us sinking to the ground. I brushed back the hair from her forehead and slid the gag away. "You okay?"

She nodded, her eyes suddenly dull. She was going into shock. I gave the daemon a hard look. "You guys are assholes."

He shrugged. "Yeah, but what are you gonna do?"

A shadow slipped past the corner of my eye. I stiffened and then forced myself to relax. Friend or foe, I wasn't sure.

Azule had seen it too and he nudged the others. "Wolves," he hissed. I perked up at this, craning my head for a better look, but the creature was gone.

"This is the Borderlands. Why wouldn't there be wolves?" Cigarette mashed the stub out with his foot. "Are we about ready to do this?"

I shared a glance with Katy and she shook her head at me. "Let her go—unharmed—and I'll willingly come with you." Even as the words left my mouth, I wondered how true they were. After all, my body *was* still lying in bed in my apartment. However real things seemed, I couldn't actually be hurt here, could I?

Suddenly, golden eyes gleamed out from the shadows behind the daemons. They glittered like hard drops of amber—wolf eyes. One of them dropped into a slow, lazy wink, and then I saw a mouth parting into a familiar canine grin.

Relief flooded my limbs. Surely if Brandon were here, that would mean Brystion and Robert couldn't be too far behind. I resisted the urge to look around, instead leaned in close to Katy.

"Brandon," I breathed in her ear. She jerked back and I gestured at her to be quiet.

The daemons were still arguing among themselves. "Get ready to run," I whispered. Katy nodded as I slid into a crouch. I glanced back at where I'd seen the wolf, but he was gone again. And then a howl sounded through the valley, echoed by the mournful shiver of a bow being drawn over the strings of a violin.

Startled, I listened as the eerie duet swept over us, while the daemons froze in place. "Melanie," I murmured.

She emerged from the shadow of the trees, the notes spilling from her instrument in a flurry of silver sparkles. The violin glowed, a heady halo of mist and light enveloping it as she played.

"Gentlemen," she said, nodding at me with a toss of her flame-gold hair. "I believe you are late."

"I told you she wouldn't come alone," Hzule snapped, glaring at me. "Late for what?"

"Your ass-kicking," Robert rumbled from above, gliding down to separate us from the daemons. I glanced past him, Brystion's name on my tongue, but one look at the angel's suddenly unsheathed sword had me swallowing my questions. This is what he did, after all.

Cigarette pursed his mouth as though he were going to say something else. In the end, he shrugged. "Oh, fuck it." He snapped his fingers, a puff of fetid smoke exploding from his palm. The angel moved forward, and I shoved Katy out of the way, grunting as a smaller, blue daemon grabbed the back of my head.

The sound of a sword slicing into something meaty rushed by me, followed by a gurgling moan. A large, and furry, and *growling* mass bounded into the fray—Brandon to the rescue.

"Lok'tar ogar!" The daemon holding me pulled my head back, exposing my throat.

"Victory or death," I retorted at my captor hoarsely. "For the Horde. And for the record, shouting World of Warcraft battle cries kind of kills the whole 'imminent death' expectation."

The daemon paused. "What server are you on?" he demanded.

"Blackhand."

"Righteous. Guild?"

I couldn't imagine what the hell that mattered at this point, but it was keeping me alive so that was a bonus. I'd gladly spit out the rest of my Warcraft stats if it bought me a few more minutes. "Yeah," I coughed. "Elfhunter-Bitches."

He blinked and then grinned, tapping himself on the chest. "No shit. I'm TartBarbie. Undead DeathKnight."

I stared at him. "TB? Seriously? I'm Baconator. Blelf Warlock. You did a hell of a job tanking on that raid the other night."

"Yeah, I *am* pretty awesome." He glanced over his shoulder, releasing me. "Look, if I'd known it was you, I'd never have agreed to this. Go on." He nudged me with a leather boot. "I'll tell them you got away."

I didn't have to be told twice. "Thanks," I said softly. "I'll make it up to you, somehow."

"No worries." He winked. "See you next Thursday."

I took off toward another copse of trees. I wasn't prepared to fight anything, and until the dust settled a bit I couldn't see the wisdom of running back into it just to get my head snicker-snakked off. I circled as quietly as I could, spying Katy crawling out of the action, arms draped across Brandon's back. I sighed. One thing taken care of anyway. Melanie was still wrapped up in the dust, but her music hadn't stopped.

"But dude, she's a *guildie*! I couldn't just kill her for reals." My daemon friend's voice cut off with a grunt.

Shit. Time to go. I ducked behind an outcropping of boulders, hands scraping over the moss. And then I was faceplanting into the leaves as Hzule bulldozed into me. Tiny pinpricks needled into my arms, holding me immobile.

"Let me go," I snarled, kicking him in the shins.

"It's too late for that. I've had enough of your bullshit. Fuck the money." His scaled lips pulled back in a mocking rictus of a grin. "Shall I be sporting, little rabbit? Give you a ten-second head start?"

"Fucking bastard," I slurred, my mouth suddenly feeling stuffed with cotton.

"Oh, you say the *nicest* things," he burbled. He lowered his face to mine in the mocking pretense of a kiss, one clawed hand fumbling at the waistband of my jeans. "You won't feel a thing."

"No, but you will," Bryston's voice declared from behind us. Hzule shoved me away, and I stumbled, crying out as my head slammed into a rock. Dizzy, I tried to get up to avoid being trampled. My vision began to blur.

"She's mine," Ion snarled, his form shifting slightly into something dark and then back again. I blinked rapidly, cursing at my inability to focus. They circled me, somehow ending up on the ground with the incubus pounding the other daemon's face.

"Not for long," Hzule cackled. "He'll see to—" His words ended with a burbling chuckle as Ion crushed his windpipe. A wet, guttural sound and then all was still.

My eyes rolled back as my limbs started twitching violently. I wondered if my real body was seizing or if this was a side effect of being on the CrossRoads with my Shadow Self.

"I've got you." Bryston wrapped his arms around my shoulders and pulled me tight, holding me as the tremors built up and then dissipated. "I'm sorry," he murmured.

I turned toward him, the haze starting to lift. My eyes widened at his appearance. "Jesus Christ, Bryston. Did it do that to you?" Dark purple blotches webbed across his cheekbone, blood vessels shattered against the delicate paleness of his skin.

He squinted one eye at me, an amused gleam residing there despite the heavy, swollen lids. "No—well, not all of it. I took him by surprise, so the most he got was this slash on my forearm." He raised it closer to my face and I winced at the deep gouge bleeding openly over his flesh. It dripped, red and vibrant, onto my shirt. "As for the rest of it?" He smiled ironically. "Let's just say that pindancer of Moira's packs a wicked punch when he wants to."

"He *beat* you?" Cold rage swirled through my veins, my own plight suddenly forgotten.

"If you want to call it that," Bryston snorted, rubbing his wrists. They were red and chafed—rope burns. "That's why it took me so long to find you. I felt you as soon as you reached the CrossRoads, but . . ." He shrugged, his gaze rueful. "Robert took a little convincing. By way of a certain werewolf and violinist, I might add."

I eyed him dubiously, my fingers tracing the still-swelling lump at the base of his chin. "We need to get you to a doctor or something—whatever they have here."

He shook his head, getting to his feet. "There's no time for that. The others are waiting for us."

"I didn't realize Melanie and Brandon were coming too. I thought it would just be you and Robert," I said, wincing as I stepped on a jagged rock. The soles of my feet started to sting.

"Once I figured out where you were, Melanie told Brandon we'd found Katy, and he Contracted her to make the Door." He snorted. "He doesn't have the angel's gift for violence, but there's still something rather convincing about a mouth full of teeth that gets a man to think things through."

"Brandon *bit* Robert?"

"Just a little. It seemed to help." Brystion coughed something rude into his sleeve.

"And Katy?"

"See for yourself," he said, smiling gently as he pushed back an overhanging branch, revealing the clearing. Two daemons lay dead in a pool of blood and scales; there was no sign of TartBarbie. I hoped he'd gotten away. The brimstone scent still hung heavy in the air, but that too was fading. Katy crouched beside Brandon, leaning into his furry shoulder.

"Abby?" Melanie swept past Robert and Brandon and threw her arms around me. She punched me hard in the shoulder, carefully maneuvering her bow away from the blood on my sleeve. "Next time just call me, you idiot." Behind her, the angel loomed, displeasure filling his eyes.

"I'm sorry. They said they'd kill her if I brought anyone else." I brushed my fingers over my shirt as though I might wipe away the blood. "It's not mine," I said quickly when his eyes narrowed.

"Stupid thing to do," Robert said, wiping his sword clean on the grass. "Especially after everything we discussed this afternoon."

"I find I remember things better when I'm not getting my head slammed into walls, you know." I knelt down beside Katy. Brandon's tongue lolled at me, a wolf's laugh. "You okay?"

"Yeah." She gave me a small smile. "But if you don't mind, I think I'd like to go home. My mom is going to shit a bird if I don't get in before curfew."

I resisted the urge to say I told you so. After all, what good would it do? She was here, albeit in a way she'd probably rather not repeat, and there was no closing the jar now. Melanie's gaze darted between Bryston and Robert. Her eyes met mine and she nodded, raising her bow to the violin. "That's an excellent idea, Katy. I think the Hallows would be a good place to land, don't you?"

"Ah, what about me?" I said suddenly. "I mean, technically I think I'm still asleep in bed."

Bryston froze, staring at me. "You're where?"

"Asleep. I can't really travel through the Doors directly and I couldn't think of any other way to get here—"

"Stupid girl," he snarled. "No, you can't go back through the Door."

"Why are you getting mad at me? You're the one who *showed me* how to do it."

"Maybe you two would like to clue the rest of us in on the situation?" Robert said, sheathing his sword. "We're wasting time."

"I told you before," Bryston snapped at the angel. "She's a Dreamer. An *untrained* Dreamer. She managed to break through her dreams directly into the CrossRoads."

"That's not possible," Robert scoffed, but there was doubt tingeing the words.

"Actually," Brystion said. "It is. Dreamers can weave their dreams into reality." His gaze met mine, suddenly dark and unreadable. "Or at least their version of it."

"Huh?" Melanie blinked at me. At least I wasn't the only one who was out of the loop.

"It's a Shadow Self," the incubus sighed. "But real enough, for all that. If she dies here, she dies there. But in either case, her Shadow Self won't survive the transition to the mortal world."

I shivered. "Well, that settles that, then. How do I get back?"

"I'll have to take you back to the Dreaming." he said. "Though we'll need to get closer to the CrossRoads. I don't think I can do it from the Borderlands."

"You're assuming I'll let you do it at all," Robert drawled.

Melanie rolled her eyes. "Don't be such an ass, Robert. Who else is going to do it?" She gave me a sour look. "Though if you'd just said something . . ."

Robert suddenly looked very tired. Moira's disappearance was clearly taking a heavier toll on him than he'd let on. "Fine. I need to report this anyway, and Katy should get home. But you two had better show up tomorrow at the Judgment Hall for the Hearing." He fixed his gaze directly on Brystion. "I entrust her to your protection," he muttered softly. "*Don't* make me regret it."

The incubus raised a hand to his heart. "On my honor," he said, his mien suddenly formal.

"For all it's worth," Robert snorted dryly. "Okay, let's get out of here." He gestured to Melanie, who began to play, the air shimmering with fresh power. Within moments, a silver outline shone between the edges of two trees. Helping Katy to her feet, Robert supported her as he led her through the Doorway, followed closely by the wary werewolf. Melanie mouthed a good-bye to me, tipping her head at both of us before she slid through the portal. Her music faded away along with the Door.

"Are you ready?" Brystion looped the fingers of his good hand through mine and we set off through the underbrush. He peered upward through the trees, eyes darting into the dimly lit sky as though seeing something I couldn't. "I'm not going to question your methods," he said finally, "but why did you leave the road?"

My face flushed. "I didn't mean to. The road just ended, and I didn't know which way to go. I tried to do what you said before and feel my way through."

His face softened. "You couldn't have known." We ducked under a rocky overhang, a tiny rivulet of crystalline water flowing down its face. "The OtherFolk use the Roads to get to different places, different worlds or planes of existence, even. When the road ends suddenly like that, it means you've come to a Doorway."

"I didn't see a Doorway. The road just ended."

Brystion held up a fallen tree branch to allow me to walk under it. "It happens that way. That's why you need to be so careful. You fall off the road or take a wrong turn and there's no telling where you'll end up. As places go, I suppose this one wasn't too bad."

"Except for the daemons," I added wryly. "Although I wish I'd had shoes with me. I didn't realize I was going to be hiking through the woods." I winced as I narrowly side-stepped something blue and thorny.

"You want me to carry you?" He waggled his eyebrows at me, his expression bordering on a leer.

I snorted. "Only if you're dying to. I'm a little wobbly, but I think I can manage."

"Mmmm . . . well, honestly, I was just looking for an excuse to grope your ass anyway." He winked, scooping me up. "God knows I could use the pick-me-up."

"I'll bet." I wanted to protest, but instead my arms slid around his neck. Might as well enjoy the ride. "That's a hell of a shiner," I said, pointing to his eye.

"It'll heal faster when I can feed." His hands tightened on my hips, but it wasn't suggestive, just gently questioning. "And I *will* have to." He nuzzled my ear. "Soon. I used up the last of my power to find you. I won't be able to get back to your world without it. Of course, that's assuming I even *want* to go back," he said dryly. "Things seem to be heating up in a rather uncomfortable way."

"I almost forgot about the feeding thing," I said, realizing it was true. "Between Katy and everything else. Not that I'm backing out." I turned his head toward me so I could catch his gaze, my tone serious. "I keep my promises."

The incubus's nostrils flared. "I know," he said softly. "Let's go."

"Are we close enough?"

"Yes," he whispered, his mouth lowering. My eyes closed at the brush of his lips and the taste of his tongue as it slipped past mine. He shifted and the CrossRoads fell away into the darkness.

Fourteen

My vision rippled as the CrossRoads looped into the darkness like a silver ribbon. Something fluttered in the distance, my nightmares battering against the edges of my mind with their ravenous mouths. I closed my eyes and pressed my face into Bryston's shoulder. His throat rumbled, a questioning hum vibrating against my cheek.

Immediately, the shadows receded; relief swept through me with an almost violent twitch. I watched as a cocoon of light enveloped us, warding off the gloom. "What's that?" I pointed to the shimmering glow that webbed its way in pulsing beams around us. The magical illumination bled across his face, causing his swollen bruises to shine in stark relief against his skin.

"A shield of sorts. It will keep the nightmares at bay for a little while."

"Can you afford to do that? I thought you were running out of energy."

"Nearly," he conceded. "There's a bit left in reserve— enough to get us to your Heart, anyway."

"Small favors."

He shifted his hands, relaxing his fingers so that my

weight was comfortably supported. "I'm going to be fairly
weak when we get there, so just bear with me. Once I get my
strength back, we'll figure out the rest of it." He nuzzled my
ear gently. "And keep in mind that I'm going to be horren-
dously jealous of your time, Abby."

I flushed like a schoolgirl. Christ, all I needed was a short
skirt and pigtails and my transformation into bumbling
idiot would be complete. I peered out past the ambient
cocoon. The darkness was fading, leaving us in a cold, gray
fog.

"First things first," I said. The mist was shedding
around us, sloughing away like the fine tufts of a dandelion's
late bloom. "'Anyone lived in a pretty how town, with up
so floating many bells down,'" I quoted, glancing down to
see the house. We hovered above it for a moment, and then
the roof grew larger, expanding as we descended. "There's
more here now." I gestured at the edges of the yard. And
there was. Where before the clearing had been empty,
now the beginnings of what looked to be wild rosebushes
sprouted up between towering willow trees.

"How odd," I murmured.

"Your Heart is responding to you. Now that you've
acknowledged it, it will shape itself to your will."

"I didn't know I could do that." My gaze strayed to the
far side of the clearing. It was still cloaked in shadow but if I
stared long enough I could almost swear I saw the gossamer
silhouette of an ancient oak, its branches twining together as
though hiding a secret.

Brystion followed my line of sight and smiled. "You'll
see, Abby. You're a Dreamer. Now hold on, we're going to
land."

My grip tightened around his shoulders, but I shouldn't
have bothered. The incubus spun us gently onto the silver
grass, the shield dissipating like fireflies into the mist. He

slumped beside me as he set me on my feet with a tired grin. "Safe as houses," he quipped.

The gate still remained locked and I frowned. I hadn't had time to get back here since the other night, and I certainly hadn't had time to figure it out when I was attempting to break through to the CrossRoads. I eyed the sandy road with a shiver.

"Seems we're at a bit of an impasse," he said, mouth pursing as he ran a finger over the gate. "Still."

I shook the lock with frustration. "Well, doesn't that just suck. You picked a hell of a Dreamer to set your cap for. I'm not entirely sure why you bother, honestly."

The edges of his pupils flared golden, capturing me in their aching brilliance. "Can't you tell?" I blinked stupidly and then his lips ensnared mine. Unbidden, I wrapped my arms around his neck as his tongue lingered like liquid velvet in the dark recesses of my mouth. His hands crept down the ridge of my spine, fingers cupping my ass. I moaned, a soft sound of longing, and he pulled away with a knowing grin. "Protest all you want, Abby, but in the end, you'll be begging for me." His voice lowered as he bent to suckle at my neck. "I swear it."

"Mmmmm." I tipped my head back to allow him greater access, shuddering when he dipped to my pulse point, teasing it with a wet tickle. "And how do I know you're not just using me, seducing me for your own nefarious purposes?"

"You don't." His hips ground into mine, the hard outline of his erection rubbing against my belly. "If it makes you feel any better, I can't really seduce anyone who doesn't want to be seduced. And you"—he ran his tongue along my collarbone—"have been practically praying for it since we met."

My belly quivered, butterflies born of anticipation and arousal sending sharp waves of heat through my limbs. I gazed up at him. "You look like shit." The words tumbled out of my mouth before I could stop myself, but he only laughed.

"I imagine I've looked better," he admitted, touching his swollen eye.

"So now what?"

He shrugged. "That's up to you. I wouldn't mind getting washed up, though."

"Open Sesame," I intoned dryly at the gate, unsurprised when nothing happened. "Enough of this," I snapped at it, jerking back hard on the bars. "Open or next time I bring a blowtorch and melt your ass down." I blinked as the hinges squeaked in response, the lock turning with an audible click. "Damn. If I'd known it would be that easy, I would have tried that sooner."

"You are Mistress here," he murmured. "You just needed to find your voice." He took my arm and led me to the front door. It was a gallant gesture, but his muscles trembled with the effort. I flushed with shame at the thought of my earlier words. The incubus had already given up so much for me—how could I do any less? I stiffened my shoulder, offering him a subtle sort of support, but if he noticed, he didn't say anything.

My thumb traced over a rough spot on the rail, the splintered tips pricking my flesh. Even this was mine. I snorted softly, remembering the day I'd ridden my bicycle off the stoop, cracking my chin on the rail. The back wheel had flattened as it wedged between the railroad ties and the brickwork of the front walk, punctured by a loose nail. And I . . . I had wiped the blood off my face with the back of my hand, marched straight back into the house, and tried to convince my mother that I needed some glue to fix my bike.

What I'd gotten was a trip to the ER and six stitches, but there's twelve-year-old indignation for you.

It was dark inside, but everything burned with familiarity. I hit the light switch on the wall and watched as
the foyer flooded with golden ambiance. My eyes welled
up, and I pulled away from Bryston. Stumbling past him,
I clutched at my grandmother's circle quilt, which was
casually draped over the back of the worn leather sofa in
the living room. "It's like home," I said hoarsely, staring
down at the quilt.

Christ, it even had the stain in the corner.

I rubbed it against my cheek, closing my eyes. "It smells
like my mother." I sighed, wiping away my tears. "I haven't
seen this quilt in years. It got lost when we moved to the city
so I could go to the dance academy."

"Memories can be very powerful," he agreed, his breath
suddenly hot in my ear. I shivered, the heat from his body
rolling over me. His arms slid around my waist and he
moved his chin to rest gently on my shoulder. I let out a soft
grunt, leaning into him.

"I had visions of setting up a Dream for you when we
got to this point. Something horribly romantic." His cheek
brushed mine, setting off another wave of flutters. "Very
old school, a seductive dance of music and sex, our bodies
twisting in the dark to the thrum of the beating of our hearts.
Doves flying. Heaving bosoms."

"And listening to Tom Jones as we bump uglies in front
of the roaring fire? Sounds like someone's been reading too
many romance novels."

"I like the classics. Ah, well," he sighed, his grip tightening for a moment. "I'm afraid you're going to have to forgive
me. You just taste so damn good." He nipped at my ear,
lightly at first and then harder, his hips pressing into my ass.
I let my head tip back as his fingers worked up my neck to
the soft edge of my hair, stroking, pressing, pulling, over my
scalp and by my ear . . .

"Wait!" I jerked my head away. "Don't touch me there—please."

Realization crept into his eyes as he released me, chagrin edging his face. "It's not there, you know. Not if you don't want it to be."

My hands flew to my head, the quilt dropped and forgotten. Frantically I looked for a mirror. The bathroom had one. I raced down the hall, heedless of the remaining dark, and flipped on the bathroom light. Fingering through my hair, I peered at my reflection, searching for the bare patch.

Nothing . . .

I looked again, but the skin was clean and whole, fully covered in hair.

"The Dreaming is controlled by you," Bryston said from the doorway. He was watching me intently, focus switching between the mirror and me. "Or it can be. Particularly your Heart. You are here as you wish to be, as you truly are, or as you truly see yourself. They're not always the same."

"And what about you? Are you affected by my Dreaming?"

He averted his gaze, shifting away. "I'm beyond it, at the moment. But yes, it is possible for you to . . . influence my appearance somewhat, though I'd rather you didn't."

"Of course." His skin seemed to be paling rapidly, its amorphous fading more pronounced. Now or never, I supposed. "What do you need from me to . . . feed?"

"Your climax."

I blinked. "My what?"

Amusement lit up his face. "I think you heard me. Mind if I use the shower? I'd like to wash off the blood."

"Sure. There should be one upstairs, assuming nothing's changed." I slipped up the stairs in front of him, his eyes raking over me like burning coals. "I'll start up the water for you." Did dream houses have hot water heaters? "How is, uh, the climax thing supposed to work?"

"The usual way, I'd imagine," he retorted dryly as he followed me into the bathroom. "It's a trade-off, really. The better the orgasm, the more energy you produce, the better I eat. So it behooves me to make sure you have the best damn orgasms possible."

"Ah. And here I thought you said I didn't need to have sex with you."

An ineloquent *hmmmph* emerged from his throat. "You're dreaming," he pointed out. "Technically we won't actually be having sex. But you're right. All I need is the orgasm, however you produce it, so if you'd like to go solo . . ."

A strangled snort worked its way through my nose. I turned the hot water on, felt the pipes clank in their old way as the water came hissing out. There was a slight breeze behind me, followed by a soft whoosh. I turned my head, and swallowed.

The incubus was naked, bloodied and utterly magnificent, from the dark hair that poured like liquid silk over his shoulders to the pale musculature of his chest and abdomen. My gaze lingered over his slim waist, dropping lower toward the dark thatch of hair below his belly button. My cheeks heated considerably as he coughed, and I jerked my focus back to his face.

"Ahem. First things first." He kicked away his clothing, eyeing himself in the mirror with a frown. One hand traced the dark bruise on his cheek. "I owe him for that one," he muttered dangerously.

I could only nod dumbly at this, unable to tear myself away from the perfect sculpture of his ass. It had lived up to its promise and then some.

"Are you done?" Brystion's voice trembled with laughter lightly brushed with lust.

"No," I breathed, my heart racing beneath my rib cage.

"I'll be waiting," he said slyly, brushing past me as he glided toward the shower. The mirror had fogged up with steam, but I wouldn't have said that it was the hot water causing it. I watched him pull back the light blue curtain, my blood simmering in response. He winked at me and drew it back into place, groaning softly as the water hit his skin.

I unbuttoned my jeans slowly, some small part of me wondering if this was wise, but I was past caring. After all, it was still a dream, right?

Undoubtedly there would be repercussions, but right now, for this moment, I was going to take what was offered and not look back. The denim fell to the floor in a heap, followed quickly by my bloodstained shirt. My bra. My Hello Kitty panties. It was just me now, standing on the damp tile with nothing between us but that curtain, the water beading against it in constant taps.

Now or never, Abby.

I pushed back the curtain and stepped into the tub. I didn't look at his face. I wanted this, yes, but I'd lose my nerve if I actually admitted what I was doing. Chickenshit of me, but there it was. A crimson trickle trailed into the water at the bottom of the tub, and I remembered the ugly gouge on his arm. Instinctively, I turned toward it, but it seemed smaller than before, less angry.

"I heal fast," he softly answered my unasked question. "Come here, Abby." It was more than a request but less than a command; I followed it anyway, moving as close to him as I dared. His hand reached down beneath my chin, tipping my face up. "No regrets," he murmured. His golden eyes pinned me where I stood. "Understand?" I nodded as he bent forward, his lips brushing over mine, and then all I could taste were the rivulets of water sliding between our mouths and the sweat from his skin, tinged with coppery blood.

Brystion grunted, running his fingers down my neck to my shoulders, pressing forward in bold strokes along my arms. He briefly traced the curve of my breasts, and I shuddered as his thumbs teased my hardened nipples. His lips curved into a smile, but his tongue never stopped its gentle exploration, even when his fingers dropped lower still, lingering on my hips before sliding toward my ass.

For a moment I hovered, as his touch stripped away the last of my hesitation like the faded skin of some desperate reptile. He drew back, his fingers skimming my jaw.

No regrets.

I launched myself at him, taken aback at my own ferocity, months of inner turmoil threatening to explode upon us. I kissed him frantically, my hand reaching to the base of his neck, trying to pull him closer still. My breasts brushed his chest as my hips began to sway against him in the most ancient of erotic motions. Soft, urgent sounds escaped my throat, but were battered against his mouth, becoming a muffled cry as he turned me around so I was facing the backsplash. A hand glided over my neck, lingering, stroking, claiming.

"You know, for an incubus you seem to be rather interested in my neck. You sure you're not a vampire?"

Filtered through the steaming hiss of the water, his answering chuckle was rich and throaty. It rippled around me. He slanted his lips over my collarbone, his teeth grazing the skin. "Vampires don't have complete jurisdiction when it comes to blood," he said mildly. "Just as incubi don't hold dominion over sex. The lines between us have always been a bit blurred." The nips became harder, more insistent. He worked his way higher, suckling and licking the water droplets from the sweet spot just below my ear, nuzzling my earlobe with an unfamiliar tenderness.

I tipped my head forward, resting it on the cool porcelain. The water sluiced over me like a gentle rain, leaving my skin slick and gleaming.

"You might even call us cousins of a sort," he continued, splaying his fingers over my breastbone, playfully reaching down to tweak a peaked nipple. I gasped, an electric rush cresting down my spine. The hum of unadulterated male satisfaction rumbled from his chest.

"Cousins?" My legs were quaking now, my knees heavy and weak. He roped his arms around mine, lifting them up to press my palms flat against the tiles before grinding his erection into the hollowed cleft of my ass. I gave a small snort of surprise. When had *that* happened?

"Life versus lust—they're practically the same thing, if you think about it. Or at least they ought to be." I twisted my head toward him, torn between annoyance and arousal. A wicked grin pulled up the corners of his mouth as he watched my helpless squirming with that hungry, half-lidded gaze. "But given the choice, I think I know what I'd rather feed on."

"Indeed," I whispered hoarsely, as his tongue darted between my lips and cut off the rest of my words. What *was* that delicious thing he was doing with his hips? And why the hell were we even *still* having that conversation? "Given the choice, I think you talk too much, incubus."

"That's about to change," he murmured, his voice husky, turning me to face him. He dropped one hand, spreading me wide even as he lifted one of my legs to wrap around his hip. "I'm going to need to get you off quickly, Abby, but I'll make it up to you. Promise."

I could only moan in approval, my hand snaking down to press his fingers harder against me. He shuddered, growling in appreciation. I arched my back when he finally grabbed my hips and thrust inside. Small ripples of heat flooded my belly, the beginnings of the first swells of climax pulsing.

"Please," I begged. He kissed my neck, the blood thrumming in my ear as my world narrowed until there was nothing left but the movement of his body with mine.

"Now, Abby," he grunted, pinching a stiff nipple. I toppled over the edge with a keening cry. His hands were iron, supporting me as I rode out the waves of my pleasure.

I had no words, just animal sounds, guttural and chuffing, a rush of air filling my lungs as I tried to breathe. His body stiffened as he found his own release, his teeth biting into my shoulder with a tender fierceness. Thick billows of steam enveloped us, and I felt the slick tiles fading away beneath my shoulders. Panic tipped the edge of my voice. "What's going on?"

He arms coiled around my waist. "Oh, shit. Hold on, Abby." And then we were sinking, floating, *falling*. Naked and entwined, the darkness swallowed us up. We were hurtling toward something. It looked like my bedroom with me lying there, but the unicorn was gone. No —he was at the foot of the bed, blue eyes staring at me intently. And then there was nothing at all.

I sat up with a jerk, rubbing vainly at my eyes. I was back in my room, away from the Dreaming, blissful and sore. And naked. I glanced down and blinked. What the hell? Bryston cracked his eyes open and grinned at me. "You're beautiful when you're groaning my name, did you know?"

I flushed despite myself. "Never mind that, what the hell just happened?"

"You pulled us through the Dreaming." His lips pursed with amusement. "I've always prided myself on being good in bed, but I've never been *that* good." He propped himself up on one arm, leaning forward to kiss my naked thigh. "And your orgasm was just . . . delicious." His voice was all male now, smugness and satisfaction rolled together with a hint of vulnerability.

"You're missing the point, Brystion. How did I manage to pull you with me? I can understand waking up from the Dreaming, but why are you here? And where the hell are my clothes? Not that I'm complaining," I added hastily.

He flopped onto his back, arms folded beneath his head. His abdominal muscles flexed as he breathed. They were exquisite. I tore my gaze away.

"Does it matter?" he asked softly. "I've never seen it done before, but I know it happens sometimes. You know the fairy tales, right? When the women wake up and their dream lovers are laid out beside them? It appears as though that might be real." He reached up to play with the loose strands of my hair.

"So I've gathered," I said dryly, snuggling against him. A stray thought pushed its way to the forefront of my mind, awkward and ugly. "Ah . . . I'm not really on birth control right now, you know."

He chuckled, nipping at my ear. "I can't procreate via mortal means."

"Mmmm," I muttered. "How does that work? I thought incubi and succubi worked together to get women pregnant."

He made a noncommittal noise. "Well, I suppose that's one option, but it's a very ugly way of going about it. Besides, that would mean one of my sisters would have to steal the seed of a man, fuck *me*, and then I'd fuck you. Not very romantic," he said reprovingly. "Never mind the fact that I wouldn't fuck my sister, I sure as hell wouldn't subject my TouchStone to it." There was an edge to his voice, an undercurrent that clearly noted my entrance into dangerous waters.

"Did you get enough to . . . ah . . . eat?" I slid down beside him, enjoying the way we fit together. "Because we can do it again, if you need."

His lips twitched, a soft flare of gold starting to circle his dark pupils. "A bit of dessert wouldn't go over too badly," he murmured, his hand curving around the back of my head. "But I'll leave it entirely up to you. In theory, we haven't actually slept together, so if you'd rather not complicate things further, I'll understand."

"Easy is for pussies," I muttered, nuzzling his palm with my cheek. "And I'm *not* easy."

"Never that," he agreed softly, his arms wrapping around my waist to pull me closer. I rolled, flexing my hips until I was straddling his waist, bending over to kiss him again. "Never that, love."

I arched a brow. "Love, is it? I must have been better than I thought."

"Figure of speech." His arms slid over my back to gently pull me forward so I was comfortably splayed across him. He kissed me again, but it was more of a question this time, a soft probing. "You're tired." He tucked the loose strands of hair behind my ear. His fingers brushed the scar and I pulled away slightly, still shy. "I forget sometimes, just how fragile mortals are. And yet, you bear our burden willingly, so there must be iron beneath the silk."

"The only metal in me is stainless steel." I tapped the scar ruefully. "And I hardly think that counts."

"Whatever you say," he said, a trace of his old arrogance seeping out, "but you sell yourself short by far." He toppled me over to my side, curling his naked body around me. "It's nearly three A.M. Sleep now."

I started to protest, but my eyes were already shutting. Feeling safe for the first time in ages, I drifted off. And this time I didn't dream at all.

Fifteen

I was wrapped in his scent, curled beneath a blanket of sunlight and cinnamon. Wriggling in the sheets, I sighed and opened an eye to watch him sleep.

Or I would have—if he'd been there.

A familiar smell worked its way into the room, and I frowned. Was that bacon? I pondered this anomaly for a moment and then decided that maybe I really should get up and see what was what.

"Chaste?" A soft, flutelike voice sounded gently in my ears.

What the . . . ?

I barely managed to turn my head before a sharp pain pierced through the softer part of my backside. I shrieked, rolling away hard enough to tumble to the floor with a thud.

Bryston bolted in from the kitchen, frying pan in hand. He was still gloriously naked.

Clutching the sheet over my chest protectively, I waved my fingers at the bed, caught between panic and momentary glee that he was actually still here. "Something bit me!"

The incubus relaxed. "Ah, yes. Nice pet you have there."

I tore my eyes away from his sculpted abs, confused. "What?"

"The unicorn," he said dryly, gesturing at the bed with the frying pan. "Seems he has a thing for . . . uh . . . asses." He held in a laugh before turning around to show me the porcelain perfection of his own. "As you can see. His name is Phineas, by the way."

I looked at the reddish-purple bruise on Bryston's left cheek. "I didn't know he could talk." I glared at the unicorn, ignoring the way he leered at me from the edge of the bed. "You little shit. You've seen me naked!"

Scrambling to my feet, I craned my neck to look at my own reddening welt. "That better not scar," I warned him. He just sniffed and then leaped to the floor.

I rubbed at the spot with a grimace before turning my attention back to Bryston. So damn easy to just let my eyes linger over his body. Our eyes met for a moment and whatever else I'd been going to say flew out the window.

His gaze flared into something bold and appraising, and I realized I was still mostly naked. "See something you like?" The crooked smile that turned up the corner of one cheek made it perfectly clear that at least *he'd* found something worth staring at. Well, that and the erection that was standing at about half-mast. I sighed, almost in disbelief.

I had a naked incubus in my bedroom. With a frying pan of half-cooked bacon and a hard-on. And a unicorn bite on his ass. Christ, this was turning out to be a weird morning.

"You look ridiculous," I mumbled, feeling a strange relief flood through me. Suddenly shy, I drew the sheet up around my shoulders. "I thought maybe you'd left."

"I thought about it," he admitted, "but your dreams indicated breakfast was a better choice. Besides, my alternatives are rather limited at the moment."

"You sure know how to make a girl feel good." I clutched the sheet a little tighter.

"It's a gift."

"Modest too, I see." I sat up straighter, glancing at the floor to find my clothing, but it was bare. I'd forgotten we'd *fallen* into my bed, sans undies. I waved my hand at him imperiously. "Go on and cook me my bacon, incubus."

"Oh, I'll cook your bacon," he muttered, ducking back out to the kitchen.

"We're going to have to find you some clothes for the Hearing," I called after him. "As much as it pains me to say it."

A noncommittal grunt was the only reply, so I kicked the covers back and set about getting dressed. Practicality warred with curiosity for a moment. What *did* one wear to a Hearing? It was early in the morning, true, but who was to say Robert wouldn't just show up and drag us away? Then again, I snorted softly, my only competition would be a naked incubus. Even a sheet would be better than that. In the end I went with a long, loose peasant skirt and a muted silk tank top. It was still late August in Portsmyth, after all, and that meant humid. Never let them see you sweat and all that shit.

I was finishing up with the last buckle of my sandals when the phone rang. I jumped, my hands trembling as I answered. "Hello?"

"Abby, it's Mel. You doing okay?"

My eyes darted toward the kitchen. Bryston's head popped around the doorjamb, but I waved him off. "Um, yeah. I think so. Can you do me a favor and bring some extra clothes over?"

Silence.

"Clothes? For you?"

"No." I felt my face burning, and I scowled into the

phone. "Brystion's still here and he's . . . ah . . . kind of naked."

"I see." Her voice wavered in vague amusement. "You've got some brass ones, that's all I can say."

"It's not like that," I snapped. "After you guys left, we ended up here, and now he has no clothes, so if you wouldn't mind, be a dear and bring some stuff that you think might fit."

"No need to get snippy," she huffed. "I'll be over as soon as I can."

"Thanks." I rubbed my face as we hung up, hoping to ward off the mounting tension in my head. Something soft brushed my leg and I looked down at the unicorn. "I suppose you're hungry?"

"Yes." His voice was a soft bleat this time, but there was something rather unrepentant about the tone.

"Why didn't you tell me you could talk?"

"Didn't seem like the right time." He waggled his chin at me. "Besides, this way I could look at your ta-tas without you caring. Hubba hubba." His lips smacked. I aimed a kick at his rear flanks, but he gracefully darted away into the kitchen.

"Nice." I followed him with a sigh, captured for a moment by Brystion's wondrous naked ass standing in front of the stove. He should have looked silly, and in a small way he did, but there was something horribly sexy about it too. "I didn't think you could cook, what with the whole dream thing."

"The mind boggles." He rummaged through one of the kitchen drawers and found a couple of forks and some plates before ducking into the fridge. "Wow. This thing really has nothing but crap in it. No wonder you're so damn thin." Without waiting for a reply, he pulled out the milk, some shredded cheese, butter and . . . eggs? "You're going to eat one of my omelets," he continued.

"I am?"

"Unlike some people, I don't let my TouchStones starve."

Ouch. "Well, I'm sure Moira has her reasons," I said lamely. "At least, I hope she does." He grunted, cracking the eggs into a bowl and whipping them madly.

"That's no excuse," he muttered, flipping on another burner. It flared to life and he threw a second frying pan on top of it, adding some milk to the eggs as he waited for it to heat up.

"I can't cook at all," I said, a touch of awe creeping into my voice. "Or at least, not very much."

"Then you're going to learn." The eggs burbled into the pan with a hiss. "Spatula?"

"Ah—over there, next to the microwave." He retrieved the utensil and set about expertly rolling the eggs. Envy ate my heart. "Whoever knew an incubus could do all this?"

"One of my previous TouchStones was a chef. Her dreams were very . . . educational."

My mouth twitched. "I'll bet, but I don't really think I want to know."

"Probably not," he agreed, setting down the finished product on a plate. I couldn't help but want to bask in his pampering. After all, no one had cooked me breakfast, even a late breakfast, since . . .

Since Mother died.

It was a sobering thought, and I thrust it away. "You know your way around the kitchen, incubus, I'll grant you that."

"Brystion," he said shortly. "It's Brystion. Or Ion, if you prefer. But I'm a person, not a thing."

"Sorry." I flushed, looking down at the plate, the omelet gleaming golden. "You gonna eat anything?"

He shook his head. "Your dreams were enough."

"My dreams?"

"I drank them, remember?"

I flushed. "Is that what you meant? I thought that was just a . . . a euphemism." I frowned, the beginnings of some decidedly unpleasant thoughts niggling their way to the front of my brain.

"Not entirely." He shifted the frying pan uncomfortably in his hand. "But it's what I am, Abby," he chided. I turned away from him, unable to bear the quiet patience of his voice or the infinite sadness he tried to mask. He set the pan down on the stove, fishing the bacon out of the grease and slapping it onto a plate before moving toward me. "No regrets, remember?"

"I know," I said numbly. "You're just so casual about it, I guess. It's a little unnerving."

His fingers traced the line of my jaw. "You were magnificent," he whispered. "Even were you not my TouchStone, I would seek you out again."

"Well, it's not like you have much of a choice now, is it?" My chuckle was brittle and hollow. "Besides, things are never that simple."

"They could be, if you let them, or we could be so much more." His fingers stroked upward gently. "There *is* something we should discuss. I should have mentioned it before, but I didn't realize how things would go between us."

"Do tell," I drawled. "But Ion, I'm not sure I can handle much more right now. Shit is flying at me left and right. Can you at least wait until I'm done eating?" I pulled away from his touch, ignoring the aching quiver in my skin, and turned on the kettle. "I need some normalcy right now."

"All right." He turned away without another word. There was a slamming sound, metal scraping over the burner, and I winced. I found a mug, tossed a couple of tea bags into it, and ignored the voice in the back of my head that said I was an ass. After all, there was a naked man in my kitchen! With bacon!

A naked man who was only cooking me breakfast because he saw that I liked it in my dreams, I reminded the voice. Which he only saw because he slept with me—

The voice shut up. Almost.

You let him, stupid. He never claimed he was there for anything else.

This time, I was the one who went silent. There was a rap at the front door, and I found myself glad for it, glad for anything to distract me from the broodiness that now filled my kitchen.

I peered through the keyhole, sighing with relief to see Melanie out front, a canvas duffel bag slung over one shoulder. "Thanks for coming." I undid the latch.

She raised a brow at me, pressing the bag into my hands. "Are you sure I'm the one you should be thanking? Sounds like you had quite the evening."

I scowled at her. "I've already got enough innuendo in the apartment as it is, so do me a favor and shut up."

Melanie smirked, craning her head past me. "I didn't know what would fit, so I brought a bunch of stuff. You decent in there, Ion?"

"That depends on who's asking." The incubus lingered at the opening of the kitchen, leaning on one arm against the doorframe, the other hand casually holding a dishrag over his important bits. Our gazes met but his eyes remained dark, as if daring me to have a reaction. My upper lip curled. I threw the bag of clothes at him, not bothering to watch to see if he dropped the towel to catch it. The hitch of Melanie's breath was more than enough to tell me anyway. A jolt of possessiveness flared tightly in my chest, but I schooled my face as best I could. Damn the man, anyway. The floor by the kitchen creaked, and I shot a glance over my shoulder to see Brystion's retreating backside as he ducked into my bedroom.

Melanie's lips pursed. "I think my assumptions may have been a bit off."

"Tell me about it." I sank into the battered cushions of my faded green sofa. "The last few days have just been a nightmare. Literally, in some cases," I snorted, sobering for a moment. "I need to get out of here, Mel."

"Well, you're welcome to come crash at my place for a few days if you think it would help. There's always a few OtherFolk coming and going, though, so I don't know how comfortable it would be for you."

I rubbed my temples with the base of my hands, the tight strains of an oncoming headache starting their telltale throb across the top of my skull. "No, I mean out of this whole damn town, this situation. I'm in way over my head."

"Don't you think you're overreacting a tad? You have a knack for it." Brystion's voice drawled softly behind me.

My head snapped toward the incubus, barely registering the way the jeans clung to his hips or the delectable press of the dark T-shirt against his chest. "Not really. I'm scared shitless, if you want to know the truth." My eyes narrowed. "What, you couldn't taste that last night? Or maybe you like drinking fear?"

He jerked as if he'd been struck, his gaze hardening as it rested on us. Rested on *me*. "As you will, Abby." He strode past us and out the door, bare feet slapping on the wooden steps. I ached to watch him go. I ached to call him back. To apologize for the flash of hurt that had blazed in those haunted ebony eyes. But I was a chickenshit coward, after all. I pressed my hand to my forehead with a groan.

"Abby?"

Melanie. Fuck. I'd forgotten she was even there. I gave her a shaky laugh. "It's been a hell of a couple of days, Mel."

Her hand patted my shoulder. "You want me to get you something to drink?"

"My tea." I stood up. "I left it in the kitchen. I'll get it." Her cell phone rang and she waved me off, struggling to dig it out of her purse.

I left her there on the couch, listening as she answered it, her usually chipper voice somewhat dimmed. The unicorn was nose-deep in a bowl still, his tail flicking back and forth contentedly. The kettle was whistling now and I poured it into the mug. I tipped a bit of milk into it and stirred. My movements were numb. I blinked as I went to throw the spoon in the dishwasher.

A tray sat next to the sink, containing another perfectly formed omelet and several pieces of bacon organized in a smiley face. There was toast and juice and what looked like a mimosa in an elegant champagne flute. Where the hell had he found champagne? I glanced at the refrigerator in bemusement.

He'd made me breakfast. And not just *any* breakfast. This was the kind of breakfast you fed a lover the morning after sex, the kind of breakfast that promised to turn into another sort of meal altogether. I eyed a bowl of grapes, my lips twitching.

"Nice work," the unicorn grumbled at me from my knees. "He's a way better cook than you are, you know."

"I've figured that out, thanks," I retorted. "And I don't recall asking your opinion."

"Never stopped me before." His blue eyes sobered. "Take me with you."

Visions of trying to hide a tiny, ass-biting unicorn in the grocery store or RadioShack filled my head. "Take you where?"

"To the Hearing, stupid head. I might actually come in useful."

"Somehow I doubt that," I murmured under my breath.

"I heard that. But you're my TouchStone. I'd rather not see anything happen to you, honestly."

"I can't imagine why. After all, it's not like I'm a virgin or anything."

"Exactly," the unicorn said sagely. "It's refreshing. First time I've been able to be myself in ages. None of this 'pure and chaste' bullshit."

I opened my mouth to say something rude, but Melanie's sudden appearance in the kitchen stopped me cold. Her lower lip trembled and my heart dropped to the floor. "What is it?"

Her eyes darted between me and the unicorn for a moment before focusing on me. "I'm sorry to interrupt, your . . . uh . . . conversation."

My gut twisted, cold lancing through me like a knife. My fear and anger were so strong I could taste it. "What is it?"

"It's Charlie. She's missing. They think she was murdered."

Sixteen

Abby?"

I looked up from where my hands rested on my knees long enough to see Melanie approaching before I glanced away. I'd been in the tiny room for hours, but what the hell we were waiting for I couldn't have guessed. As holding cells go it was nice enough, but polished wood and brass fittings aside, I would have given anything not to be there at all.

After the news of Charlie's disappearance, we'd taken a few moments to catch our bearings and then Robert was at the door, demanding Brystion and I present ourselves at the Judgment Hall immediately. Which, of course, didn't work out quite as planned. Shortly thereafter I found myself strong-armed through the streets by an extraordinarily pissed off archangel with Melanie trailing behind. My initial inquiries about Charlie were met with silence, but a not-so-subtle pressure upon my wrist made no bones about his grief.

I'd barely had a chance to *try* to sort things out before we'd arrived, at which point I'd been tossed into the holding room without so much as a bathroom break. Apparently part of the Hearing involved character witnesses, and not the kind I was allowed to be present for. Four hours of stewing in my own juices had left me with a raging headache and a sick sort of anger. Not to mention my earlier spat with Brystion. Had he actually left me to face the Hearing alone? Or was he out there now, spilling my secrets to the Faery liaison?

I snarled at myself for being such an idiot.

"What do you want?" I scowled at the door as it shut behind Melanie.

"Aren't you just a bottle of sunshine?" she retorted, rubbing at her temples. "It's almost time. I just wanted to see if you needed anything. Brystion hasn't shown up yet, but they're going to question you without him. Katy already told them about the daemons, and Robert presented your suspicions about the paintings." She paused, shifting restlessly, as she eyed the door. "So, *do* you need anything?"

I waved her off with a sigh. Tensions were high all around. "A pee break would be nice. I get they need to keep me separate from the others, but the prisoner treatment is getting a bit old."

"That's Robert's doing. I think he forgets we're just humans." She rolled her eyes. "But I wouldn't be too hard on him. He's pretty torn up. Here." She thrust her purse at me. "I thought you might want to freshen up before they call you in."

"It's not a fashion show, Mel. They can take me or leave me."

Her eyes narrowed and she shoved it back into my lap. "Take it, Abby. I *insist*."

I clutched the purse on my lap, bewildered. "It's not even my purse, Mel. Why the hell would I want—"

"Take the purse, doll." The unicorn's muffled voice sounded from the bag. Startled, I nearly threw it across the room. Opening the leather hobo, I snorted as Phineas poked his head out. "'Bout time you figured it out," he muttered. "She's only been trying to get me in here for the last two hours."

"At least you've had your freedom," I said. "And the use of a bathroom."

He shuddered, craning his head behind him. "You try having a stick of lip balm half up your ass for forty-five minutes and then we can compare notes."

"Sounds like a personal problem." I glanced up at Mel, but she was already disappearing through the doorway. I saw her shake her head at someone outside, but within moments she was gone, leaving us alone.

"It took a lot of guts for her to get me in here," Phineas muttered. "Don't fuck it up."

"I wasn't planning on it. Not that I know what's expected of me."

"It's like she said." The unicorn snorted, impatient with my ignorance. "You're going to be interrogated. You can't really blame them for that. The Faery Queen's daughter is missing and *you* were likely the last person to see her. Just answer their questions and be honest. Unless, of course, you really did do something to her," he amended hastily. "In which case, lie your fucking ass off."

I shot him a look that would have melted an iceberg. "Remind me never to hire you as my defense."

The doorknob turned with a slight screech, and I shoved Phineas back into the purse. He whickered in protest and then went quiet. I had no idea how having him here would be to my advantage, but I wasn't about to turn down an ally.

The door swung open, revealing a sullen Celestial. He was a strapping sort of brute, with a spiked tangle of russet hair and a five o'clock shadow maybe three hours too late. I didn't stand up. I'd had enough of being polite, and I'd be damned if I'd snap to just because of their say-so. Unperturbed, he motioned at me to follow him, ignoring the sour smirk I gave him. Slinging the purse over my shoulder, I shuffled to my feet. I didn't recognize him, but that didn't mean anything. Any OtherFolk denizen could come and go as they pleased in the Judgment Hall, assuming they had reason to be there.

I glanced up at the dark, stained-glass windows as I trudged behind the winged angel, pretending not to notice the dread rooting down my spine, prickling over my skin like a death sentence. The Judgment Hall was impressively understated in stone and wood with a hint of the same bits of magic that filled the Marketplace, mostly in the form of witchlight sconces. An ancient air haunted the place, lurking in the shadowed corners like it had found its roots within the crumbled remains of some secret, pagan sanctuary.

I'd only been here once before, but that had been with Moira and under far different circumstances. I'd perched in a small seat beside her on the dais at the front of the room, like some kind of exotic pet. It had been awkward at first, but after a few curious glances I'd been mostly ignored as Moira went about listening to complaints. An execution had been scheduled that day, but thankfully it had been postponed. I had no desire to be *any* part of that. Not that the bloodstained and battered stone block to the left of the dais left any less of a sinister impression.

The angel stopped at the sculpted doorway that led into the main hall, gesturing me inside with a polite flourish. There were two main sets of seats, large and bulky, almost like ancient marble church pews. They were currently filled, one row after the other. OtherFolk. Mortals. Things I barely recognized as being sentient. I swallowed as they turned to face me.

"Go up to the front," the angel commanded softly, his hand hovering by my elbow.

"I know where it is." I shouldered away from him before he could touch me. The last thing I needed was for that instant TouchStone thing to start working its mojo. Head held high, I strutted down the aisle, feeling like some kind of retro-virgin-sacrifice-slash-bride.

A crescent-shaped table stood at the front of the room, flanked by thirteen empty seats in quiet array, each normally filled by a Council member. The seats were supposed to be a matched set of the three paths—the right-most side of the table was for the Light Path, the left for the Dark Path, the middle for the Fae. The center is where Moira sat, but then, that was the reason we were all here, wasn't it?

The Petitioner's Throne that the angel had directed me to was by itself, centered before the crescent. Made of gilded marble and solid stone, it reminded me of a medieval version of an electric chair. Certainly not one meant for comfort, anyway.

Murmurs rippled through the chamber as I made my way to the dais. I tried to keep my eyes straight ahead, but I couldn't help the nervous slide of my vision, vibrating with the recognition of so many people. Brandon. Melanie. The Gypsy. The PETA pixie. The hag. Alisair. I blinked. Even Katy. Our gazes met and she gaped at me, her blue eyes wide and terrified.

"Be careful what you wish for," I muttered, but there wasn't much sympathy in my voice.

I spotted Robert at the corner of the crescent and swallowed my anger. "Charlie was my friend too," I said to him as I approached. The electric blue of his eyes damn near lashed out with tiny lightning bolts, but he deliberately turned his back, wings shifting with a feathered shuffle.

"Whatever." I hugged the purse to my chest and slumped into the seat.

"Ahem." I turned about until I spotted an elderly Fae striding toward me, purpose driving each precise, clicking step. A severe bun balanced perfectly upon her head, with nary a stray bang out of place. Shot with silver, the delicate shade of gold gleamed beneath the witchlights like the burnished edges of my grandmother's old Christmas ornaments. It was unusual to see one of the Fae showing her age. In fact, I couldn't recall a time when I'd ever caught one with more than a few wrinkles here or there—most of the time they wore a Glamour. Either she had dropped hers, or this woman was *really* old.

"Abby Sinclair?" Her voice was sonorous, lilting with the delicate accent that the more noble Fae often possessed.

"Yes," I nodded, easing back into the chair in an attempt to seem relaxed. I probably failed miserably, but she was kind enough not to show it.

"Roweena DuMont." She inclined her head gracefully, hand extended. Her fingers wrapped coolly around mine, as though the blood were sluggish in her veins. "I'm the Fae liaison for this case. It is of utmost importance that you answer all questions as truthfully as you can." I almost laughed aloud. I'd never yet met a Faery that could give anyone a straight answer, and yet somehow I was expected to tell them everything I knew?.

"Yeah, okay. What do you want to know?" I could be a good girl if I needed to be. I even did my best to keep the sarcastic twang from my voice.

Her face hardened into smooth marble. "Do you understand the seriousness of your situation, mortal?"

I shrugged, ignoring the grunt of warning from my lap. "I understand that one of my best friends is missing. I understand that Moira is missing. I understand that the succubi are disappearing. And," I said softly, "I seem to be the common factor."

"Moira is the Queen of Elfland's daughter," Roweena said, her lips pressed together tightly. "The gravity of that cannot be overlooked, regretful as your friend's situation may be. Moira is the reason I am here."

Robert tensed, his wings flaring in and out, feathers trembling. I knew he was hurting, and the better part of me wanted to go to him, but I quashed it. Displaying emotion would be seen as a weakness in this place.

"I know about Moira," I said, "but this has to come as a package deal. *You* may be willing to overlook the rest of it, but I can't. And I'm not going to. You want my help finding Moira, you're going to need to compromise."

Roweena's eyes narrowed shrewdly. The Fae couldn't resist a bargain and we both knew it. "What are they to you, these Dark Path succubi? The angel's TouchStone I understand—such mortal bonds are rich in emotion." Her hand waved at me carelessly. "But to care for those of the Dark Path? That seems a bit extreme, doesn't it?"

"I gave my word to a friend," I said stubbornly, ignoring Robert's disbelieving snort. "And even if that wasn't enough, I feel it's my duty to try to help."

"Your duty?"

"Moira's not here," I pointed out. "Brystion came to her for help. I think it's what she would want me to do in her stead."

"Ah, yes," she said. "The incubus. Where *is* he? I would have thought he might be here, given the situation."

"I don't know." I bit the inside of my cheek, not wanting to admit just why that was.

"So he just wandered off after taking you . . . home?" Robert sneered at me, the innuendo hanging there like a bad joke.

It was none of their business and easy enough to sidestep. I gestured toward Melanie. "Ask her. She saw him at my apartment when she stopped by this morning."

Robert's mouth pressed together sharply as Melanie nodded. Her word would be hard to gainsay, especially given she had also been present during Katy's rescue, not to mention she was notorious for never taking sides.

"My guard did not see anyone enter your premises last night," Robert pointed out. "No Doors created or closed."

"He didn't come through the CrossRoads," I said. Flushing at the memory of the night before, I allowed my gaze to drift to Roweena. Time to put up or shut up. "He came through me—I did it."

The elven woman whipped toward me, her lips twitching like a hungry rabbit. "You did? How?"

"I pulled him through the Dreaming."

"Preposterous," Robert scoffed. His hand caressed the hilt of his sword, his face reddening.

"I'm his TouchStone," I pointed out, ignoring the sudden intake of breath around the room. "But I don't have a Contract to prove it. I've been told that changes things a bit."

Roweena looked at the angel sharply. "I believe you neglected to mention that in the report, yes?" She retreated to the stone table to scratch out a note on a piece of parchment. "Just how many OtherFolk are you TouchStoned to in that manner? Without a Contract, that is." There was a curious bent to her expression as she said it, a feral gleam in her smile as she leaned forward.

"Just two after Moira. That I know of," I amended hastily. No need to accidentally get caught up in a lie. "I think." I winced, sheepish. "How can I tell?"

Roweena's gaze narrowed into that of a hawk. "You can't. Therein lies the problem with KeyStones."

"KeyStones?" The word was unfamiliar to me, and yet there was a pull to the syllables, a reverberation through my bones that had a terrible ring of truth.

"They're very rare." Her voice had dropped as she watched me and I fought the urge to squirm like a little kid who'd been caught doing something she shouldn't. "Most of the time KeyStones are places—sacred groves, ancient monuments, that sort of thing. They are little pockets of time and space in the mortal world where OtherFolk might dwell without the need for a TouchStone. It's not uncommon for us to build on top of or around such a place." She cocked a brow at me. "The Hallows, for example, or even the Marketplace. And *sometimes*, KeyStones are people."

I mulled over this new bit of information for a moment. It explained the unicorn and the incubus, so that was helpful. The idea of having a string of OtherFolk dependant on me for their movements between the worlds was not. "And that means what for me?"

"It means you're going to have to be very careful. There's a very good chance you'll burn out if you're too free with your charms, so to speak." The quill scratched against the parchment again. "I wonder if Moira knew what you were. Who else are you TouchStoned to?"

A soft thud landed at my feet before I could answer. Bloodstained sheets. The crimson splatters still looked damp. I stepped back instinctively, not wanting to touch them. "Charlie?" I croaked out, the sight choking the words from my mouth.

Robert moved toward me like a freight train made of feathers. "These are her sheets. *Our* sheets. She was taken from our bed while she slept." He loomed over me, the heat from his skin searing me. "I need to find her, Abby."

"As you were," Roweena snapped at the raging Celestial. "This is immaterial."

"It is *not!*" He jabbed a finger at me. "And we are wasting time."

Part of me wanted to point out that he hadn't seemed nearly as concerned when Katy was taken the day before, but that would have been unfair. Or at least dreadfully unwise, given his current state. I could be as snarky as anyone, but I had no desire to lose my head either.

"Is it any coincidence that Moira went missing at about the same time the succubi began disappearing? And then that damn incubus shows up, simple as you please, to seduce her into doing his bidding." He leaned in close to me, his eyes maddened with grief. "I know you have something to do with it, Abby. You and that Dreameater you're fucking."

"I am *not* fucking him!" My voice echoed through the chamber, reverberating off the wall and sizzling with anger. Technically it was the truth. Dream sex, maybe, but I wasn't going to apologize for what happened in my dreams. "And there was nothing simple about the way he showed up," I argued. "It sure as hell hasn't been a walk in the park. I'd rather it had never happened at all, if you must know."

"Wish I'd known that sooner," Bryston's low voice rumbled behind me. "And saved myself the trouble of rescuing your ass last night."

I started, dropping the purse to the floor. Phineas squealed and tumbled from the leather hobo with a baleful snort. Robert took a step toward the incubus, hatred stamped across his face.

"Stand down," Roweena commanded, "or I'll have you removed from this proceeding." Robert glowered, and I had to turn away from the haunted ache reflected there. It was love that motivated him, and I could not fault him for that. The Fae stared down at me, one brow raised at the unicorn. "Something we should know?"

"Nice one." The unicorn glared up at me before bowing slightly to Roweena. "Phineas," he announced, "Abby's personal adviser. And she is also my TouchStone."

"Indeed." She eyed me thoughtfully, a finger pressed to her lip. "This is more complicated than I thought," she said, rubbing at her temples with a weary hand.

"Join the club," I retorted. I shifted in my seat and exchanged a glance with Bryston. "So, do I TouchStone everyone I touch?" I tried to chuckle, but it stuck in my throat. "I mean, wouldn't that make it hard to . . . I don't know. Live?"

"It's possible, but the actual act of becoming a Touch-Stone isn't driven by mortals. You are merely the conduit. The OtherFolk must actually engage the process."

"That would mean they would have to know what I was."

"Yes, but you still have to allow it." Her lips compressed in disapproval. Clearly daring to TouchStone anyone other than the Protectorate had been a major no-no. But I had known that, hadn't I?

I gestured at the unicorn. "Phineas was unintentional on my part." My eyes flicked back toward Bryston. "As was he."

"And they were transcribed upon physical contact?"

"Yes. I was trying to capture Phineas when that one happened."

"You were trying to *capture* a unicorn? I find it rather difficult to believe that a TouchStone of Moira's would ever stoop to such a thing."

"In truth, my Lady, it was more of a rescue," Phineas interjected smoothly. "And of course, the TouchStoning was completely driven by me."

She raised a brow at this. "You purposely TouchStoned a nonvirgin?"

"It was more a means of escape at the time. Better that than being daemon hors d'oeuvres."

"Practical little thing." Roweena's mouth twitched. "And the incubus? What cause would you have had to touch him?" Her eyes lit on Brystion with a dark glitter. "Or maybe I should ask, what cause would the incubus have had to touch you?"

Brystion's shoulders slumped. "I needed to—"

"Seizures." I stood up suddenly. "I have seizures. He came into the store to find Moira, and while we were talking, I had one." My gaze drifted toward him, watched him school the flash of surprise on his face. "Brystion was able to catch me before I hit the floor."

"Yes," he said wanly. "Under the circumstances, I thought it might be a bit awkward to have the Protectorate's TouchStone spill her brains out all over the counter. Bad form, you know."

"Wouldn't be the first time," I muttered, fighting the urge to touch my scar.

Roweena stared at the three of us for several moments. "This is the most ridiculous thing I've ever heard," she finally exploded. "Which means you're either all very good liars, or you're all telling the truth."

The unicorn coughed. "Well, technically, I can't lie, so that would mean—"

"I *know* that," she snapped, her arms crossing in frustration. "I'm sorry, Robert, but your charges of coup are unfounded. There is nothing I can do. While you may find the situation repugnant, that is not really your concern. " She gestured at us carelessly. "None of the parties involved appear to have any reservations from what I can see or a need to break the Contracts." Her eagle eyes zoomed in on us. "Or lack thereof, as the case may be. Do they?"

"No." My legs trembled with sudden relief. "I've got it under control."

"But what about Charlie?" Robert pushed past us as though we hadn't said a thing.

"Use your head, angel. If Charlie were dead, would you be able to travel the CrossRoads as you have been?" Phineas stomped a hoof, fixing Robert with a withering stare. "My TouchStone may or may not be guilty of many things, but accessory to murder isn't one of them."

"Shut up." I nudged the unicorn with my knee, ignoring his indignant squeal, and looked at Robert. "I already told you everything I knew about Moira the other night. I mean, the Midnight Marketplace continued to open, so I just figured she'd be back later. That means she's still alive, doesn't it?"

"There's different levels of alive," the angel said sourly. "And most of them aren't very good."

Roweena winced at his words but shook herself. "We cannot allow ourselves to think in that fashion. If the Royal Court even remotely suspects she is . . . dead . . ." She shuddered. "Well, it certainly doesn't bear thinking about."

"We've got bigger problems," Brystion interjected brusquely, shifting in front of me. I absently noticed he'd found shoes somewhere as he tossed something onto the table. "This is the badge the daemons were wearing last night. I went back to the attack site this morning and found it on the body of the one I killed."

Roweena's nose flared. "Disgusting things." Gingerly, she turned it over, her face suddenly paling as she looked at Robert. "Is this right?"

The angel exhaled sharply, tracing the mark branded into the leather.

"What is it?" I glanced between them. "What does it say?"

"Many of these sorts of mercenaries wear the mark of the one who purchased their services," Robert said, the words appearing to choke him. "Daemon battles are often too fluid and fast to change sides. It makes them easier to identify between the fighting. Not that they seem to care much who they kill."

I asked the question even though I was pretty sure I wouldn't like the answer. "And whose mark does that one bear?"

He let the circle fall to the table, his icy gaze capturing mine. "One Maurice Delacroix. Former lover and ex-TouchStone of the Protectorate."

Seventeen

Maurice?" My voice sounded thin against the sudden explosion of murmurs in the room. I thought back to that little photo from Moira's office, the way Maurice's hand was entwined with hers. "But that makes no sense. I mean, you all said he disappeared, but . . ." I slumped back in the chair. "I guess if he sees me as a threat, then okay, but why attack Charlie?"

"And more importantly, why is he actually still alive?" Roweena snapped. "He should have aged to death months ago."

Bryston frowned, sharing a glance with me. "Aged to death how? Abby and I found a picture of him from over a hundred years ago."

"It's the Contract," I said dully. "All that agelessness bullshit, all those little perks? They all go down the shitter if I leave Portsmyth. I'll age a year for every minute I'm out there. Maurice had the same deal, I'm guessing."

"Yes," Roweena said softly. "And he tried to leave. It wasn't pretty."

My bullshit detector went off in about a thousand different directions at *that* particular statement, but I didn't want to call her on it. Not that I thought she was lying exactly, but the Fae had a way of twisting words into a type of truth. But there was no way there wasn't more to this story than she was saying.

"And you say you took this off one of the daemons?" Roweena turned toward Bryston. He nodded.

"Hzule," I said. "I recognized him from the Marketplace the other night."

"Then they've been targeting you longer than we thought," Bryston said sharply, his jaw tightening.

Roweena fixed me with suddenly defensive eyes. "We're going to need to make sure you're guarded at all times."

"I will see to it," the incubus interrupted, with an even deeper chill to his voice. "Unlike some, I guard my Touch-Stones with my life."

"I'll kill you for that." Robert launched himself toward us, his wings snapping open like a crack of thunder.

"Bring it," Bryston sneered back, already moving into a protective stance.

I looked askance at Roweena, pressing myself back against the chair as the angel steamrolled past. Phineas gave a sharp whinny and ducked behind the seat. "Aren't you going to stop this?" I shouted at her, wincing at the sound of Robert's fist against the incubus's chin.

Roweena returned her attention to her parchment, her expression bored.

"Fine," I muttered, realization shooting through me. She was waiting to see what we'd do. What *I'd* do. Another goddamned test. But what was I going to do? The other night, the two of them had responded to my anger and stopped, but that was before they'd come to blows. And now, Bryston straddled Robert, his dark eyes whirling with gold-tinted fury.

I was at my own CrossRoads, I thought grimly. Fae.

Incubus. Angel. Which Path would I choose? My eyes met the amused gaze of Roweena. Clearly she expected me to ask for help.

Not this time, honey.

My earlier words to Katy swept through my mind and I stood up, my hand resting on the cool marble. "I choose the Fourth Path. Humanity."

Roweena's mouth gaped slightly, but I shoved past her, wedging myself between the two men. I didn't have a bucket of water to toss on them, but I remembered my grandmother twisting my ear when I was a child and how goddamned much it hurt. I grabbed an ear from both and pulled, hard. "Both of you, knock it the fuck off."

An elbow cocked me upside the head. Pain lanced through my skull, and I swore, arms windmilling to catch my balance. The floor shot up to meet me despite my skilled flailing, and I rolled to catch the brunt of the impact on my shoulder. My breath pushed out in a gasp, and the telltale aura edged around my vision.

Robert and Brystion both squatted over me, their lips moving. But there was only the ringing in my head and my own voice screaming silently at them. My body stiffened and I plunged into darkness.

Silence. Darkness. Shadowed wings like midnight moths brushing against my face. Where was I? I tried to open my eyes, but I had no eyes to open, no mouth to speak through, no ears to hear with. Flat and empty, my skin stretched over the hollowed canvas. Inside, I was screaming, my mouth eternally open, eternally silent, each shallow breath like sucking in gasoline and linseed oil through cotton mesh, hot and unbearable.

"Tell him . . ." A face . . . my face? Vacant doll's eyes, burning in agony like crisping paper in a fireplace. "Tell him," it whispered, the bond snapping into place between us.

* * *

"Is she awake?" The voice was quietly grim. I heard soft footsteps. A door closing.

"Imma wak." My mouth felt like it was full of sand. A sweeping whisper pressed past my lips, echoing in an eerie nasal whistle. Something cool tickled over my tongue and it took me a moment to recognize it as a plastic straw, dripping ice water into the abused reaches of my throat.

"Sip it slowly, Abby."

I coughed, wincing at the burning scrape of air in my lungs. I swallowed, the chilled liquid leaking steadily until I'd had enough. I swatted at the straw, but my hands were swollen and clumsy. What the hell?

I sat up. Correction. I *tried* to sit up. The resulting head spin promptly caused me to roll over on my side and dry-heave, sternum aching with each violent contraction. A dull pain throbbed on the side of my head. I reached up, tried to feel the scar. "What's on my hands? Why can't I see?"

"We had to put gloves on your hands to keep you from scratching yourself." Bryston's words were low and soothing in my ear. He caressed my temple gently and I sighed, the warmth of his skin a welcome balm to the pain. "And as to why you can't see . . ." The incubus chuckled. "Well, it would probably help if you opened your eyes."

My eyes? "I'm such a dumbass," I complained, cracking one open at him. I squinted, preparing myself for harsh light, but I was only met with shadows.

"But a cute dumbass." His lips twitched and I frowned. They were upside down. Or I was upside down, really. I was lying on my back on the floor, my head cradled in his lap. "What happened?" My eyes darted to the sides but nothing was there. "Where are the others?"

"We're still at the Judgment Hall. You had a seizure." His face darkened with thinly suppressed anger. "Silly, stupid girl. Whatever possessed you to step between a fighting angel and an incubus?"

"I needed to stop you," I sighed, closing my eyes again. "Roweena wasn't going to do it, that's for sure."

"No. Do you want to sit up?"

I thought about it. I thought about it some more. "Not really."

"Fair enough," he said. "Do you remember anything from during your seizure? Anything at all?" His voice remained calm but had an undercurrent of tension.

"I'm not sure. Most of the time when I have a seizure it's like I can see what's going on around me, but I'm powerless to stop it, or to do anything. Like I'm watching it all happen from a distance. It makes me disconnected, I guess, but this time . . ." I shifted, my hip grinding into the floor. "I was trapped. I couldn't move, couldn't breathe. I don't really know how to explain it." I gazed up at him, taking in the stiff edge of his jaw. "That wasn't just a random question, was it?"

He shook his head grimly as he pressed something into my hand. "Look," he said. There was something terrifying in his face the way he said it.

I struggled to sit, and his arms came beneath me to raise me up. I glanced down at my wrapped fingers, unable to feel what he'd placed in them. "Feathers?" Large and scarlet, the pinions looking like spilled blood over the black leather of the gloves. "Where did they come from?"

His eyes bored into mine, unblinking. "You tell me. You brought them from the Dreaming during your seizure."

Something clicked in the back of my mind. "They look like—"

"Sonja's." He glanced away from me, but I saw the ache in his eyes. "I'm sure of it. Please, Abby, I *must* know. Did you see her? Did she say anything to you?"

I twisted the feathers between my fingers, brushing their

delicate softness across my unfeeling palm. "I don't know what I saw," I said finally. "Everything was frozen in place. I couldn't move, no matter how much I struggled . . . wait." I shivered. A dark voice, whispering into the shadows . . . *Tell him* . . . "Yes, she did. She just said, 'Tell him.'" I swallowed hard as I looked at the feathers again. "Jesus, Ion. I think I TouchStoned her."

He froze. "How is that possible?"

"You're asking *me*? I mean, what other explanation could there be for the feathers?"

"Did she say anything else? Anything at all?" His hands tightened on mine.

I shrugged helplessly. "Not that I remember. I'm sorry."

Disappointment flickered in the depths of his eyes, but he contained it quickly. "It's not your fault. It's mine, really—all of it."

"What are you talking about? What's your fault?"

He waved me off. "Never mind. At least I've still got hope she's alive. Do you think you're feeling okay now? We really need to discuss this with Roweena and Robert."

"You two worked out your lover's quarrel?"

He flushed slightly. "Something like that," he muttered. "Let's just say we're going to try to behave a bit better."

"Do tell," I drawled. "What changed your mind?"

"Watching you hit the floor when his elbow clocked your stubborn excuse for a head. Nothing like seeing your only connection with the missing Protectorate spill her brains out to make you realize how much of a fucktard you're becoming."

"Is that all?" I snorted. "Robert's going soft."

"It's not all," the incubus said softly, his hands sliding tighter against my waist. His lips brushed over my forehead. "Abby, you were completely out of control. And that scream . . ."

"I don't usually scream when I seize." I frowned. "How long was I out for?"

"Two hours, after you stopped moving. The feathers showed up toward the end of your seizure. One moment you were pounding the floor with your fists and the next you started scratching at your face, only the feathers were sticking out between your fingers."

"Crap." I glanced down at my watch. "It's five-thirty already. I'd forgotten how long they left me in that little room back there."

"I'm sorry for that too. I shouldn't have left you."

"But you discovered the mercenary mark," I pointed out. "That has to count for something."

He shook his head. "No. Roweena was right. We cannot leave you alone now. As long as you're alive, Moira still has a connection to Portsmyth and the CrossRoads. We lose that and the Fae are going to swarm all over this place like hornets on a caffeine buzz."

"Now there's an image I could live without. What's Roweena going to tell them?"

"She's going to try to give you a few days to recover, but she's got no choice other than the truth at this point."

"What are they going to do with me?" I rolled over onto my side, adjusting my head to rest more comfortably on his knees. "I doubt they're just going to let me break her Contract."

"Not a bloody chance in hell, Abby." His gaze drifted toward the closed door. "I don't know what to do. Are you sure you can't leave town? Some loophole, maybe?"

I shook my head wearily. "No. It's an ironclad deal, and I signed it. Eyes wide shut and everything. Besides, whatever else I am, oathbreaker isn't it."

"No, you're not. Cranky, maybe." He grinned slightly. "But I'd say that's understandable under the circumstances."

"Yeah, well, I'd rather not be in these circumstances, no offense." I sipped at the water. "I've got this envelope back in my apartment with all the information regarding my mother's estate. I'm supposed to go back home and meet with the attorney to finalize things, but I can't. How the hell am I supposed to tell him that I'm bound by a magical geas set by a damned faery?" I let my voice go nasal, pinching the bridge of my nose. "I'm sorry, Mr. Jefferies, I'd love to come by the office and finish that paperwork today, but I'll be dead by the time I get there. Or at least horribly old." A sigh escaped me. "It doesn't really matter, though, does it? This is just the way it has to be. I was stupid and scared and desperate and I signed."

"And you'll be free at the end of the Contract?"

"That's the theory. But honestly, I did some reading up on this Faery Contract stuff, and I don't think I'm going to like the end of the road." I shuddered, thinking of the Devil's tithe. "I know Moira's old school, but I hope like hell she's not *that* old school. I'd rather avoid being a human sacrifice, you know?"

"One step at a time," he said, his voice becoming thoughtful. He reached out so that his fingers rubbed the back of my neck. "Let's just get the others back, and then we can check the specifics of your Contract."

"I know what the specifics are. And I'm not interested in breaking it." My lips turned up in a sad attempt at joviality. "Besides, if I break it, I don't get my wish."

His hand paused, lingering at the collar of my shirt. "Wish?"

"Yeah. That's the door prize. I put up with all this bullshit for seven years and, at the end of it, I get a wish." I held up my hand. "And please, I really don't want to hear how I was probably tricked, or that things never work out the way you want them to. It's about the only thing I've got left going for me."

"I won't." He started a gentle massage at the base of my skull. If he had any other thoughts on the matter, he didn't voice them, but his eyes grew distant.

The skin tingled where he touched it, the waves of longing rolling down my spine. "You're going to have to stop that," I said wryly. "It's going to be hard enough to try to figure out what's going on without constantly wanting to throw myself on the bed for your pleasure."

"I prefer up against the wall, myself."

I snorted. His hand stroked downward to the small of my back and remained there, the heat searing across my flesh. "Bryston," I warned, fighting the urge to rub myself against him. There were things that needed to be said. "Listen. I wanted to thank you for the other night. For saving me and Katy, I mean."

Something sad flickered over his face. "What choice did I have?" His lip curved as he gently removed the gloves from my hands. He raised one to his mouth and kissed my fingertips with a hint of mischief. "When this is over, I'll show you the Dreaming properly."

"Sounds heavenly," I said, my voice dreamy. My head still felt like it was stuffed with cotton, my words stilted and woolly on my tongue. "Just you and me and no Faery politics. And lots of sex," I added hopefully. "The kind where there isn't any pain or expectations. Normal stuff."

"Pain?" There were entire volumes of meaning written into that one word, but I didn't know how to address it.

"Mmmm. Yes. Or at least the kind that doesn't involve the forceful taking of my blood."

"Just how hard did you hit your head?"

"Never mind." I closed my eyes again. "Contract gone

bad a while ago. I didn't insist on the correct wording and the asshole decided to take more than he should have."

"More what?" The chill in his voice almost made me shiver. I should have heeded the warning, but I pushed onward.

"Blood, of course. I Contracted with a vampire my second night in Portsmyth. I was clueless and he took advantage of that." Ion's fingers stiffened in my hair, the stillness in him charging like a lightning bolt. "I'm over it, so don't go all he-man on me now."

His fingers started their light massage again, brushing over my forehead. "What was his name?"

"I'm not that stupid. I tell you that"—I yawned, stretching slightly—"you're going to go beat the mother-fucker's head in. And as much as I might not mind seeing it happen, I don't think we're in a good spot for that. Besides, Jett doesn't hang around the Hallows much anymore." Crap. "Did I just say that out loud?"

"You certainly did," he crooned, an echo of male smug-ness ringing through the words.

"Please don't. I really can't handle being responsible for one more person right now. I'm a big girl. I can live with my mistakes. Or most of them."

"Tell me what happened, then." The kneading dropped toward my neck, his thumbs tracing over a hard knot close to my shoulder. "All those *sordid* little details."

"Why don't you just go look them up in my dreams? Or my nightmares. Same thing in this case."

"I could, but I'd rather hear it from you. Did you sleep with him?"

"Yeah, I did. Wasn't all that great, though." I thought about it for a moment. "Well, okay, it was probably better than a regular guy, but it was just kind of . . . empty. I've had one-night stands before that were more fulfilling, and some that were less, so really, it wasn't a big deal. By the end of the night, he signed off on the Contract and kicked me out the door and that was that." I turned toward him, attempting to sit up.

His face shadowed over. "You don't ever let anyone in, do you? Nothing shatters that shell—not even a Contract that probably was equivalent to rape."

I blew out sharply. "Rape? I don't think so. He took advantage of me for sure, but I signed the thing. It's not on him if I didn't read the fine print. And as for not letting it bother me—I don't know how to answer that. I definitely had a dark moment or two after it, but let's be honest, shall we? The last thing I remember of my mother was having her brains explode over my face. There is *nothing* that will ever compare to that in the internal darkness and angst scale. An oversexed vampire rates pretty damn low, comparatively."

"There is that."

"You were right, though," I said. "About me running away. I was. I have been ever since the accident. Since I realized that I was never going to be what I wanted to be." I tapped on my plate. "Some things can't be undone, but that doesn't mean I want to accept it either."

He kissed my forehead firmly, his mouth drifting down over my nose until it captured my lips. I allowed myself to respond to it, something visceral catching hold in my chest, burning through my lungs like a tongue of flame.

"I know," he murmured, the words muffled. "And I had no right to say it like I did."

"It's true, though. I crashed on Mel's couch that night and cried myself to sleep and then just wandered around the next morning, trying to figure out where I fit in."

"And you found Moira?"

"Yeah. I didn't even know what I wanted to do, but she had an apartment-for-rent sign up. Something about it . . .

I just ended up in the store and she was there and I guess that was it." I let my head drift onto his shoulder. "She was . . . kind to me, offered me the place at a reduced rent, but I don't know. The more I think on it, I have to say there was an air of something desperate about her." I frowned. "Whatever was going on with her, it was happening well before I ever entered the picture." Another thought crossed my mind. "There's one thing that confuses me about all this though. If I'm a KeyStone—and I'm assuming Moira figured it out pretty quickly, since she offered me her Contract a few hours later—why didn't I TouchStone Jett? I mean, we had sex. If my TouchStoning is triggered by touch, shouldn't he have bound to me too?"

Bryston's eyes narrowed. "It's like Roweena said. You have to be receptive to it. On some level with him, you weren't, regardless of what level of physical intimacy you had."

"Probably a good thing. After all, I could be Touch-Stoned to Robert now too, eh?"

"Hardly bears thinking about." His mouth quirked up in a mocking grin. "But right now, I think we should get you home."

"I suppose. I could really use something to eat too." My belly rumbled in protest. "I didn't get a chance to eat anything all damn day, not since your breakfast, anyway. Help me up."

I flushed beneath the weighted look of his eyes. "There's a good Italian place around the corner from the Pit. They deliver." I looked around. "Where's Phineas? We probably need to get something for him too."

Bryston shrugged, rubbing his hand over his backside with a curious expression. "He left with Robert and Roweena. I think they were going to come up with a plan. I wouldn't worry about him too much. He seems to be able to take care of himself."

"And the others? Melanie?"

"They were told to leave as soon as you hit the floor. Of course," he snorted, "Robert threatened them with death if any of them mentioned what they saw, which means the entire town should know the story in about two hours."

"That's something, I suppose." A wave of light-headedness swept over me. "Ah, you know, I think I need to sit down again. How much longer are they giving us in here?" He led me back to the center chair, and I slumped. Brystion handed me my forgotten cup of water, his attention on the front doors, mouth curving.

"They didn't say, but it sounds like they're still arguing. We've got a little time, I think."

"Time for what?" I sipped at the water.

He knelt between my thighs. "Nothing in particular," he murmured, his hands sliding along the outsides of my calves. "Call it a short recess."

"We shouldn't," I whispered hoarsely as he leaned toward me, his arms raised to frame either side of my head. His lips brushed mine lightly, dusted the skin of my cheek to move down my neck. I moaned, the wet slide of his tongue over my collarbone enough to make me tremble with longing. I arched my back, heedless of the way the back of the chair ground into my shoulders.

"No."

His mouth curved into a wicked smile, teeth gleaming in the darkness as he glanced up. I swallowed, some secret part of me knowing this battle was lost and had been the moment he stepped into the bookstore four days ago.

The ridges of his abdomen pressed through his thin cotton shirt, the heat from his skin searing me with each ragged breath I took. My fingers traced the seamed edges of the cloth bunched up at the small of his back, clutching at it in a futile attempt to remain calm.

"Moira said it wouldn't be a good idea," I said.

He blinked in surprise and pulled away, the golden nimbus of his eyes fading. "Moira actually told you not to sleep with me?"

I scowled. "Not you specifically, you pretentious ass. She just said I shouldn't get . . . involved. You know, given that other thing with Jett."

The incubus snorted, shoulders relaxing. "Well, then, I suppose there's only one thing left to decide."

"And what's that? If I prefer asking permission to begging forgiveness?"

He gently pressed a finger to my lips, his voice smug and husky with desire. "Do you want me?"

Cheeky bastard.

"Yes." I shivered as I stared into those dark eyes, watching as they flared with new light.

One brow arched in amusement. "Then we can argue about it later."

"You're assuming I'm even going to *want* to talk to you later," I grumbled.

He chuckled and the sound rippled down my spine like liquid lust. "I never assume anything, Abby. Besides, it's a little late to be arguing about it now, don't you think?"

"Probably," I muttered, sitting up. "But as enjoyable as this is, I'm not exactly one for public acts of ravishment." My mouth quirked up at him. "The walk of shame afterward is a right bitch."

He pulled back and then gently tugged me to my feet, but not before giving my ass a pinch. I wanted to hit him. I wanted to run away. I wanted to throw him on the floor and tear his clothes off. In the end, I did none of these, choosing instead to give him a sour smile.

"Come on, *incubus.*" I gestured at the door. "Let's go."

If he took offense at my words it didn't show, but a flicker of amusement danced behind those golden eyes as he drifted past me.

"Later," he promised.

Eighteen

The waning evening sun shone through the Judgment Hall, the sunlight watering down through slatted windows that spoke of arrow slits and protection from sieges. Oddly appropriate, given the circumstances, but not in a particularly comfortable way.

I winced at the glare, sucking in a deep breath to ward off the swimming feeling in my head. Bryston's hand was at my elbow, a subtle guide and burning reminder of what was left unsaid.

Roweena slid gracefully toward us like a ghost. "I see you are awake. How are you feeling?" Her gaze moved to the cluster of feathers in my hand, giving rise to the question she really wanted answered.

"They're his sister's. I . . . um, seem to have Touch-Stoned her—during my seizure."

"Troubling." Her eyes searched my face, but I just held out the feathers to her. She frowned, chewing on her lower lip, but didn't touch them. She looked strangely uncertain, and that wasn't a good sign. The Fae were almost *always* certain.

Roweena's expression became grave. "I don't know if

Brystion told you, but the full Council has been contacted. I've tried to stave them off to give you some more time, but they cannot wait any longer. It will take them a while, however, to fully assemble, so I think you've got a day or two to find Moira. After that . . ."

"I guess my character witnesses weren't that good," I sighed.

"On the contrary," she said, "most of them were excellent, but there's no denying the Queen. She will stop at nothing to get her daughter back."

"Then why isn't she here now?" I challenged. "Why wait almost four months before coming to look for her? Why isn't the Council here already?"

"Time travels differently on the CrossRoads. You know that," Roweena explained. "And I do not speak for the Queen. She makes her own decisions."

"What about Maurice? Wouldn't he be the obvious one to track?"

"He is an unfortunate presence," the Fae agreed. "I am waiting on the Council's word on that, as well."

I thought back to the note Moira left me, with its hastily scrawled message. If she had been kidnapped by Maurice—or anyone for that matter—why would she leave a note? Something about her oddly phrased words churned in the back of my mind. "Even that phrase from the note she left." I turned around slowly, twisting the feathers. "Hold *back* the fort instead of hold down." Such a simple mistake, but Moira had never been that sloppy before. It had to be intentional.

"She was likely in a rush," Brystion observed. "Surely it's a common error."

"Even if that were true, why wouldn't she have at least told Robert?" I eyed the angel. "You said it yourself—she would never go anywhere long-term like that without telling you."

Phineas sidled up to us, rearing on his hind legs to sniff at the feathers. "What if Maurice was already there?"

"I didn't see her leave," I admitted. "And it wasn't uncommon for her to keep weird hours. But if he forced her to write the note, why would it be so sloppy?" I shook my head; the answer suddenly snapped hard. "Fort! That's it. The wording *wasn't* a mistake." I caught the liaison's eyes. "She doesn't want the Queen to come."

Roweena blinked slowly. "It is true that Faery hills are sometimes known as forts," she said. "If this is the case, there is a much larger game being played." I nearly choked on the obviousness of that particular observation.

A sudden weariness swept over me. I was tired of not having answers, and every way I turned only made things less clear. Phineas brushed his horn against my leg. "Come on, Abby. Let's take a walk."

Leaving the others to continue their conversation, the unicorn and I paced the outer perimeters of the hall.

He paused by the edge of a shadowed alcove, his hooves echoing on the marble. "You don't have to do this all alone, you know. Faery tales aside, there's no particular grace in being the solitary hero."

"I've hardly done anything that counts as heroic," I said wryly, crouching down beside him.

"Bah," he snorted. "The concept is nothing more than a word for stubbornness. You've got that in droves. The only real trick is using what's at your disposal."

Puzzled, I followed his gaze back to where the others were standing. They weren't all there, of course. The Gypsy, in particular, was missing, but Melanie and Robert were still there, of course . . . and Katy. I guess she wasn't that tired after all. "Looks like Katy made herself comfortable, eh?" The young blonde was leaning up against the wall, her face animated in that way only the truly innocent have. Then again, it may have had more to do with the way Brandon was protecting her, his eyes burning with a hunger that had very little to do with grandmothers or woodsmen.

Phineas waggled his beard at the odd pair. "The better to eat her with," he chortled.

"Ah, well, Brandon is a good sort. I don't think he'll lead her too far astray." I paused, looking at the little group. "You really think they'll help?"

"Abby, they're just as scared as you are. *No one* wants the Faery Queen here. We've all got lives too, you know." I thought for a moment, hesitating.

I approached them cautiously, catching Mel's wry smile with my own. "Are you all right, Abby?" She hugged me unexpectedly, and I returned the embrace.

"Guess I scared you more than I thought."

"I've seen some weird shit over the last few years, but . . . well, let's just say I'd rather not see another seizure of that caliber again, and leave it at that."

"You and me both," I agreed, turning the feathers over in my hands.

"Hey, Abby!" Katy waved me over. I moved to where she and Brandon were standing. Melanie drifted in my wake. "We, uh, that is, Brandon thought we might be able to help track Moira down?"

I pursed my mouth at Phineas. "I'm listening."

"We can offer you a base of operations," Brandon explained. "And we can help you search, or at least set up some kind of watch list. You know, interview the rest of the populace, so to speak? Find out if anyone knows something."

I nodded slowly. "It's not a bad idea, actually." As a bartender, Brandon had to know a lot of people. And *everyone* rambles at a bartender at some point. "I don't suppose you've actually got any information about any of this already?"

He shook his head regretfully. "Wasn't really paying attention before. But I'll see what I can find out."

"And as far as a base of operations goes . . ." I chewed on my thumb. It tasted of leather and something else. Wet feathers? Suppressing a shudder I turned back toward him. "I had thought that maybe the bookstore would work. But now . . ."

"Nah. Use the Hallows." The werewolf shrugged, winking at me. "It's well stocked and centrally located."

Roweena perked up and nodded at this. "I think that's an excellent idea. When the Council convenes it would be good to have a collaborative show of effort."

I snorted. "Covering our asses, I guess."

"Just so," she agreed sagely, her face a study in blankness. "And the Hallows would be better defended, as well. After all, don't you live above the bookstore?"

The thought of having all those nymphs and satyrs partying below me made me cringe. God knows what would be banging on my door at any given hour. "I see your point," I said.

"So, what is it that we need to do first?" Katy's face quivered with anticipation.

"Consolidate information, I guess. I'm assuming you guys put together a timeline while I was out?" My gaze flicked toward Robert.

"It's got some gaps, but yes. Just help me find them," he said quietly, his burning edge of judgment fading into a sad resignation. "My Charlie and Moira. That's all I want."

"I will. We need to start by finding out how those paintings fit in. If we can track down Topher too, that will speed things up, but his assistant said he wasn't in town. So, I guess we could take a look through some of the books in the

Marketplace. We might find something there about magical paintings." I yawned, rubbing at the back of my head. "And to be honest I really need something to eat and some rest." Time may have been of the essence, but I wouldn't do anyone any good if I had another seizure because I was strung out. I was TouchStoned to four OtherFolk now. I didn't know what my limit was, but I could definitely tell I was tiring because of it.

Melanie dug into her purse. "I've got a granola bar." She tossed it at me.

I unwrapped it dubiously. "It looks healthy."

"You never know," she retorted, "but then, I'd hate to see you die from eating something without bacon in it."

"One does one's best," I agreed, taking a bite.

"Shit," she sighed as her phone started ringing. "Give me a sec." She flipped open the purple RAZR. "*Moshi-moshi,*" she quipped, her face shadowing within seconds. "Ah, yes, just a moment." She held out the phone to me. "Speak of the devil, it's Topher. He said you weren't answering your cell."

"I didn't have time to grab my phone this morning." I held it to my ear. It smelled faintly of cinnamon lip gloss. "Hello?"

"Abby? I need to talk to you." Topher's voice was low and furtive.

"I tried to stop by the Gallery yesterday, but your . . . *assistant* wasn't all that helpful."

"She told me," he said gruffly. "But I've been kind of indisposed."

"That's fine, but Christ, Topher, things are getting serious. There's something wrong with those paint—"

"Hush. Listen to me, Abby, and listen very carefully. Stop poking around. You're going to get into some seriously bad shit if you don't."

"You know something." My voice was quiet, surprised.

The line went dead for a moment and I would have thought he had hung up if not for the heavy breath rattling through the earpiece. "Can you meet me tonight? Somewhere safe?"

I glanced over my shoulder, waving everyone into silence. "Okay," I said, "Come by the Marketplace. It's as safe as anything else, and I've got research to do."

Another pause. "All right. I'll try. But I think they're watching me. Don't trust anyone. There are spies on all sides."

"Erm. Okay?"

"I have to go. I'll see you later." He hung up with an eerie little click, like in the movies where you know the big bad is just lurking around somewhere. I handed the phone back to Melanie.

"Is everything all right? You look pretty pale."

"Yeah, I'm fine." It was a blatant lie, but she didn't push the issue. "You gonna swing by tonight?" I left my tone casual, but anyone who really knew me would have understood the message beneath. I needed her watching my back.

"Of course," she said airily. Her smile never made it past her mouth.

"We'll find Charlie," I promised, grabbing her wrist. "We'll find them all."

"I hope so." She nodded at me and exhaled with a slow hiss. "I need to go cancel my gig tonight, but I'll catch up with you at the Marketplace later."

"You promise too much," Bryston murmured to me as Melanie walked away. His voice tickled the back of my neck, but that didn't stop the frown I slanted at him.

"Well, it's better than the alternative." I thrust the feathers at him. "Here. You might be a better custodian for these." He let them slip between his fingers, the crimson edges sparkling in the witchlight like dried blood.

"Do we really have time for this?" Phineas's horn brushed my ankle. "Honestly, children." The unicorn glared up at me and I sighed.

"This isn't finished," I said softly, pinning Brystion with my gaze.

He nodded, a light circle of gold flaring about his pupils. His jaw tightened. "When you're done with Topher, let me know. I've a few things to tell him myself."

"Just remember, he's our only real link to what's going on," I muttered dryly. "He won't be of much use to us if he's unconscious."

"Says you," he retorted. "I'll bury my way into his god-damned dreams if I have to."

"If you could do that"—I raised a brow at him—"why haven't you?"

He scowled. "Well, for one thing, I can't find him in the Dreaming. He doesn't burn brightly enough. And for another, I've been a bit busy, if you haven't noticed. Mostly trying to save your ass."

"Not like you've been doing that out of complete altruism," I pointed out.

"No," he admitted. He moved closer, his fingers creeping between mine. I stiffened and then folded them into my hand. "No regrets," he whispered.

A jolt of electricity ran down my spine. The rest of his words hovered unspoken. I laughed shakily, ignoring Phin's eye roll. "No." Whatever else was coming along, I couldn't deny that there was something growing between us. I wouldn't have called it love, exactly. I mean, shit, it had only been a few days, but the TouchStone bond was mighty intimate. And ours wasn't even a contractual one at that. On the other hand, I wasn't so stupid as to pin a "might be" on anything as fragile as dream sex and metaphysical orgasms. Time would have to reveal the rest. I squeezed his hand, enjoying his warmth.

"You're not to leave my side, understand? Unless Robert is with you. Come on." He tugged me back toward our little cluster of allies. "Let's go get you recharged." Wearily, I clung to his hand like it was the only solid thing left in my world.

Nineteen

Nothing. Not a damned thing." I slumped against the wall, tempted to toss the latest tome across the room. The Marketplace was subdued tonight. Apparently news of Charlie's disappearance and my required presence at the Hearing had traveled through the CrossRoads on the wings of a burning butterfly. The few customers that had shown up were only there to gawk; my Gypsy friend hadn't even made an appearance. I felt a slight pang at seeing his corner empty, but I couldn't blame him. He hadn't looked too happy about being at the Judgment Hall, and probably with good reason.

I sighed, tossing the next pile of books on the floor, watching as they thudded next to Bryston's leg. The incubus had set himself up behind the counter, sorting through the indexes as fast as I could pass them to him. "This is hopeless," I said. "Forget needle in the haystack. This is like a needle in a vat of silver toothpicks."

Melanie shifted beside Bryston to pick up another book on *trompe l'oeil*. "If I ever read one more alternate ending to *Dorian Gray* it will be too soon. There has to be more than this. Are you sure that's the last of it?"

I chuckled, but there wasn't any humor in the sound. "This is everything I could find about magic paintings that I couldn't Google. And where the hell is Topher?" I glanced at my watch. "It's almost one A.M. as it is. If we don't leave the store by then we'll be stuck here until it opens again tomorrow."

"Is that how it works?" Bryston traced his fingers on the counter.

I flushed. "I'm not entirely sure, but believe me, I have *no* desire to spend a full twenty-four hours here again. I've done it once and that was plenty."

His mouth curled. "You're going to have to tell me that story, one of these days."

"Not that exciting, really." I glanced at my iPod, cheerfully chugging away to Amy Winehouse's "You Know I'm No Good" before changing over to Stevie Wonder's "Superstition." Somehow terribly apt and not overly reassuring. "What about magical paint?" I tapped on a page that told a Chinese legend of a boy and his enchanted paintbrush.

"We're doomed," Melanie groaned. "There's no way we can possibly try to come up with every variation of curse or spell that could be used with all the stuff here."

I grabbed a handful of peanut M&M's from the candy dish on the counter. "So this is pretty much a waste of time, isn't it? I mean, do we actually have any real idea of what we're looking for?"

Phineas opened an eye from where he was dozing on the corner of the counter. "Duh. No. Whose bright idea was this?"

"Mine," Bryston snarled back. "Why hasn't that shithead artist come by yet?"

I stared at my watch. It was 12:50. Shit. "And obviously too late to try to go to the studio. Unless you want to try breaking in."

Melanie rolled her eyes. "I hardly think we're in any shape for that. I'm practically passing out as it is."

"Well, it *has* been a rather long day," I said, my voice dry. Of course, I'd had the benefit of a four-hour nap and a plate of chicken parmesan, so it sounded easy enough. "But what other choice do we have?" Before she could answer, the cell phone at my side vibrated gently against my hip. I flipped it open, not recognizing the number.

"Hello?"

"Abby? It's me."

"Topher? Where the hell are you?"

"I can't talk, Abby. I won't be by tonight. I can't . . . I can't get away. Where will you be tomorrow?" His voice was hoarse and tight, just like before, like he was whispering in a dark corner.

"The Hallows. We'll all be there, actually."

"I'll be there." His tone grew urgent. "If I can't, you need to tell him—" The phone went dead.

"Tell who what?" I repeated stupidly. "Tell who *what*? Fuck!" I slammed the phone shut. "He's not coming."

"The hell he's not." Brystion shot to his feet. "I'm going to go find that asshole right now."

"No," Phineas snapped, rising to his hooves, "you're not. You're going to take Abby upstairs and guard her ass. And make sure she sleeps."

"Excuse me?" All eyes turned as a cloaked figure peered through the doorway, scaled feet sparking against the stone. The hood fell away when he approached the register to reveal my would-be daemon savior of the night before. I blinked. "TartBarbie?"

"Brigadun," the daemon hissed at me. "TB is just my handle online."

Brystion shot me a withering look. "Let me guess. You're TouchStoned to him too?"

"Oh, no," the daemon said brightly. "Nothing like that. I just tried to kill her." He held up a clawed hand as Bryston started to close in. "Aw, come on, dude. It was a job. I'm here on good faith."

"How convenient. Where are the others?"

Brigadun shrugged. "Rayo and Turnip got away, but they're hurt real bad. Thanks to the angel's handiwork, I'm thinking. He's pretty righteous with that sword, you know." His voice became dreamy. "He'd be great at DPS." The daemon frowned, looking at Bryston, and inched backward. "And Hzule wasn't looking too good either."

"Not having a throat will do that," Bryston said dryly. "Why are you here?"

Brigadun shuffled toward us, throwing something onto the counter. It was his mercenary badge, the same symbol on it as the one Bryston had found earlier. "I'm quitting the job."

I stared at it. "Where is Maurice?"

"I don't know. I only ever met him once and he didn't show his face," Brigadun said. "We were just supposed to capture you. Alive," he added, his face somewhat apologetic. "But I don't want to do that anymore."

"First daemon to say *that*," I muttered. "What *do* you want?"

"Just to be left alone and go back to the way things were." He fidgeted with his cloak. "I mean, I'm all for a little tank and spank, but I kinda prefer a pixel death to the real thing."

"Less mess that way, I suppose," Melanie deadpanned, eyeing him curiously. "You're a funny sort of daemon."

He flashed her a grin. "You have no idea, babe. Anyway, as I was saying, I'm leaving town for a bit. I just wanted to make sure there weren't any hard feelings."

My eyes narrowed. "And they just let you go?"

He smirked. "Oh, no. Once they found out I'd set you free, they decided to kill me. Technically, I'm due to be executed in, oh"—he glanced down at his watch—"about fifteen minutes. So with that in mind, I'd kind of like to get out of here."

I exchanged a glance with Melanie. This whole thing smelled like a setup, but the idea of trying to take him hostage didn't really appeal to me either. If he really was being hunted, it was probably unlikely that the other daemon mercenaries would give two figs if we captured him. On the other hand . . .

"Give us something we can use first. If you can't tell us where Maurice is, what *can* you tell us?" I popped another M&M. "I don't suppose you know anything about magical paintings?"

The daemon shifted uncomfortably, pulling on the sharpest horn hanging from his chin. "There's a garage across town that Maurice was using for storage. I can tell you where that is."

"You mean you can show us." Bryston glowered at him from where he was leaning against the counter. "That way, if we discover you're just feeding us bullshit, I can beat you senseless right there. Saves me the trouble of hunting you down," he added pleasantly.

"Erm, yeah. Okay. I can do that."

I glanced down at my watch. "Crap, guys—we gotta go or we won't be doing anything until tomorrow night. Come on." I pushed the rest of the books hastily into a corner and snagged my iPod, herding everyone out the door as fast as I could. "Not that I don't enjoy everyone's company, but all things considered, I'd like a bed tonight."

"Me too," Bryston leered, his eyes flashing gold for a moment.

"Is that all you ever think about?"

"Incubus," he pointed out, tapping his chest.

"Yeah, yeah," I muttered, my fingers brushing the stone wall as the door disappeared. The moon was full tonight, illuminating everything in a wash of silver. It made the proud edge of Ion's jaw gleam beneath his lips. I had the sudden urge to kiss it. "So what now?" I dialed Robert's cell, texting him when he didn't answer. Might as well let him know we were on to a lead.

Melanie rubbed her elbows in the evening chill. "How far away is this garage? Walking distance?"

"Yeah, maybe a mile or so," Brigadun admitted.

Phineas snorted. "I vote for a cab. I've got short legs, you know."

"Seconded," Melanie said.

"Not going to let me carry you?" I said it jokingly, but the unicorn stiffened.

"I'm not a Chihuahua, you know."

"You hump my leg like one," I retorted. "But in either case, I'm not sure the cabs are running this late. You might just have to hitch a ride in my purse."

I turned back to Brigadun, blinking as I realized he'd thrown on a Glamour. Innocent blue eyes gazed up at me, framed by beautiful blond curls. Great. A cross-dressing daemon? Her boobs would have poked my eyes out if she had been any taller. "And here I thought you were going to try to attract *less* attention."

I scooped up Phineas and tucked him into my purse with minimum fuss. Together, the five of us slipped out of the courtyard and down the street, letting Brigadun take the lead.

The night air was chilly, but my blood was thrumming with the possibility of finding answers and that shook off any chance of being cold. Melanie's arm slipped through mine on the right. I couldn't help but feel strangely grateful at the act, as our shoes tapped in time on the sidewalk. Brystion loomed behind us, his power uncoiling like a cloak of shadow as we passed the quiet brownstones and elegant town houses. The gentrification of past generations gleamed like ghosts in the streetlights.

We were moving away from the center of the tourist areas, though I thought I could hear the bass of a local club in the distance. Tall trees lined the streets, old oaks and graceful beeches, their leaves rustling in the breeze.

Brigadun hung back at one point to wait for us to catch up, eyeing Melanie's violin case with interest. "You're the Door Maker, aren't you? The one who won the bet with—"

"Yes," Melanie interjected, cutting him off with a warning look. "I am. And I don't like to talk about it."

"Sorry." He dropped her an abashed smile. "That's a pretty neat trick though. What's the secret?"

Melanie frowned at him, shifting as though to pull the violin farther away from him. "There is no secret. I have synesthesia," she said finally. "Or some form of it."

The daemon blinked. "You have what? Is it contagious?"

"I see music," she said, her jaw tensing. "Notes appear to me as colors." Her fingers crept up to the violinist's mark beneath her chin, rubbing it violently.

Brigudun looked at her blankly, opening his mouth to speak. I shook my head at him. "Like musical Skittles. You know, taste the rainbow? Same sort of thing." I squeezed her arm and she sighed, giving me a tight smile. I had learned about that particular quirk back at Juilliard, but I hadn't realized it tied in to her ability to make Doors.

Secrets upon secrets, and nothing I was willing to press her on just now.

At last we came to a run-down Victorian, the front porch decaying and decadent against a wall of ivy. "You're sure this is the place?" Not that it didn't look suitably spooky, but it just seemed terribly obvious. As if on cue, a loose shutter creaked ominously, tapping against the house.

"Yeah," Brigadun muttered, shifting from one foot to the other. "We only came here once or twice. It's haunted."

Melanie glanced back at the house with interest. "Really? Too bad we don't have Charlie with us." She stilled, as though she'd just realized what she'd said.

"Exorcist?" Brigadun said, impressed.

"No, she just has an affinity for the . . . dead, I guess."

"Let's go," I said gruffly. In truth, my knees were starting to quake, scenes from horror flicks rattling through my brain. The sort where you just *know* the heroine is too stupid to live. And yet, here we were.

But I wasn't alone. Phineas squirmed beneath my arm to poke his head out from the purse. "What a dump."

Brigadun gestured at us, raising his finger to her lips, crouching through a hole in the picket fence. It would have been pretty with a fresh coat of paint, but it had been left to sag and fade, rotting away from the inside. Melanie followed the daemon and then I walked behind her, with Brystion bringing up the rear.

The incubus had been silent during our walk, with none of his usual sarcastic digs. I reached back and gave his hand a squeeze.

We went around the back of the house, past a rosebush growing wildly up to the garden shed. Brigadun reached for the lock and cringed as it creaked. After a moment of silence he shrugged and opened the door, standing back to let us peer in.

A wave of turpentine and linseed oil hit me in the face, as though the scent had been trapped inside for a long time. "Man, it's dark in here," Phineas grunted, wriggling out of my purse. He pawed at the ground, his horn sparking to life with a silver halo.

"It's not much," he admitted. "And it won't last too long, but it should be enough to see what we need to." He shook his mane and hesitantly stepped forward, illuminating the inside of the shed in a pale glow.

I let out a reluctant breath and pulled the door wider. Dirty sheets covered squared-off shapes against one wall, but aside from those and an obvious pile of painting supplies, the shed was empty.

"Topher," Brystion breathed behind me, a quiet rage clipping the word with a finality that did not bode well for the painter.

"We don't know that yet," I said, but even I knew the words were nothing more than a futile hope that my painter friend was not involved. Without a word, the incubus strode toward the sheets, his jaw set grim and tight. I tried not to glance away as he pulled back the first sheet.

He let out a low cry, kneeling before the first painting. I crouched beside him, straining to make out the details. A woman's form, hunched and curled, her limbs arched in a mocking sort of rigor mortis, fingertips pressing against the canvas as though she had tried to claw her way out of it.

Melanie made a retching sound. "That's Lintane."

"You knew her?" The moment the words slipped out of my mouth I felt like an idiot. She nodded her head, her lips in a grim line.

Brystion pulled back another sheet. I forced myself to look at this one. Another succubus, I assumed, this one curled into a fetal ball, her skin sagging and dried out into flakes upon the floor. The third was winged like Sonja, but there was nothing left of her feathered limbs except some crumpled bones. I sucked in a deep gulp of air, the taste of paint thinner like poison in my lungs. "Ion?"

The incubus turned his face to me for one awful moment, and those eyes shone like they might swallow the night in their grief. Behind us, Brigadun moaned, one hand over his mouth as though he might vomit. I struggled to stay on my feet, the realization that these had been real people pinching my heart as though it might burst.

"I'm so sorry," I croaked, uncertain what to do. I reached out anyway, my cold fingers grasping Ion's. I nearly flinched from the heat beneath his skin, the grip of his knuckles grinding into mine. "It's evidence now. We should . . . save . . . them. For the Council."

At my feet, Phineas suddenly swiveled his ears. "'Ware the door!" he barked, neighing as the door slammed shut.

Bryston whirled on the daemon. "What bullshit is this?"

"I didn't know," Brigadun said, the Glamour dropping from him with a shudder. "They told me if I brought her here"—he gestured at the suddenly wide-eyed Melanie—"they'd let me go."

"And now you're going to die," Bryston snarled, lurching for him. He tore his hand from my grasp, neatly snatching at the daemon's chin horn so that he couldn't move.

"Hold up! Something's burning," Melanie said, glancing upward. "The roof. Shit. If they've set this place on fire and it hits that turpentine . . ."

"Assuming we don't die of smoke inhalation first," I added, my upper lip curling at Brigadun. "Nice job, asshole." I tried for the door, slamming my shoulder into it, grunting when it refused to budge.

"It's bespelled. I can smell it." Phineas ran toward the far wall. "There's a hole in the back. I can slip through."

"Make a Door," Brigadun begged. "Then we can all get out, and they won't have any idea."

Bryston and I exchanged a grim look. It was a good enough plan, even if I couldn't follow through on it. "Do it," I murmured to Melanie. "Get yourself out. I'll be okay.

If nothing else you and Phin can find Robert or someone else."

"What about me?" the daemon whined up at me, struggling to break free from Brystion's grip.

"What about you?" I retorted. "You don't leave until I do."

Melanie opened her violin case, fingers curling around the bow. "I need you to Contract with me," she snapped at the daemon. "I can't make a Door for myself."

"What do I need to do?"

She pulled a tiny scroll from her back pocket. "Here, just push your thumb in that bit of wax." He snatched the paper from her, pressing the scaled digit hard against the soft wax. "Now tell me where you want to go. Anywhere. Someplace safe."

"The Hallows," I shouted. "Go there."

Brigadun nodded. "Sure. The Hallows."

Ever the consummate performer, Melanie moved hurriedly but controlled, even as she started to play. The smoke grew stronger, something sooty falling from above.

"Maurice did this," I said to Brigadun, though it wasn't really a question.

He nodded, his eyes miserable. "I don't want to die." Melanie's song changed, the beginnings of a silver Door taking shape against the back wall. And then the daemon let out a gurgle as his head slid from his body, bloody ichor rolling from his neck. The music cut off with a wail, and the Door faded into nothing.

Brysion shook his hand in disgust as Brigadun's head fell with a sharp thud on the rotting wood floor. I gasped, my brain shutting down for a moment, so that time seemed to move in slow motion.

"Perfect timing," a voice growled from the shadows. I cried out as large scaled hands snatched at Melanie, slicing into her arm. Another daemon emerged from behind a loose pile of boxes, a bloody dagger dripping from his hand.

Brystion moved in front of me, ignoring Brigadun's now twitching body. As he engaged the daemon, he pushed me back toward the painting of Lintane, my bad knee twisting so that I stumbled. My face pressed against the canvas, the woman's fingernails like brittle seashells.

From a distance, I could hear Melanie shrieking at me to get up, her voice wavering in pain, but all around me were shadows, the glint of scales lighting up against the flames. I rolled away from the painting, glancing up to see Melanie driven to her knees, the violin twisted in her hands as she tried to hold on to it.

With a crunch of bone, her fingers snapped as the daemon snatched at her wrist and bent it back. "No!" Her eyes rolled up to the back of her head and I shot forward to catch her before she faceplanted into the floor. The daemon leered at me, waving the violin just within arm's reach. "Not my violin," Melanie sobbed, struggling in my arms. From the corner of my eye, I caught Phineas bolting through a tiny hole at the bottom of the shed. "Help," I muttered, knowing he wouldn't hear me.

Brystion growled and moved to intercept the new daemon, his hand grasping the other's wrist, trying to wrench the violin away. The knife-wielding daemon staggered to his feet, one arm hanging loose at his side.

"Brystion!" The words crackled from my throat a second too late, the knife slashing wide and fast, embedding itself in Brystion's thigh.

He grunted, trying to whirl upon the attacker and yet not let go of the violin. My hands scraped the rotting floorboards as I tried to pull Melanie away. My fingernails bit into something hard, a handle.

I wiped soot out of my eyes. Brystion's form was

wavering in the heated air, the Glamour getting fuzzy at the edges. I thought I caught a glimpse of something black poking through the seams of his skin, but then he was rolling on the ground with the other daemon, the violin forgotten.

Without even realizing, I grabbed the handle, dimly recognizing it as a rusted triangle hoe. And then I was on my feet, swinging it toward the violin-stealing daemon's head. He shouted something, the words lost in the cracking of the rooftop, as a rain of sparks fell down upon us. A siren wailed in the distance.

I swung again, the impact vibrating up to my elbows as the ancient hoe shattered against the daemon's head. A rotting beam collapsed and then another and he faded into the smoke, violin still in hand. A moment later, a voice rattled off something in Latin, and then he brushed by me and crashed through the door, fresh air flushing in.

"Brystion," I yelled, trying to pick Melanie off the ground. "We have to get out of here. *Now*," I coughed.

He shifted to his feet, limping over to where Melanie and I were. He dropped the knife that had been embedded in his leg, while behind him, the prone forms of Brigadun and the other daemon lay motionless. I turned away before I could see the bloody details.

Without a word, the incubus picked Melanie up, cradling her shock-ridden body gently against him. I followed, chucking the splintered remains of the hoe to the floor. The clean air swept through my lungs, making me gasp even as I staggered away. "What about the paintings?"

"Let them burn," he said shortly, his leg buckling slightly. Melanie moaned, a guttural sound of heartache. The red flashing lights of an approaching fire truck reflected off the nearby houses, the strobe effect making me dizzy. I glanced back at the shed and realized that if mortal authorities found evidence of nonhuman bodies in there, things were not going to go over well.

I tugged on his sleeve to bring that little fact to his attention, but the explosion as the shed launched itself to the moon left the words ash in my mouth. I had only a moment to wonder just how much turpentine had been stored inside, and then the blast hit me in the back, thrusting me to my knees. I caught a whiff of brimstone. Maybe daemons were flammable too? In front of me, the incubus stumbled, pressing his body into the side of the house and hunching over Melanie.

Something sharp prickled into my palms and I realized I'd fallen onto the rosebush, its thorns lancing deep. My head throbbed with the smoke and the roar of the fire trucks, and yet all I could see was the dark crimson of my blood streaming from my fingertips, dripping onto the grass as though I might empty myself unto the earth.

Twenty

The door to my apartment gave a welcoming creak, but it might have been the crack of doom for all the comfort it brought me. Brystion and I limped into my living room, a bloody, stinky mess of smoke and daemon ichor, grass stains and gashes. Whole in body, if not in heart, anyway. Phineas had not returned, and Melanie . . .

I'd let the ambulance take her away to the county hospital where I couldn't follow. A quick phone call to Robert ensured she would be well guarded, and Brystion managed to wheedle our way out of too many questions. Just some concerned citizens walking home from the local bar, smelling something funny . . .

I don't know if I would have bought it myself, but the incubus could be mighty convincing. He somehow managed to flash a brilliant smile despite his pain.

Melanie's hand was broken, but it was the violin she was inconsolable about. "Find it, Abby," her shattered voice shivered beneath the wail of the sirens. "My soul is inside it. The daemons have my soul."

Her words continued to echo in the back of my mind, hollow and aching, swirling with the disappearence of

Phineas. The tears rolled hot and wet down my chin. Silent, fragile at first, my throat locked into a whispering sob. I fought to hold it back, knowing that if it was allowed to come forth, all my grief, all that reality would have to be looked at, analyzed, and accepted. My gaze fell to the manila envelope on the table, and my limbs started to shake. "I can't do this, Ion. I can't lose anyone else."

Bryston's lips pressed gently on my temple as he pulled me even more tightly against him. "It's all right," he murmured. "I've got you. Let it go, Abby. Let it go."

With a hoarse cry, I shattered, as though his words gave me final permission. My knees buckled as helpless rage and anger, as a sadness I had no words for, poured from me.

She's gone. We're sorry, Abby, but we had to bury her last week. You were still in a coma, hon, and well . . . we didn't know if you'd wake up . . .

My head shaking in disbelief as the world broke into thousands of pieces, put back together like a retarded Humpty Dumpty, eggshells becoming nothing but powder, the yolk spilling down the wall. My body trembling uncontrollably, eyes rolling into the back of my head, voices screaming beside me. Pain as my head cracked the side of the hospital bed, my mouth dribbling a cocktail of spit and vomit . . .

She's seizing! Get a doctor!

. . . and then nothing but blessed darkness as consciousness slipped away . . .

"She's gone." I mouthed the words, but no sound emerged. "She's gone." I tried harder this time, wincing at the pathetic tone. I closed my eyes against it. "She left me," I whispered again.

Bryston turned me around, one hand snugly around my waist, the other cradling my head against his chest. This last act of tenderness did me in. I erupted into sobs, hard, ugly noises muffled in the cloth of his shirt. He was kissing my forehead, fingers running through the tangled mess of my hair.

"She didn't mean to leave you," he whispered. "You know that."

"My fault," I gasped. "I was driving. All my fault. If I had just paid more attention to the surroundings. We were arguing . . . and those motherfucking headlights came from nowhere . . ." I cringed beneath the memory of shattered glass and twisted metal, a high-pitched scream that just went on and on before I realized *I* was the one screaming. And Mother . . . Mother wasn't moving at all, her face a pulpy mess of blood and tissue . . .

I choked on the emotion and fled into the bedroom, into the bathroom, barely making it to the toilet. In moments there was nothing left in my stomach, but I still sat there, heaving painfully. I welcomed it. It was something real to focus on, a problem I could at least pretend to fix, or wait for it to pass.

My arms trembled, smearing spittle over my lips as I wiped my mouth with the back of my hand. "You want any help?" Bryston's words were as soft as a caress.

I shook my head, trying to give him a smile and failing utterly. A question formed in his eyes, but he didn't ask it. He just returned the gesture with a small smile of his own. Without a word, he slipped past me to the bath, and the shower came to life.

I sighed, slumping against the cold tiles, my head on my knees. For a moment, I wondered what it would be like to just curl up on the floor and melt away into nothing. But no, there was no honor in that. Groaning, I stood and staggered to the mirror.

I looked like hell. Between the smeared makeup, the tear

streaks, the swollen face, and the rest of it, I was surprised Brystion hadn't run screaming into the night. "Must be True Love," I muttered, stripping off my filthy tank top. It was stained with vomit and sweat and reeked of fear. Numbly, I kicked it away, my skirt getting the same treatment.

Beside me, the incubus had done the same, bruises scattered along his shoulders, scratches etched into his arms from the other daemon's claws. The wound on his leg had started scabbing over. My mouth opened, a worthless apology dangling from my tongue, but he merely shook his head and slid back the curtain, gesturing at me to follow.

There was nothing sexual about it this time, just my weary hand slipping into his for balance. Carefully, we washed each other, each breath pushing air to another sore spot. I forced myself to look at each of his wounds, knowing full well that I had none on myself, save from the thorns . . . and those were my fault.

I let him wash my hair, watching the soap bubbles run down the drain with the last of my emotions. He gently massaged my scalp before tipping my head back into the water for a final rinse. And then the water was off and he had a towel around me, ruffling it over my skin, tsking at the first sign of goose bumps. Snagging a towel of his own, he murmured something before disappearing into the bedroom, a gust of cool air taking his place.

Left with nothing but a weary silence inside, I dropped the towel, wrapping myself in my old bathrobe. I suppose it wasn't exactly haute couture, but it wasn't like I had anyone to impress. I finger-combed my hair, studying my scar in the mirror like I always did. With a sigh, I covered it back up. I may have earned the damn thing, but that didn't mean I was ready to display it.

Emerging from my steaming cocoon of comfort and

lavender shampoo, I padded into my bedroom, turning on the small light next to my bed. The faint smell of something warm and breadlike emanated from the kitchen. I poked my head around the corner.

Bryston looked up as I peered past him, his lips twitching when my gaze fell on the tightly wrapped towel at his hips. "I made you some toast," he said softly. "And some tea." He gestured at the mug as though uncertain of my reaction. "Hardly a gourmet meal, but you need a little something in your stomach. Go lie down; I'll bring it in."

I retreated without hesitation to the shelter of my bed. The blankets were still wrecked from yesterday morning. I couldn't help the quiet chuckle falling from my lips, remembering Bryston holding the frying pan. How quickly things had changed.

I slid under the sheets, tucking the coverlet up around my shoulders. The faint beacon of his scent still ghosted there, and I pressed it to my cheek, wondering if that's how it was for women visited by incubi—to just wake up to an empty bed with only a barest hint of their dream lover drifting over their skin like a heady perfume.

I glanced up to see Bryston standing in the doorway, amusement etched across his face. He held a tray with a plate and a steaming mug. He carefully set it down on the table next to the bed, before sitting beside me. His back was still damp and the hair on his shoulders gleamed. "You need anything else?"

"Just let me see if I can keep this down," I said wryly, clutching the teacup between my fingers. The mug was uncomfortably hot, but I didn't want to put it down. I sipped it slowly, my eyes shutting as the sweetened liquid slipped into my throat, chased by something with a bit more kick. "Added a little something extra, I see," I murmured, turning my head to face him.

"Whiskey." He gave me a lopsided grin. "You look like you need it." It roiled in my belly for a moment and then settled pleasantly.

"Mmmm." I took another sip. "It's pretty good." Suddenly ravenous, I snagged the toast, finishing it up in short order, the second piece following suit. He watched me eat in silence, leaning forward to brush a few stray crumbs from my robe, the back of his knuckles grazing my chin. I froze, the heat from his hand matching the burning fire in my belly. I raised the now trembling cup to my lips, washing the last of my toast down a throat suddenly far too dry.

"Do you want me to go?" he said softly, his thumb arching forward to stroke down my cheek. "I can guard your dreams tonight."

I could feel the tips of his fingers tremble; my nerveless hands carefully replaced the mug on the table. The last of the day's angst was gone, wrapped in this single moment when I realized just how badly I wanted him, wanted to lose myself in the mindless warp of pleasure. His eyes were flushing gold, belying the question. Capturing his hand against my mouth, I gently kissed the tip of his thumb.

I twisted so that my knees were folded beneath me, our faces at an equal height, still pressing his hand to my mouth. "Are you sure?" His voice was a whisper, seductive and soothing, his other hand already hovering at the edge of my robe, fingers sliding beneath the collar, running over my neck, pausing at the pulse point of my throat.

In answer I shifted to let the robe drop from my shoulders, exposing my flesh to him, nipples hardening in anticipation, a flush of heat fluttering from my belly. I shuddered as his hand dropped even lower. I moved toward him, our mouths meeting in a flurry of kisses. Within moments the robe was gone, and he was stroking me, questing along every inch of my skin, setting me on fire with each touch.

I fumbled at his waist, the hot hardness of his erection launching into my hands as I pulled the towel from his hips. He was a velvet rock in my palm. I squeezed him, smiling at the husky groan that tore from his throat, dark and rich as honey. With an oath, he tumbled me back onto the mattress, hands jerking my hips upward, my knees open and welcoming. He hovered above me, his cock lightly stroking over my sex, hot and wet and slippery with desire. I arched forward, my hand on his ass, pressing him low and close.

Our eyes locked. The question reasserted itself and I only smiled at it, my mouth moving against his. "No regrets," I murmured fiercely, pushing him down as I snapped up to meet him, taking him into me with a soft, shuddering moan. Without further prelude, he thrust against me, taking me forward and upward, rolling me over so I was on top, driving into him. His hands were on my hips, a litany of soft words tumbling from his lips. I could not have said what they were, only that I was swept away by the golden nimbus of his gaze, and knowledge of him moving inside me, and for that moment I knew I was truly and utterly alive.

He was peeling me away from myself. One layer at a time, I was exposed, laid bare and open beneath the heated scrape of his fingers. Every stroke was like a brand, burning his mark into my skin. He bent me beneath his will and I broke myself upon him, aching and hungry. Was I dreaming? Awake? I couldn't bring myself to care anymore. Brystion had spun a web of desire about us, entwining strands of lust and the delicate beginnings of some deeper, unnamed emotion into a pulsing nebula of light and shadow.

"Abby . . ."

My name echoed from his lips like a prayer, murmured in gentle refrain. His mouth trailed across my throat, beneath my chin. It lingered on my cheeks, my eyelids, my forehead. My eyes fluttered open to catch his, half-lidded and golden in the dim light of my bedroom. Something flickered over his face—uncertainty, perhaps—but it was quickly replaced by a far more primal mien as I arched my back in anticipation.

"Shush." I didn't want any words, nothing to shatter the fragile shell of ignorant bliss carved around me.

The frantic pace of our earlier coupling had dispersed, the edges of passion blurred. We were merely naked now, wrapped in cotton sheets and shadowed hues as the night slipped away into the waiting morning.

Dawn . . .

He leaned forward on one elbow, his long, sculpted body curled about me like a cat, possessive and warm. The rainy scent of his midnight hair filled my lungs. His free hand continued to roam over my skin, pausing to cup a breast or brush the curve of my hip, trailing down the length of my thigh. I reached up to twirl those silken curls around my finger and watched his expression change yet again as he shut his eyes, brushing my palm with his lips. I wanted. I ached.

"Come here." I tugged gently on the lock of hair, my lips already parted. His teeth flashed white, his smile teasing and predatory as he watched me silently plead for his mouth. He nipped lightly at my jaw and gave me what I wanted, his tongue probing deep. His fingers traced over my belly before slipping between my thighs.

I bit down on his shoulder; his sweat and skin mingled on my tongue. He reared back, gold flaring from his eyes. "No mercy."

"Wasn't asking for any."

His mouth twitched. "Works out nicely, then," he snarled, his hands capturing mine, pinning me to the bed. I squirmed, laughing despite myself, but the sound inflamed him and he bit at my mouth, sucking hard on my lower lip. "Mine." It wasn't really a question, but there was a purring rumble to the words that reverberated through me with a tender sort of uncertainty.

"No," I murmured, kissing him back, as my legs drew up around his hips. "Mine." His grip relaxed just a touch around my wrists. I wriggled them free and wrapped them around his neck, snagging into his silken hair like the reins of a horse. "Now," I whispered, pulling him down to me. "Now!"

With a cry he thrust into me. I clung to him, unable to do much more than hold on. His hands stroked down, fingers biting into my ass, spreading me wider. For a moment I hovered on the edge of oblivion. Captured beneath him, my body started that familiar tightening. His movements were a blur.

"Abby . . ." My name echoed between us like a prayer, and I answered with a mewling cry, tumbling over the precipice again. Pleasure swept over me, vibrating though the marrow of my bones as I lost myself to it. The bed wailed beneath us, and the headboard slammed into the wall with a rattle as Brystion followed swiftly behind. He stiffened, a hoarse groan escaping him as he released into me.

Aching and sore, I dissolved around him, our bodies slick and worn. His breathing slowed in time with mine so that we were boneless, merging into a single entity.

With a soft sigh, he brushed his mouth over mine again and slipped from my body to roll onto his side. I shivered, every nerve under my skin still on fire, even as some hidden part of me sagged in disappointment at the emptiness he left behind. He curled around me, one hand pulling up the sheet to tuck it around us, the other moving over my shoulder in tiny circles.

"Dreamer," he whispered, a gentle smile on his face.

"You've undone me utterly, woman." I mouthed his ear, suckling the lobe between my teeth so that he trembled in response. He tipped his head back as though he were offering his throat to me, his eyes half-lidded and languid. It was deceptive, such submission, but I continued to run my lips over the salty edge of his jaw, wondering when the trap would be sprung.

"But such lovely bait," I murmured, leaning forward to kiss him. Inhaling deeply, I pressed my face into his hair, willingly captured in the haze of midnight rainstorms, crushed rose petals, and the distant tang of the sea.

I didn't remember him tasting like this in my dreams. There had always been the hint of something shadowed beneath the honeyed flavor of his skin, but it hovered out of reach, masked by a barrier I couldn't quite penetrate. And now he was here beneath me, and that exquisite darkness embraced us both. .

He looked at me shyly, as though guessing the question written across my face.

"In the Dreaming, we can only take from what is given to us," he admitted. "I can change it, manipulate it to my lover's will, but I cannot create something new." There was something curious in the tone of his voice. He lifted me up so that I straddled him, his hands running over my thighs. "I tasted the way you wanted me to taste."

"And now?" I cocked my head at him.

His lips curved into a slow, lazy smile, turning his head to kiss my hand. He drew a teasing finger down my rib cage, running it in small circles over the flat of my belly. "And now . . ."

Sprung!

I nearly laughed aloud when his hands ensnared my wrists, powering me onto my back with predatory ease before kissing me soundly again. My eyes closed and I nuzzled him closer as he slid beside me. "How does it work? The creation of your kind?"

"Ah," he said. "We're born of the Dreaming. My mother was a Dreamer—a poet, I suppose."

"You suppose?"

He shrugged. "I didn't really know her all that well. Sonja and I were just afterthoughts for her, I think. Bastard offshoots of inspiration, maybe, or the metaphysical equivalent of a man's seed running down his lover's thigh." His words went flat and monotone, his hand stilling on my shoulder. "Sonja's father was an angel, hence the wings."

"He wasn't the same as yours?"

His hair tickled the back of my neck as he shook his head. "No," he said, the sound muffled in the pillow. "My father . . . well, honestly? I don't really know who or what he was. Something daemonic is the best I can come up with. Certainly not Celestial." There was more than a trace of envy in his words, and I could detect the bitterness of what was surely the pinnacle of sibling rivalry.

"And your mother never told you?"

"I don't think she even knew I existed." He shifted me around so I was facing him, one hand sliding over my cheek. "I was never a baby, Abby. I didn't have a childhood, or at least not one you'd recognize as such. I just came into being, much like you see me now. One moment I didn't exist and the next . . ." He sighed. "Sonja found me lurking in the dark corner of my mother's Dreaming. Born from her Heart, I was never allowed to reenter." He snorted with a touch of irony, something painful lancing through me at the hollowness of the gesture. "None of us can . . . something about the creation process, I guess . . . the stuff of what we're made. Maybe we'd just get reabsorbed if we went back. Didn't stop me from trying though."

I reached out to stroke his face, my fingers lingering

on the plump curve of his lips. "I'm sorry. That sounds horrible."

"It's what I am," he said softly. "But I wouldn't take it amiss if you might offer me a bit of your Heart to retreat to, now and again. Incubi have no Dreaming Heart of their own. If we did . . ." He shifted again, wrapping me tighter into his arms. "If we did, perhaps we wouldn't be the parasites we appear to be."

"Parasites?"

"Nothing of me is mine," he said brusquely. "I can only be as my Dreamers wish, bound by their wills to suit their pleasure. My appearance, my skills, my mannerisms—all of it taken, stolen from the dreams of mortals."

"Even me?" Had I inadvertently thrust my will upon him? *That's a new look for him . . . he used to be blond . . .* Melanie's previous words winged their way through my mind. "Oh, God. I'm sorry. I didn't know."

"You couldn't have. It's all right," he mused, one hand trailing through my hair. "I'm used to it."

"How do I stop?"

The incubus stilled, his head tilting back on the pillow. "We break the bond."

I couldn't think of anything to say to this, so I kissed him. "No. You are what you are," I said. "There's no shame in that. And if it makes any difference to you," I said, letting my hand drift to rest on the pulse on his neck, "I don't know who my father is either."

"At least you knew *what* he was," he pointed out dryly, giving my hair a gentle tug. "No chance of a tail sprouting out of that perfectly delicious ass, anyway."

"Hardly perfect," I retorted, my cheeks flushing as his hand strolled casually down my spine to the small of my back, fingers swirling over the spot in question. "Mmmph," I muttered. "And even so—human or not—it still leaves me in the dark about my heritage." My head tipped forward to rest on his chest again. "I used to pretend I was a princess," I said dreamily. "I was always wondering if my daddy was a fleeing prince or a secret agent or some such thing."

"You never know," Brystion said, resting his chin on my head with a contented sigh. "And your mother never told you?"

"No." I frowned. "But then, I suppose mothers have their reasons, don't they? Guess I'll never know, now." I worried my lower lip. "There's one thing I'm confused about, Ion. How did I become a Dreamer? Or if I have been all along, why now? Before I came to Portsmyth, I'd never even heard of the OtherFolk or the CrossRoads or anything else."

He lightly stroked the curve of my hip, but it was soothing now. "Dreamers are born, but not all of them Awaken. In your case you probably poured all that energy"—he kissed my head—"into your dancing. When you . . . lost that, it had to go somewhere. When did you start having the nightmares?"

"After the accident," I said softly. "I had been hoping that visiting my mother's grave would have helped them, but it didn't. All of it just sort of came on at once—the seizures, the dreams." I shuddered. "It's pretty awful, really."

His hand went still, the heat from his fingers suddenly burning like a bonfire. "Would you give it up, if you could?"

"Give what up?" I raised my head, confused. "I don't follow."

"The Dreaming. Would you give it up for a chance to go back to what you were?"

A warning bell went off in the back of my head. "Just what are you asking? Back to what? Before the accident, you mean?"

"Well, it wouldn't be exactly the same. But you'd be free of the nightmares, anyway. Maybe even the seizures, if it's done right." His voice got even lower. "You'd be free of all of it."

"Would it bring my mother back?" I swallowed the bitterness, looked up at the ceiling. "But I don't know. I don't think you can ever really go back to the way things were." On the other hand . . . to be able to dance again. My heart ached with it, the longing to see if such a thing were possible. "You're not telling me something." I glared at him. "What else would I have to give up?"

He snorted. "Me, for one. You wouldn't be a TouchStone anymore, but then, isn't that what you really want? To be normal again?"

"Give you up? As in what, never see you again?" My upper lip curled. "The tit dries up and you move on to someone else, is that it?"

"No," he snapped. "That's not it." His body twitched as though I'd slapped him, muscles coiling in an effort to sit up.

"Then what?" I turned in his arms so that I pushed him back down on the bed. "What is it that you're trying to say?"

"Never mind." He shook his head. "It was wrong of me to suggest it. I don't think it's even possible." I stared at him, utterly bewildered, but he merely chuckled. "Let's worry about it later," he said. "After we find Sonja and the others. Then maybe we can talk about it." He gathered me back into his arms. "It's getting late."

"Late," I snorted, "hell, it's early morning."

"Rest, then. I'll guard your sleep."

"You're a stupid man, Ion," I muttered, my eyes already closing. "For all that you're an incubus, I'm not sure you know the first thing about romance, but we can talk about that tomorrow too."

"Tomorrow," he agreed, his hand stroking my forehead. He curled around my back, his broad chest cradling me against him.

"Ah, and you can have it, you know," I yawned.

"Have?"

"The spot. In the Heart of my Dreaming. It's yours, anywhere you like." He said nothing, but his body froze, his breathing suddenly stiff. Finally, his head dropped on the pillow, a soft echo of thanks falling from his lips, so faint I nearly mistook it for a sigh. Without another thought, I slipped away, not even the lure of the Dreaming able to pull me away from catching an actual chance at rest. The barest hints of dawn crept through the slats of the blinds.

Dreamless, I slept.

Twenty-one

I started awake with the phone screaming for my attention. Bryston's arms tightened around me and I relaxed, suddenly realizing where I was. "I have to get it." I kissed him and squirmed free. He made a little *mmmmph* noise, rolling over on his side. I paused for a moment, my gaze lingering over the bed-swept hair, drifting over his sculpted jaw. His face seemed quieter now, all dulled edges and drowsy vulnerability.

The phone rang again and I tore myself away, snagging it from the dresser.

"'Ello?"

"We're ready, Abby," Robert said, his voice terse. My momentary postcoital bliss screeched to a stop as my brain shot back into high gear. I gazed at the clock; it was nearly two in the afternoon. Nothing like a little metaphysical pickle tickle to make you lose track of the important things.

"Have you heard from Melanie at all?"

"They discharged her this morning," he reproached me. "She's not really speaking to any of us at the moment."

"All right, I'm heading down there right now. Did . . . did Phineas ever show up? He didn't come back here last night." I flushed guiltily. Not that I'd even checked—some TouchStone I was. I pushed the thought away when he grunted in affirmative.

"He's here, but you'd better hurry. He's gone through at least half a bottle of rum on his own, and I don't think he's got any plans of stopping." There was a pause. "And you might want to tell him that if he bites me again I'm gonna rip that horn off and shove it up his ass."

I sniggered despite myself, dashing into the bathroom. Brystion lifted his bleary head as I passed. "Yeah, it's one of his more endearing qualities. He humped your leg yet?"

"No comment."

I eyed my snarled hair with a sigh. "Is Topher there?"

"No. He called the bar a little while ago—wanted to know if you were there. He sounded real edgy though."

I grimaced. Something told me the artist wasn't going to show, especially if he knew any of the particulars from the shed the night before. There was very little doubt in my mind Topher was intimately involved in what was going on with Maurice. I hadn't quite worked it out, but the connection was there. I sighed, realizing I'd missed part of the conversation. " . . . and Roweena sent a report back to Faery. We found one of the succubus paintings mostly intact from the shed."

"Shit. We'll take a closer look at it when we get there. Maybe Brystion will be able to tell us something." He grunted a good-bye and I hung up the phone, peering around the doorway. "Get up, we're fucking late."

The incubus propped himself on his elbows, his eyes suddenly lazy. I was naked, of course. In real life, people can actually walk around their bedroom without draping a sheet around them first. Didn't stop the flush from creeping up my face as he watched me. Finally his lips pursed and he snorted softly. "Fucking late, eh? Who's that?"

I threw a towel at him, rolling my eyes. "Seriously. It's afternoon. Why'd you let me sleep in?"

"Didn't mean to," he grumbled, sliding out of bed. "I think you needed it though." He bent over obligingly to drag Melanie's duffel bag out from where he'd stowed it beneath my bed. I sighed, wondering just how bad it would be if I just threw all that responsibility to the wind and spent the rest of the day banging his brains out.

"Duty calls," I murmured, slipping past him to pull out a pair of Hello Kitty panties from the top drawer. I shook them slightly. At least these were mostly free of fur. I quickly threw on the rest of my clothes, a simple pair of jeans and a tank top. I splashed a little water on my face, and rimmed my eyes with kohl, spearing my hair into a bun. I glanced at myself in the mirror and snorted.

Abby Sinclair, urban geisha. Bringing SexyBack to an OtherFolk apocalypse near you.

"Good enough. You ready yet?"

"I'll do." His T-shirt clung to his chest as he leaned against the doorframe. The openness of a few moments ago was gone; his eyes contained that familiar guardedness. Funny how two people can be so close and yet so far apart. A pang of sadness took root in my gut, and I couldn't help but wonder if that was always going to be the case. His lips curled up, as if seeing my thoughts. He extended his hand to me, the smile lighting up his face like the sun. "No regrets," he murmured.

My fingers interlocked with his and I stared up at him. "No regrets."

Tension hung over the Hallows in a miasma of grim smiles and worried brows. I shrugged off the weight of the circumvented stares, a wave of eyes upon me as I approached the bar where Robert and Brandon held court among a group of angels and a contingent of elves in Armani. Court business, I supposed. I wetted my lips, trying not to notice the way my mouth suddenly went dry. Strange how quickly enemies become compatriots given a serious enough situation. The Paths didn't like to mingle more than they had to, but the root of it was that *no one* wanted the Faery Court coming down on them.

"Took you long enough." A small hiccup burbled by my knee as I watched Brystion head toward the back of the club.

"Be polite, Phin. It's hard enough to see them all staring without feeling like I'm two years old." He staggered slightly and I scooped him up. "And why the hell are you drunk?"

"Sue me." The unicorn cracked open one bloodshot eye. "It was a hell of a night, Abby. There were daemons everywhere—the mercenaries. I tried to get back to you, but they had me cornered for hours in the back ally of the Spank Bank."

"I'm sorry," I said, stricken.

"You should be." He buried his face in my shoulder. "I'm not meant for that."

My fingers drifted through the cirrus fluff of his mane and I shifted him on my hip. "Why the XXX movie theater?"

"Unicorn," he pointed out with a grumpy snort. "Figured it would be the last place they'd look."

"Clearly they know your tastes," I muttered, spotting the PETA pixie approaching. She gave me a friendly wave and sat down next to me at the bar. "Hello?" I hesitated. "Why are you here? Not that I'm not grateful or anything, but I didn't think this was your fight."

"That depends on who you ask, I guess." She scooted her pet seal onto the counter. "Seabert didn't think much of that daemon the other night." When I didn't respond she frowned at me. "Asshole broke my wand. I want him to pay for it."

"Ah . . . he's kind of dead, already."

"Damn. Well, that's all right. Daemons tend to breed a lot. I'm sure he's got family who will step up to the plate. And if not, that's why I brought the Cousins." She gestured over her shoulder at the corner by the stage where two . . . somethings sat. Horses with flippered legs. And yet they had human torsos . . .

I swallowed hard. "They don't seem to have any skin."

"Why would they? They're Nucklavee, after all." Her mouth curled into a feral grin. "Nasty fuckers too."

"You're pretty hard-core for being in PETA," I said. "I thought you guys were all love the earth and shit like that. Unless I've misunderstood what the acronym stands for."

One perfect brow cocked at me. "Yeah, well. It's not called People for the Ethical Treatment of Assholes, now is it?" She flittered into the crowd, leaving me and the seal to stare at each other. It made a disparaging bark as I set Phineas next to it on the bar.

My glance fell on a huddled form on the stage. Melanie. She cradled her splinted arm tightly against her chest, her eyes dull as she stared at the amp next to the mic stand. "Give me a sec, Phin?"

I hurried to her side, climbing onto the stage with a little grunt. The skinless giants eyed me curiously, but I tried not to look at their thick yellow veins or the way they pulsed with black blood.

Melanie blinked at me, the bags beneath her eyes dark and empty. "It's okay," I murmured as she stumbled forward. I hugged her hard, feeling her shudder against me. "We'll get it back," I promised her, but even I could hear the hollowness beneath the words. Despair lanced over her features.

"I'll die if we don't." Her eyes went blank. "I damn near lost my soul over that instrument—it's a part of me now. If it's broken, it won't just be a matter of me not being able to open the CrossRoads again, but I think I'll be . . . broken too."

"It just doesn't make any sense," I muttered. "You had a painting done by Topher, so clearly there's still a connection there, but then why didn't they just take you?"

"The only one who's going to be able to answer that is Topher," she said savagely, wincing when her arm brushed my thigh. "And he's got a lot to answer for."

"How bad are your fingers?" I'd been hedging on the question, not entirely sure I wanted to know the answer. I knew all too well what the loss of one's limbs could do to one's talent.

"Bad." She gestured up toward the bar. "Robert says he can get me in with one of the Royal Healers, as a favor to Moira."

"I'm surprised they haven't already." And I was. Usually the OtherFolk were fawning all over her.

A grim snort escaped her. "I'm a marked woman now. No one wants to take the risk of helping me. Just like they won't want to help you," she added. "Fairweather friends. Be careful of that, Abby. Whatever they tell you, the OtherFolk only watch out for themselves." Her shoulders sagged. "Though I'm not sure they know how to do anything else."

"I'm not sure they've got much of a choice," I sighed. "But speaking of that, I suppose we ought to get this thing started. All I need now is a master plan."

"Got anything in mind?"

"Sit back and wait for my new special power to show up? Seems to work that way in all the Faery tales, doesn't it?" I crossed my arms. "What do you think? Will I be able to shoot fire out my ass or just control all the werewolves in the neighborhood through the awesomeness of my Sex-Fu?"

The ghost of a smile crossed her face. "I'll be sure to pick up a bag of marshmallows. I'd really dig an ass-fire s'more right about now."

"You and me both." I gave Melanie's good hand a gentle squeeze and left her there, heading back up toward the bar. Phineas appeared to be in a heated argument with the seal, but it looked rather one-sided. I cleared my throat to get everyone's attention.

Nothing.

I frowned. "AHEM!"

"Amateur," Phineas grumbled, trotting to the center of the bar. His legs wobbled uncertainly, but he shook himself and then reared up a bit, letting out a belch that would have knocked over a sailor.

The elf next to us jumped, his silver eyes startled. One by one, the others turned toward us. A taint of fear rode the air, the stink of it on my tongue.

"Ye're on, babe," the unicorn muttered. Bryston glanced my way from where he had been talking with Robert. He gave me a faint smile, his head tipping to indicate I should go on. Melanie still hadn't moved from the stage.

"I . . . uh . . . well." My voice faltered and I shook myself. "Thank you all for coming," I said.

"What's the plan, Abby?" Brandon wolf-grinned from behind the bar, canine teeth gleaming under the lights. He had Katy pressed tight against him, one hairy paw wrapped protectively about her waist.

"This is what I know," I continued, scooting behind the bar to use the special whiteboard. Carefully I drew out the timeline. "Here is when I signed Moira's Contract and here"—I wrote the date two months later—"is when she disappeared. Somewhere in between that"—I gestured toward Bryston—"is when Sonja went missing. Before that, other succubi were also apparently disappearing."

Bryston nodded grimly, moving up to the bar with Robert, the two men peering at the whiteboard. "I was attacked two nights ago. Or really, they mistakenly took Katy for me." I put another dot on the timeline. "And then Charlie." My gaze darted sharply toward the angel. I flinched as his eyes went cold.

"I don't understand," the pixie said, leaning on the bar to interrupt. "How does the succubus fit into this?"

"The paintings." Some of the stares went blank. "Topher Fitzroy did a series of paintings of TouchStones several weeks after Moira . . . left—one of me, Charlie, and Melanie. But there were portraits of others as well. One of them is of Sonja." I didn't look over at the incubus, but I could sense him tense as I said it. "One of them was Moira. And last night we discovered the three paintings of the dead succubi."

Robert pulled up the sheeted remains of one of the paintings. I braced myself as he uncovered it, the brighter lights of the bar making it seem obscene. The angel did not react, as though it were nothing more than disrobing a corpse in a morgue for identification. The unfortunate Lintane had not changed her position behind the canvas, her naked form still arched in terror.

The elf beside me blanched and I finally looked away. Robert covered it back up and laid it gently on the floor where it sat like the pink elephant in the room, everyone's eyes continually drawn to what was hidden beneath.

"No wonder the little shit hasn't shown up here," Brandon snarled, tongue idly running over a sharpened canine.

"No." I gave them the rest of the information from the night before, skirting over Brigadun's betrayal. I glanced back at the painting, unable to continue. Phineas nudged my arm and took up the tale as best he could, ending with the theft of Melanie's violin.

"Guess that kills the option of just making a Door into the Gallery," Brandon sighed. "Assuming that's where we would find him."

"The bigger thing is finding Maurice." Robert fiddled with one of the markers. He eyed the elves with a sour smile.

"It begs the question though," Phineas said. "Just who was Sonja's TouchStone when she disappeared? Assuming she had one?"

Bryston shook his head helplessly. "If I'd known that I would have started there."

"I believe I can answer that," a low voice came from the doorway. I turned, my mouth gaping as I saw Topher standing there, his face gaunt and eyes bright and blood-shot. He raised his hands in a "no harm" fashion, fingers splayed. "I was."

I could only stare at him, my knees beginning to wobble. "Well, isn't that a perfect bitch," I said aloud, the warning voice in my head sending out a five-alarm bell.

And then all hell broke loose.

Twenty-two

Daemons poured in the front door, leaping around the hunched figure of the artist. I had no idea how to react to the panic around me, but Bryston had no such handicap. Swearing, he flew over the bar and grabbed my hand, leading me toward the stage. Melanie had pressed herself behind one of the curtains, her face paling.

"We have to get out of here," Ion shouted.

"Tell me something I don't know," I muttered, shuddering as Robert's maddened cackle echoed through the room. I spared a glance toward the Celestial. His wings were spread in a formidable rage, his long sword glowing as he cut a swath through the daemons. Blood splattered over the floor and walls like a daemonic carwash. If daemons washed their cars in their own blood, that is.

I tripped, biting hard on my lip as I kicked a severed daemon head out of my path. I slipped on the wet hardwood as a high-pitched whinny sounded. I turned to see Phin rearing on the bar, his horn jabbing madly at a cluster of grinning daemons. "Phineas!" I shrieked, watching in horror as one of the daemons snatched him up by the tail. He let out a squeal of fury, teeth bared as he kicked out with sharp hooves.

Ignoring Brystion's shout of warning, I lurched toward the daemons, crying out as I slammed into a table. I fell to the floor, rolling off Katy's prone form. I shook her but she didn't move, and then a clawed hand gripped my shoulder, hauling me to my feet. "Ion——" Another hand covered my mouth, pinching my nose hard as I attempted to bite it.

"Quiet there," said a guttural voice, the daemon's lips pulled back. I kicked out and down, trying to remember what soft bit you were supposed to target when you were attacked. Ah. Eyes! My free hand was still free and flailing, but I shoved it back, driving with the sharp nail of my thumb into the fleshy mass between the eyelids. There was an audible pop, viscous fluid burning over my skin as my attacker screamed and released me.

Shaking off the egg-white chunks from my hand, I fled toward the bar. Bodies were everywhere, but how many were dead versus injured I wasn't sure. It wasn't like I'd ever been in a battle before.

"Shit." Something squishy wobbled beneath my foot. I glanced away quickly. One of the Armani-clad elves hadn't been quite fast enough.

The pixie swooped above me, displaying some extraordinarily pointy teeth. Whatever she'd said about a broken wand, she must have had a spare since she was going all Harry Potter with a Barbie-pink monstrosity, flashes of silver sparkles raining down on another daemon. Her "Cousins" were . . . well, they were eating someone. One of them had a nasty cut on his equine flank, ebony blood dripping onto the hardwood as he gleefully ripped into the unfortunate victim's chest.

I ducked behind the bar, struggling to avoid a cluster of claws. A furry and growling mass bounded past me, tail slapping me upside the face. Spitting fur, I crouched against the wall. "Brandon," I gasped. "Katy's out there——" The wolf bared his teeth at me and disappeared into the fray. There was no sign of Phineas except for a pile of white hair and a few choice blood splatters.

"Abby, come with me." Hard fingers curled above my upper arm.

"Topher?" I shot him an incredulous look. "This is madness. You have to stop it."

He shrugged with weary acceptance. "I cannot, but if you leave with me, the rest will retreat."

I hesitated, watching in horror as the tattered remains of my friends were encircled by the daemons. Brystion and Robert were back-to-back, Robert still swinging his sword and Brystion slamming the business end of a mic stand like a club, an unconscious Phineas cradled in one arm. For a moment they were frozen in time, and I marveled—two sides of the same coin, each an exact opposite on the Paths. Topher nudged me again. "They're outnumbered. Come with me and they'll survive. *He'll* survive."

"How do I know this isn't a trap?"

"Don't be stupid," he murmured. "Of course it's a trap." His mouth curved into a lopsided smile, all the more painful for remembering it bestowed upon me in friendship. Or so I'd thought.

"Fine." I spat the words between gritted teeth. "Call them off."

"Good girl." He raised his head, some tiny gesture fluttered at his side, and the fighting stilled. The daemons retreated a pace, weapons raised to the defensive. They surrounded Topher and me, their backs to us as though flanking us like flower petals made of blades. Questioning glances spiked toward us, echoed by sighs and groans and a sobbing gurgle from the floor.

A throbbing began beating at my temples. I swallowed and turned away from the carnage. The pixie huddled in the corner, one gossamer wing bent defiantly. A golden spill of hair was cradled in Brandon's lap, the werewolf's eyes haunted and sorrowful. It lanced me to the core, the accusatory anguish nestled there, but I'd already done what I could. Still, it smacked of betrayal, even to myself. Topher's fingers dug into my shoulder, and I spoke. "Brystion, Robert—put your weapons down."

The two men stared at us, neither lowering their guard. Topher cleared his throat, his smile broadening. "Everyone ease up. She's coming along quietly."

"Abby, no!" Brystion's eyes widened, his face disbelieving. "You cannot go with him." He took a step toward the bar, ignoring the daemons' weapons as they pressed tight against his chest.

Topher's mouth tightened. "You're TouchStoned to him, aren't you?"

I hesitated, my gaze meeting Brystion's for half a second. He snarled, but nodded once.

"That won't do," Topher mumbled to himself. "Goddamned KeyStones." He jabbed something sharp against my throat. My eyes pressed down, catching sight of the jeweled pommel of an elaborate dagger. "Maurice will not be pleased at your insubordination, *incubus*."

The world froze, chilling me in the depths of my bones. My focus found Brystion's midnight gaze, but the flash of admission had already come and gone. The last piece of the puzzle slammed into place. Beside him, Robert growled a heated promise of death.

Bile choked my throat and I retched, swallowing back the urge to vomit. "No," I whispered, my knees starting to buckle, images of this morning playing through my head. My skin twitched in response, recoiling.

"Break the Contract." Topher shifted, impatient with my histrionics.

The edge of the knife sliced at my neck. "I don't know

how. There isn't one." I gasped, the pain clearing my senses.
I had a different sensation to channel—ice exploding into a
burning rage.

He frowned. "Maurice never said anything about that.
State it aloud that you release him, then. It might hurt you,"
he conceded. "Possibly kill him, but I think you'll live." His
face grew closer to mine. "You'd better live."

"Funny words for a guy who's threatening to slice my
throat," I retorted.

"I can cut you pretty badly and you'll live for a while,"
he pointed out. "Don't make me." His words were cold, but
his eyes . . . his eyes were white and open and pleading. "I'm
begging you," he whispered. "Break it, Abby."

I spared a glance back at Bryston, my upper lip curling. "Pie crust promise," I spat. "Easy to make and easy to
break." He winced, but I was past caring. "The bond has
been satisfied. I release you." A snapping sound like the
crack of a whip hit my ear and I shuddered. Bryston let
out a choked growl, backing away. The sight of it pierced
through me, despite my anger. "Looks like I should have
trusted my Heart after all," I muttered.

His head jerked up as though he'd been struck, but before
I could say anything more, Topher grabbed a hank of my
hair. "Good enough, honey. Let's go." He pulled me along
behind him, the daemons slowly falling in after us. Topher
grimaced and then shook his head. "On second thought, I
don't think you need to be awake for this."

I struggled, wanting to bite the smirk from his face.
"Asshole."

"Probably," he shrugged. And then the dagger hilt arced
by my face, an explosion of pain slamming into the side of
my skull. I had a dull vision of Bryston being held back by
Robert, and then the darkness swept me away and I knew
nothing.

✳ ✳ ✳

Wet.

A soft squelching bristled distantly in my ears. It should have been a gentle, soothing sound, but my head was on fire, my ears ringing with pain. There was a hollow roaring in the distance, accompanied by a cool dampness on my forehead and another wet spot on my cheek. "Mmmmph," I whispered hoarsely. I tried to open my eyes, but they were stuck together.

"Hush," Topher's smooth voice trembled. The moist blotting motion on my skin came faster now. "Nearly done, so please lie still."

"The hell I will," I croaked. I wrenched open my eyes, as flakes of . . . something . . . floated past my face. I tried to sit up, but my limbs refused to obey. Confused, I looked past my torso. My head felt very far away as I realized I was tied down. My legs were bound together at the ankle with duct tape and again at the thighs and knees. And I was naked.

I blinked for a moment as this information assimilated itself in the hazy remainder of my mind, glancing down again to confirm it. "Son of a bitch!" My arms were loosely bound behind me, and easy enough to pull apart, but the artist held them in a grip of iron.

"That's quite enough of that," he scolded. "You'll spoil the paint."

"The what?" I could only stare dumbly as he gestured at the mirror on the wall. Naked indeed. Bound. There was dried blood all over my temple, from where I assumed the fucker had cold-cocked me, a grim reminder of what had kept my eyes shut. Topher held a paintbrush and he'd clearly been running it down my flesh, but whatever was on the bristles was clear and shining and not really a color at all. Goose bumps broke out all over me.

"This how you get your kicks?" My upper lip curled.

"Did you have fun raping me?" In truth, aside from my head and the discomfort of being tied I didn't feel too bad, but I wasn't just going to sit here meekly. Besides, the angrier I got the less likely I was going to think of Brystion, and based on the knot in my chest right now that would be a very good thing.

"What do you take me for?" He sniffed. "I merely needed you to be still so I could finish my work."

"And I needed to be nude for that?" I spat at him, baring my teeth when he backhanded me across the face. His eyes widened and for a moment he seemed completely mad, but there was nothing mad about the way his jaw clenched, or the purely clinical way his vision strolled over my prone limbs. I rolled the blood in my mouth, not particularly interested in his answer.

"Yes, well, I assure you, there's nothing I'm interested in less than ravaging *you*," he sneered. "I've got a much bigger reward coming. Wasting you on something as pathetic as fleshly needs isn't something I plan to do."

"What is that shit?" I gestured at the paintbrush with an air of disdain.

"Ah," he said delightedly. "Succubus blood, actually." He dipped the brush into a dubious-looking ceramic container. "Very hard to get. Pure muse," he chortled. "Distilled from the source."

My heart clamped around my throat. "Jesus," I whispered. "Is that . . . Sonja's?"

"No, no, no, no," he muttered. "Sonja is the anchor. Can't possibly bleed her. Besides," he sighed, glancing behind me, "I don't think she's going to last too much longer anyway. Best to hurry this up, eh?" He bent forward again, lovingly applying each stroke on my face with a graceful hand.

I shuddered and rolled my head away to see Sonja's

portrait. Her wings drooped in defeat; her eyes were dark and empty. "Oh," I murmured. "I'm so sorry." Regardless of her brother's actions, she clearly had very little choice in the matter and was now paying the price.

"Don't be, my dear." My head snapped toward this new voice, and I frowned at the ancient man limping toward us. "It was the fate she deserved."

"Maurice, I presume?" I kept my voice casual, but I couldn't tear my gaze away from his face. He was so like the picture from Moira's office, but his hair hung long and thin and wispy. Thick eyebrows and sunken cheeks showed the passage of time, but the beetle-bright eyes held a malicious sort of charm.

He leaned heavily on his cane as he bent to peer at me. "Not much to look at now, are you?" He wheezed hard, his rotting teeth glinting from between his lips. I winced at the stink of his breath, which was hot against my cheeks.

"I imagine I've looked better," I admitted, fighting the urge to squirm away. "But then, I suspect the same can be said of you."

His eyes narrowed, but I merely glared back at him. "You think you know it all, don't you? You think that illusion of time she sold you will be worth anything when you go to leave?" A humorless chuckle escaped him, spittle flecking his lips. "You're a KeyStone. The Fae will *never* let you go."

"Jealous, much?"

"You know nothing," he sneered. He glanced over at Topher. The painter studiously looked everywhere but at me. "A moment, if you would."

Topher nodded, carefully placing the brush into a glass cup. "I can't wait too long. If it dries out on her skin too much we won't be able to use it."

Maurice grunted at him, slumping down on an empty

stool as Topher left. The old man's mouth pursed in sad amusement. "You put up quite the fight, you know. Far greater than the other two. Hell, even Moira hardly managed anything at all. Rather pathetic for a Protectorate, wouldn't you say? Although, given her condition . . ."

"Moira," I gasped, turning my head to where he pointed. The other paintings leaned haphazardly against the wall. Charlie's was the same as I remembered, but her eyes were widened in panic, one hand pressed up against the canvas. And Moira was . . .

"Pregnant," I whispered. The elven woman sat before her mirror. The same one as in the bookstore, in fact, one hand cupped around the swell of her belly. Her face held an infinite sadness—anger and hurt lurking within—mixed with a mother's tender ferocity.

"She wasn't showing when Topher painted her," Maurice said, his dark eyes boring into me. "That started after the fact. I'm surprised she's even managed to carry it this far. But I suppose I have you to thank for that, my dear. You're quite the TouchStone, from what I hear. I wonder where all that lovely power comes from, eh?" His voice was low and crooning as he lowered his mouth to mine. "I could take it, you know. I know how . . . perfection in the art of removal."

I recoiled and then thought better of it. Slamming my head forward I clamped down on his lips, tearing at them in feral satisfaction when he screamed. He punched me in the head, wiping away the blood on his chin, the tattered remains of his lower lip ragged at the corner of his mouth. "You filthy bitch!"

I blinked owlishly, my body stiffening as I retreated into myself.

I was dimly aware of him standing over me, a litany of profanities showering me like snow, but I was past hearing and certainly past doing anything about it. For a moment it felt like I was standing at a very great distance, watching him slap my face, screaming something about not dying on him yet. Inwardly, I smirked. *Not likely.*

Spittle and blood spattered his lips, dripping in my mouth. Abruptly, my body relaxed and I shuddered, pain racking my limbs as I was shoved back into place.

"Stop . . . shaking . . . me," I mumbled.

Maurice slumped. "Join me," he said suddenly. "You're a KeyStone. If you were free and clear of Moira's influence, you wouldn't be limited to this town, to this life. OtherFolk would trip over themselves trying to Contract with you." His mouth slipped into an easy smile. I could see a ghost of an old charm, something he was used to wielding as a weapon. Even at his advanced age it was formidable. "You could name any price you wanted."

My head spun with a muzzy sort of comfort, even though my inner voice was screaming at me to get up. "If that's the case, why would I need to join you at all?" I went to rub my eyes and then realized I was still tied up and settled for rolling my face against the table. "Let's cut the crap and pretend we're never going to work together and move on. What do you really want?"

He gave me a sour look before glancing up at Moira's painting. "How much do you know of the Faery Court? How it works?"

I stifled a snort. "Nada. There's a Queen. Everyone is scared shitless of her. That's it."

He bared his jagged teeth at me, and spun away to pace in front of Moira's painting. His feet slapped hard against the linoleum. I had the distinct impression this was something he'd done a number of times. There wasn't a trench burned into the floor or anything, but the rhythm of his legs spoke volumes.

"Why?" he muttered at Moira. "You aren't as stupid as all that to choose an untrained child." He paused in front of the Fae woman, her cold eyes glittering down at him. "What is she to you?"

"Good question," I slurred, my eyes growing heavy. "If she answers you, let me know. In the meantime, I've got places to go and people to do—so if you wouldn't mind moving this along? Otherwise, I might just have to die of boredom to escape."

"The Steward," he snapped. "The Steward is always mortal. But to think she was grooming *you* for such a thing is laughable."

"I get that a lot," I retorted dryly. I knew a steward ran the day-to-day stuff for a king or queen, at least as far as medieval terminology went, but what would that have to do with me? Or Maurice, for that matter. "I don't get it. I haven't even been to Faery." I paused, as it suddenly struck me. "TouchStones. The Steward is the Faery Queen's TouchStone?" I snorted. "You don't aim small, do you?" He stepped toward me and I hurried to change the subject.

"What about Brystion?" The words slipped out before I could stop them.

"What about him? I hadn't realized he would prove so tenacious. But he did what he was supposed to—more or less." He sneered at me. "You were merely a complication— and quite clearly an easy one to remedy."

I blanched, remembering Brytion's words to me on the dock. Hatred sparked to life in my chest. *This is a complication I don't need, Abby.* Shamed at my idiocy, I turned away. He'd known all along . . . and yet I'd fallen for it.

"I'm sorry to interrupt, but if we don't get this finished the paint will be wasted." Topher slid up next to us with an apologetic simper.

"Very well." Maurice stared down at me for a long

moment and then shook his head. "I don't think we'll be getting anything out of this one. Let me know when it is done." He shuffled out of the room, leaving Topher to reclaim his seat.

"I trusted you," I said softly, hoping I might be able to convince him to let me go. "We all did."

Topher's hands stilled for a moment. "I know. And I also know that it doesn't matter what I tell you right now, but I do have my reasons for it." He slopped another slimy trail across my cheek, chewing on his tongue as he concentrated. He bound my wrists tighter this time, draping a sheet over my prone form.

"Why? Why are you doing this?" My gaze flicked to Sonja. "You were her TouchStone. How could you do that to her?"

He studied his hands. "I can't paint anymore," he said finally, putting the brush down. The handle struck the edge of the table with a ring of finality. Sighing, he picked up a rag and started tying it over my face, covering my eyes. "So they don't get damaged," he explained.

Damaged from what? Fear swept over me.

Keep him talking, Abby . . .

Trying to keep the tremble from my voice, I turned my head toward him casually. "Bryston said you couldn't paint," I agreed. "Looks like he was right." The hot stink of Topher's breath brushed against my ear as he tightened the rag.

"Watch yourself." The lilt in his voice became dangerous and feral. I'd touched a nerve. "But as to why I'm doing this?" A sad chuckle escaped him and in my blindfolded state it was like I could hear every rattled nuance of it, from the way it guttered in his mouth to the low vibrato in his chest. "I owe Maurice a debt."

"Must be one hell of a debt." I choked, hysteria

threatening to bubble over. "What'd you do? Welch on a bet?"

"I had pancreatic cancer," he said shortly. "He had the cure. A cure," he corrected himself. There was the sound of liquid sloshing, something grating on the floor. "And pay my debts, I have. The cost for my life was my talent." His laughter was humorless. "I'm not sure how fair the trade was, honestly, but I am alive, so there is that. Tell me something, Ms. Sinclair—are you so ready to stare death in the face that you wouldn't give up everything you had to jump at the chance of being able to live?"

The hairs on the back of my neck prickled. The words were so close to what Bryston had said to me just a few hours ago. "Once I might have said yes," I said slowly. "But to betray those I love to do it? I'd rather die."

"And so you shall," he said amiably. "Not right away, of course," he assured me, patting my cheek. "In fact, I imagine it will take a rather long time, most likely through starvation. I doubt you'll last as long as Sonja though." I heard the smug pride in the words, and I fought back the urge to vomit.

"Are you going to capture Melanie now?" My lips moved numbly, trying not to babble.

"No point. Last night was a clusterfuck of rather epic proportions, due in no small part to *you*. But no matter," he said. There was a note of doubt rippling beneath the cocky tone of his words. "Her violin was really all we needed, wasn't it? I'm sure she won't last too long after we destroy it."

"But why capture any of us at all? Maurice already had Moira."

He looked at me as though I was daft. "Control," he answered softly. "What better way to make sure Robert behaved himself than to capture you and Charlie? Or to try to bribe his way into the Faery Court?"

In answer I lashed out with my feet, wriggling like a worm on the sidewalk, burning with the need to smash his face in.

"Now, now," he admonished. "Are you ready? This won't hurt a bit. Or maybe it will, but in either case, I'm sure I don't care. You're the last of them and as soon as you're finished I'm out of here and heading for a beach somewhere. Fuck the lot of you."

"Talentless hack," I spat.

"It's true now, but then at least I'll be alive. Off you go." His fingers dug into my hip and my shoulder, heaving my body with a slight grunt.

I was falling. In a matter of seconds, I was unable to see, everything felt like it was moving in slow motion. The sweat of my fear stung the cut on my head, my eyes burned with rage and unshed tears, and a wretchedness of shame at my own stupid ignorance.

I didn't have time to think on it. I plunged into something cold and fluid. It wasn't quite water and it smelled a bit like the succubus blood on the paintbrush, but more elastic. Instinctively I kicked, flailed, and my mouth clenched tight. Topher gripped my head and held it beneath the surface. To breathe was death; my heart lurched painfully against my ribs. I could hear him shouting something, but it was all a fog as my senses dulled, faded. Liquid poured in through my nose and mouth.

Air! My body was screaming for it, but there wasn't any, and still the artist pushed me down. Then I was sinking, everything fading into black. Something battered at the edges of my consciousness, images of Bryston and his gleaming golden eyes filling my senses, and my heart shattered.

Twenty-three

Nothing but darkness, cold and velvet black. It was quiet and comforting; my mind felt sluggish as I curled around myself like some kind of fetus, cradled in the dark womb of the ocean. My lungs stung with each shallow breath full of burning pain. It was easier to just lie here in that strange torpor. Something niggled in the back of my mind. Something I needed to do. Someone I needed to save? I closed my eyes and drifted away, rocked to sleep in the shelter of the cool waves.

Abby.

I rolled over, brushing the seaweed from my face.

Abby.

The voice was getting persistent. Who was it? I was sure I knew. My eyes fluttered open. Everything was as it should be. Cool. Blue. Softly lit. Protective and safe. I closed my eyes again, nestling into the soft scales of my tail, and gently told the voice to hush. I was a mermaid, like I'd always been. I rolled back into the welcoming shadows.

* * *

Abby.

The voice nudged me again. I stretched, ignoring the way it still hurt to breathe. I didn't know how much time had passed in the darkness. A haziness wafted over me as I swayed back and forth, weightless and quiet.

Wake up, Abby.

The voice was softer now, pleading and desperate. What was I supposed to do? It hovered on the edge of my memory, dangling like a worm on a hook.

You seem to be doing an awful lot of sleeping considering you're a mermaid. Maybe Topher should have painted you as a sloth, the voice muttered dryly in my mind. It was delicate and feminine and vaguely sarcastic, but there was a brittleness to it.

Who are you? I thought back, not pondering on the ridiculousness of having a silent conversation with myself.

There was a pause. *Sonja.*

"I don't know any Sonja," I retorted aloud.

For someone who's sleeping with my brother, you're not very bright. And to be perfectly honest, I don't care if you know me or not. But we need you, Abby, so please wake the fuck up.

"Brother? What brother?" Everything was jumbled. And then I froze. "Brystion?"

Bingo! No, wait, Abby—don't do that!

Too late. The memories came pouring in, my blood suddenly churning, as I pushed through the membrane of the blue pearl encapsulating me, feeling its slimy walls reclosing in my wake. I glanced up, up, up . . . so far up as to see the rolling of the breakers and the shadow of a ship. Up, up, up. My tail flicked, propelling me forward, my heart longing for the surface and the man that was surely waiting for me. My love, my—

I shrieked silent bubbles as the first grazing slide of teeth sliced into my arm. Ebony red blood billowed like falling silk from the injured limb. I gazed at it incomprehensibly, and then twisted away as another cut of pain shredded the base of my tail. Sharks—great whites, hammerheads, tigers . . .

Nightmares.

My lips formed the word as my mind screamed at me to move, swim, do *something*. I couldn't see anything in the blackness, couldn't find anything but the pearl down below, welcoming me, winking its blue light like on the porch back home.

Hurry, hurry, hurry . . .

I kicked my fins, graceful even through the pain. Shadows everywhere, sharp and vicious, nothing but hungry mouths and gaping maws, silver-gray dorsals cutting through the water like living blades—coming for *me*. Those hideous dark eyes were dead and lifeless and utterly without mercy. Sobbing, I pressed onward, my hands scraping at nothing, pulling myself through the weighted thickness of the pearl.

It swallowed me up. I nestled at the bottom, staring as the shadows neared, circled, and then swept by. Safe.

Idiot.

"I didn't know," I said, my voice marred and hollow-sounding in the water. My arms folded around my shoulders, my mouth sucking numbly at the wound on my wrist. The blood tasted salty, foul.

I tried to tell you. Sonja sounded weaker, more distant, than before.

"I'm sorry. I'm so sorry." I was babbling, my mouth running, running, running, trying to match the litany of thoughts in my head. Who was I apologizing to? Bryston's face slipped past and I paused. Where was he? Was he starving? Lost? Waiting for me? I thought of the Heart of my Dreaming, pictured him standing there, outside a dark and dusty house. I shivered as he raised his head, eyes dull and lifeless, as the sharks swam around me.

Betrayer.

The image washed away in a flush of anger.

"Where am I?" My brow furrowed as I wrapped my hands around my bleeding tail, trying to staunch the blood with some seaweed. It burned. I hissed with the sting, eyeing another cautious shadow as it floated by. Instinctively, I crouched away from it. Everything seemed so horribly familiar about this, like I'd been here forever, a mermaid enclosed in a blue pearl at the bottom of the sea. Waiting for . . . ships . . .

"Painting," I breathed. "I'm in the motherfucking painting."

Memories crashed down around me, the last few days flashing by—the incubus, the unicorn, the bookstore, Moira. I glanced around the pearl, fury and anguish racking through my chest. It wasn't safety; it was a goddamned prison. I lashed out at it, watching as my fist punched through the filmy surface. Immediately, a shadow approached, not hurrying, merely watching. Waiting.

I waggled my fingers at it, pulling them back hastily as it sped toward me. Painting or not, I had *no* desire to find out what would happen if I actually lost limbs or bled to death here. I pushed back a strand of tangled hair in impatience.

Well, at least you're not a crier. The other one wouldn't stop wailing long enough for me to get a word in edgewise. Sonja's voice echoed dimly in my mind, her tone dry.

"I do my best," I shot back, tightening up the seaweed bandage over my tail. The scales were marvelous, silver and gleaming, but I couldn't bear to look at them. They were just an illusion, after all. The thought was bitter in my mouth.

"So now what?" I peered into the darkness outside the pearl. "And what do you mean, the 'other one?' "

The angel's girl. His TouchStone. She went a bit mad, I think. The voice paused. *Not that we all haven't, but I think they roughed her up pretty good.*

"We who? And why can't I hear her?"

She's gone . . . silent. They both have. The succubus paused again, but this time the silence became ominous.

"Are they dead?" I could hardly get the words out, but I had to ask. "They can't be, can they? I mean Moira can't— wouldn't I feel it?"

Probably. But it depends on the closeness of the bond. They're just . . . elsewhere. They have retreated into themselves, like you did when you first got here. Moira needed to concentrate on her baby. Charlie just couldn't hack it. Though maybe it was the ghosts that did her in.

I shook my head. "English, please. This whole thing effs up my head."

Explanations are hard to come by in this place, the succubus snorted, *but I'll do the best I can. You're correct in assuming you're in the painting. You are. In fact, if you concentrate hard enough you can actually look out of it and see through to the other side.*

Startled, my gaze shot up. "How?" I demanded as I squinted into the darkness.

Relax and try to—oh, shit, I don't know—try to become one with the canvas. It happens that way for me.

"Ooohhhhmmmm," I muttered sarcastically while I eased my tail beneath me, slumping as I stared at the inner walls of the pearl. My vision drifted after a bit, following the glowing patterns rippling on its surface. There. I blinked and suddenly I was flat. Horribly flat, in fact. Everything went hazy and warped as I stared around the edges of Topher's art studio. A dim light burned in the corner; the tub he'd drowned me in was empty.

Drowned.

I felt sick, the churning waves of nausea burning a hole in my stomach. I retreated from the wall, my awareness slowly shifting back to the pearl. "That's awful."

Tell me about it. I've been trying to get your attention for days now, but no one could see me in the damn thing. I could see all of you just fine. And my damn brother and his damn shields. I've never been able to get through them, even when we were younger—but the thing he had thrown around you was damn near impenetrable.

"Shield? Oh, you mean when he was protecting me from my nightmares? Yeah, that was part of our . . . deal." I swallowed the bitterness of *that* particular thought.

Damned inconvenient time for him to get all chivalrous, she snorted. *I had to wait until you had that seizure to get anything through—and even then I did a fuck job of it.*

"I wouldn't say that," I said, remembering the way the feathers had cut into my hands. "We took notice, anyway. Not that it's helped us any." My finger drifted along the wall of the pearl. "Too little, too late."

Sonja's brittle laughter echoed past me. *Truer words have not yet been spoken. And I should have seen it coming.*

"Topher said he was your TouchStone," I said cautiously. "I thought that meant you would always know where he was."

I'm not my brother. Whatever connection the two of you have is a personal thing. I've never felt the need to check up on my TouchStones.

"How does that work? I thought all of you traded sex for something."

Not hardly, my dear. I've no real interest in sleeping with Topher. Although he has a certain charm about him, it's his talent that I'm interested in. Or was. He's merely a shadow of himself now. Sad, really.

Her voice held a certain dispassion, but I couldn't help

but wonder at the odd little tremble behind it. I wasn't going to press the issue though. It wasn't any of my business, and I've never been one for caring about other people's sex lives, metaphysical or otherwise.

"That's what Bryston meant," I murmured, "when he said Topher couldn't have painted these pictures, that you would never have sat for him willingly."

Oh, I sat for him willingly in the beginning. But the chains here are real enough, in their own way. I heard a distant clinking and shuddered, knowing how much they had to pain her. She chuckled again, as though reading my mind. *Yes. They hurt. Exquisitely. It's my own reward though. I thought I could help him, thought I might make a difference. But in the end, I became the anchor for his madness. Ironic, no?*

"But just what is it that he's doing? Or really, what is Maurice trying to do? I'm not sure they're the same thing."

Maurice clearly has a bone to pick with Faery. Whatever he's trying to do, he's been trying it for a while. The paint . . . somehow he figured out a way to use succubus blood as a base for the painting. As far as I know, I was the only successful exchange. My sisters . . . died.

There was burning hatred behind her words, and I knew that if she ever made it out of here alive, the artist would probably not last long in the world. Not that I could blame her. Cure for cancer or not, there was such a thing as honor, and none of this struck me as particularly honorable, especially given the sacredness of the bonds between OtherFolk and their TouchStones.

Still, I thought of my mother and the way she'd died, and Bryston's words echoed back to me. Would I give up what I was for another chance at somehow bringing my mother back to life? Moira's wish hovered just out of reach, teasing me with its closeness.

"That's different," I muttered. "I'm not going to kill anyone for it." And yet—what *would* I do to set things back? "The past can't be changed," I said savagely, my heart aching.

I wrapped my arms about my tail, rocking back and forth. "So how do we get out of here? And for that matter, where are we? Aside from the painting thing. We can't just be trapped in the canvas." I breathed deeply as I watched the shadowed sharks. "I'm bleeding pretty well for just being some cadmium red."

So many questions.

She was getting irritated with me. I could understand that, but I needed more information. After all, not knowing enough is what got me into this mess in the first place.

We're in some kind of Shadow Realm. It's small and contained, just a pocket tethered on the CrossRoads somewhere, but it's not . . . normal. We seem to almost be in the Dreaming, but the paintings only have one-way Doors. And no, there's no way out. It's completely sealed as far as I can tell. She paused. *And oddly enough, I think you and I are TouchStoned, though I can't imagine how.*

"The feathers," I said. "I ended up touching you and we linked. I'm a KeyStone, you know."

Huh. I thought Maurice was lying about that. For all the good it does us. Guess we can just sit around and jabber at each other until one of us starves to death.

I shook my head. "No. There has to be a way out."

She didn't answer and I realized her attention was fixed on something else. I stilled, outside voices reaching my clogged ears.

"I know she's here, you lying piece of shit." Bryston stepped into view, dragging Maurice behind him. Both of them looked like they'd seen better days. The incubus in particular was sporting a bloody contusion on the underside of his chin.

"Bryston," I breathed, pressing myself up against the edge of the pearl. Anger and hurt and disgust at my desperation shot through me. He'd *used* me. Seduced me. Lied to me. *Betrayed* me.

On the other hand, I was stuck inside a painting.

I decided I had no shame when it came to trying not to die. I pounded my side of the canvas. "Please," I cried. "I'm here. I'm in here!"

He can't hear you, Sonja said glumly. *I've been trying for ages, like I said.*

"We'll just see about that," I muttered, opening my mouth to scream again.

Hush! I want to hear what's going on.

I tucked my aching tail under me and leaned closer.

Maurice's words garbled as though his mouth were stuffed with cotton, but judging by the look on Bryston's face I knew nothing good was said.

"There's nothing you can do, incubus. They're all beyond your reach, and once Sonja dies, the Shadow Realm will close forever." The old man leered up at Ion, his mouth splitting wide in a toothy, blood-smeared grin. "Whatever you do to me, she'll be dead, either way. They all will."

Bryston's eyes narrowed. "Where is she?"

"Right in front of you, of course," came the mocking retort. "Where she's always been."

Bryston glanced at Sonja, turning away with a hiss. "Motherfucker." His eyes flicked toward mine, pain flooding me as our gazes met. It sounds stupid—I was in the painting after all—but he stepped toward me, his fingers curling at his sides. Even through the fishbowl I could see them clench and unclench, biting into the rivets of his jeans. "What have you done to her?" he said hoarsely.

"Like that, do you?" Maurice chortled. "She ran into

some of my little pets, as you can see. They don't fuck around, do they?"

"All that blood . . ." Brystion's eyes blazed as he reached up to touch my painting.

Maurice shrugged. "The fun part is that they're of her own making, you know. Succubus blood seems to have this delightful way of bringing one's nightmares into reality. A real bonus to have discovered that particular trait, don't you think?" He elbowed Brystion, ignoring the way the other man's jaw tightened.

"This was *not* part of the bargain," Brystion said hoarsely. "My sister for the TouchStone of the Protectorate, yes, but you promised me you wouldn't hurt her. Just hold her for a bit. Not this . . . perversion."

"A fine one you are for talking bargains," Maurice spat. "Why don't we ask Hzule what the original Contract was for? Oh, wait, you killed him, don't you remember?" His smirk deepened. "Fell in love, did you, daemon? I'm sure it will sting a bit once she's dead, but I imagine you'll get over it. Your kind always does. Besides, I have nothing to do with her pain." He waved his hand carelessly at me, his mouth a sly curve. "She controls how much power they have over her. Apparently, they have a lot more than I reckoned for. But that's all right."

What is he talking about?

"Your *brother* set us up." I bit down on my lip, ignoring the little billow of blood spilling from my mouth. "I thought he was trying to find a way to release you. Apparently I was the price; I guess you don't come cheap," I snorted. I shouldn't have been surprised though. After all, he *had* told me he would do anything to save her. But it still hurt like a bitch.

The incubus stiffened at Maurice's words. "You know *nothing* about it, old man."

Maurice coughed, his gnarled hands pushing back his thinning gray hair. Pointing a trembling hand at Moira, he shook his head. "That bitch is carrying my child. She *owes* me. You think I *wanted* to age like this? Love, hell." His gaze turned wistful. "How many years did I serve you faithfully? How long did you plan on deceiving me with your Faery lies? Did you think I would just stand by and let you replace me with some . . . some interloper? The Stewardship belonged to *me*. All you had to do was keep me by your side. We could have had the world at our feet," he said softly.

Moira obviously said nothing, but damned if a flicker of something didn't spark in the depths of her eyes. Her hands tightened on her belly, her mouth thinning.

"She can hear you," Brystion said wonderingly.

"Of course she can," Maurice snorted. "They all can. Even your little mermaid."

Ion turned toward me, something pleading in his face. "I know you probably can't forgive me, Abby, but I had no choice." I made a *hmmmph* sound in the back of my throat. I'd heard *that* one before. He tipped his forehead so it rested on mine. "I have no regrets, save this."

Goddess, he's into you. Sonja's thoughts flitted by me like the buzzing of bees, a mixture of envy and sisterly protectiveness. On impulse, I pressed up against the canvas, willing him to feel me, willing him to pull me through. He stared at me for a moment before letting his hand drop.

"Set them free." His voice fell to a low whisper. "I'll do anything you want, if you set them free."

Maurice's eyes narrowed, one hand drifting up to cup Brystion's chin. "Will you now? I wonder if an infusion of incubus blood might not sweeten the deal. Or perhaps that lovely sexual Glamour. Who knows what magics I might be able to work with such a thing."

Brystion's gaze never wavered from mine, but his

nostrils flared ever so slightly. "Whatever you need," he said dully.

"Let's go discuss it elsewhere. Little rabbits have big ears, you know," Maurice murmured, his fingers sliding to the back of Brystion's neck. The incubus stiffened, but allowed himself to be led out the door.

My head snapped toward Moira's painting. "Wake up! You have to wake up!" I thought she stirred, but it was only for a moment and then she settled back into stillness. I punched through the pearl in frustration. I heard Sonja sigh, and I glared in her direction. "Knock it off. We have to do something."

What do you want me to do? I've tried everything I can so far.

"Not good enough," I snarled. "If Melanie were here she could make us a Door."

If she had her violin. And knew where the hell we were.

"And her hand wasn't busted," I added. I paused, tapping my fingers on my hip. "I don't suppose you saw what they did with it?"

He locked it away. I suspect Maurice is going to try to bribe Melanie with it. He's rather manipulative, if you hadn't noticed. A strange sense of excitement hovered beneath the words. *Do you think she could do it, if she had the violin?*

"I don't know. How hard would it be to make a Door into a Shadow Realm? If we're partially in the Dreaming, would Doors even work here?"

Making Doors is tricky . . . you need a focus of sorts, especially if you've never been there. Even if she had her violin, how would she know what to look for?

I glanced up sharply, trying to remember Moira's painting. The creepy mirror. "She'll have one," I said grimly. "The mirror in Moira's painting is real. It's in the Pit. If Melanie uses that for her focus, she might be able to call one up that way. And then, if the paintings are connected somehow, maybe we could move between them."

Someone strong in the Dreaming might—or a creature of it. Hells, if it weren't for the chains, I could do it. But even if I did, there's no way out.

Her words rolled about my head. "I'm a Dreamer," I said finally. "According to your brother, anyway. But I don't know how to manipulate my own dreams, let alone a place like this."

Bummer.

"I'm your TouchStone right? That means you can touch my dreams?"

Yes, but I already told you, the shields—

"Are no longer there," I interrupted. I paced back and forth in the pearl, blood agitating around me. "I broke my TouchStone bond with Brystion, so we should be free and clear. Can you reach the Heart of my Dreaming?"

She paused. *Yes, I think I could, being that we are connected. But you'd have to be asleep for that. And to what end?*

"If it were that simple you would have been able to escape when I was asleep before. And I don't think it's quite the same here." I exhaled abruptly, bubbles whirling away in the darkness. "What if I could pull you through? To where I am, without the chains?"

Without the chains? Yes, I think I could slip into your Heart from here. But how?

"Brystion and I. We, uh, discovered that I could pull him out of the Dreaming when we were, uh, you know," I added hastily.

She snorted. *That's a bit different. High emotion, sexual energy—these things will often open a conduit. What did you have in mind? Planning on bedding me?* A hint of amusement crossed over and I frowned.

"If I have to. Although I'm not sure how I'd do that from

here. No," I sighed, "I'm going to have to find some other emotion to pull you through."

What emotion is that?

I looked back through the pearl, the mere whisper of a shadow flicking by.

"Fear."

Twenty-four

It was quiet when I slipped out of the pearl, the heaviness of the sea bearing down upon my hapless form. I was going to have to embrace the mind-numbing terror, the inner coward that I had become. It was part of me, after all.

It was time to submerge myself in the aching realms of my nightmares and willingly seek all that I had shut out in the hopes it would be enough to free the succubus. If Sonja could get to the Heart of my Dreaming, she'd be able to leave, to escape to the CrossRoads.

That was the theory, anyway. I didn't want to think what the reality might be.

You realize that once I leave here, the anchor will be gone and this Shadow Realm will drift? You could be lost forever.

"*You* realize you're dying and we're going to be stuck in that boat regardless," I retorted. "At least this way, even if it doesn't work, I'll know I tried *something*. It's the best chance we've got." *Except for Brystion*, my mind reminded me. I told my mind to shut the hell up. "Are you ready?" I wasn't even sure who I was asking, but I said it anyway.

Yes.

My heart pounded against my rib cage, and I swallowed

hard, flicking my tail in rapid succession. Up and up and up. My lower half undulated out the rhythm and then the shadows loomed before me. Without giving myself time to think, I threw myself directly into the gaping maw of my inner madness, let the shining flash of serrated knives rend the flesh from my bones.

. . . my mother, her head cradled in my lap, blood pouring from her mouth, nothing but an empty husk. Her hair falling out, clumps of brown and pepper, scattering over my legs. Her mouth curled into a rictus of a grin, her front teeth broken and ragged. "Empty," she whispered, her breath rattling in a singsong whistle . . .

. . . Me, standing on the stage, staggering. My knee giving out beneath me, bone splintering as the flash of spotlights sheared across my vision, the crowd gasping. The first row sitting there like zombies, waxen and unmoving, as my head hit the floor. My skull splitting, the metal dented open, and the maggots pouring out . . .

. . . Me, alone in the Heart of my Dreaming. The house is empty and dark. I call out someone's name, but there is no answer. Something moves. "Brystion?" His golden eyes flicker over me with contempt, his upper lip curled. "Your dreams are dead," he mutters. "And so are you." He turns away, fading as he walks behind the house, the silver glitter of the CrossRoads taking him. "Don't leave me," I sob. "Please don't leave me alone . . ."

A flash of light burst through my head, gold and bronze and scarlet, like sharp needles behind my eyes. The clink of iron falling away to the floor. A beating of tattered wings buffeted my face, something warm in my arms. Sonja's dark gaze was grave as she leaned forward. Her mouth brushed over mine, the barest hint of tongue on my lips, and then she was gone in a haze of feathers, the water around me bleeding with them.

I sank, slipping away from the circling sharks, my bones hanging from their mouths. I was being devoured, my life shredded, my dreams disintegrated. Raw and exposed beneath their attack, I no longer cared.

"Moira," I called out softly as the sharks pressed me back down toward the pearl. "I'm done." If she stirred at all, I didn't notice. I just let the soft blue of the pearl envelop me. My eyes closed as I listened to the lullaby of the ocean. The Shadow Realm was adrift now, set free by my own hand. I wondered dimly if I was aging. Had I violated my contract with Moira by traveling beyond the boundaries of Portsmyth? The thought of aging to death in a matter of hours or days made me laugh. A little late to worry about it now, wasn't it? Maybe mermaids were immortal and it didn't matter.

Maybe this was my ticket out of this whole thing. What had Brystion asked me? Would I be willing to give it all up for a chance at normalcy? My fingers trembled and I hunched my shoulders, my hands folded to hug my arms.

"Maybe . . ." I whispered. I could feel the scales from my tail flaking off and drifting away on the tide. The empty places burned and itched, but there was nothing I could do. Rolling over, I let the darkness overcome me, slipping away into a welcoming oblivion.

"Hello, pretty."

I blinked, consciousness dragging to the forefront of my brain. I slid over to the fishbowled canvas, pressing my face against the surface. Dark clouds floated across my vision, making everything blurry. A man stood outside my painting. He seemed vaguely familiar, but . . .

Fuck. It was Maurice. But a young Maurice—robust and

straight-backed. Gone was the thinning hair and sinking jowls, the wrinkled lips and sagging brows. Everything was new and handsome, but his eyes burned horribly cold and hard. He stroked the canvas and I recoiled, even though I knew he couldn't touch me.

"See what you and your lover have given me?" he murmured. "I sucked the incubus dry, and in return I'm supposed to let you go free. But honestly, my dear, I don't think you're going to last too much longer. Seems almost a pity to let you suffer, doesn't it?"

He leaned in close, his voice low; I could almost smell his fetid breath. "Besides, I rather like the idea of Moira watching you die, knowing it's her fault. And bargain or not, I don't mind breaking my word for the sake of revenge." His eyes lingered on Moira's portrait. "She spurned me, you know. I, who was never anything but utterly loyal to her, refused to lift that pathetic geas. The Stewardship should be *mine*." He pursed his lips sensuously and I started, the movement so much like Bryston's as to be a mirror image.

Maurice turned away. "Did you want to see him, usurper? Your poor little daemon? He's quite different now than how you remember. I stripped all that lovely Glamour away—or almost all of it. Pathetic creature is still trying to hold on to his mortal appearance." He motioned down by his feet, and I turned to see . . . something. It was dark skinned and hairy one moment, naked and flesh colored the next, its skin rippling as though something was trying to escape. It was also unconscious.

My mind reeled. "Ion?"

There was a flash of a movement as Maurice turned to look at Sonja's painting. He stood in silence, but the back of his neck flooded red. Furious, he whipped around. "Where is she? Where did that winged bitch go?"

"Like I'd tell you," I sneered, even though he couldn't hear me. With a cry of rage, he leaped toward me and the world turned on its side. He had knocked the painting down. An awful ripping sound filled my ears, and I shrieked as my body stretched out, my skin splitting beneath the force.

With a rumble Bryston lifted off the floor, fingers like claws darting toward Maurice. I opened my mouth to shout, but the words died into silence as Maurice punctured the edges of the canvas with something sharp and shiny. Pain seared through my gut. I recoiled, catching the merest glance of the daemon at the corner of my vision.

"Bryston," I muttered, as a burbling, wet noise gurgled nearby. No—not nearby. From *me*. I wriggled, my tail burning as I tried to pull away. I slumped against the surface, the inside of the canvas, whatever the fuck it was.

"What did you do?" The words jangled in my ears. Bryston's voice—harsh, raspy, terrified, furious.

Maurice's high-pitched laughter cackled past me. "Ah, well. Took steps, I suppose you'd say. Remove the blade and she'll be dead within minutes. Of course," he shrugged, "she's going to die anyway, but now the decision is yours. Free her and kill her, or keep her imprisoned and watch her slowly bleed out." He whirled on Moira's painting. "All this could have been avoided if that stupid bitch had just given me the child."

Bryston snorted, one clawed hand snagging the madman. "I'm going to eat your soul now," he said pleasantly. I shivered, thinking how the daemon assassin had said the same thing to me. Horrified, I watched as Bryston lowered his mouth to Maurice's, his eyes still dark and cold. He would take no pleasure from the act. Their lips touched, and Maurice made a strangled sound, grappling at the incubus's shoulder.

The door banged open behind them, followed by a shriek.

Sonja. But the succubus wasn't alone. Robert and Phineas poured in past her, Roweena close behind. The Faery woman gestured curtly, fingers snapping. The angel launched himself at the two men, solid arms struggling to pull Brystion away. The incubus roared in anger, muscles taut in Robert's meaty grip.

Melanie slid in behind them, her hand surprisingly whole. "I'll be taking my violin now," she said coldly.

"It's destroyed," Maurice spat, wiping the blood from his mouth.

"I'd know if it was, but nice try." She lifted her head, meeting Maurice's gaze with a secret strength. "Shall we make a bargain? Give me my violin and I'll open a Doorway to wherever you want. I'll let you escape."

"There's no need for this," Brystion intoned grimly. "I'll kill him before he makes it past the CrossRoads. He's a dead man."

Phineas stepped between them. "This isn't your vengeance to take," he said. "It's Moira's."

"Look at what he's done to Abby!" Brystion snarled, pointing at me.

"Is she dead yet?" the unicorn asked bluntly, his nose quivering. His horn glowed faintly blue in warning.

"No."

"Then quit wasting time with petty revenge and let's see if we can save her." His eyes flicked toward the other paintings. "Save them all." He looked past Brystion, eyes focusing on something else. "Where's the mirror?"

There was a grunt of assent and then Brandon carried Moira's mirror into view. "You're sure this is going to work?" the unicorn muttered to Sonja.

She shrugged. "It's the best Abby and I could come up

with. We think the paintings are connected in the Shadow Realm. If Melanie can conjure up a Door between them, I think we can pull everyone out."

"Whatever you do, do it fast," I muttered, as pain shot through my midsection. I was openly bleeding now, and the shadows were scraping past the outer membrane of the pearl. "And really, it's not like Charlie has a damn knife in her gut, is it?" Uncharitable maybe, but I was past caring. I shifted, trying to breathe carefully.

Bryston's eyes flicked toward my painting. "I can swim."

"So can I," Robert snarled.

Roweena rolled her eyes. "I'll sign Melanie's Contract to create the Door. We'll get Moira out first and then Charlie. And then, if we can pull the knife out, that should free Abby enough to try to get to the surface."

Phineas took a closer look at the blade, his face close enough that it nearly touched mine. "She's still got plenty of energy." His eyes narrowed at Maurice. "Spitting mad at you though."

"Enough," Bryston snapped. "How do we get the violin, Maurice?"

"It's locked in the chest behind the door," Sonja said, her wings folded behind her. Robert pulled the chest away from the wall. It was small, a bit larger than a standard violin case, but the wood seemed to shiver with an unearthly light. Magic, for sure. "Topher never got a chance to push it into its painting."

Maurice snarled at her. "We had problems with inanimate objects going through the process," he admitted. "I didn't want to risk it just yet, though I suspect the soul trapped inside the thing would have been enough. Not that it makes any difference," he said softly. "It can't be unlocked by mortal means. Not even *I* have the key to open it."

"Somehow I doubt that," Robert retorted.

Melanie glanced up from where she'd been staring at her own painting, a rapt sense of horror and curiosity written across her face. "Shut up a second, all of you." Tracing a finger over the painted mouth of her face, her brow furrowed. "The key," she said slowly. "G-A-G. I thought this was just a joke that Topher played on me . . ."

She stepped back and hummed. An eerie vibration hovered through the room, my bones trembling with it. Maurice paled, his face draining of blood. "That fucking painter!" Melanie's mouth split into a wide smile, the humming becoming a soft croon.

From the corner of the room, the chest shook like some sort of medieval pager, grinding against the floor. Robert smirked over at Maurice. "Seems you had a key, after all."

And there it was, golden and lovely, the heavy gilt of the handle appearing in the lock with a flurry of sparkles.

"Mortal means are my specialty," Melanie said softly, kneeling beside the chest to turn the lock. "There you are," she murmured, pulling out the violin. She held it in the crook of her arm, her fingers caressing the neck tenderly.

"They were notes," Sonja said wonderingly, her eyes brightening. "Can you do it? Can you open the Door?"

Melanie wiggled her fingers. "They're stiff, but they should be able to make it work. They'll tire easily, though, so I don't know how long I'll be able to keep it up." Her shoulders rose apologetically. "The elvish Healer couldn't quite fix it all in such a short time." She ran the bow over the strings, creating a mournful sigh of harmony. One eye cocked open at Maurice. "Tie him up or gag him or something. I'd rather not have him breaking my concentration."

"Easy enough," Robert muttered, slamming Maurice upside the face with a broad fist. Maurice slumped to the floor, putting up no resistance as the angel trussed him quickly.

"All right." Robert moved in front of Moira's painting, bowing slightly. "Mistress, we're going to get you out."

Melanie shut her eyes in concentration. A faint glow crossed the reflection of the mirror, a silver nimbus etched against the dark wood.

"Moira first," Phineas reiterated, "and then Charlie. And then—"

"And then Abby," Brystion said firmly. He knelt down before me. "Nearly there, sweetheart," he murmured. "It's going to hurt when they pull the knife, but I need you to fight, Abby." His finger stroked my cheek. "I'll meet you on the other side. Now, Mel. Open the Door."

Melanie nodded silently and the tune changed.

Phineas whinnied, bugling a challenge. "The mirror in the painting," he shouted. "It's glowing. Go, Ion!"

Brystion wheeled, throwing himself headlong into the real mirror without hesitation. It didn't shatter, but then, I didn't really expect it to. I craned my head to try to see more, but there was only gray, the fishbowl effect growing worse. *So cold* . . . My fingers twitched, numb and icy, but the moment the incubus set foot through the mirror I felt an answering tingle in my blood.

A ripping sound. A grunting wail of pain. Moira crying out. The wavering squall of a newborn baby. Muffled voices raised in anger, wavering at me as though my ears were stuffed with cotton. Shit.

" . . . going back in . . . there's a Door into Charlie's . . ." The remainder of the words faded away. The darkness was closing around me and my breath was slowing. I felt like a goldfish on the floor of a bathroom, each laboring exhalation slamming into my lungs, or maybe gills. Either way, it was sucking majorly.

There was another shredding of canvas, followed by Robert's cry of relief. Sobbing, choking noises—Charlie.

And then there was silence, the world tilting on its edge again. Phin's voice came from nearby, low and even. "Your turn, Abby. Brystion's gone through to get you."

"He's going to look a little . . . different," Sonja's voice interjected. "But don't let it alarm you. " She paused. "I'm going to pull the knife out. We need you to swim up to the ship. That's where he'll be." I made a small sound of alarm and she sighed as though she'd heard me. "The sharks are yours, Abby. They only have as much power over you as you allow."

She took a deep breath. "Three. Two. One."

The knife blade slid out and my body burned in agony.

Twenty-five

Water rushed to fill the empty space left behind by the blade, warmth pouring from me in a flurry of red. Instinctively, I clamped my hand across my belly, my life leaking between my fingers.

"Swim!"

Phin's voice pulled me out of my stupor. Dimly I thought of the story of The Little Mermaid. The original one, where every step was like stepping on knives. Little girl currently had *nothing* on me at the moment. I would gladly have traded fins for feet as opposed to the exquisite gut wound I was now sporting.

I pushed myself through the water, each movement stretching across broken muscle and fiery skin. I wondered if the asshole had stabbed anything really vital. Stupid thing to wonder, given the situation, but calculating how long it was going to take me to get to the surface was at least somewhat safer to think about than . . . them.

The shadows still swarmed above me, but they looked larger and sated. And why wouldn't they be, really? Hadn't they nearly devoured me before? The darkness stretched out, an eternal road of black. I was definitely swimming slower now, but my veins were thrumming, my blood pulsing in an easy cadence. Bryston was above me—he had come for me, was *waiting* for me.

I let the rest of the memories, the pain, and the night-mares go. All of it washed away like mud down a river, eddying and pooling in places, but loosening the tension, setting me free. I pressed onward. The sharks parted for me, fins lazy, eyes dull and dead. One of them still had a mouthful of flesh hanging from its teeth.

It snapped toward me and then away. I cleared my mind of everything but *him*. My body was sluggish, despite the way the cool chill of the water dulled my pain.

Hurry, hurry, hurry. The words drummed again and again until at last I saw it—moonlight through waves, white light filtering down.

The current had taken on a stronger pull than before, the last twenty feet or so in particular. I could feel the swells pushing by me in deep pulses. The waves would be awful up above and for a moment I hovered on uncertainty.

Hurry, hurry, hurry . . .

The ship was heaving wildly, the sky purple and dark. There, wavering on the prow, skin shone in the moonlight, a hand outstretched.

Sonja had said he would look different, but his face was masked in darkness, the wind whipping his image into a frenzy of salt spray. I didn't care. I just wanted to be wrapped up in his arms again, out of the water, out of the shadows. I wanted to be in my own bed with a hot toddy after a warm shower, wrapped in sheets and sex. My mouth trembled with desire, tasting it, longing for it.

I burst through the waves, calling out, a strange warble vibrating from my throat—the delicate song of the siren. Bryston's golden eyes sparked from the shadows; they were brighter than I remembered, vivid and glowing. Another wave swept me up, slamming me into the side of the ship. I clung to the barnacled wood, my fingers slicing open on shellfish and crustaceans. "Traitors," I muttered. So much for the romantic image of the mermaid arising to the edge of the ship on a graceful wave.

"Throw me a goddamned rope!" I wasn't sure if he could hear me, given the howl of the wind, but he signaled my words with a shrug.

"I tried to bring one, but it couldn't come through the mirror." His voice was husky, a midnight fury laced with the metallic edge of bullets. He paused. "Hold on! I've got something here, but it won't be quite long enough, so you're going to have to time it with the waves."

"You'd better not be talking about your dick. I mean, you're well hung and all, but it's a Shadow Realm, not Fantasyland," I snorted, trying not to laugh. The painful burble in my lungs spoke of something worse happening.

"Just take it," he snapped, "and don't ask questions." He turned away, his back showing broad and black. There was the glitter of something white and pointed sweeping up from his head. Horns? Antlers?

"Whatever," I muttered. I'd figure it out once I was safe. Daemonic or not, he could have been farting fire at that point and I wouldn't have cared. Something long and narrow curled over the rail, a frayed handle at the end. I clung to the ship, my head turning to see when the next wave would hit, feeling the ocean gather beneath me, the hull start to descend. I ducked down a bit, releasing the wood. I was going to need a little more *oomph*.

Nervously, I sank a few feet below, gathering my strength. The sharks were nowhere to be seen and inwardly I relaxed. One last hurdle, then. If my nightmares hadn't completely subsided, maybe that last act had put them to rest for a while. I could only hope.

The surge crested and I shot upward, ignoring the pain. The last rush of blood flew from my belly, my tail pumping—quick, quick, quick—matching the beat of my heart. I rode the crest for as long as I dared, airborne as I reached the peak, water falling like rain over my back. Arms outstretched, my fingers brushed the end of the line, clawed at it, yanked on it.

Above, I heard Brystion cry out, felt the rope twist and twitch in my hands. "Oh damn—it's your *tail*." It was soft and slick with the wet, the furry tuft at the end as black as ebony. "Sorry!"

He grunted something I couldn't quite hear, a strained growl echoing past me. He shifted, and slowly I dragged up the last few feet. My fingers curled over the ship's edge, the last of my strength giving way in a rush of relief and pain. Clawed hands grasped my wrist, nails pricking my already lacerated skin, but I hardly felt it. My vision blurred and I blinked against it, trying to focus on his face. "Brystion."

"Shhhh," he murmured, pulling me forward so my upper half was resting on the deck. "I've got you, Abby."

"I hope so," I croaked. "I'd really like to get out of here, if you don't min—"

"Oh, shit!" I caught a flash of hooves and fur, and then there was a horrible shriek, high-pitched and ugly. Was the boat cracking beneath us? No, it was me. *I* was the one screaming. The boat wasn't pitching, I was sliding down the side, some enormous weight pulling me down. Dimly, I craned my neck, dully noting the massive shark tearing into my tail.

"Help me," I whispered, the last of my voice dying as I sank into the darkness of the sea, into the waiting gullet of the Great White. There was a flash of gold above me, ebony skin and hair falling, arms entwined around my shoulders, and then I was gone.

✳ ✳ ✳

. . . *he was pressing me down into the dirt, sharp hooves cutting into my flesh as he kneed my thighs apart. One clawed hand clenched around my neck, the other trailed over my ass, slicing delicately at my tender flesh. He bent down, teeth long and pointed. "You're filthy. A filthy whore, Abby Sinclair." His breath was grass, soft and tender, and all the more wretched for the pain.*

I squirmed, my legs kicking feebly. "None of that, now," he murmured. "I'm going to make you come, you know. You're going to come and come and come, and when I'm finished with you, you'll never come again. How does that sound? And then, I'll eat your soul." He paused, nipping at my ear. "You taste so delicious, Abby."

"Why are you doing this?" My voice was a whimper, pathetic and sad.

"Isn't this what you expected all along?" He chuckled. "Begging me for it? Just dying to see my true form? Well, here it is, Abby. I do hope you aren't disappointed." Thick hair rubbed over my ass, his erection sliding obscenely over the curved ridge of my spine. "Everything you hoped it would be, hmmmm?" He lipped my cheek, curving down to lick my neck.

Dirt caked on my mouth, spit and snot and blood from where I was biting my lips. He laced the other hand through my hair, yanking my head back, exposing my throat. He caressed it gently, and then paused. "Mine," he snarled, my head snapping back farther as he pulled.

"No!" I screamed.

There was a howling cry of anguish beside me. I recoiled, looking back at the daemonic golden eyes, scratching my hands across the black skin as the nightmare dissolved. "Let me go, let me go!"

His fingers were like iron around my wrist, fury dancing

over his face. I blinked and realized we were alone. The sharks were gone. The water was gone. The tail was gone. Just the two of us, naked and alone in the darkness. There was nothing left of his daemonic body—the fur, the hooves—everything was familiar, all pale skin, aching beauty, and haunted eyes.

"No." His muscles quivered beneath my fingers. I couldn't see him in the blackness, but his arms shook. "I will *not* be party to this," he snarled. "Is that how you see me? An animal? A rapist?" His voice lowered, raspy and hurt. "I have never given you a reason to think of me that way."

He shoved me away and we stood there, his eyes dark and ice cold. Sobbing, I wrapped my arms over my chest in a useless measure of modesty. "You used me," I whispered, my stomach burning. I pressed one hand over the wound. "You lied to me. You were going to—"

"Is that what you think?" His face bunched in contempt. "You're a Dreamer, Abby. Your nightmares—your *dreams*—are your *own* doing." He gestured at the darkness. "Even now, I guard you from them."

"I hardly think *that* constitutes guarding," I said, my voice strangled. I rubbed my neck, touching the swollen marks.

"Why do you think the sharks didn't attack you when you swam to me?" His eyes narrowed.

"What the fuck do you call what just pulled me off the ship?" I sank to my knees, my legs giving out at last. He looked at me dispassionately, not even a twitch to show any concern.

"That one—that last one—didn't get created until you saw me, touched me." His words were full of scorn, his voice one of contempt. "And you wonder why I wasn't eager to show you what I am." He shook his head, a ring of finality to his words. "So be it." His nostrils flared. "I gave it all for you, Abby. I let that fucker Maurice take all of it, to save your life. I let him *use* me, and still I came for you."

Shame flooded my heart. I peered up at him through dirty fingers, flinching beneath the ice. A gleam of silver flared behind him. "Ion," I whimpered, one hand reaching out for him. My fingertips nearly brushed the fine hairs dusting his pale muscles, but he sidestepped me at the last moment.

"If you ever touch me again, I'll kill you."

He gestured at the newly formed Door with a graceful hand. "Melanie has made us a way out. I suggest you take it before you bleed to death."

I glanced down and saw that I was still oozing. I staggered to my feet, my calves shaking. "I'd carry you, of course, but I'm rather through with that." He gestured at the door again. "Go on. I'll see myself out."

My hands rose over my mouth, my vision a hazy blur of tears as I did what he'd always accused me of doing. I fled through the Door without looking back.

I was warm, wonderfully warm wrapped in sheets and comfort. There was a purring sound beside me, coaxing me forward.

"There now, that's better." The purring stopped, and I felt something soft tickling my chin and nuzzling my cheek. "Ah, damn . . . she's crying again. Wake up, Abby."

I blinked, realizing the unicorn was right. Tears were rolling from beneath my lashes. I gave a shuddering sob, my fingers wiping gently at my temples. With effort, I opened my eyes.

I was in a bed—my bed. I went to sit up, grunting at the sudden spike of pain. "Don't move, Abby. You're still wounded." My hand traced down my breastbone, as I numbly pulled back the sheets, noted the stiff bandages around my abdomen.

I slumped, propping my head on the pillow with a hollow sigh. "How long?" My voice was hoarse with disuse. There was an uncomfortable silence. "How long?"

"Two weeks," he murmured. "Melanie wanted to take you to the hospital, but the blade that injured you was magical and needed an elvish Healer to mend you." He snorted dubiously. "Good thing you're so stubborn."

"I feel like shit," I said. The inside of my mouth was gummy, cotton and crap all rolled into one.

"You've slept for a while," he admitted. "They've been keeping you in some sort of stasis to let you heal, but Roweena removed it this morning. She said you would probably wake up in a bit."

I nodded, my hands tapping idly over the bandage. I hissed at the pinch of pain, but it didn't feel as bad as I thought it should. "Must have been a hell of a healing spell." Part of me wasn't sure I liked the concept of Faery magic done to me while I was unconscious. On the other hand, I wasn't dead, so that was a plus right there.

"How's Brystion?" I said it casually, ignoring the twisted feeling of my heart. The unicorn gave me an odd look, shifting his legs underneath him and taking a sudden interest in his tail.

"Ah, well. Ahem. That is to say"—he shook his head, mane splaying like fine dandelion fluff—"he's gone. Completely and utterly gone. Truth be told, we sort of hoped you'd be able to tell us."

I turned away, my eyes staring unfocused at the blinds. "How would I? I'm not his TouchStone anymore." I rubbed my eyes, resolving not to cry. "I don't remember anything past that—just going through the Door."

Phineas nodded. "Complete chaos, honestly. You spilled

out of a massive hole in the painting a damned bloody mess. I thought Roweena was going to have an apoplexy at the sight. Brystion stepped through after you and asked Melanie to make him another Door." He nuzzled my hand. "She's been here too, you know. They all have."

I bit my lip. "Except for him." Damn. So much for not crying. The salted dampness ran to the edges of my mouth. Idiot. In the end I really didn't have anyone to blame but myself, though how I was supposed to have controlled my own nightmares from manifesting, I had no idea. Still, if it really *had* been my subconscious forcing him into such a thing . . . I shuddered.

"Except for him," the unicorn agreed.

The ache of misery filled my face and stretched it taut. "You can leave too, you know. You don't need to be stuck here anymore."

"I know," he said softly. "I could have broken our bond whenever I wanted to. But the truth is, I don't want to. It's interesting here. Of course, you *are* a pretty shitty cook."

I smiled despite myself. "I'll learn," I promised, "but stay out of my underwear. It's kind of nasty."

"Fair enough," he snorted, his ears flattening as someone tapped lightly at the bedroom door. He cleared his throat. "Enter," he said imperiously, winking at me.

Robert poked his head around the door frame, his face brightening when he saw me. "I thought I heard voices. Good to see you're awake." He gracefully slipped into the room, crouching down beside the bed. "How are you feeling? Up to having visitors maybe?"

I frowned at him. "For a little bit," I nodded, wondering at his demeanor. "But I'm not sure you're someone I want to see right now, no offense."

"Robert's been guarding your apartment," Phineas admonished as the angel's face darkened. "It's a rather high form of flattery to get the Protectorate's own bodyguard watching over you."

I snorted. "Or maybe it's a punishment, eh? Let your guard down around Moira and they dumped me on you? Replaced you with something better?"

Robert's jaw tightened. "Perhaps." He inclined his head as though acknowledging the point. "But I can't say I didn't deserve it, Sparky. I was . . . wrong."

"How's Charlie?" I ignored him.

"She is . . ." His mouth twitched and he pulled hard on his lower lip. "She's doing okay. She wasn't badly injured, but she is having a lot of issues sleeping." He bent down, his forehead touching the back of my knuckles. "I was wrong about you, Abby. I know that now." He kissed the tips of my fingers, but it was less an erotic gesture and more a promise of sorts. "Thank you," he murmured. "You have brought my heart back to me—both of them."

A polite cough drew our attention back to the door, and a sunbeam of a smile lit up Robert's face as he saw Moira framed just inside the doorway. The elvish woman was still slight, even given her recent pregnancy, but her dark blond hair was perfectly smooth and gleaming. The rest of her was just as flawless, from the honeyed skin to the arched cheekbones with her succulent lips and delicately pointed ears. Her eyes were slanted and a brilliant green. I was surprised to see her like that, but I tried not to let it show. Moira had rarely displayed herself to me without some form of Glamour.

A delicate spring-green dress clung to her hips, ribbons at her arms and her ankles. It should have looked ridiculous, but on her it was as though she would simply float away on the breeze with each gliding step. She placed one hand on her protector's head, caressing the dark locks fondly.

"I'd like a moment or two alone with Abby, Robert.

If you don't mind, that is." It was phrased as a request, but there was nothing particularly questioning about it. Robert gave her a rueful smile, quite assured of his place. He nodded politely at me and left, the door clicking closed behind him. Moira gave the unicorn a pointed look, but he simply bleated.

Her smile turned up, exposing feral teeth. "Now."

I nudged Phineas with a tired hand. "Go on," I said, my eyes flicking toward the Protectorate. "Girl talk. I'm sure you understand."

He snorted but hopped off the bed. Trotting over to the door, he pawed it gently with a hoof, sighing as it opened and then closed again, his tail swaying gently behind him.

"Strange little thing," Moira muttered, sitting down on the bed beside me. She reached out with her hand, brushing the hair from my brow. Her touch was soothing, and I let myself lean into it. We sat there like that for a few moments, and I became vaguely aware that I probably hadn't bathed in a while. Bad enough to be in the company of mere mortals, but she didn't appear to notice.

"How's the baby?" I hadn't seen it since the night of my escape. Or heard it, rather, but I suspected it had been bundled off rather quickly with Moira at the time.

Her face lit up in a gentle smile. "Ah, the wee little thing is quite well. The Queen owes you a debt, you know."

"Not me," I said brusquely, pulling away from her hand. "Brystion is the one that did it. He's the one who rescued you."

She cocked a brow, her head tilting to one side. "Yes," she nodded. "It's true. The incubus *is* the one that came through the Doorway to find us. But who was it that set that in motion? Who was it that searched for me? Who stood in the face of quite a bit of prejudice?" Her gaze turned toward the door before fixating back on me. "I'm very well aware of what you had to go through to free me . . . and what you had to give up."

I stared at her. "Are you?"

"I am," she said coolly, all princess and Protectorate now. "And I want to offer you the chance to break the Contract."

"I did that poorly, huh?" I tried to roll over onto my side but winced at the pain and settled for just looking away.

"I'm sorry for that, too," she said, eyeing my stomach. "But no, that's not why I'm offering it. In truth, it's because I was not able to honor the terms of our agreement. If you wish to break with me, there are no repercussions to the act, save that you'll get your freedom." She held up a hand. "Though I'd imagine you'll have several offers within the hour. My part of the bargain included making sure *you* were taken care of, that you were given correct information, that your word would be honored among my people. I have failed you in that regard, and therefore failed in my position."

"Well, you were kind of captured in a painting," I pointed out dryly. "A bit difficult to rule the roost from there."

Moira's hand rested on her slim belly. No new mama look for her, obviously. Somehow I doubted there would be stretch marks either. Bitch.

"Aye. But even . . . before all that. I should have taught you more. I brought you in uneducated and threw you to the wolves."

"Trial by fire," I said softly. "I've had a lot of that lately." I paused, unsure of the next question, but the hell with it, really. I wanted to know. "Why did Maurice do it? And, um, what happened to him?"

"Maurice and I were lovers. TouchStoned for a long time—several hundred years as you mortals reckon it."

"So, lovers," I prodded, knowing this part. "And then, something happened?"

She sucked in a deep breath, suddenly looking far more uncertain than I had ever seen her. "Yes. I don't know. He changed, I guess. Or I did. Even for my kind, love is never sure, never eternal. He became power-hungry and angry. He wanted me to take him to Faery. To live."

"He wanted to become the Steward," I mused. "A modern-day True Thomas. And you wouldn't agree?"

"It's the Queen's decision, and I am not yet Queen. Once accepted to the Faery Court, you become part of it. I wasn't sure I *wanted* Maurice as a permanent fixture. So, I let him go. He left before I could terminate the Contract completely and tried to leave the city. The geas snapped into place before I could stop it. I was able to track him down later and break it properly, but by then it was too late."

She rubbed at her eyes with a weary hand. "And then you showed up, all Dreamer and Nightmares wrapped into one, so jaded and so strong. I had to take you, KeyStone and all."

"You could have at least told me what was going on," I said, not bothering to keep the sullenness from my tone. "And you didn't answer my question. Where's Maurice?"

"He's being . . . taken care of," she muttered grimly, looking away. "Needless to say, his ill-won youth will not gain him anything where he's going. He has a lot to answer for, between the daemon assassins and the draining of the succubi." Her lips twisted wryly. "Not to mention our imprisonment."

"What about Topher?"

"That is for Sonja to decide. She was the one most wronged by him—and he was her TouchStone."

I struggled to sit up, my legs shifting to the side. She reached out a hand to steady me. I suppose I should have felt grateful, but I didn't.

"Knowledge is power, Abby. If I choose not to reveal

certain things, it is my right to do so—but in this case it's to protect you." Her clear eyes became serious. "I know that sounds dubious, but the more involved you get, the more tangled the web. I'd like you to take a few days to think about my offer. See how you're feeling. If you choose to go, there will be no hard feelings. If you choose to stay . . ." She shrugged, her mouth curving into a secret smile. "Well, I'll do better by you this time."

I snorted, reaching down to take a sip of water from the cup on the nightstand. It tasted as though it had been there a while and I quickly put it down, making a face. She chuckled and took the cup, swirling her fingers around the rim, a sprinkle of silver fluttering from her perfect nails.

"There, now," she murmured, "that should be better." She handed me the glass with a little wink. "A little extra something to help you rest."

I sniffed it. "What is it?"

"A sleeping draught, mixed with a painkiller." She eyed my bandaged stomach cautiously. "I don't want you pushing it."

"No, thanks." I set the cup on the table and slumped back into the pillows. "I've been asleep long enough."

"As you wish." She nodded, not seeming to take offense. Gathering up her skirts, she smiled again. "I truly am in your debt, Abby."

I grunted at her. "If I choose to stay on as your Touch-Stone . . . I'll want a few changes."

She hesitated and then nodded. "Such as?"

"Freedom." Images of my mother's manila envelope appeared in my mind, echoed by Maurice's mad ravings. "I have some personal business I need to deal with, and I think I've earned the right to move outside the boundaries of Portsmyth, don't you?"

"Perhaps—I shall see what I can do." A tapping at the

door caught her attention. "But I have a few changes as well." She opened the door, bowing slightly as a tall, muscular elvish man entered the room. No Armani suits for this one, judging by the blue Celtic tattoos scattered over the rough planes of his face. Definitely of the warrior caste then.

"Prince," she murmured.

"Princess." He nodded to Moira before turning to face me. A leather patch covered his left eye, but the right gleamed a silvery blue as it assessed my pallid form. Whatever decision he came to was hidden in the deep bow he gave me, a cluster of dark braids slapping lightly against his leather vest.

"This is my brother, Talivar. He has agreed to protect you during your time with me."

I frowned suddenly. "A bodyguard? But I don't think I really need—"

"There are no arguments here, Abby. You are not required to be his TouchStone. In fact, Melanie has agreed to do so in your stead, but you have no choice in this if you want to continue your duties with me."

I glanced back at Talivar. He was certainly easy enough on the eyes, anyway, and I didn't doubt the man could be lethal. But it seemed like just another complication, another level of complexity I wasn't sure I wanted. Bryston's dockside words haunted me still. To hell with it, then—a complication for a complication—maybe it would all even out. "Melanie?"

"All things come with a price," Moira said softly. "The price of her Healing was Talivar's Contract."

I rubbed at my head. "All right," I sighed as he nodded and retreated from my room. "But I don't want him crashing on my couch long-term. I have limits, you know."

Her mouth quirked up as though she had expected nothing less. "I'll leave you to your rest, then."

"One last thing." A sudden wariness paused over her face. "Maurice wanted the baby. He said this wouldn't have happened if you gave him the baby."

She drew herself up. "I know what he said. He was hoping to use it as a bribe to get in to Faery, or to save his life."

"It was his, wasn't it?" She ran her fingers down her bodice, but said nothing. My eyes narrowed as I watched her. Strange to see Moira dissemble like this. I cocked my head. "No?"

"No." She hesitated, letting out a rueful laugh. "I know you've probably wondered why I didn't go to the Faery Court when all this trouble began."

"The thought had crossed my mind once or twice."

Her lips pursed. "How eager would you have been to run back home to your mother and tell her you'd gotten knocked up after an illicit affair?" I blinked. "Aye," she snorted. "That's about what I thought. There are other things at work here than just sheer elvish arrogance."

"Whose is it then?" I felt a flash of desperation, remembering Bryston's initial eagerness to see her that first morning. But no, he'd been in love with Elizabeth, hadn't he? He said he'd cheated though. I swallowed. Shit. But that wasn't right either. He couldn't make children that way.

She chuckled again, seeing my face, but there was no humor in it. "The incubus is yours, Abby. He always was, from the moment he touched you."

I made an inarticulate sound of protest, letting out a shuddering sob. Bryston would never be mine.

"No," she shook her head, reaching for the door. "The father of my child is Robert."

Twenty-six

Two months later...

I swept the last of the dust from the counter. The door chimed and I looked up with a weary smile. It was nearly 1:00 A.M., after all, and the Midnight Marketplace would be closing soon. The red-winged succubus strutted in, the motion of her movements so much like her brother's I had to look away.

"Dead in here tonight, huh?" Her voice had the same mocking lilt to it as Bryston's too. A few months of *not* being trapped in a painting had done wonders for her. Her feathers had grown back, slick and fat and brilliant; the hollows of her cheeks were less pronounced; her eyes were dark and merry and full of seductive promise. I'd never had the courage to ask her just what had happened to Topher. Not because I didn't want to know—I did— but not badly enough to dim the peace she'd apparently found. Somehow I doubted he'd ever made it to that beach.

"It's okay." I shook the cloth out. "I don't mind the quiet nights sometimes. Not that it matters, really. I'll get to sleep in tomorrow—Katy's working the Pit's morning shift."

Sonja's upper lip curled in amusement. "And here I'd thought she'd be in the Hallows twenty-four-seven."

"She's there a lot of the time," I admitted. "But she comes to help out now and then." I snorted softly. "She and Brandon are working on some kind of TouchStone dating service."

"More power to them," she muttered. "Kind of takes all the fun out of it, if you ask me." She licked the corner of her mouth like a feral cat, eying one of the nearby shelves curiously. "Wow. There's some really weird shit in here."

I shrugged. "I just work here."

"Of course you do."

Our eyes met, smiles cracking at nearly the same time. Just like that, the tension dissolved and we were merely friends, bound by more than survivalist instinct. We'd broken the TouchStone bond when I'd awakened, but it was still nice to see her.

She primped her hair with a careless hand. "Have you thought of a costume yet?"

"Ah. You know, costume parties really aren't my thing. I might just skip it."

"It's one of the biggest parties of the year," she prodded. "And one of the four nights when the CrossRoads are open to all travelers. Halloween, Samhain, All Hallows' Eve—whatever you call it, it really is quite the . . . experience. You've got an open invitation to the Hallows, don't you? The guest list is going to be extensive and hard to get on."

"Well, that's fine with me because I'm not going." Sonja pouted prettily, but I held up a hand. "What can you do?" I bent down and grabbed my coat off the floor, gently nudging the snoozing unicorn from the sleeve. "Time to go, Phin," I said, slipping the jacket on. It was warm and smelled like cinnamon and violets. He shot me a disgruntled look, but shook it off, yawning disdainfully.

Ever my shadow, Talivar removed himself from his position beside the fireplace to pace three steps behind me. It had been creepy at first, given his mostly silent demeanor, but I'd learned to ignore it, even if he *had* been crashing on my couch every night.

At least he didn't snore.

I turned out the light and the four of us walked to the door, slipping out into the chilly mid-October air. Goose bumps rippled down my back, but it was refreshing, full of rustling leaves and the scent of green things fading away.

"Did you want to come upstairs for a bit?" I didn't have much to offer company these days, but I suspected she wasn't really here for purely social reasons. I tapped the silver doorknob three times, watching as the Door melted away into the stone wall. Moira had made some nice concessions for me in the last few weeks—a way to open and close the Marketplace on my own was one of them.

"Nah, I'm hunting tonight. I just came by to see if you were ever planning to go after my brother."

I raised a brow, my hands jammed into my pockets. "I think he made his position pretty damn clear. Besides, I'd rather not have him kill me right now. I just finished healing a short while ago, you know?"

"You say it so convincingly. And yet for all that, I suspect he's been lurking about."

I hesitated. In truth, I was sure he had been. I'd taken to visiting the Heart of my Dreaming most nights, and there were little signs of him everywhere. One night there were rose petals strewn up the stairs into the bedroom. Tiny little sugared things, pink and moist and beckoning. When I reached my bedroom, they disappeared, leaving me in darkness.

Another night, I found the old stereo turned on, one of my mother's Tom Jones albums spinning softly, the

entire house filled with the soothing timbre of his voice. I
hadn't let it play for long. There was a fire in the fireplace,
built up and crackling with warmth, golden light spilling
over the soft blue woven rug on the hardwood floor. I had
spent many evenings as a child like that. And yet, this was
different. Slower. Seductive. Gently wooing, perhaps. I
smiled inwardly, thinking of that long-ago request. Maybe
Sonja was right.

"What difference does it make to you?" I questioned.

"It doesn't really. I just don't like to see him moping."

Something tightened in my chest. "You've actually seen
him?"

"Not exactly. I can just feel him poking around the
corners of your dreams sometimes. Not that I visit there
often," she said hastily. "Once was enough, thanks. But he's
hurting, Abby." Her eyes softened. "After everything he
did to help free me, it seems the least I could do."

"Sounds like stalking to me." I scowled.

Her head tipped up at me, staring until I flushed. "You
know better," she said. "I think the two of you need to talk."

I gestured at the apartment and snapped my fingers
angrily. "He knows where I live, Sonja. Ion can stop by
whenever he likes—or even meet me at the Hallows if he
prefers. I wouldn't even know where to begin to find him."

"He's a man. Men are stupid. He'll admit he's wrong,
but you'll have to pin him to the wall to get him to do it."

I shook my head. "Oh, no. I'm not playing that kind
of game with him. Or with anyone, for that matter. What
happened that night is between us, and I'll thank you to
stay out of it. It's over," I said firmly. "And I don't want
to hear anything melodramatic. No stories about how he's
dying, or how he's trapped in my dreams or any of that type
of bullshit. It's not up to me to convince him of anything."
I chewed on my lower lip. "I don't work that way."

"All right," she said finally, a curious light drifting through the hollowed shadows of her eyes. "But what if you're wrong?"

"I'm not his savior," I retorted.

"Did you ever think he might be yours?"

I looked down at my feet and when I glanced back up, the words died in my mouth as I realized she was gone. "Damn it."

I turned to head up the stairs. Phineas tripped up the steps behind me, scooting under my feet as I slid the key home. "Maybe I should just install a cat door and save us both the trouble." I glanced behind me and shook my head as Talivar followed us inside. He'd wait until I'd settled down for the night before taking care of himself. I'd told him not to worry about it, but on this point he was unmoving and I'd long since given up trying to convince him of anything else.

"Hmmmph," Phineas grunted, his hooves thumping through the kitchen. He was cranky whenever I had to wake him up like that, but he'd get over it. "She's right, you know. He really was pretty good for you." He looked mournfully up at the stove. "And he could cook too." His sapphire eyes gleamed with hunger. "I could really go for a cheeseburger right now."

I shuddered. "Doesn't that bother you?"

"What?" He sat down in front of the fridge.

"Eating meat like that. It's kind of cannibalistic."

He shot me an unfriendly look. "I've yet to ask for a plate of unicorn flank, so calm down. We can't all be so lucky as to live on saffron and violets." He waggled his beard. "And you're changing the subject."

"Whatever." I was too tired to argue with him. "I'm going to bed."

"Suit yourself," he said. "I think I'm going to play some World of Warcraft."

Strangely enough the unicorn had shown an amazing aptitude for computer games. I'd lost my taste for them after Brigadun's death, but they utterly fascinated Phin. Of course, I hadn't figured out how he managed to make the game work, what with him not having hands and all, but he was happy. It kept him quiet and out of my underwear drawer and those were really the only things that mattered. I gestured wearily at him and stumbled back to my bedroom.

My answering machine light blinked from across the room. I played it back as I got undressed. A message from Melanie. Two from Charlie. Neither was an emergency and both were going to wait until I woke up eight hours from now.

Melanie and I had slipped back into our usual state of friendship. If things still seemed a little strained with the forced Contract between her and Talivar, well, that was something we were working on as best we could.

Charlie, on the other hand . . .

I let my hair drift down from its bun. Total clusterfuck there. I had no idea if she knew her lover had cheated on her, and I really didn't want to know. But Moira had been right. Knowledge was power, and if Robert kept a slightly more respectful tone around me these days, well, I wasn't going to look too closely at it. Still, it sucked royally to have to look at your friend and lie—or at least pretend not to know.

I wished Moira had never told me, but anyone who saw the baby would probably be able to tell. There was a definite resemblance in his chubby face. If he sprouted wings the jig would be up.

I quickly washed up in the bathroom, wiping at my face with a damp cloth. My reflection looked the same as it always did, trapped in that strange half-life of nonaging. I'd had that part of the geas reinstated when I formally re-signed Moira's Contract, though she had limited that particular perk only to the inner regions of Portsmyth. It seemed like the status quo thing to do, and if I had to give up another six and half years of my life, I might as well come out of it looking as good as I had going into it.

As for the rest of it, I hadn't decided on either the wish or whatever sort of boon the Queen might decide to offer me. I preferred *not* to think about it, honestly. Gifts freely given are one thing, but gifts offered under duress are another animal altogether. At least this time Moira had made the extra effort to train me once or twice a week. And the fridge had better food in it now too.

The thought of food turned my thoughts to Bryston. Not for the first time, and probably not for the last time.

I'd had a lot of time to think about him, my eyes drifting down to that spot just below my sternum. I lifted my shirt, staring at it in the mirror like I'd done nearly every night— another scar to live with. My fingers traced the silver oval left by the knife. It was almost like a tattoo, perfectly round, but with one little jagged edge at the bottom. No, it wasn't likely I'd be forgetting that night. I let the T-shirt drop. I needed a shower, but I needed sleep more.

I caught my own gaze and held it. "Are you in there, you bastard?" I said it half seriously, but a flutter of anticipation took wing in my chest. Was there a hint of something there? Would I see a flick of disdainful arrogance, a flare of gold? I turned away before anything had the chance to manifest. I was ever the coward, as Bryston had pointed out. "Still running away," I agreed, turning off the light.

The manila envelope from my mother's attorney seemed to echo the sentiment. I'd moved it from its little domain in the kitchen once Talivar moved in, but this time I left it in plain sight on my nightstand. So far, I'd still managed to ignore its presence somehow.

And yet, tonight I was drawn to it. Maybe it was the conversation with Sonja, or maybe I was just tired of being afraid.

Sucking in a deep breath, I carefully pried it open as though it might suddenly grow teeth and bite me. Snorting at myself, I pulled out the letter, a standard sort of legal thing, wishing me well and stating that my signature was still required for the release of my mother's estate and asking me to call at my earliest convenience.

"Not just yet," I murmured. I shook the envelope and realized there was something else in the bottom. Cold metal fell into my hand, sliding through my fingers. A key to a lockbox, undoubtedly residing in the bank back home—and a silver necklace.

I stared at it bemusedly, taking in the shining blue topaz amulet, so similar to the one Phineas wore around his own neck. I certainly didn't remember my mother ever wearing it. I ran my fingers over its smooth curves, wondering at its origin. Why had Mr. Jefferies sent it to me? I reread the letter but there was no mention of it at all.

"Is a puzzlement," I declared, tossing the envelope back on the nightstand, the key and amulet clustered together upon it. A small victory, perhaps, and maybe a hollow one, but for now, it was enough to have acknowledged her death, even in this fashion. Baby steps and all that. The scab wasn't really ready to be pulled off, but it was a start.

Besides, I had bigger fish to fry.

I turned off the light and slipped beneath the covers, huddling into a soft cocoon of warmth. From underneath the door I could see the flicker of light indicating Phin was still happily immersed in his game. Well, that and the occasional cry of "DPS, my ass. Motherfucking Death Knights."

I rolled over, tucking the blankets around my shoulders,

and let my mind drift away. What if Sonja was right and Bryston really was as hurt as she said? I still had no way to explain the nightmare I'd had about him. But more to the point, he blamed me for that which I could not control. Or was I just making excuses? Were dreams truly the window into the mind's soul, or just mere instruments of processing?

My thoughts continued to chase themselves round and round, an endless circle of fox and hound, chicken and egg, each answer leading to another question. I was not going to find satisfaction by myself, that much was certain. It occurred to me that I hadn't dreamt of him once in the last few weeks. In fact, with the exception of the visits to my Heart, I'd barely dreamt at all, let alone been exposed to my nightmares. Was he even now guarding my dreams? He'd had no cause to do so.

I opened my eyes for a moment, staring into the darkness. There was only one place to find the answer, and it wasn't going to be here. "We're going to have this out tonight, Ion. One way or the other." I felt foolish saying it like that. I had no idea if he could hear me, but I didn't care.

"Do you hear me?" I let my voice drop to a whisper. "I'm coming to find you."

I exhaled sharply and shut my eyes again, this time falling quickly into sleep, my journey sped by purpose and possibility.

Twenty-seven

The house was dark and creaked something fierce when I opened the front door. The noise wasn't quite a warning and not really a threat, merely a shadow of its normal self. I moved forward, brushing away the cobwebs that clung to my hair as I crossed the threshold.

I slipped into the main hall, past the familiar rugs, bookshelves, and dusty fireplace. Even the small bowl of potpourri on the wooden end table—strawberries, with a hint of cinnamon. My mother's scent haunted me here. The smell was cloying; it distracted me with memories I couldn't afford to pay attention to.

The shadows drew my gaze up the stairs to the bedroom, but even though I could feel his presence in every corner, I knew I would never discover him there. It would be too easy then. No, to find Brystion, I was going to have to go deeper.

What was the line from that Narnia book? *Farther up and further in . . .*

I pressed through the kitchen, a hanging crystal winking a dim purple in the hazy candlelight from the window. The rest of the dreamhouse sat in silence, doors closed and quiet. The crickets' song called my attention outside toward the garden. I inhaled sharply, tasting Bryston on the damp breeze that blew in from the open window.

Dark. Earthy. Hungry.

"Where are you?" I asked the silence, but there was no answer. Not that it mattered—I hadn't expected one. Sonja had warned me as much.

Abby . . .

"Bryston." I said his name, the sorrow and loss I'd felt over the last several empty weeks bubbling up, tingeing the flavor of the word with an aching echo of that night. I slid open the screen door, my shoes sounding sharply on the stone patio. Heedless of my passing, the fireflies continued their celestial mating dance, fading in and out of the growing darkness.

I traveled down the steps cut into the hillside and through the damp grass—grass that became taller and thicker until I was weaving through prickly thorn trees and past an ivy-covered gate. I hadn't come this way before, but its familiarity stung me to the core and brought a lump to my throat. From dreams into nightmares, I supposed. Still, it was a bit unnerving to actually see it. I'd always confined myself to the House proper, not willing to venture forth into the wilderness that was slowly swallowing it.

The brush became overgrown and harder to push through as the light faded faster. I let out a desperate groan, somehow knowing that if I didn't find him by the time the dream evening was gone, he might slip away forever. The sleeve of my sweater snagged on a low-hanging arch of rock. I pulled away, feeling it start to unravel.

"Please." I tripped over a gnarled tree root, stumbling to my knees. I glared at it in betrayed frustration—dream trees weren't supposed to do that. "Thanks a lot." I brushed a stray twig from my hair, wondering what the hell had possessed me to wear such inefficient shoes.

A snap of branches sounded behind me and I started, my ankle twisting sharply. I could feel his presence in the shadows, darker than before. I knew he was there, watching me struggle but offering no hand to help me up. Clearly he had not forgotten our last words and they hovered between us like the cord of a whip, tangible and taut. I fought the urge to flee. I fought the urge to beg. I fought the urge to reach out and touch him.

The breeze pulled the hair away from my face and I looked up at him, seeing him fully for the first time. My heart ached. I hadn't understood what he meant about feeding before, not really. But this . . . this was an incubus bereft of dreams.

His skin was midnight blue, almost deep enough to be black, but it glowed in the moonlight with tiny crystalline scales. They were curled in delicate patterns across his face and abdomen like the gossamer strands of some celestial spider's web. He looked so different, and yet, his arms were familiar to me, and his hands, and the rippled muscle of his chest as he breathed. All of it was still Bryston.

My fingers pressed to my lips as my eyes roamed over the rest of him, catching the details of what I hadn't been able or willing to see before. He had the hind legs of a stag, curved and cloven and furred, a dusky lion tail twitching by the left hock. Great antlers swept up—wicked, glittering, and crystal pale—bursting from his brow and tangled in the blue-black of his hair. His ears were pointy, cupped hollows with a hint of deer, but his face . . . oh! His face was the same—from the arrogant pout of his lips to the angled edge of his cheeks. His eyes remained dark and haunted, only the merest ember of gold shining.

"You're beautiful," I murmured, taking a step closer.

His nostrils flared, and his left hoof stomped a warning, but he didn't retreat. I reached out and he flinched. "Don't."

I left my hand where it was, my gaze never faltering. His breath misted slightly, and I wondered at the crisp chill in the air. Surely it hadn't been there before. "Do you live here now?"

"You offered it to me." His voice was bitter, his mouth a pencil-thin line. "What choice do I have?"

"You have the choice to live your own life," I pointed out dryly. "Moping about my Heart doesn't seem like a particularly proactive way to go about anything."

"Easy words from someone who can't even see herself in a clear light," he retorted, but there was an uncertainty behind it. "You think me a monster. Admit it."

"I've never copped to being something I wasn't. Just avoided what I couldn't admit to—survival mechanism, I guess. And I don't see you as a monster, Ion." I hesitated. "Although when you threatened to eat Maurice's soul, that kind of threw me. I didn't think you did that sort of thing."

His skin appeared to darken. Was he blushing? "I'd forgotten you could see me."

"Can you actually do that? Eat souls, I mean."

"I suspect so." He looked away, one hand clenched against his chest. "I don't know what side I fall on, which Path I belong to."

I watched him for a moment, wondering at the grief in his eyes. How long had he hated himself?

"Which one do you want to belong to?" I stepped closer to him again and this time he didn't back away. "Who do you *want* to be?"

He remained silent, paralyzed between hope and fear, eyes wide and gleaming.

"You could come back, you know." I said it quietly, casually, my pale fingers drifting over the dark skin of his shoulder. The muscles trembled beneath my touch. "We could start over, be ourselves without the pressure of the sky falling on top of us to push us together."

"You don't mean that," he said, his voice carefully braced on the edge of flight. "You can't."

"Of course I can. Would I be here otherwise?"

"It is your Heart that makes you so compassionate. Your need to fix what is broken."

I laughed but there wasn't any humor in the sound. "I can't fix myself, Ion. What makes you think I could fix you?" I brushed the hair away from his forehead and placed my fingers at the base of his antlers. "I've missed you."

One silver brow rose, the emotions flattening on the perfect beauty of his face. "Don't you get it?" He whirled away from me, lowering his antlered head. I fought the urge to flinch from the glittering points. "You Dreamed me as someone who hurt you, ravished you, *cut* you. You're a Dreamer. Your dreams can become reality, especially to one who . . . who is connected to you."

"That makes no sense," I snapped, shame pricking me like the point of a needle. A memory of teeth rippled across my skin, remembered fear making me harsher than I should have been. "You're not connected to me at all." I winced beneath his stare, regretting the words the instant they left my mouth.

"Perhaps I was mistaken, then. I will not trouble you further." He skittered sideways, as though he might melt into the moonlight.

"Hold up there, bucko. You think because I dream of maggots pouring from my head it means it's going to happen? You think that imagining someone I care about attacking me is something I intended?" He shuddered beneath the onslaught of my words, but I pressed forward. "Newsflash for you, incubus. I wasn't aware of doing *anything* right then." I wiped my hand over my face. "What is it you want me to do, Ion?"

"I don't know." He leaned against the side of a fallen elm, one arm holding on to a curved branch. "Why are you here? I lied to you, stole your faith, your friendship . . . your lust." His eyes drifted partway shut, taunting me with a touch of his old arrogance.

"Yes. And I suspect that, had things not turned out the way they did, Moira would be looking to nail your ass in front of the Council. But they took into account the circumstances. I don't think they're completely happy with you, but there's no ill will on the part of the Protectorate." Sonja had seen to that matter almost immediately, pleading clemency for her brother far more eloquently before the Council than I ever could. Of course, I'd still been in my sleep-induced coma, so the point was completely moot.

He snorted. "I could give two shits about what the Protectorate thinks. Why are *you* here?"

My teeth ground together. Confession time. "You know, if you're just going to play hide-and-seek with me all night, you could have just left me in that damn painting and saved us all the trouble. I'm a little short on mental floss, at the moment." I exhaled sharply. "The more important question is why do you *think* I'm here?"

"I have no idea what you're talking about," he said, his face suspiciously devoid of emotion.

"Oh, of course not." I moved closer to him, ticking off on my fingers. "Let me guess. You're like a thousand years old, but you've never found love, right? Never found a single woman in *all* that time who made your loins quiver and completed your soul, or whatever bullshit you happen to need? Well, except one and you had to cheat on her."

He blinked, dry amusement flickering across his countenance. "Actually," he said slowly, "I'm only about thirty-five as far as your years go. Then again, I'm not really sure what you're accusing me of. It's a Contract you want then?"

"Don't be such an ass." I rolled my eyes and yanked hard on a lock of that perfect hair. "Come here," I insisted, leaning up to kiss him.

His lips met mine for an instant, fierce and possessive, hands digging into my hips so that I slid against the hardened muscles of his torso. He uttered a low groan and it pulsed into my mouth even as the curved length of him brushed against my belly.

Brystion . . .

He thrust me away, ignoring my cry of protest. His eyes flashed feral and golden now, his chest rising and falling in painful counterpoint to the pounding of my heart.

"I cannot stay with you," he said finally. "Not like this . . ."

"I don't understand." I swallowed against the tightness of my throat, his words pricking the edges of my heart.

"Just . . . this." He gestured at me. "It's all I can ever be to you, Abby. All I know is of the flesh, the hew and the thrust of pleasure. An incubus is not meant for more."

"And if I don't want more?"

His eyes narrowed. "You can't lie to me—not here. Not for long anyway," he snorted. "And when the moment is over . . . what then? When the ripples of gratification have faded away, the heat of passion cooled . . . when you realize that I will not grow old with you, or have children?" His expression turned rueful. "And however you might feel about these things now, I have tasted them in your dreams . . . and those do not lie."

He captured my hand to rub it against his cheek. "And perhaps, in truth, it is I who want more," he said. "More for you, anyway."

The heat from his skin jolted down my arm in a warm flush that fluttered wildly between my thighs. He kissed one finger and then another, his grasp locked around my wrist. "I don't want you to be anything you're not," I whispered. "Ever."

He groaned, harsh and guttural, as he leaned forward, his mouth trailing hot and wet over my ear. "I could give it up for you—what I am. You have the power, Dreamer."

"I have nothing," I insisted. "I have a wish, given to me by the daughter of the Queen of Elfland—and not one I can use for quite some time. Besides"—I kissed his collarbone with a sigh—"if you're going to play Angel to my Buffy, you should know this type of stuff never works out once one person becomes 'normal.' Could you have rescued me if you were human? Could you have protected my dreams?"

"No," he admitted. "But don't you see? If you weren't a Dreamer, we wouldn't even be having this conversation. I would have given you to Maurice the moment I could have reasonably done so." He went still and stared at me. "And I would have left you to rot inside that painting without another thought."

I exhaled painfully, the truth of it all the worse for the gentleness in his voice. "But you didn't."

"No. But I tried. I didn't know about the paintings or Moira or the rest of it. I just knew Maurice had my sister. And he had agreed to release her in return for you." His gaze locked into mine, cold and black. "I knew about the other daemons. I knew they were going to try to take you. I knew."

"But . . . you brought us the assassins' marks. You fought for me and Melanie in the shed."

He raised a clawed finger to my lips. "Yes. By the time I discovered Maurice's duplicity, I knew I couldn't go through with my side of the bargain. But it was too late."

The minutes ticked by, my heart hovering on the edge of disappointment and acceptance. "All right," I said finally. "I'm not sure what you want me to say."

"There is nothing. I cannot be what you want; I can only be what I am." His ears twitched in the darkness. "And that, I fear, will not be enough."

I withdrew a pace, letting his words roll over me, even as I decided to let him go. "The Heart is a fickle thing, Ion," I murmured. Our eyes met, a flicker of understanding crossing his face. "You'll always have a place in mine."

He touched me then, one awkward stroke of his hand against my cheek, and for a brief moment I felt as though I was exactly where I was supposed to be. I stepped forward into his arms despite myself, feeling them part before me and then encircle my waist. "Show me, Ion," I whispered. "Show me what you are."

The leaves crunched beneath me, dry and harsh, but it didn't matter. My clothes had disappeared into the twilight of the Dreaming, my back was pressed into the soft loam of the earth. The fragrance of the woods, thick with spruce and hemlock, honeysuckle and mint, cocooned around us; still, it was the heady flush of Brystion's scent that captured me most. I was wrapped in it, embraced by the masculine pulse of his desire, tasting it as he savagely nipped at my mouth. It was dark and shadowed, like drinking midnight wine made of lust and moonbeams, salt and ashes. It prickled over my flesh with the delicate brutality of thorns, delicious and sinful and utterly *him*.

He hovered over me, his teeth grazing the pulse of my neck, fingers roaming over my thighs, my hips, my belly, hot and possessive. I quivered, moaning as his hand captured a breast and rolled the nipple taut until I cried out and writhed beneath him. His grip was like iron, pinching me to stillness; his other hand pressed between my thighs, knuckles parting them wide to find me slick and ready. He growled as he slipped a finger inside, stroking, teasing me until the blood was singing in my ears.

He bit my shoulder again, harder this time, and I felt the fine brush of his furred hindquarters sliding gently against my skin. "Goddess save me to think Maurice was right," he muttered hoarsely, "but I do love you, Abby."

I froze, the words ringing true in the depths of the Dreaming, filling me with a terrible clarity.

"Bryston . . ." I stumbled over his name, squirming at the feel of his shaft rubbing against me in earnest.

A heartbeat. Another. The moment drew out, long and quiet, and it felt as though the entire forest had stopped moving, watching us.

"Abby." His breath was hot in my ear, his voice stricken as he waited for me to continue, waited for . . . what?

Permission? Rejection?

His grip relaxed ever so slightly, and I took his face in my hands to meet those aching, beautiful eyes, my heart breaking into a thousand pieces. "No . . . regrets."

His ears twitched in the darkness and I heard the jangle of the bells hanging from the tips, the sound pulling me back to that first morning, echoed in the way the door chimes had rung out as he stepped across the threshold.

He uttered a low cry, and I knew I'd shattered the illusion. The truth melted away the dream like snow beneath the brilliance of the sun. I kissed him fiercely, our tongues and moans mingling with the frictionless slap of flesh meeting flesh. The leaves beneath me became rose petals, crushed blossoms of pink and red, swirling about us in a riot of color. And then we were falling, fading away into the shadows . . .

* * *

We *rolled . . .*

I was falling, snared in the web of dreams, twisting, turning, bound and slipping and then . . .

And then Bryston was there, tumbling into the warmth of my bed, his arms wrapped around my waist. His shape had changed, back to his mortal semblance, porcelain and familiar.

"So sorry," he murmured, his lips brushing over my face. "I'm so very sorry, Abby."

"I'm sure you'll find a way to make it up to me," I sighed, arching my back. His skin was hot, burning, as I slid against it. He was still inside me and I clamped down around him, the tremulous pulse of another wave of pleasure starting to crest. His hips jerked forward, a growl rumbling from his chest. I exhaled sharply, breath ragged in the stillness of the shadows, but I could hardly hear it from the blood pounding in my head. His fingers slid down past my ear and traced the line of my jaw, the tip of his thumb drifting over my lips as he turned my face to his.

Bryston's eyes smoldered, alight with a dark desire that had nothing at all to do with being sorry.

"Yes," he agreed, a flicker of impudent humor glimmering in the golden depths of his gaze, hued with an unfamiliar tenderness. One corner of his mouth kicked up into the beginning of a sad smile. "I'm sure I will."

Twenty-eight

Morning was peeking from beyond the shadows of dawn when the barest whisper of breath against my ear pulled me from a haze of slumber. "You're leaving," I murmured with a strange certainty, rolling over to see Bryston perched on the edge of the bed staring at me.

"I wish you could see what I see when I look at you," he said finally, neatly avoiding my statement. He snagged the afghan off the floor to wrap around his waist. I eyed it with a raise of my brow, not really remembering how it got there.

"And what's that? Besides a grumpy ex-dancer with a penchant for bacon?" I propped myself up on my elbows, poking him with my big toe.

"Dreamer," he snorted, giving me a rueful glance. "I have to go. The CrossRoads will close soon."

"Keep the blanket," I said dryly, pushing the bitter-sweetness of the moment away. That he had not chosen to renew our TouchStone bond hurt more than I thought it would. "That walk of shame is a bitch, isn't it?"

His mouth twitched. "You have no idea." His eyes alighted on my nightstand. "What is that?"

I frowned, following his gaze to the necklace, silver

winking in the dawn. "Ah. It was my mother's, I guess. I found it last night in the letter from her attorney."

He strode over to take a closer look. "It would suit you, I think," he said suddenly. "May I?"

I shrugged, nonplussed, as he brushed the hair from my shoulders and gently fastened it around my neck. "I wasn't really planning on doing anything with it, honestly." I pulled it away from my chest, its weight heavy in my hand. "Solid thing, isn't it?"

"And a guaranteed 'plus-four' against incubus seduction, I'll wager," he said softly. The awkward pause lasted several minutes and then he shook his head. "I will have Sonja stop by later. I think she would be excellent at teaching you to control your nightmares."

Somehow I thought she might not see it that way, but I wasn't going to argue the point. I bit down on my tongue before I could embarrass myself by asking him to stay. He'd clearly made up his mind, and if it wasn't quite what I'd hoped for, at least we were on the same footing. Who was I to deny him his own personal quest for . . . whatever he was looking for?

With a sigh, I slid off the bed and found my bathrobe. The least I could do was see him out. Besides, I didn't need Talivar going all WWE on the incubus in my living room.

"Let me go first," I advised Bryeton. "I've got a . . . a guest. Sort of a permanent bodyguard. Moira's idea, you understand."

He raised a brow but allowed me to push past him. The kitchen floor creaked as we crept through. Phineas was no-where to be seen, though a slight snoring from beneath the tablecloth was more than enough to answer that particular question.

Talivar was waiting for us, of course. The elven prince sat in his usual place on the couch, bristling with a lethal sort of quiet. Of course, the effect was slightly lessened by the tousled fall of his hair and the bleary yawn that escaped him, but I decided not to point that out. Bedhead had no truck with elven princes, of that I was quite sure.

His polite cough still had me blushing, though that irritated me more than anything else. Shit if I was supposed to apologize for what I did in my own bedroom.

I gave the elf a sour look, frowning at the sudden gleam of amusement in his good eye. Behind me, Brystion grunted in that oddly possessive male way of greeting and I hurried us along before it could escalate into anything more.

The autumn chill drifted in and lingered at my ankles as I opened the door. I shivered. "Guess this is it," I muttered, hugging my arms to my sides, debating the wisdom of saying anything about letting wild things go free. "Will I see you again?" The words fell from my lips before I could stop them.

"Only in your dreams," he said slyly. And then he gently kissed my cheek and slipped down the steps and into the morning, his breath fogging in the air. A slurry of silver sparked up as he faded through the Door at the garden gate, and I sighed.

"Will this be a common occurrence?" Talivar asked. I closed the door behind me, strolling slowly back into the living room where he stretched gracefully. "Not that it's any of my business, but I like to be aware of who's a stranger and who's a guest."

I shook my head. "No. He won't be coming back."

The elf made a disbelieving sound but said nothing else, sagging back into the couch with another yawn. He seemed suddenly very out of place, wrapped in the archaic tunic and leather vest. I decided to take pity on him.

"Are you hungry?"

"Breakfast would not go amiss. I'm afraid I've not much

to offer by way of cooking skills, though I can field dress a mean coney," he added helpfully.

I chuckled despite myself, gesturing at him to follow me into the kitchen. "That's all right. I've been told I make pretty lousy omelets—but my scrambled eggs are to die for."

I paused outside the entrance to the Hallows, the heavy thrum of the music beating a sharp, muffled cadence through me. Unconsciously I let my hips sway to it, even as my fingers touched the silvered panel beneath the lock. "Meet me at the Crossroads," I murmured, stepping back as the familiar glow brushed past me in a flutter of butterfly brilliance. It tickled past my skin, tingling over my face as I stepped inside.

Brandon and Katy had outdone themselves. Clearly the decorations they'd purchased from the Marketplace had gone to good use if the dancing stars and spiders on the ceiling were any indication. Up on the stage, Melanie was in usual form, belting out Rilo Kiley's "Under the Blacklight" in her rich, throaty voice. A throng of masked dancers paid her court in a haze of graceful limbs and elegant movements.

I brushed the remainder of the silver sparkles away from my store-bought Pirate Wench costume (COMPLETE WITH GENUINE FAKE BOOTY!), my mouth curving into a smile as Talivar awkwardly took my elbow.

"Grrr. Argh," I murmured at him, his one good eye rolling in a suffering sort of tolerance beneath his tricorne hat.

Much to his dismay I had let Sonja talk me into showing up after all, but for this one night the Hallows had a dress code. And not just any sort either. Glamours were strictly forbidden, leaving the OtherFolk to such mundane devices as Scotch tape and crepe paper.

Some of the results were rather unintentionally hilarious—elves dressed as accountants or pixies as IT consultants. The vampires in particular seemed to take great delight in strutting about with rubber stakes and mallets, pretending to be slayers. Brandon still sat behind the bar, decked out as a grandmother, of course. Katy wore a red cloak and big smile and not much else. Even Phin had gotten into the spirit of things, although I wasn't entirely sure covering his body with bacon and calling himself a daemonic hors d'oeuvre really counted.

Talivar had taken my request without much more than a protesting grunt, but then, he already had an eye patch, so I figured a justacorp and hat wouldn't be *that* much of an imposition. I caught the ghost of an occasional smile cracking that handsome veneer time and again, so I supposed he was loosening up at least a little bit.

A figure brushed by me, and I looked up to see the Gypsy stroll by, his arm linked gallantly through that of a pale woman. She was short and voluptuous, with fat black ringlets and ebony wings folded neatly against her back. Her laughing violet eyes glowed, and her generous mouth lifted in laughter. The sheer joy in his face reflected in hers as though she were the moon herself.

I felt a momentary twinge of envy. Brystion hadn't come back, of course, though Sonja certainly had held up his end of the bargain well enough. Girlfriend was kicking my ass quite nicely as far as the Dreaming went. It was a bittersweet taming of my nightmares, but I can't say I was completely unhappy with the arrangement. Trust and lust may rhyme perfectly well in the scheme of poetic definitions, but some days poetry just isn't enough, and I'd had my fill of emotional wangst to last me for quite a while.

"Did you want to dance?" Talivar held his hand out with grave interest when Melanie started up a slightly maniacal rendition of *Danse Macabre*. I shrugged, surprised at the unexpected grace in his movements when he spun me out before leading me into a gentle waltz. Warrior-poet, indeed.

And if he caught the silhouette of a certain Captain Jack Sparrow prowling on the outermost edge of the crowd, he chose not to disclose it. My gaze met the other pirate's, his eyes sparking gold for a moment and then he was gone, swallowed up in the haze and jumble of the other dancers.

A secret smile crept over my face as I watched the Gypsy lead his angel to the dance floor beside us. It seemed as though my friend had found what he was searching for, after all. And CrossRoads help me, one day so would I.

Here is a sneak peek at
the next book in
the fantastic urban fantasy series by

Allison Pang

Coming soon from Pocket Books

Run, Abby."

Sonya's warning slid around me with a wash of power. Startled, I shot up from where I huddled beneath a cluster of fallen logs, narrowly escaping a swipe of claws. I ducked, the sharpened talons slicing the air with a deadly whistle.

Grinding my teeth, I narrowed my eyes and concentrated, letting my own form shift. Small, furry, fast . . .

Hare.

The Dreaming rippled. I bounded away, sleek and long, haunches bunching and then springing forward, propelling me into the darkness. Sonja's low growl of frustration echoed behind me. I didn't know exactly what form she'd taken, but my rapidly twitching nose instantly recognized the acrid scent of something feline.

The urge to go to ground vibrated through my little body, but I pushed forward, leaves sliding beneath my paws. All around me were shadows, as my nails dug into the moist earth. The scenery blurred past in a haze of ragweed and pine trees, needles brushing my fur. I couldn't hear Sonja anymore and I paused, my ears rotating to cup the darkness. The faintest breeze caught my attention, and I instinctively flattened against the grass as Sonja swooped past, this time in the form of a barred owl.

She wheeled, but I took off toward the tinkling stream nearby. Shedding the last vestige of the hare, I leapt towards the surface, my skin sluicing into scales as I slithered into the depths. My gills opened, sucking in the water, my pink salmon belly scraping the gravel.

"Good! Very good." Sonja applauded from the banks. The succubus had shifted into her normal form, the blood-red feathers of her wings shining in the moonlight of the Dreaming. "You can come out now, Abby. I think that's enough for tonight."

My tail flicked me through the current as I changed again, pulling together the part of what made me, *me*. Emerging from the water, I squeezed the drops from my hair and brushed it away from my face with my fingers. "I'm getting better." I pulled the Dreaming around me until I was dressed in a pair of jeans and a shirt.

Sonja nodded cautiously. "You are, but you're still barely tapping your potential." She gestured around us with a hint of frustration. "These are *your* Dreams. You limit yourself to your own sense of physics. Becoming a rabbit was fine and you've certainly improved your shifting ability—but why not change the ground, or the trees? If you're ever going to really, truly defeat your nightmares, you're going to need more than just a few parlor tricks."

"I don't think that way. You know that. We've been through this how many times now?" I glanced down at my feet, watching the water flow over my toes before giving her a wan smile. "Have patience with me. I'm new to this." One dark brow rose at me sourly, but she let the lie pass without comment. In truth it had been over six months . . . six very *long* months. She was frustrated, I was frustrated.

She sighed, looking at my woeful expression. "You'll get there. You just need to concentrate."

I waggled my nose. "Is *that* all there is to it, Endora?" My eyes narrowed as I stared at her, the power rushing through me, a thin rivulet of the Dreaming taking form in my mind.

Just a small change, perhaps.

The succubus glanced over her shoulder with a surprised laugh. Her scarlet wings now gleamed a brilliant purple. "Not bad," she admitted, ruffling them with a shiver, a flush of crimson staining them back to their normal shade.

Her face sobered. "But seriously, Abby. You have enough potential to make a first class DreamWalker. With the right training, you'd be able to slip in and out of the Dreaming at will . . . and not just into your dreams, but others as well."

I shuddered, wondering what that might be like for a moment. My lip curled in distaste as visions of accidentally stumbling into someone's personal porn theater crossed my mind. "Ah. Yeah. You know, I'm not really trying for that sort of thing. Let's just stick with what will keep me sane."

"Suit yourself, but you might change your mind some-day."

"Not likely."

She held out a hand to pull me from the stream, and we slowly ambled back toward my Heart. My gaze slid toward the dark forest behind the house. Brystion had made good on his promise to be scarce and I'd barely seen a sign of him, short of the occasional sound of bells echoing like some distant memory through the trees. The few times we'd run across each other at the Hallows had been polite, if a bit strained. I didn't usually hang around to listen to him sing, and he avoided flaunting whoever his latest TouchStone was to my face, a fact for which I was utterly grateful.

Sonja snorted at me and I flushed. "Have a good night. We'll try again tomorrow."

I waved at her, watching as she passed back through the Gate, fading away in a slurry of silver. I often wondered how she could manage the CrossRoads directly like that, but I supposed it was just what succubi did.

I reached out and stroked the Gate of my Heart with a curious finger, the rusted metal flaking into my hand. Physics or not, it still seemed so real here. And as far as confronting my nightmares . . .

I pushed the thought away, my eyes glancing over at the rocky path that led to the sea. So far I'd managed to stay far enough away from those particular memories, but sometimes it was just easier to not think about them.

"Always the coward," I muttered, rubbing my face before shutting the Gate and locking it tight. I didn't mind leaving it open when I was here, but now that I knew there were things actually wandering around in the Dreaming, I disliked leaving it gaping like that.

The fact that I might have been locking the incubus inside didn't bother me so much. He certainly could make his own way through if he wanted to. My gaze drifted over the thick cluster of hemlock behind the garden and the heady taste of jasmine suddenly grew heavy on my tongue. Not one of my flowers, surely. I took a step towards the trees, the scent growing stronger. Tempted, I gave the darkness a wry smile and shook my head. "No games tonight." And I meant it.

Besides, the one time I'd actually given in I'd wandered for hours, emerging back at my house richer only by the number of brambles stuck in my hair. I debated mooning the woods, but in the end, I merely entered the house, gently closing the door behind me. And if I thought I caught my name whispered on the breeze, I chose not to acknowledge it.

✳   ✳   ✳

Poke.

Something sharp prodded my back. Bleary, I shifted away from it.

Poke.

"Phin, if that's you, you'd better have a damn good reason for pulling me out of my training." I yawned the words and attempted to roll over.

"I thought you might want to know he's awake again." The tiny unicorn clambered over my hip.

"And he won't go back to sleep for you?"

"Abby, in case you haven't noticed, I don't have hands. But I *do* have teeth, so unless you want that delicious ass of yours blemished, I suggest you get your butt out of bed. Little angel wants his mama and Talivar's out somewhere."

I groaned. Some bodyguard. "He had to go back to Faerie for a bit. He should be back in a few hours. What time is it?" I cracked an eye at the clock. Four A.M.

Shit. "Fine. But I'm *not* his mama."

"You're the only thing here with tits. Close enough." Phineas grinned, wriggling under the warmth of the sheets I left behind. "Mmmm . . . cozy," he sighed, laying his head on the pillow.

"Don't push your luck." I glared at him, gathering my robe around my shoulders. Sure enough, now that I'd managed to pull myself out of the hazy state between awake and Dreaming, I could hear Benjamin's wailing cry down the hallway. "I'm not sure I get paid enough for this," I muttered. But who was I kidding? Moira said jump, I jumped. Why should the job stop at a little thing like childcare?

I padded down the hall, yawning again. "I'm coming, sweetie," I said, wincing as his voice jumped two notches from "slightly pissy" to "full-on-mega-howl." Upon entering the room and switching on the nightlight, the reason became evident. Wedged up in one corner of the crib,

Benjamin had managed to get one of his limbs wrapped around the bars. The fact that the limb in question was a neatly feathered wing made very little difference to the furious little eyes peering at me from a squinched-up face.

Angel, indeed. Spitting image of his father.

Startled by just how much he thrust that chin out like Robert, I tsked at him soothingly, gently extricating the wing without knocking any feathers loose. His volume lowered about two decibels and I picked him up to rest his head on my shoulder. He snuffled, dark hair damp against my neck, his mouth rooting to take hold of my collarbone. "That time again, is it?" I patted his back and covered him with a blanket, starting up what had become a twice nightly ritual of pacing.

This time Benjamin wasn't having any of it, though, so I quickly changed his diaper for good measure and then the two of us headed into the kitchen so that I could warm up a bottle. I continued rocking side to side as the pot on the stove began to heat up. The fridge, of course, always had his milk in good supply, though what it was, I wasn't entirely sure. Moira wouldn't hear of giving him mortal formula, but I'd never actually seen her carrying a breast pump either. In the end, I supposed it didn't matter. Whatever it was seemed to keep him healthy and it's not like I'd even know where to begin to find food for a half-angel/half-fae child anyway. Based on the amount the little booger was going through, I could only imagine his metabolism was higher than a mortal child's, although his somewhat limited development was troubling. At eight months, a human baby would have been at least starting to wean, and certainly not requiring twice-nightly feedings. On the other hand, human babies couldn't fly, so maybe the comparison was unfair.

Two weeks ago, Moira had been called away to the Faery

Court to give her testimony about Maurice's betrayal. Thankfully, I'd been spared that particular requirement, but the offshoot was to stay behind and continue to run things—including the task of being Benjamin's nanny. Talivar had been happy enough to take the night shift when he was around, but when the infant had sprouted wings a few days ago, the prince had decided it was worth the risk of leaving us behind to tell his sister directly.

Regardless of what the Protectorate had told me, the knowledge of who was Benjamin's father wasn't for public consumption . . . but feathers would be hard to hide for too long.

Benjamin began to whimper. The bottle was nearly warm now, so I shushed him until it was the right temperature. I retreated into the living room, and curled up on the sofa. He popped his lips at the sight of the bottle and suckled greedily. "Better be careful," I warned him. "Keep eating like this and you'll be too heavy to fly."

If he heard my words, he studiously ignored them, eyes closing in contentment. "Silly boy," I murmured, shifting him so that he was crooked in my elbow, my arm on the sofa edge. Now that his needs were fully taken care of, I blinked sleepily myself, just now noticing the burning sand grinding my eyes. "Not yet," I sighed. "Gotta get you all tucked in first, eh?" I glanced down at the pile of loose papers on the coffee tables and snorted. I turned the lamp to its dimmest setting and grabbed the top few sheets.

Might as well try to get some work in.

"Dear Abby . . ."

I rolled my eyes. Just my luck to be stuck with the same name as the columnist. I couldn't recall exactly when the first letters started showing up, but shortly after Moira had gotten things squared away upon her return, I began to find them. At first, they'd be randomly slipped under the door of the Midnight Marketplace, or even sometimes at the Pit, but as I tentatively began to answer them (with Moira's full blessing, of course), they started showing up on my pillow, in my bathroom, taped to the fridge. I drew the line when I found the one in my underwear drawer.

Or really, Phineas blew a gasket.

"I don't mind you having your hobbies," he'd exploded at me that morning, "but god damn if you could keep them out of your lingerie?"

Even aside from the fact that he wasn't actually supposed to be *in* my underwear, this was one time I agreed with him.

I formally set up a separate address at the Marketplace, with occasional diversions to the Hallows and made it clear that any letters randomly showing up in my sheets were going to get burned.

Still, the flow kept on here and there, though how useful my answers were I had no idea.

I was hoping you could settle a little issue between me and this ghost I'm living with.

"Not bloody likely," I muttered.

I'm a brownie, and I used to work for Mr. Jefferson. Now technically, brownies work until their chosen masters pass on and then we are set free. But in this case, Mr. Jefferson did not fully move into the light and his ghost haunts the place and refuses to let me go . . .

I groaned, placing the letter on the cushion beside me. I hated these types of questions. Not as much as the Touch-Stone ones or the star-crossed lover ones, but without knowing both sides of the story, how was I supposed to answer this?

Even if I meant well, there was no telling what the repercussions would be if I gave them the wrong advice. "Tomorrow. Have to find ghost whisperer, Benjamin. Remind me."

Benjamin's jaw was slack now, the nipple hanging off his lower lip, milk in the corners of his mouth. "Alright, little man. Back to bed with you. And Auntie," I amended.

"Here, I'll take him." Talivar emerged from the dark kitchen with a quiet grace. The elven prince had finally relaxed his rather minimal dress code of tunics and torcs a few months ago, just as he had relaxed his vigilance. Things had quieted down considerably and although he continued to watch over me, I could tell he was getting bored.

With a little shopping help from me he had taken casual chic to an entirely new level. Even now in jeans and a black T-shirt, he cut a nice figure in the dim light, his long hair tied back in a loose queue, pointed ears poking between the strands. He still retained the leather eyepatch, though. My threats to glitter it up had been met with a slightly chilly smile, and in the end I'd decided to leave well enough alone.

"Ah. I didn't hear you come in." I peered up at him blearily. "Good trip?"

He shrugged. "There is much to discuss, but I think it can wait until tomorrow." His eye fell on the baby, a strange expression ghosting over his face. "Moira wasn't overly happy to hear about the wings, as you can imagine, but she'll manage."

I grunted, not really sure I cared about anything other than getting back to my bed. Not at this hour, anyway. "When do you think the trial will wrap up?"

He frowned, gently taking Benjamin from me. The elf cradled his nephew's head with a careful hand. "Maurice is not being overly cooperative, as we suspected. Moira has given her testimony, but . . ." He hesitated. "Well, the truth of it is our mother is not doing as well as she might. Moira is keeping an eye on her."

"Translation: Things are fucked," I quipped with a sigh. "I already know where this is going." Visions of raising

Benjamin to his college years filled me with a weary sort of resignation. "What are the chances I'll be seeing Moira again before my Contract is up?"

He snorted. "Well enough, I'm thinking. The Queen won't keep her there forever."

"Small favors. But I still think we need to tell Robert. Benjamin is his son and however uncomfortable that makes people, he should know. After all," I said dryly, "who's going to teach him to fly?"

Talivar shifted Benjamin to his shoulder and shook his head. "We do not recognize paternal claims in Faerie, Abby. All lineages are drawn through the mother. By that logic, I'm actually more closely related to my nephew than Robert is."

"Yeah, I can tell, what with those *wings* and all," I muttered. "Still makes no damn sense."

"Yes, well, we're a rather promiscuous bunch. We cannot trust our wives to be faithful, any more than our wives could trust us. At least this way I know my sister's children are related to me. But my wife?" He shrugged at my raised brow, a wan smile on his lips. "My hypothetical wife, anyway. She could take a hundred lovers over the course of our marriage and I would have no right to gainsay her that."

"And that doesn't bother you? Knowing that you have no real acknowledgement of your own children?"

He looked down at the baby, his gaze distant. "Children are rare and precious to our kind. We tend not to look too closely at where they come from. And that, I think, is enough for one evening. Or morning, as the case may be," he noted, glancing at the false dawn through the blinds. "I'll tend to him now. Hopefully your rest wasn't disturbed overly much."

"Mmmm . . . you're assuming I *like* to be awakened by a horn half up my ass."

"Probably depends on the horn," he murmured, an

uncharacteristic smirk crossing his face before he slipped back through the kitchen and down the hallway to the baby's room. I watched him go, rubbing my eyes again. He didn't have Ion's blatant sexuality, but there was an ethereal beauty to him, nevertheless.

A pang of sadness twisted in my gut and I told it to shut the hell up, ambling back to my bedroom to try to catch a few more hours of shut-eye. Today was Katy's eighteenth birthday, after all, and I had things to do—party plans to set in motion and a werewolf to keep under control. My duties didn't get put on hold simply because I had a messy private life.

Phineas was unabashedly drooling on my pillow, his equine mouth half open. "Lovely." I grimaced, snatching up a spare from the closet. I hunched beneath the blankets, wrapping them partway about my head as though I might shut out the memories.

The unicorn snuggled closer, making kissy sounds.

I shoved him away. "You're an ass. See if I make you any breakfast."

"Be still my wounded heart," he retorted. "However shall I manage without a plate of burned bacon?" There was a snuffling sound and a sigh, and then a miniature chainsaw revving next to my ear.

Out of a perverse sense of revenge I nudged him with my shoulder. "I've got to try to find a ghost whisperer today, if I can. Remind me when you wake me up again."

There was a sudden silence. On instinct, I jerked my backside away from him, peering out of my nest to catch him midbite. The unicorn gave me a sour look, curling his upper lip in distain. "Almost got you," he mumbled, flopping onto his back with his legs spread obscenely. "Just ask Charlie. She's always talking to dead people."

I frowned. I hadn't spoken to Charlie in quite some

time. At least not in anything that didn't end up being awkwardly . . . awkward. "Charlie as in 'the girlfriend of the angel who cheated on her with my boss and whose baby I'm taking care of'?"

"Yeah." His mouth pursed. "Hmmm . . . yeah, I could see where that might be a problem. Good thing I don't have to talk to her, though . . . eh?"

"Nice." I slouched back down and rearranged the blankets, rolling to the other side to keep my posterior out of range. "Whose side are you on anyway?"

"Thought you'd have figured that out by now," he yawned, one eye cocking open to wink at me. "Mine."

Fantasy.
Temptation.
Adventure.

**Visit PocketAfterDark.com,
an all-new website just for Urban
Fantasy and Romance Readers!**

- Exclusive access to the hottest
urban fantasy and romance titles!

- Read and share reviews on
the latest books!

- Live chats with your favorite
romance authors!

- Vote in online polls!

 www.PocketAfterDark.com

26119